Serpent's
Reach

Serpent's Reach

C. J. CHERRYH

Nelson Doubleday, Inc.
Garden City, New York

Published by arrangement with
DAW Books, Inc.
1633 Broadway
New York, New York 10019

Serpent's
Reach

"HYDRI REACH: QUARANTINED. Approach permitted only along approved lanes. SEE: Istra."

—*Nav. Man.*

"HYDRI REACH: CLASSIFIED: Apply XenBureau for information."

—*Encyclopaedia Xenologica*

"HYDRI STARS: quarantined region. For applicable regulations, consult Cor. Jur. Hum. XXXVII 91.2. Native species of alpha Hydri III include at least one sapient species, majat, first contacted by probe Celia in 2223. Successful contact with majat was not made until Delia probe followed in 2229, and majat space was eventually opened to very limited contact under terms of the Hydri Treaty of 2235, with a single designated trade point at the station of beta Hydri II, locally called Istra.

"The entire region is under internal regulation, assumed to be a majat-human cooperation, and it is thus excluded from Alliance law. Alliance citizens are cautioned that treaties do not extend to protection of Alliance citizens or property in violation of quarantined space, and that Alliance law prohibits the passage of any ship, or person, alien or human, from said zone of quarantine into Alliance space, with the exception of licensed commerce up to the permitted contact point at Istra, by carefully monitored lanes. The Alliance will use extreme force to prevent any such intrusion into or out of quarantine. For specific regulations of import and export, consult

ATR 189.9 and supplements. The nature of the internal government is entirely a matter of speculation, but it is supposed on some evidence that the seat of government is alpha Hydri III, locally called Cerdin, and that this government has remained relatively stable during the several centuries of its establishment . . .

"Majat are reported to have rejected emphatically all human contact except the trading company initially introduced by Delia probe. The Kontrin company is currently assumed to be the government of the human inhabitants. Population of the mission was originally augmented by importation of human ova, and external observation indicates that colonization has been effected on several worlds other than Cerdin and Istra within the quarantine zone.

"Principal exports are: biocomp softwares, medical preparations, fibers, and the substance known as lifejewels, all of which are unique to the zone and of majat manufacture; principal imports are metals, luxury foodstuffs, construction machinery, electronics, art objects."

—XenBureau Eph. Xen. 2301

"MAJAT: all information classified."

—XenBureau Eph. Xen. 2301

"The fact is . . . we've become dependent. We can't get the materials elsewhere. We can't duplicate them."

—report, EconBureau, classified.

"Advise you take whatever opportunities exist to establish onworld observation at Istra, even to clandestine operations. Accurate information is of utmost importance."

—classified document, AlSec

BOOK ONE

1

IF IT WAS ANYWHERE possible to be a child in the Family, it was possible at Kethiuy, on Cerdin. There were few visitors, no imminent hazards. The estate sat not so very far from the City and from Alpha's old hall, but its hills and its unique occupation kept it isolated from most of Family politics. It had its lake and its fields, its garden of candletrees that rose like feathery spires among its fourteen domes; and round about its valley sat the hives, which sent their members to and from Kethiuy. All majat who would deal with Men dealt through Kethiuy, which fended one hive from another and kept peace, the peculiar talent of the Meth-marens, that sept and House of the Family which held the land. Fields extended in one direction, both human-owned and majat-owned; labs rambled off in the other; warehouses in yet a third, where azi, cloned men, gathered and tallied the wealth of hive trade and the products of the lab and the computers, which were the greatest part of that trade. Kethiuy was town as much as House; it was self-contained and tranquil, almost changeless in the terms of its owners, for Kontrin measured their lives in decades more than years, and the rare children licensed to replace the dead had no doubt what they must be and what the order of the world was.

Raen amused herself, clipping leaves from the dayvine with short, neat shots; the wind blew and made it more difficult, and she gauged her fire meticulously, needle-beamed. She was fifteen; she had carried the little gun clipped to her belt since she had turned twelve. Being Kontrin, and potentially immortal, she had still come into this world because a certain close kinsman had died of carelessness; she wished her own replacement to be long in coming. She was a skilled marksman; one of the amusements available to her was gambling, and she currently had a bet with a third cousin involving the target range.

Marksmanship, gambling, running the hedges into the fields to watch the azi at work, or back again in Kethiuy, sunk in the oblivion of deepstudy or studying the lab comps until she could make the machines yield her up communication with the alien majat . . . such things filled her days, one very like the other. She did not play; there were years ahead for that, when the prospect of immortality began to pall and the years needed amusements to speed them past. Her present business was to learn, to gather skills that would protect that long life. The elaborate pleasures with which her elders amused themselves were not yet for her, although she looked on such with a stirring of interest. She sat on her hillside and picked an extraordinary succession of leaves off the waving vine with quick, fine shots, and reckoned that she would put in her required time at the comp board and be through by dinner, leaving the evening free for boating on Kethiuy's lake . . . too hot during the day: the water cast back the white-hot sky with such glare one could not even look on it unvisored; but by night what lived in it came up from the bottom, and boats skimmed the black surface like firebugs, trolling for the fish that offered rare treat for Kethiuy's tables. Other valleys had game, and even domestic herds, but no creature but man stayed in Kethiuy, between the hives. None could.

Raen a Sul hant Meth-maren. She was a long-boned and rangy fifteen, having likely all her height. Ilit blood mixed with Meth-maren had contributed that length of limb; and Meth-maren blood, her aquiline features. She bore a pattern on her right hand, chitinous and glittering, living in her flesh: her identity, her pledge to the hives, such as all Kontrin bore. This sign a majat could read, whose eyes could read nothing of human features. Betas went unmarked. Azi bore a tiny tattoo. The Kontrin brand was in living jewels, and she bore it for the distinction it was.

The tendril fell last, burned through. She clipped the gun to her belt and smoothly rose, pulled up the hood of her sunsuit and adjusted the visor to protect her eyes before leaving the shade. She took the long way, at the fringe of the woods, being in no particular haste: it was cooler and less steep, and nothing awaited her but studies.

A droning intruded on her attention. She looked about, and up.

Aircraft passing were not unusual: Kethiuy lake was a convenient marker for anyone sight-navigating to the northern estates.

But these were low, two of them, and coming in.

Visitors. Her spirits soared. No comp this afternoon. She veered from the lab-ward course and strode off down the slope with its rocks and thread-bushes, tacking from one to the other point of the steep face with reckless abandon, reckoning of entertainments and a general cancellation of lessons.

Something skittered back in the hedge. She came to an instant halt and set her hand on her pistol: no fear of beasts, but of men, of anything that would skulk and hide.

Majat.

She picked out the shadowed form in the slatted leaves, perplexed to find it there. It was motionless in its guard-stance, half again as tall as she; faceted eyes flickered with the slightest of turns of its head. Almost she called to it, reckoning it some Worker strayed from the labs down below: sometimes their eyes betrayed them and, muddled with lab-chemicals, they lost their direction. But it should not have strayed this far.

The head turned farther, squaring to her: no Worker . . . she saw that clearly. The jaws were massive, the head armored.

She could not see its emblems, to what hive it belonged, and human eyes could not see its color. It hunched down, an assemblage of projecting points and leathery limbs, in the latticed play of sun and shade . . . a Warrior, and not to be approached. Sometimes Warriors came, to look down on Kethiuy for whatever their blind eyes could perceive, and then departed, keeping their own secrets. She wished she could see the badges: it might be any of the four hives, while it was only gentle blues and greens who dealt with Kethiuy—the trade of reds and golds channeled through greens. A red or gold was enormously dangerous.

Nor was it alone. Others rose up, slowly, slowly, three, four. Fear knotted in her belly—which was irrational, she insisted to herself: in all Kethiuy's history, no majat had harmed any within the valley.

"You're on Kethiuy land," she said, lifting the hand that identified her to their eyes. "Go back. Go back."

It stared a moment, then backed: badgeless, she saw in her amazement. It lowered its body in token of agreement; she hoped that was its intent. She stood her ground, alert for any shift, any diversion. Her heart was pounding. Never in the labs had she been alone with them, and the sight of this huge Warrior and its fellows moving to her order was incredible to her.

"Hive-master," it hissed, and sidled off through the brush with sudden and blinding speed. Its companions joined it in retreat.

Hive-master. The bitterness penetrated even majat voice. *Hive-friends,* the majat in the labs were always wont to say, touching with delicacy, bowing with seeming sincerity.

Down the hill a beating of engines announced a landing; Raen still waited, scanning the hedges all about before she started away. *Never turn your back on one;* she had heard it all her life, even from those who worked closest with the hives: majat moved too quickly, and a scratch even from a Worker was dangerous.

She edged backward, judged it finally safe to look away and to start to run . . . but she looked now and again over her shoulder.

And the aircraft were on the ground, the circular washes of air flattening the grasses near the gates, next the lakeshore.

A bell rang, advising all the House that strangers had come. Raen cast a last look back, finding the majat had fled entirely, and jogged along toward the landing spot.

The colors on the aircraft were red striped with green, which were the colors of the House of Thon, friends of Sul sept of the Meth-marens. Men and women were disembarking as the engines died down; the gates were open and Meth-marens were coming out to meet the visitors, most without sunsuits, so abrupt was this arrival and so welcome were any of Thon.

The cloaks on the foremost were Thon; and there was the white and yellow of Yalt among them, likewise welcome. But then from the aircraft came visitors in the red-circled black of Hald; and Meth-maren blue, with black border, not Sul-sept white.

Ruil-sept of the Meth-marens, with Hald beside them. Raen stopped dead. So did others. The welcome lost all its warmth. Save under friendly Thon colors, neither Ruil nor Hald would have dared set foot here.

But after some delay, her kinsmen stepped aside and let them pass the gates. The aircraft disgorged more Thon and Yalt, but there were now no welcomes at all; and something else they produced—a score of azi, sunsuited and visored and anonymous.

Armed azi. Raen stared at them in disbelief, nervously skirting round the area of the landing; she sought the gates with several backward glances, angry to the depth of her small experience of

Ruil, the Meth-marens' left-hand line. Ruil had come for trouble; and the guard-azi were Ruil's arrogant show, she was sure of it. Thon would have no reason.

She put on a certain arrogance as she walked in the gates. Sul-sept azi closed them securely after her, leaving the intruder-azi outside in the heat. She wished sunstroke on them, and sullenly made her way into the House, the whole day spoiled.

2

IT WAS A LASTING strangeness to see Ruil-sept's black among the white-bordered Sul cloaks—and as much so to see Hald red-and-black; and incredible to find them admitted to the dining hall, where House councils and dinners took place simultaneously.

Raen sat next her mother and found security in her—Morel, her mother, who had gotten her of an Ilit who himself was bloodkin to Thon; she wondered if any of these present were distant relatives. If it were so, her mother, who would know, said nothing, and deep-study had given her no clues.

Grandfather headed the table . . . more than grandfather, but that was shortest: eldest of Meth-marens, *the* Meth-maren, who was gray-haired and bent with the decades that he had lived, five hundred passes of Cerdin about its sun: eldest of all Sul-sept, of Ruil too, so that they had to respect him. Raen regarded him with awe, seldom now as he came out of his seclusion in westwing, rarely to venture into domestic concerns, more often to Council down at Alpha, where he wielded the power of a considerable bloc of votes. Meth-marens, unlike other Houses whose members were scattered from world to world across the Reach, stayed close to home, to Kethiuy. Of the twenty-seven Houses and fifty-eight septs within those Houses that composed the Family, Meth-maren Sul was the only one whose duties rarely took him elsewhere, away from Cerdin and the hives. The Family's post was here, between the hives and Men, while Meth-maren Ruil hovered about the area of Alpha and guested where they could, Houseless since the split.

Hald remembered that day, that Meth-maren and Meth-maren had fought. Hald had bled for it, sheltering Ruil assassins; and it was a powerful persuasion that brought Halds and both septs of Meth-maren again under the same roof.

It had taken all the influence of Thon and Yalt together to persuade Grandfather to accept this gathering, Halds and the divided Meth-marens at the same dinner table, carefully separated by Thons and Yalts. It needed a certain bravado on the part of Halds and Ruils to eat and drink what Sul gave them.

Raen herself felt her stomach unsettled, and she declined when the serving-azi brought the next elaborate dish. "Coffee," she said, and the azi Mev whispered the order at once to one of his fellows: it arrived instantly, for she was eldest's great-granddaughter's daughter in direct descent, and there was in the House a hierarchy of inheritance. She was to a certain extent pampered, and to another, burdened, for the sake of that birthright. It mandated her presence at table tonight in the first place, and made it necessary to mix with her elders, most of whom had resentment for the fact. She tried to bear herself with her mother's studied disdain for the proceedings, but there was a Ruil across the table, cousin Bron, and she avoided his eyes when possible: they were hot and insolent.

"We hope for a reconciliation," the Thon elder was saying, at the other end of the table. He had risen, to begin what he had come to say. "Meth-maren, will you let Ruil speak here? Or would you prefer intermediaries still?"

"You're going to say," Grandfather intoned in his reedy voice, "that we should take in this left-hand branch of ours. It diverged of its own accord. It's not welcome in Kethiuy. It's trouble to us, and the hives avoid it. Ruil-sept alienated them, and that wasn't our doing. This is hive territory. Those who can't live under those terms can't live here."

"Our talents," said Tel Ruil Meth-maren, "lie with other hives, the ones Sul can't manage."

"Reds and golds." Grandfather's chin wobbled with his anger. "You deceive yourself, Tel a Ruil. They've no love of humankind, least of all of Ruil. I know you've had red contacts. It's rumored. I know what you're up to and why you've gone to the trouble of drawing Thon and Yalt into this. Your plans to build on Kethiuy lake are unacceptable."

"You're head of House," Tel said. He had an unfortunate voice, nasal and whining. "You ought to be impartial to sept, eldest. But you carry on feuds from before any of the rest of us were born.

Maybe Sul sept feels some jealousy—that Ruil can handle the two hives Sul can't touch. They've come to us, not we to them. They preferred us. Thon saw; Thon will witness it. All within the Pact. Redhive has promised us its cooperation if we can secure that holding near its lands, on the lake. We've come *asking,* eldest. That's all. Asking."

"We support the request," the Thon said.

"Yalt agrees," said the other eldest. "It's good sense, Meth-maren, to end this quarrel, and to get some good out of it."

"And does Hald ask the same?"

There was silence. Raen sat still, her heart pounding.

The Hald eldest rose. "We have a certain involvement here, Meth-maren. The old feud has gone on beyond its usefulness. If it's settled now, then we have to be involved, or the Meth-marens will have peace and we'll have none. We're willing to forget the past. Understand that."

"You're here to stand up with Ruil."

"Obligation, Meth-maren."

They did not say friendship. Raen herself did not miss that implication, and there was a space of silence while Ruil glowered.

"We have opportunities," the Hald said further, "that ought not to be neglected."

"At least talk on the matter," said Yalt. "We ask you to do that."

"No," some of the House muttered. But Eldest did not refuse. His old eyes wandered over them all, and finally he nodded.

Raen's mother swore softly. "Leave," she said to Raen. And when Raen looked at her in offense: "Go on."

Others, even adult and senior, were being dismissed from what was becoming elder council. There was no objection possible. She kissed her mother's cheek, pressed her hand, and sullenly made her retreat among the others, younger folk under thirty and third and fourth-rank elders, inconsiderable in council.

There was a muttering gathering in the hall just outside, her cousins no happier than she with what was toward.

No peace, she heard. *Not with Ruil.*

And: *Reds and golds,* she heard, reminding her of the hillside and the meeting which had diverted her. She had told no one of that. She was too arrogant to contribute that meaningless fragment to the general turmoil in the hall. She skirted the vicinities of her chattering cousins, male and female, and brushed off the attentions of an azi, walked the corridor in a fit of irritation—both at being cast out and at reckoning what Ruil-sept proposed. Kethiuy lake belonged to Sul-sept, beautiful and pristine. Sul had cared to keep the shores as they were, had labored to make the boat-launches as inconspicuous as possible, to keep all evidence of man out of view. Ruil wanted a site which would obtrude into their sight, to plant themselves right where Sul must constantly look at them and reckon with them. This business of reds and golds: this was surely something Ruil had concocted to obtain backing from other Houses. There was no possibility that they could do what they claimed, interceding with the wild hives.

Lies. Outright lies.

She shrugged past the azi at the door and sought the cool, clean air of the porch. She filled her lungs with it, looking out into the dark where the candletrees framed Kethiuy lake; and the ugly aircraft sat in her view, gleaming with lights.

Armed azi, as if this were some frontier holding. She was indignant at their presence, and no little uneasy by reason of it.

A step sounded by her. She saw three men, the one nearest in Hald's dark Color. She froze, recalling herself unarmed, having come from the table. Childish pride held her from the flight prudence dictated.

It was a tall man who faced her. She stared up at him with her back to the door and the light from the slit windows giving her a better look at him: mid-thirties, beta-reckoning; on a Kontrin, that could be anywhere between thirty and three hundred. The face was gaunt and grim: Pol Hald, she recognized him suddenly, with the *déjà vu* of deepstudy. The two with him, she did not know.

And Pol was trouble. He had lost kin to Meth-marens. He was also reputed frivolous, a libertine, a jester, a player of pranks. She could not connect that report with that gaunt face until quite suddenly he grinned at her and shed half a dozen apparent years.

"Good evening, little Meth-maren."

"Good evening yourself, Pol Hald."

"What, should I know your name?"

She lifted her head a degree higher. "I'm not in your studytapes *yet,* ser Hald. My name is Raen."

"Tand and Morn," he said with a shrug at the kinsmen at his back, the one young and boyish, the other lean-faced and much like himself, like enough for full kin. His grin did not fade. He reached out with complete affrontery and touched her under the chin. "Raen. I'll remember that."

She took a step backward, feeling a rush of blood to her face. She had no experience to deal with such a move, and the embarrassment became rage. "And who sent you out here, skulking round the windows?"

"We're set to watch the aircraft, little Meth-maren. To be sure Meth-maren hospitality is what it should be."

She did not like the sound of that, and turned abruptly, seized the door handle, afraid for the instant they they would stop her; but they made no move to do so, and she delayed to glower resentment at them, determined to make it clear she was not being chased off her own doorstep. "I seem to have left my gun inside," she said. "I usually carry it for pests."

Pol's gaunt face went serious then, quite, quite sober.

"Good evening, Meth-maren," he said.

She opened the door and went in, into the safe light, among her own kin.

3

THERE WAS THE DRONE of an engine toward dawn. Aircraft taking off, Raen thought, turning in her bed and burrowing into the pillows. The talk down in the dining hall had gone on and on, sometimes loudly enough to be heard outside the doors, generally not. The gathering in the hall outside had drifted off at last toward duties or pleasures: there was a certain lack of law in the House, younger men and lesser elders piqued by their exclusion, seeking to make clear their displeasure. A few became drunk. A few turned to bizarre amusements, and the azi maid who had bedded herself down in Raen's room had fled here in panic.

Lia had taken her in, Lia her own azi, a female nearing her fatal fortieth year. Raen blinked and looked at Lia, who had fallen asleep in a chair by the door, while the fugitive maid had curled up on a pallet in the corner . . . dear old Lia was upset by the commotion in the House, and had surely taken that uncomfortable post out of worry for her security.

Love. That was Lia, whose ample arms had sheltered her all her fifteen years. Her mother was authority, was beauty, was affection and safety, but Lia was love, lab-bred for motherhood, sterile though azi were.

And she could not slip past such a guard. She tried to rise and dress in silence enough, but Lia wakened and began to fuss over her, choosing her clothes with care, wakening the sleeping maid to draw a bath and make the bed, supervising every detail. Raen bore this, for impatient as she was to learn how things stood downstairs, she had infinite patience with Lia, who could be hurt by refusal. Lia was thirty-nine. There remained only this last year, before whatever defect was bred into her, killed her. Raen knew this with great regret, though she was not sure that Lia knew her own age. She would on no account make a day of Lia's life unhappy; and on no account would she let Lia know the reason of her attitude.

It's part of growing up, her mother had told her. *The price of immortality. Azi and betas come and go, the azi quickest of all. We all love them when we're young. When one loses one's nurse, one begins to learn what we are, and what they are; and that's a valuable lesson, Raen. Learn to enjoy, and to say goodbye.*

Lia offered her the cloak of Color, and she decided it was proper to wear it; she fastened it and let Lia adjust it, then walked to the window, where the first light of dawn showed the landing.

One aircraft still remained. It was not over.

She went out into the corridor and down, past the council room where a few of her elder cousins and relations lounged disconsolately. They were not in the mood to brief a fifteen year old, be she heir-line or not; she sensed that and listened, heard voices still talking inside.

She shook her head in disgust and walked on, thinking of breakfast, though she rarely ate that meal. Lessons, at least, were still suspended, but she would have traded a week of holidays to have Ruil and their friends out of Sul's vicinity. She recalled the three Halds and wondered whether they were still occupying the porch.

They were not. She stood on the porch with her hands on her hips and breathed deeply. The area was clear and the azi were heading out to fields as they did every morning. A golden light touched the candletrees and the hedges at this most beautiful hour, before alpha Hydri showed its true face and scorched the heavens.

There was only the single aircraft befouling the landscape.

And then she saw movement at the corner of the house.

An azi, sunsuited at this hour.

"What are you doing there?" she shouted at him. And then she saw shadows skittering in a living wave across the lawn, tall, stiltlike forms moving with eye-blurring speed.

She whirled, face to face with an armed azi, and cried out.

BOOK TWO

1

RAEN STUMBLED, SKIDDED, came to a halt against a projecting rock. Pain shot through her side. The cloth clung there. The burn had broken open; moisture soaked her clothing. She felt of it and brought away reddened fingers, wiped a smear on the rock which had stopped her, fingers trembling. She kept climbing.

She looked back from time to time, on the lowlands, the forest, the lake, on all the deceptive peace of Kethiuy's valley, while her breath came short and balance nigh failed her on the rocks. They were all dead down there, all her kin: all, all dead—Ruil sept held Kethiuy for its own, and Sul-sept bodies were everywhere. Only her own was missing from the tally, and that from no act of wit, nothing of credit: burned, she had fallen, and the bushes by the porch had sheltered her.

They were all dead, and she was dying.

There was no relief from the sun up here; it burned in a sky white with heat, blistered exposed skin, threatened blindness despite her cloak that she had wrapped about her face. Stones burned her hands and heated the thin soles of her boots. Her eyes streamed tears, seared by the dryness and the glare. Her chance for shelter was long past, at the beginning of the climb. If Ruil sought her, they would find her. She left a trail for any groundsearch they might care to make, smeared on the rocks from her hands and her side. And from the air, Ruil might well manage heat-sensors for night tracking. There was no hope of shaking them if they wanted her.

She kept running, climbing, all the same, because there was no going back, because it was less her Ruil cousins she feared than red-hive, the living wave that had poured over her into Kethiuy, spurred feet trampling her among the bushes, deadly jaws clashing. There were deaths and deaths, and she had seen them in plenty in recent hours, but those dealt by majat were cruelest, and majat trackers were those she most feared, swift beyond any hope of escape.

A second fall; this time she sprawled full length, and from this impact she was slow in rising. Her hands shook now as in ague, and there was skin gone from her palms and her knees and elbows, cloth torn. Thirst and the blinding heat of the rocks were more painful than the abrasions, but even those miseries were devoured by the pain that stitched her side. She drew breath with difficulty, reaching for support to hold her on her feet.

She was running again. She could not remember how, but she faced a climb, and her mind was forced to work again. She used hands as well as feet, and managed it, slowly, tottering on the brink, slipping, gaining another body's length. There had been other refuges, the woods, the road toward the City. She had chosen wrong. Her mother, her uncles—they would have done otherwise, would have tried for the City. She had made a panic choice, the hills, hide and seek in the rocks, the high places, hard ground for their vehicles. But most of all the hills were blue-hive territory, old neighbors. Red-hive would not readily venture *their* borders, not for all Ruil's urging.

Panic choice. There was no help up here, nothing human, no way down, no way back. She knew what she had done to herself, and the tears that ran her face were of rage as well as the heat.

There was another gap in her memory, and then a bald hill swam in her sight. Here was the boundary, the point-past-which-not for any human. Majat trails ran through the gap, converging here. Raen caught her breath and felt her way along the rocks and down, into the shadows, set her feet on that well-worn track and looked about her, at tilted, tumbled rocks, flinching from the white sky.

Here was the refuge. No one would come here rashly; no one would likely take the trouble and the risk. It was a private place, for the private business of dying, and she knew it finally, that dying was what she had left to do. She had only to sit down and rest a while, while the blood kept leaking from her side and the sun baked her brain. Of pain there could be no more to endure. It had reached the top of the curve, and lessened even from standing still; there was only the need to wait. Her mother, eldest, her kinsmen and her azi

. . . there was no grieving for them: their pain was done. Hers was not.

Balance failed her. She moved to save herself, fearing the fall, and that move led to the next step and the next. Her vision went out for a moment, and panic and failing balance drove her stumbling and reaching for the rocks which she remembered ahead. She hit them hip-high, braced herself, recovered a blurred vision of daylight and kept moving downhill. It was a little death, that dark, that blindness; the real one was coming, deeper and larger, and already the heat of the sun seemed less. She fled it, fighting each dark space that sent her staggering and reeling from point to point.

Thorns ripped her arm and her clothing. She recoiled and fought past the edge of the obstacle, blinked her eyes clear. She knew the meaning of the hedge, knew that here was the place she must stop, must. Her frightened body kept moving with its own logic, heedless of dangers; her mind observed from a distance, carried along help-lessly, confused . . . and suddenly, in grim rage, found a focus.

The pact of Family had failed; it was murdered, with her mother, Grandfather, her kin . . . slaughtered by Ruil and Hald.

There was an older Pact, that which was grafted into the very flesh of her wounded hand, chitinous and part of her, living jewels.

She was Kontrin, of the Family which ruled the Hydri stars, which had won of majat the rights of settlement and trade, the serpent-emblemed Family, which lived where other humans would not; she was Meth-maren, hive-friend.

A great many fears diminished in her. There was a place to go, a thing to do, a means to make Ruil suffer.

Her mother smiled grimly in her mind, encouraging her: *Revenge is next only to winning.* Raen's mouth set in a rictus between gasp and grin, seeking air, a little more life, and someone else's death.

The blacknesses came more frequently now, and she hurled her-self from rock to rock, tumbling from one winding turn to the next, fending off thorns with her chitin-shielded right hand . . . majat barriers, these ancient hedges.

"I'm from Kethiuy!" she shouted at the grayness which hazed her senses, the cold that numbed the pain and threatened her with los-ing. "Blue-hive! I'm Raen Meth-maren! *Kethiuy!*"

The black edges closed on her sight.

She thrust herself toward the next hedge, and heard rocks shift and rattle above her, stones which she had not stirred.

They were all about her, tall leathery shapes, hazy shadows, shimmering with jewels in the blinding sun.

"Go back," one said, a baritone harmony of pipes. "Go back!"

She saw the dark opening in the earth, and held her bleeding side, flinging herself into a last, frantic effort. She could not feel her legs under her. There was no more heat nor cold, nor up nor down nor color. Her body hit stone. Her wounded hand slicked wetly across it and the gray itself went out.

2

WORKERS TUGGED AND ARRANGED to satisfaction, careful not to further damage the fragile structure, delicate as new eggs. Worker palps busily gnawed away the ruined clothing, laved off the foul outsider smells and cleaned the spilled life fluids from body and limbs. Warriors still milled about the vestibule, disturbed by the invasion, seeking directions. Confusion reigned throughout the sector.

A Worker took the essence of the problem and circled its companions, squealed a short burst of orders to clear the trafficway, and scurried off. Worker was already in contact with Mother, after that subliminal fashion which pervaded the hive, but that kind of communication was not sufficient for details. There was need of direct report.

Other Workers delayed it briefly, chance encounters in the dark corridors. *Human-in-hive,* they scented, among other things of life fluids and injury. Alarm spread. Warriors would be moving; Workers would be throwing up barricades, sealing tunnels. Worker kept travelling, original and most accurate carrier, and obsessed with urgency. Its personal alarm was chiefly distress for the untidiness, a vague sense of higher things out of control and therefore threatening the whole hive: chaos was already loosed and worse might follow.

Dim glow of fungi and the sweet scent of Mother pervaded the inmost halls, near the Chamber. Worker passed others, Egg-bearers— touched, smelled, conveyed the alarm which sent them hastening away. A Warrior shouldered past, bluff and hasty, returning from its own inquiry. Its message was of sense to Warriors. Worker rejected it, although it bore upon its own, and scurried on, forelimbs tucked, into the Presence.

Mother sat in a heaving mass of Drones and attendants. The smell was magnetic, delirious. Worker came to Her in ecstasy, opened its palps and offered taste and scent, receiving in turn.

Mother thought. The shifts of chemistry swirled dazzlingly through Worker's senses. She spoke at the same time, sound which occasionally ascended to the timbre of human names. Communication wove constantly between the two levels, intricate interplay of sound and taste.

Heal it, the decision came, complex with the chemicals necessary to the performance of this task. *Feed it. This is of Kethiuy hive, the young queen Raen. Workers of blue-hive have encountered her before. I taste injury, abundant life-fluids. Warriors report red-hive intrusion in the Kethiuy area. Accept this intruder.*

Queen. The scent touched off reactions in the chemistry of Worker, terrifying changes—communicated also to the Drones, who shifted uneasily and sought touch. The hive-mind was one. Worker was one complex unit of it. Mother was a master-unit, the key, which made sense of all the gatherings. Others moved closer, compelled by the intimation of understandings, Workers and Drones and Foragers and Warriors, each sharing this intelligence and feeding into it in its own way.

Kethiuy. That was a Drone, who Remembered, which was a function of Drones. Images followed, of the land before and after the human hive called Kethiuy had been built . . . domes, one at first, and then others, and trees growing up among them. Blue-hive's memory was as long as its members were brief: a billion years the memories went back, and the specific memory of Kethiuy saw the hills rise and the lake form and drain several times, and form again. Drone-memory extended even back into hives older than Kethiuy's hills, into days of dimmer and dimmer intelligence; but these memories were not at issue: humans were brief upon the earth, only the last several hundreds of years. The hive sorted, comprehended, knew Sul-sept of Meth-maren hive and all its issue, its bitter rivalry with Ruil and Ruil's allies. Human thought: intelligence served by peculiar senses, a few more than the hives possessed, a few less, and contained by single bodies. The concept still troubled the hive, the idea that individual death could extinguish an intelligence. It was still only dimly grasped. Mother in particular put it forward, the impending death of an irreplaceable intelligence.

Queen, Worker insisted, perturbed.

Dying, another Worker added, with an implication of untidiness.

No rival, Mother reassured the hive, but distress persisted strongly in her taste, permeating all consciousness. *We perceive that red-hive is massing in the vicinity of Kethiuy; golds are stirring; and now there is a human injured, perhaps others as well. We have not enough information. Red-hive is involved where red-hive does not belong. Red-hive has a taste of hostilities, of strange contacts, human contacts. The Pact is at issue. Feed Kethiuy's young queen. Heal her. She is no threat to me. She is important to the hive. She contains information. She is an intelligence and contains memory. Tend. Heal.*

Worker departed, one part of the Mind, bent on action. Others raced off on their own missions, impelled by their own understandings of what Mother had said, reactions peculiar to their own chemistries and functions.

Then the Mind did a very difficult thing, and lied to itself.

Mother directed certain three Warriors, who rushed from the Chamber and from the hive and out into the heat of the day. Beyond the thorn-hedges, beyond the safe boundary of the hills, they stopped, and began purposely to alter their internal chemistry, breaking down all the orderly complex of their knowledge, past and present.

The hive lost them, for they were then mad.

They died, wandering inevitably into red-hive ambush in the valley, and red-hive could only believe the lie which it read in the chemistry of the slaughtered blues, that blue-hive had tasted the death of the young queen of Kethiuy hive, that no such survivor existed.

3

"WHAT IS THIS?" Lian muttered, looking about him at the Council, the many-Colored representatives who settled into place beneath the serpent emblem of the Kontrin. Suddenly there were new faces, new arrangements of seating. His blurred vision sought friends, sought old allies. The eldest Hald was gone; a younger man sat in his place. There was of the blue of Meth-maren . . . the black-bordered cloak of a Ruil; of several of the oldest septs and Houses . . . no sign, or younger strangers wearing their Colors. Lian, Eldest of the Family and first in Council, looked about him, hands trembling; and, having almost risen—he sank down again.

He began to count, and took reckoning what manner of change had come on the Family in these chaotic days. Some of the House eldests looked at him across the room, glances carrying question and appeal: he had always opened the sessions . . . seven hundred years in the Council of Humans on Cerdin, the assembly of the twenty-seven Houses of the Family.

"Uncle," said Terent of Welz-Kaen. "Eldest?"

Lian turned his face away, hating the cowardice which must now be the better part of common sense. Assassins had been planted. A purge had been carried out with extreme efficiency, not at one point, but at many. One had no idea where matters stood now, or what the count of votes would be on a challenge. There was something new shaped or shaping, dangerous to all who stood too tall in the Family. One did well now to wait and hear others' decisions.

Lian felt his age, an incredible weight on him, memory which confused one with too many alternatives, too much of wisdom, experience heaped on experience, which always counselled . . . *wait and learn.*

"Eldest!" the Malind elder called aloud, dared rise from her seat, marking herself among dissenters. "You will open the session?"

The whole hall was waiting. He declined with a gesture, hand trembling uncontrollably. There was a sudden murmur of surmise in the hall, dismay from many. He looked last on Moth, aged Moth, seeming older than he in her face and her brittle movements, but she was half a century younger. Her pale eyes met his, shrouded in wrinkles.

She bowed her head, having taken count as well as he; her hands occupied themselves with some minute adjustment in the trim of her robes.

Of those who had come first into the Reach, first humans among majat, there had been few survivors. Even immortality did not stand well against ambition.

This morning, in Council, there were fewer survivors still; and new powers had risen, who had waited a century in patience.

The new Hald rose, bowed ironically, and began to speak, setting forth the changes that were already made.

4

RAEN LIVED.

She discovered this fact slowly, in great pain, and on the verge of madness.

That she was Meth-maren, and therefore no stranger to majat at close quarters . . . this saved her sanity. She was naked. She was blind, in absolute darkness, and disoriented. She suffered the constant touches of the Workers the length of her body, wetness which worked ceaselessly on her raw wounds, and over all her skin and hair; an endless trickle of moisture and food was delivered from their mandibles to her mouth. Their bodies shifted above and about her, invisible in the dark, with touch of bristles and grip of chelae or mandibles. They hovered, never stepping on her, and their ceaseless humming numbed her ears as the dark numbed her eyes.

She was within the hive. No Kontrin had ever gone within a hive, not since the first days. The Pact forbade. But the blues, the peaceful blues, so long Kethiuy's good neighbors—had not cast her out. Tears squeezed from her eyes. A Worker sipped them instantly, caressing her face with feather-touches of its palps. She moved, and the humming at once grew louder, ominous. They would not permit her to stir. Raw touches on her wounds were constant. She flinched and cried out in agony, and they hovered yet closer, never putting full weight on her, but hindering each movement. The struggle, the needed coordination, grew too much. She hurt, and surrendered to it, finding a constant level for the pain, which finally merged with the sound and the sense of touch. There was neither past nor future; grief and fear were swallowed up in the moment, which stretched endlessly, circular.

She was aware of Mother. There was a Presence within the hive which sent Workers scurrying on this mission and that, to touch her and depart again in haste. In her delirium she imagined that she sensed the touches of this mind, that she was aware of things unseen, the movements in countless blind passages, the logic of the hive. She was cared for. The dark was endless, the touches at her body ceaseless, the sound only slowly varying, which was like deafness, and the touches became numbness. It was, for a long time, too difficult to think and too hard to struggle.

But from the latest sleep she wakened with a sense of desperation.

"Worker," she said into the numbing sound, on a delicate balance of returning strength and diminishing sanity. "Help. Help me." Her voice was unused, her ears so long assaulted by majat-song that human words sounded alien in her hearing. "Worker, tell Mother that I want to speak with her. Take me to her. Now."

"No," said the Worker. It sucked up more air and expelled it through chambers, creating the illusion, if not the intonations of human voice. Other sound fell away, Workers pausing to listen. Worker harmonized with itself as it spoke, the chambers all working in intricate combination. "Unnecessary. Mother knows your condition, knows all necessary things."

"Mother doesn't know what I intend."

"Tell. Tell this-unit."

"Revenge."

Palps swept her face, her mouth, her body, picking up scent. Worker could not comprehend. Majat individually had their limits. A Worker was not the proper channel for an emotional message and Raen knew it, manipulated the Worker with confusion. She had been cautioned against it from infancy, Workers going in and out of the labs, near at hand: *never play games with them*. Again and again she had heard the dangers of disoriented majat. It might call Warriors.

It drew back abruptly: she suddenly missed that particular touch. Others filled the gap, constantly feeling at limbs and body.

"It's gone for Mother?"

"Yes," one said. "Mother."

She stared at the blind dark, hard-breathing, euphoric with her success. She moved her hand with difficulty past the hindering limbs and palps of Workers, felt of her wounds, which were slick with jelly . . . tested her strength, moving her limbs.

"Are there," she asked, "azi within call?"

"Mother must call azi."

"I shall stand," she declared, rationally, firmly, and began to do so.

Workers assisted. Palps and chelae caressed her naked limbs and urged her, perhaps sensing new steadiness, conscious direction of her movements. Leathery bodies, chitin-studded, pushed at her. She trusted them, despite the possibility of pain. Their knowledge of balance and leverage was instinctive, none truer. With their support she stood, dizzied, and felt about her in the featureless dark. The floor of the chamber was uneven. Up and down seemed confused in the blackness. Her ears were still numbed by their voices; her hands met jointed palps and the hard spines of chelae. The Workers moved with her, never overbalancing her, supporting her with unfailing delicacy as she sought a few steps.

"Take me to Mother," she said.

The song grew harsh and ominous. "Queen-threat," one translated. Others took up the words.

They feared for Mother. That was understandable: she was female, and of females, the hive held only one. They continued to groom her, wishing to feed her, to placate her. She turned from their offerings, distressing them further. She was in pain and her legs trembled under her. The burn on her side had opened in the exertion of rising. They tended this, keeping it moist, and she could not fend them from it. The touches on raw flesh were familiar agony. She had time to reckon what might come of an intruding female, that there would be no welcome: she refused to think it. Mother must control all that happened here. Mother had tolerated her this far.

Then Worker must have returned; she reckoned so from the commotion that had broken out in the direction of the principal draft. "Bring," a voice fluted, human language, of courtesy. "Mother permits."

Raen went toward the voice, guided by delicate touches of bristling forelimbs, feeling to one side and the other in the blackness, following the currents of moving air. The tunnels were wide and high . . . must be, to afford passage to the tall Warriors. And once, when the right-hand wall vanished suddenly at a steep climb, she fell, in great pain, her body abraded by the hard earth. Workers chittered alarm and lifted her at once, steadied her more carefully as she climbed. The air began to be close and warm. Sweat ran on her bare skin, and distressed the Workers, who tried frantically both to walk and to remove the untidy moisture.

The tunnel seemed all at once defined, the first light her unused

eyes had perceived in uncounted days. It was the only proof she had
had that she was not blind, and yet it was so very faint she doubted
that she perceived it at all . . . circle patterns, oblong and irregular
patterns. She realized with a surge of joy that she *was* seeing, realized the shapes for apertures, opening onto a faint greenish phos-
phorescence, in which majat shadows stalked, bipedal, deceptively
human in some poses, like men in ornate armor. Raen hastened,
misjudged, almost lost her senses in the warmth and closeness of this
place. She gained her balance again, aided and supported into the
Presence.

She filled the Chamber. Raen hung in the grip of the Workers,
awed by the sight of Her, whose presence dominated the hive, whose
mind was the center of the Mind. *She* was the one, if there was any
single individual in the hive, with whom they of Kethiuy had so long
dealt . . . the legends of all her childhood, living and surrounded by
the seething mass of Her Drones, a scene of fever-dreams, males
glittering with the chitinous wealth of the hive.

Air stirred audibly, intaken.

"You are so *small*," Mother said. Raen flinched, for the timbre of
it made the very walls quiver, and vibrated in Raen's bones.

"You are beautiful," Raen answered, and felt it. Tears started
from her eyes . . . awe, and pain at once.

It pleased Mother. The auditory palps swept forward. Mother inclined Her great head and sought touch. The chelae drew her close.
Mother tasted her tears with a brush of the palps.

"*Salt*," said Mother.

"Yes."

"You are healed."

"I will be, soon."

The huge head rotated a few degrees on its circular jointing.
"Scouts report Kethiuy closed to them. This has never happened
since the hills have stood. We have killed a red-hive Worker on
Kethiuy's borders. Young queen, majat Workers do not enter an
area until Warriors have secured it. We tasted in it traces of greens,
of golds, recent in red-hive memory. Of humans. Of life fluids.
Greens deal with golds and avoid us. Why?"

Raen shook her head, terrified. Her mind began to function in
human terms. Majat were still in the valley, when the Pact dictated
restrictions. Red-hive. Ruil's allies. The whole Family might have
risen against Ruil; it had not; it had agreed, and red-hive remained.

She forgot the other questions, ignored logic. Reason could not be on her side. "I'll take Kethiuy back again," she said, knowing that it was mad. "I'll get it back."

"Revenge," Mother said.

"Yes. Revenge. Yes."

More air sighed into Mother's reservoirs. "Since before humans were known, blue-hive has held this hill. Humans came. We majat killed the first. Then we understood. We understood stars and machines and humans. One Family at last we permitted, all, all, red-hive, blue, green, gold . . . one human ship to come among us, one human hive. One ship, which brought the eggs of other humans. We were deceived so. Yet we accepted this. We permit Kontrin-hive to trade and breed and build, instead of all other humans. We permit Kontrin-hive to keep order, and to keep all other humans out. So we have grown, majat hives and Kontrin. We have gained metals, and azi, and consciousness of things invisible; we have enlarged our hives and sent out new queens beneath other suns. Azi work for us with their human eyes and their human hands, and trade gives us food, much food. We can support more numbers than was so in many cycles. We have ridden Kontrin ships to Meron and to Andra and Kalind and Istra, making new extensions of the Mind. We have been pleased in this exchange. We have gained awareness far surpassing times before humans. Your hives have multiplied and prospered, and increased nourishment for ours. But suddenly you fragment yourselves, and now you fragment us. Suddenly there is division. Suddenly there is nest-war among humans; this has been before: we have seen. But now there is nest-war threatened among majat, as it has not been since times before humans. We are confused. We reach out to gather the Mind and we have grown too wide; the worlds are too far and the ships are too slow to help us. We do not gain synthesis. We failed to foresee, and now we are blind. Aid me, Kethiuy-hive. Why are these things happening? What will happen now?"

Drones sang, and moved, a tide of life about Mother. The Drone voices shrilled, much of the song too high for human ears; sound drowned words, drowned thought, grated through bone.

"Mother!" Raen cried. "I don't know. I don't know. But whatever is going on in the Family, we can stop them, blue-hive could stop them!"

Air sighed. Mother heaved Herself lower, and breathed a bass note that made silence. "Kethiuy-queen, Kethiuy-queen—is it possible that our two species have overbred? What is the proper density of your population, young queen? Have you reached some critical level, which humans did not foresee? Or perhaps the equation for both our species is altered by some complex factors of our association. This should not have happened yet. We reach for synthesis and do not obtain it. Where is human synthesis? Have you the answer?"

"No." Raen shivered in the battering sound of Mother's voice, conscious of her own inexperience . . . of that of all men with majat. She reached in the utmost irreverence and touched the scent-patches below the compound eyes, imprinting herself as her kinsman would do with majat Workers, establishing friendship. Mother suffered this without anger, though the jaws might have closed at any instant, though the Drones were disturbed and disturbance ran through all the others. "Mother, Mother, listen to me. Kethiuy was blue-hive's friend, we always were, and I need help. They've killed —everyone. Everyone but me. They think they've won. Ruil sept has brought red-hive in with them. And do you think that Ruil will ever send them away again, or even that they know how? No, they're not going away. Ever. Red-hive will always be in Kethiuy, in our valley, and the Family isn't going to stop them or they would have done something by now."

"This seems an accurate estimation."

"I can take it back. If blue-hive helped me, I could take it back again."

Mother lifted up Her head, mandibles clashing. While She considered, She brought half a dozen new lives into the world. Workers snatched these up and carried them away. Drones groomed Her, uttering soft, distressed pipings, that shrilled away into higher ranges.

"It is very dangerous," Mother said. "Intervention violates the Pact. It adds confusions. And you have no translation computers. Without precise instruction, Warriors and humans cannot cooperate."

"I can *show* them. They can work that way. I can guide them. Some know Kethiuy, don't they? They've been there. And the others can follow them."

Mother hesitated. Again the head rotated slightly. "You are right, young queen, but I suspect you are right for the wrong reasons. All, all Warriors know Kethiuy. We do not fully understand how your thoughts proceed. But you can serve as nexus. Yes. Possible. Great risk, but possible."

"I can't yet. A few days, a few days, and then I'll be able to try. I'll need a gun, azi, Warriors. Then we can take Kethiuy back. Kethiuy's azi will join the fight when they have orders. Revenge, Mother! And blue-hive can come and go in Kethiuy when they please."

There was again long thought. Air sucked in, gusted out, sucked in again, and the songs of the attendants rose and fell. "I breed Warriors," She said. "This aspect of the hive is needful in these circumstances." While She spoke, She produced several eggs more. "I cannot breed azi. The azi will be irrevocable losses. There can be only one attempt on Kethiuy. Blue-hive has deceived red-hive concerning your presence here. Your death was reported. Warriors went out unMinded in this cause. But Warriors who go with you into Kethiuy cannot go unMinded; they could not then remember their mission or focus properly. There are reds full-circle of Kethiuy. Once you meet them and once blue-hive Warriors have fallen, you cannot retreat here. Taste will betray your existence here to red-hive and they will come here very quickly, for we have admitted a human to the inner hive, and there is strong sentiment against this practice. Therefore we will be fighting both here and there, which will require all our Warriors engaged at once. If we lose many Warriors in this action, we will face further attack from red-hive and others without sufficient time for new to hatch. Tell me, Kethiuy-queen, is this the best action? Perhaps you could find Drones and reestablish elsewhere with better prospect. You could produce Warriors of your own, young queen. You could buy azi. You could make a new hive."

Raen looked up into the great moiré-patterned eyes, in which she existed only as a pattern of warmth. "Red-hive is breeding Warriors too, won't that be so? If they've been expecting to attack Kethiuy, then they'll have been breeding toward it for a long time. Years. What when they come farther than they have? You need Kethiuy in Sul-sept control. If you wait . . . if you wait, you won't have time to breed enough Warriors, and red-hive—" She caught her breath, for she suddenly sensed what key to use, the essentially honest character of the blues. "Red-hive killed humans, killed Meth-marens, against the Pact. Ruil may have led them to it, but red-hive did it, they chose to do it. Do you want them for neighbors forever, Mother? And your Warriors—do they know the ways into Kethiuy that they can't see? I do. I can get them inside, now. I can get Warriors inside. It doesn't matter how many reds are guarding the doors if blues once get in. And I know I can get you that far."

There was silence.

"Yes," Mother said finally. *"Yes."*

A haze flooded over Raen's eyes, blurring greenish radiance and majat shadows, and the glitter of the Drones. She thought that she would fall, and she must not, must not show weakness before Mother, throwing all she had won in doubt. She touched the chelae, drew back, not knowing what rituals the majat observed with Her. None hindered her going. None seemed offended. She sought the tunnel out of the Chamber. The fungus-glow was like the retinal memory of light, and in this direction lay the dark, circles, holes in the light, into which she entered, losing suddenly all use of her eyes. The air hummed with Worker songs, the deeper songs of Warriors and the high voices of the Drones. She met bristly touches in the dark.

Workers swarmed and circled her, guided, caressed, sought her lips, to know her mind, though human chemistry was chaos to them. Perhaps the scent of Mother lingered. She did not flinch, but touched them in turn, delirious with triumph. They were the substance of her dreams and her nightmares, the majat, the power under-earth, native here where men were newcomers. She had touched the Mother who had lived under the hill since before she was born, and Mother had permitted it. She was Kontrin, of the Family, and the pattern grafted to her right hand was the power of the hives, which Kethiuy had always understood, more than all others of the Family—hive-friends. She laughed, bewildering the Workers, even while her senses began to fail.

5

CHAIRS MOVED; the group settled. A female azi, engineered for functions which had nothing to do with household labor, passed round the long table setting out drinks and beaming dutifully at each.

Eron Thel patted her leg, whispered a dismissal—she was his, as was the summer house in the Altrin highlands—and ignored her familiar charms as she left, although more than one of the men regarded her retreat. He was pleased by this, pleased by the obvious attention of the others to their surroundings. The objects which decorated the meeting room were unique, gathered from worlds even outside the Reach, and met with gratifying admiration . . . nothing of awe; the envy of kinsmen in the Family was difficult to rouse, but they looked, and approved.

Awe: that was for what entered the room now, the majat Warrior who took up guard by the door. That was power. Yls Ren-barant, Del Hald, certain others . . . they were accustomed to the near presence of majat; so was Tel a Ruil, well-accustomed—but familiarity did not remove the dread of such a creature, the sense that with it, invisible, were countless others, the awareness of the hive.

"Are you sure of the majat?" the Hald asked. "It remembers, even if it can't understand."

"It carries messages only to its hive," Eron said, "and its hive has some necessary part in this meeting, cousin, a very central part, as it happens." He beckoned to it, gave a low whistle, and it came, sank down again to sit beside the table, towering among them, incapable of the chairs. It was a living recorder: it received messages; it contained one. "Red-hive," Eron explained, "is standing guard at a number of critical posts, on these grounds and elsewhere. Incorruptible guards. Far better than ordinary security. Their desires are . . . not in rivalry with ours. Quite the contrary." He opened the plastic-bound agenda before him, and the others anxiously did the same. They were a mixed group, his own comrades, and some of the older representatives, selected ones . . . thankful to have been exempted from the general purge . . . grateful—Eron laughed inwardly, while gazing solemnly at the page before him—to have been admitted to this private meeting, the place of power where Council decisions were to be pre-arranged. He folded both hands on the agenda, smiled and leaned forward with a confidential warmth: it was a skill of his, to persuade. He practiced it consciously, foreknowing agreement. He was handsome, with the inbred good looks of all the Kontrin; he looked thirty: the real answer was two centuries above that, and that was true of most present, save a few of the Halds. He had grace, a matter most Kontrin neglected, content with power; he knew the use of it, and by it moved others. He was spokesman for the inner circle, for Hald and Ren-barant and Ruil Meth-maren. He meant to be more than that.

"Item one: widening the access permitted by the Pact. There has been too severe a restriction between ourselves and the hives." He reached, horrifying some of the older representatives, and laid a hand on the Warrior's thorax. It suffered this placidly, in waiting pose. "We have learned things earlier generations didn't know. The old restrictions have served their purpose. They were protective; they prevented misunderstandings. But—both majat and humans have adjusted to close contact. New realities are upon us. New cooperations are possible. Red-hive in particular has been responsive to this feeling. They are interested in much closer cooperation. So are golds, through their medium."

"Azi." The deep baritone harmonies of the Warrior vibrated even through the table surface. The elder faces at the end of the table were stark with dread. Eron watched them and not the Warrior, reckoning their every reaction. "We widen the hives," the Warrior said. "We protect human hives, for payment in goods. We need more fields, irrigation, more food, more azi. You can give these things. Red-hive and Kontrin—" More air hissed into the chambers. "—are *compatible*. We group now without the translation computers. We have found understanding, identification, *synthesis*. We taste . . . mutual desire."

That was awe. Eron saw it and smiled, a grim, taut smile, that melted into a friendlier one. "The power of the hives. Kontrin power, cousins. Human space shuts us *out*. Kontrin policy has limited our growth, limited our numbers, limited beta generation growth, limited the breeding of their azi. Colonized worlds throughout the Reach are fixed at the level of population reached four centuries ago. Our whole philosophy has been *containment* within the Reach. We have all acquiesced in a situation which was arranged for us . . . in the theory that humans and majat can't cooperate. But we can. We don't have to exist within these limits. We don't have to go on living under these restrictions. Item number one in the program before you is essential: widening access permitted by the Pact. Your affirmative vote is vastly important. Majat will be willing to assist us on more than the Worker level. We already have Warriors accessible to our direction, at this moment; and possibly, possibly, my dear cousins—Drones. The key to the biologic computer that is the hive. *That* kind of cooperation, humans working directly with what has made the hives unaided by machines . . . capable of the most complex order of operations. *That* kind of power, joined to our own: majat holistic comprehension, joined to human senses, human imagination, human insights. A new order. We aren't talking now about remaining bound by old limits. We don't have to settle for *containment* any longer."

No one moved. Eyes were fixed on him, naked, full of speculations.

No, more than speculation: it was fact; they had made it fact. This, here, in this room, was the reality of the Council. Decisions were being shaped here, and no one objected—no one, staring into the glittering eyes of the red Warrior—objected. At this end of the long table, in the hands of the Thels, the Meth-marens, the Renbarants and the Halds . . . rested authority; and the others would go into the Council hall and vote as they were told, fearing for themselves what had been wrought elsewhere.

And perhaps . . . perhaps conceiving ambitions of their own. The old order had been stagnant, centuries without change; change confronted them. *Possibilities* confronted them. Some would want a share of that.

"Second item," Eron said, not needing to look down. "A proposal for expansion of the azi breeding programs. The farms on Istra . . . have applied for expansion of their industry, repeatedly denied under the old regime. The proposal before Council grants that license . . . with compensations for past denials. The facilities on Istra and elsewhere can be quadrupled, an eighteen-year program of expansion easily correlated with the majat's eighteen-year cycle of increase. The hives can be paid . . . in azi; and the population of the Reach can be readjusted.

"Third item, cousins: authorization to beta governments for a ten percent increase in birth permits. The supervisory levels of industry and agriculture must increase in proportion to other increases.

"Fourth: licensing of Kontrin births pegged to the same ten percent. There has already been attrition; there may be more.

"Fifth: formal dissolution of certain septs and allotment of their Colors and privileges to other septs within those Houses. This merely regularizes certain changes already made."

There was laughter from the left side of the room, against the wall, where some of the younger generation sat. Eron looked, as many did. It was Pol Hald who extended his long legs and smirked to himself, ignoring his great-uncle's scowl.

"Questions?" Eron asked, trying to recapture the attention of those at the table. "Debate?"

There was none offered.

"We trust," Tel a Ruil said, "in your votes. Votes will be remembered."

Meth-maren arrogance. Eron scanned faces for reactions, as vexed in Ruil's bald threat as he had been in Pol's mistimed laughter. The elders took both in silence.

Glass smashed, rattled across the tiled floor. Eron looked rage at Pol Hald, who was poised in the careful act, hand open, his drink streamered across the floor. Eron started to his feet, thought better of it, and was grateful for the timely hand of Yls Ren-barant, urging him otherwise; and for Del Hald, who heaved his own bulk about from the table to rebuke his grandnephew.

Meth-marens and Halds: that hate was old and deep, and lately aggravated. Pol's act was that of a clown, a mime, pricking at Family pomposities, more actor than the azi-performers. The poised hand flourished a retraction, buried itself beneath a folded arm. *Sorry,* the lips shaped, elaborate mockery.

Tel Ruil was hard-breathing, face flushed. Ren-barant calmed him too, a slight touch, a warning. Tand Hald and Pol's cousin Morn both looked aside, embarrassed and wishing to disassociate themselves. Eron scanned the lot of them, smiled in his best manner, leaned back. Tel a Ruil relaxed with a similar effort. The small knot of oldest Houses at the end of the table was a skittish group, apt to bolt; those faces did not relax.

Eron relaxed entirely, and kept smiling, all cordiality. "We've begun a smooth transition. That has its difficulties, to be sure, but the advantages of keeping to a quiet schedule are obvious. There is the absolute necessity of keeping a calm face toward the betas and toward the Outside. You understand that. You understand what benefits there are for all of us. We have energies that are only grief to us, so long as we're pent within these outmoded limits. Those talents can be of service. Is there any debate on agenda issues?

"Are we agreed without it, then?"

Heads nodded, even those at the end of the table.

"Why don't we," Eron suggested then, "move on into the bar, and handle this in a more . . . informal atmosphere. Take your drinks with you if you like. We'll talk there . . . about issues."

There was a relieved muttering, ready agreement. The air held a slightly easier feeling, and chairs went back, men and women moving out in twos and threes, talking in low voices—avoiding the majat Warrior, whose head rotated slightly, betraying life.

Eron cast an urgent scowl at Del Hald, and a grimmer one at Pol and his two companions, who tarried in the seats against the wall, no more anxious to quit the room than their elders. Ros Hald and his several daughters delayed too, the whole clutch of Halds banded for defense.

But Del wilted under Eron's steady gaze, turned to Pol as he rose and caught at Pol's arm. Pol evaded his hand, cast his great-uncle a mocking look . . . son of a third niece to Del and Ros, was Pol: orphan from early years, Del's fosterling, and willing enough to put Del in command of Hald—but Del could not control him, had never controlled him. Pol was an irritant the Family bore and generally laughed at, for his irritation was to the Halds as often as any . . . and others enjoyed that.

Pol rose, with his cousins.

"The essence of humor," said Eron coldly, "is subtlety."

"Why, then, you are very serious, cousin." And seizing young Tand by the arm, Pol left for the bar, self-pleased, laughing. Morn followed in their wake, his grim face once turned back to Eron with no pleasance at all.

Eron expelled a short breath and looked on Del. The eldest Hald's lips were set in a thin line. "He's a hazard," Eron said. "Someone has to make sure of him. He can do us hurt."

"He should go somewhere," Yls said softly to Del, "where he can find full occupation for his humor. Meron, perhaps. Wouldn't that satisfy him?"

"He goes," the Hald said in a thin voice. "Morn goes with him. I understand you."

"A temporary matter," Eron said, and clapped his hand to the Hald's shoulder, pressed it as they walked toward the bar, Ros and his daughters trailing them. "My affection for the fellow. You understand. I don't want trouble right now. We can't afford it. Older heads have to manage this."

And when matters were more settled, Eron thought, Pol might come to some distant and inconspicuous end. Pol's wit was not all turned to humor . . . a child of the last great purge, Pol a Ren hant Hald, and participant in a more recent one, when Meth-marens had done some little damage. Pol Hald and Morn: Pol whose jokes were

infamous, and Morn who never laughed—they were both quite apt
to treacheries.

Eron thought this, and smiled his engaging smile, among others
who held their drinks and smiled most earnestly . . . anxious folk,
appropriately grateful to be invited here, admitted to the society of
power.

With the Halds and the Meth-marens, the Ren-barants and other
key elders here, with Thon and Yalt decimated, and their bloc
decimated . . . this gathering and the blocs they represented consti-
tuted the majority, not only of raw power on Cerdin, but of votes to
sway all the Reach.

6

"NIGHT," said a Worker.

Raen had sensed it. She had learned the movements and rhythms
of the hive which said that this was so: the increase of the traffic
coming in, the subtle shifts of air-currents, the different songs. Inside
the hive, the blackness was always the same. She had wished a piece
of the fungus to provide light, and Workers had brought it, establishing it on the wall of the chamber that was hers. By this she
proved to herself that her eyes still functioned, and gave them limits
against which to work. But that was only for comfort. She had
learned to see with touch, with the variations of the constant song of
the hive; and to understand majat vision. *Beautiful, beautiful,* they
called her, entranced with the colors of her warmth. *You are the
colors of all the hives,* the attendants told her, *blue and green and
gold and red, ever-changing; but your limb is always blue-hive.*

Her hand, covered with blue-hive chitin: they were endlessly fas-
cinated by that, which was a secret toward which majat had contributed. Kontrin genetic science and majat biochemistry . . . the two in
complement had spawned all the life of the Reach. Majat were capable of analyses and syntheses of enormous range and sensitivity, capable of sampling and altering substances as naturally as humans
flexed limbs, a partnership invaluable to Kontrin labs. But the hive,
she realized, the hive had never directly participated. The majat
Workers who came into the labs to stay were always isolated from

Workers of the hive, lest their chemical muddle impress the hive and disturb it. They never returned, but clung forlornly to human company and direction, dependent on it, patterned to the few humans who dared touch them: seldom resting, sleepless, they would work until their energy burned them out. Afterward, humans must dispose of the corpses: no majat would.

My being here is a danger to the Mind, she thought suddenly, with a deep pang of conscience. *Maybe my coming here has done what they've always feared, shifted their chemistry and affected them. Perhaps I've trapped them.*

There were azi, human Workers . . . the majat lived closely with those, unaffected by chemical disturbance.

Are they? she wondered; and then, more terrifyingly: *Am I?*

The song deafened, quivered in the marrow of the bones. Mother began it, and the Workers carried it, and the Warriors added their own baritone counterpoint, alien to their own species, the killer portion of the partitioned hive-mind. Drones sang but rarely . . . or perhaps, like much of majat language, the Drone songs were seldom in human range.

Raen rose, walked, tested the strength of her limbs. They had given her cloth of majat spinning, gossamer, the pale web of egg-sheaths. She did not wear it, for it disturbed them that she muted her colors, and nakedness no longer disturbed her. But she considered it now.

"I am ready," she decided. Workers touched her and scurried off, bearing that message.

A Warrior arrived. She informed it directly of her plans, and it hurried off.

Soon came the azi . . . humans, marginally so, though majat did not reckon them as such. Lab-bred, sterile, though with the outward attributes of gender, they served the hives as the Workers did, with hands more agile and wits more suited to dealing with humans, the new appurtenances the hives had taken on when they began to associate with humans, a new and necessary fragment of the hive-mind. Betas made them, and sold them to other betas . . . and to Kontrin, who sold them to the hives, shortlived clones of beta cells.

They came, bearing blue lights hardly brighter than the illusory fungus, and gathered about her, perhaps bewildered by the chitin on her hand, the realization that she was Kontrin, though naked as they, and within the hive. They were not bred fighters, these particular azi, but they were clever and quick, bright-eyed and anxious to serve. They were much prized by majat and must know their worth in the hive, but they were a little mad. Azi who dwelled among majat tended to be.

"We're going outside," Raen told them. "You'll carry weapons and take my orders."

"Yes," they said, voices overlapping, song-toned, inflectionless as those of the majat. There was a certain horror in these strangest of the azi. They came here younger than azi were generally sold; they acquired majat habits. They touched her, confirming her in their minds. She returned the touches, and gathered up the clothing she had been given. She wrapped it round and tied it here and there. It had a strange feel, light as it was, the reminder of a world and a life outside.

A Warrior came then, sat down, glittering in the azi-lights, chitinous head and powerful jaws a fantasy of jewel-shards. It offered her a pistol. It carried weapons of its own, besides the array nature had provided it: these items too majat prized, status for Warriors . . . empty symbols: humans had believed so. Raen took up the offered gun, found it shaped to a human hand. The cold, heavy object quickly warmed to her grip, and she took keen pleasure in the solidity of it: power, power to make Ruil pay.

"Azi-weapon," Warrior said. "Shall we arm azi?"

"Yes." She thrust her free hand against its scent-patches, reaching between the huge jaws. "Are you ready?"

A song hummed from Warrior. Others appeared, shifting from unseen tunnels into the meager light. They bore weapons, some belted to their leathery bodies; others went to the azi. The azi's human eyes were intense with something other than humanity. They grinned, filled with excitement.

"Come," she bade them.

Her word had Mother's authority behind it, the consensus of the hive. They moved, all of them, down the tunnels. Other Warriors joined them, a great following of bodies strangely silent now, songs stilled. They went in total blackness, azi-lights left behind.

Then they reached the cool air of the vestibule, and poured out under the night sky. Raen shivered in the wind and blinked, awed to find the stars again, to realize the brilliance of the night.

Warriors gathered silently about her, touching, seeking motive and direction. She was nexus, binding-unit for this portion of the Mind. She started away, barefoot and agile among the rocks.

7

STARLIGHT GLISTENED ON the lake, and bright artificial lights danced wetly at the farther shore, where Sul had never put lights. Raen stopped on the last rocky shelf above the woods and snatched a look at sights to which majat eyes were all but blind. For the first time her wounds hurt, her breath came short. Kethiuy-by-the-waters.

Home.

She felt more grief than she had yet felt. She had been out of human reference; and now the deaths became real to her again. Mother, cousins, friends . . . all ashes by now. Ruil would have spared no one, least of all eldest, so that there would be no possibility of challenge to their claim. Even yet the Family had made no move to intervene: Ruil still held here, or the hive would have known, would have told her. Red-hive remained here: of that they were sure.

Bile rose in her throat, bitter hate. She swallowed at it, and wiped her eyes with the back of her left hand, the gun clenched in her chitined right.

"Meth-maren," Warrior urged her. She scrambled down, reckless on the rocks, half-blind. Her limbs trembled with the strain, but Warrior caught her, its stilt-limbs strong and sure, a single downward stride spanning several of hers, joints bracing easily at extensions impossible for human limbs: its muscles attached to endo- and exoskeletons. Azi too swarmed back up the rocks and took her arms, helping her, handing her down to other Warriors, who urged her on in their turn Worker-fashion: most adaptable of majat, the Warriors, capable of independent judgment and generalized functions.

"This way," she bade them, choosing her way through the forest, along paths she knew. They went with hardly a crack of brush, walking as fast as she could run.

Red Warrior. It started from cover in the thickets and misjudged its capacity for flight. Blues sped after it, brought it down and bit it. The group of combatants locked into statuelike quiet for a few moments, blues bowed over their enemy, mandibles locked with majat patience. Then the head came free, and blue Warriors came to life and stalked ahead, some on the trail and some off, passing taste in weaving contacts, one to the other.

"Strong red force," Warrior said to Raen, and nervously touched palps to her mouth as they walked, a curious backward dance in the act. It interpreted aloud what taste should have told her, a mere breathing of resonances. "Ruil humans. No sense of alarm. They do not expect attack."

The blue Warriors were elated; their movements were exaggerated, full of excess energy. Some darted back, urging on those who lagged; a dark flood of bodies in their wake tumbled down the rocks and through the trees. The azi, touching each other and grinning with joy, would have loped ahead. Raen distrusted their good sense and hissed at them to hold back. She was hurrying as much as she could. Her side hurt anew. Her bare feet were torn by the rocks and the thorns. She ignored the pain; she had felt worse. An increasing fear gripped her stomach.

I'm too slow, she thought in one moment of panic. *I'm holding them back too long.* And in another: *There are grown men down there, used to killing; there are guard-azi, bred for fighting. What am I doing here?* But they were not expecting attack: the blues read so; and they would not be expecting majat. She looked about her at her companions, at creatures whose very instincts were specialized toward killing, and drank in their enthusiasm, that was madness.

They were nearing the end of the woods, where there were only thickets and thorn-hedges. "Hurry," Warrior urged her, seizing her painfully by the arm. Majat were not like men, who respected a leader: hive-mind was one. She pressed a hand to her throbbing side and started to run, spending the strength she had saved.

There were ways she knew, paths she had run in other days, shortcuts azi workers took to the fields, places where the hedges were thin. She ran them, dodging this way and that with agility that only the azi matched in this tangle. A wall loomed up, the barrier to the inner gardens by the labs, no obstacle to the Warriors, who livingchained their way up and made a way for the azi. Azi swarmed over, tugging and pulling at her to help her after, climbing over their naked and sweating bodies. She made it. The chain undid itself. The last Warrior came over, a stilt-limbed prodigy of balance and strength, pulled by its fellows.

They were pleased with the operation. Mandibles scissored with rapid excitement. Suddenly they broke and raced like a black flood in the dark, majat and azi, moving with incredible rapidity.

More red-hivers. Bodies tangled on the lawn, rolled; the wave-front blunted itself, knotted in places of resistance. There were crashings in the shrubbery, the booming alarm of Warriors, flares of weapons. Raen froze in shadow, panic-stricken, everything she had planned slipping control. Then she adjusted her grip on her gun, swallowed air and ran, to do what she had come to do.

A Warrior appeared by her, and another, half a dozen more, and some of the azi. She raced for the main door, for an area visibly guarded by red-hive. Fire laced about them, and from them. War-riors beside her fell, twitching, uttering squeals from their resonance chambers. In sanity, she would have panicked. There was nothing to do now but keep running for the door . . . too far now to retreat. She reached the door and Warriors tangled in combat about her. She burned the mechanism, and struggled with the door; azi and then a Warrior used their strength to move it. Azi and Warriors flooded behind her as she raced into Kethiuy's halls.

"Exits all covered," Warrior breathed beside her; and then she re-alized where all the others had gone—majat strategy, efficient and sudden. The main corridor of the central dome lay vacant before her . . . what had been home. Rage hammered in her in time to her pulse.

Suddenly, far off down the wings, there was crashing and shrilling of alarms, from every point of the building: blue-hivers were in. A domestic azi darted from cover, terrified, darted back again, up the stairs—and screamed and fell under a rush of majat down them.

Red-hivers. Raen whipped the gun to target and fired, breaking up their formation, even while blue-hive swarmed after them.

There were human cries. Doors broke open from westwing: Ruils burst from that cover with a handful of blues on their heels. Raen left majat to majat, steadied her pistol on new targets and fired, care-ful shots as ever in practice, at the weapon's limits of speed. Her eyes stayed clear. Time slowed. They fell, one after the other, young and old, perhaps not believing what they saw. Their faces were set in horror and hers in a rigid grin.

Then a baritone piping assailed her ears and the blues in all parts of the corridor signalled each other in booming panic, regrouping to signals she could not read. From eastwing came others, reds, golds, a horde of armed azi.

Raen stood and fired, coldly desperate, not seeing how to retreat. Some of the Kethiuy azi and the surviving blues attempted to rally to her, but fire cut them down and a rush of majat came over them.

Warrior fell almost at her feet, decapitated. The limbs continued to struggle, nearly taking her off her feet. Naked azi sprawled dead about her. She spun then, catching her balance, and tried to run, for there was no other hope. The blues, such as survived, were in full flight.

Something crashed down on her, crushing weight.

8

A SECOND TIME Raen lay quietly and waited to live or die; but this time the walls were stark white and chrome, and the frightened azi who tended her kept their eyes down and said nothing.

That was well enough. There was nothing she particularly wanted to hear. She was not in Kethiuy. That told her something. Drugs hazed her senses, keeping her from wishing anything very strongly.

This continued for what seemed days. There were meals. She was fed, being unable to feed herself. She was moved, bothered for this and the other necessity. She said nothing in all this time, and from the azi there was no word.

But finally the drugs were gone, and she waked with a majat guard in the room.

Red-hive. She recognized the badges, the marks they wore for humans, who could not see their colors. Red-hive Warrior.

She knew then that she had lost, lost more than Kethiuy.

The majat gave her clothing, gray, without Color. She put it on, and found the close feeling of it utterly strange. She sat afterward with her hands in her lap, on the edge of the bed, staring at the wall. The majat guard did not move and would not move while she did not.

There was shock attendant on regaining the human world; there were realizations of what she had lost and what she had become. She was very thin. Her limbs still hurt, although she bore scars only on her side. She held her right hand clenched in her left, feeling the beaded surface of the chitin which was her identity: Raen, Sul-sept, Meth-maren, Kontrin. They gave her gray to wear, and not her Color. There was no way to remove the other distinction save by massive scarring. A scale lost would regrow. She had heard of Kontrin deprived of identity, mutilated by assassins, or by Council order. That prospect frightened her, more than she was willing to show. It was all she had left to lose. She was fifteen, going on sixteen. She was mortally afraid.

It was a very long time before the call she anticipated came. She went with the azi guards, unresisting.

9

THEY WERE THE AUTHORITY of the Family, the available heads of the twenty-seven holdings and the fifty-odd subgrants, with their out-world branches. They wore the Colors of House and sept, and glittered with chitinous armor . . . ornament, little protection, for most was for right-arm only; and weapons in Council were outlawed. Old men and old women inside, although the faces did not make it evident . . . Raen scanned the half-circular array, the amphitheatre of Council, herself in the low center, and realized with mixed feelings that no one present wore Kethiuy blue. She saw Kahn, once the youngest in Council; at seventy-two, senior of assassin-ravaged Beln sept of the Ilit; he looked thirty. There was Moth, who showed her age most, incredibly wrinkled and fragile . . . going soon, the Family surmised. She was beyond her six hundredth year and her hair was completely silver and thinning. And Lian, Eldest of Family . . . to him Raen looked with a sudden access of hope; Lian still alive, uncle Lian, who at seven hundred had been immune from assassination perhaps because the Family grew curious how long a Kontrin could live and remain sane. Lian was one of the originals, old as the establishment of humans on Cerdin, first in Council.

And he had had friendship with Grandfather. Raen had known him from her infancy, a guest in her home, who had noticed her at Grandfather's feet. She tried desperately now to meet his eyes, hoping that about him still gathered some power to help her; but she could not. He nodded away in his own thoughts, placid, seeming elsewhere, and simply old, as betas grew old. She stared past him at the others then, altogether out of hope.

There were Eron Thel and Yls Ren-barant, allies, some of Ruil's friends. Sul had detested them. And there were others of that ilk. She had deepstudied the whole Council and all the Houses of greatest import to Sul Meth-maren, so that she knew every name and face and the manners and history of them: but the faces she should have seen were not there, and others wore their Colors. There were new representatives for Yalt and Thon, young faces. Her skin went cold as she reckoned what must have happened throughout the Family—many, many Kethiuys, in so short a time. New men had come into power everywhere, on Cerdin and elsewhere, a new party in power, and from it only Ruil Meth-maren was missing.

Eron Thel rose, touched his microphone to activate it, looked at Council in general, sweeping the banks of seats.

"Matter before the Council," he said, "the custody of the minor child Raen a Sul Meth-maren."

"I am my own keeper," Raen shouted, and Eron turned slowly to stare at her, in the silence, the consent of all the others. Of a sudden she realized in whose keeping she was intended to be, and what that keeping might be. The thought closed on her throat, making words impossible.

"That you tried to be," Eron Thel said, his voice echoing from the speakers. "You succeeded in wiping out Ruil-sept. All perished, down to the youngest, by your action. *Child* may be a misnomer in your case; some have argued to that effect. If you held the Meth-maren House, you would have to answer for its actions; and I don't think you'd want that, would you? Council means to consider your age. You'd be wise to remember that."

"I am *the* Meth-maren," she shouted back at him.

Eron looked elsewhere, signalled. Lights dimmed. Screens central to the room leapt into life. There was Kethiuy. Raen's heart beat painfully, foreknowing in this prepared show something meant to hurt her. *I shall not,* she kept thinking, *I shall not please them.*

There was the garden, by the labs. Bodies lay in neat rows. The scene came closer, and she recognized them for the azi of Kethiuy, most merely workers, inoffensive and innocent of threat to any, face after face, all of them slaughtered and laid out for inspection, one body upon another. The line went on and on, hundreds of them, most strange to her, for she had not known all who worked the fields; but there was Lia, there were others, and those faces suddenly appearing struck at her heart. She feared they would show her the bodies of her kin next, but they should have been long cremated and beyond such indignities. She hoped that this was so.

The scene shifted to the hills. Majat swarmed everywhere, reds, greens, gold. She saw blue-hivers dead. The lens approached the very vestibule of blue-hive. There were white objects cast about the entry, eggs, their fragile wrappings torn, half-formed majat exposed to the air. Blue-hive bodies were stacked in a tangle of stilt limbs, Workers as well as Warriors, and naked human limbs among them, dead azi.

Then Kethiuy again. Fire went up from it. Walls crumbled in great heat. Candletrees went up in spurts of flame.

The screen dimmed; the lights of the room brightened. Raen stood still. Her face was dry, cold as the center of her.

"You can see," said Eron, "Meth-maren's holding is abolished. It has no adult membership, no property, no vote."

Raen shrugged, jaw set, not trusting her voice. This was something in which her protests meant nothing. She was Kontrin, well-versed in the techniques of assassination and the exigencies of politics; and reckoned well her probable future in the hands of an enemy House. She had deepstudied the history of the Family. She knew the adjustments that necessarily followed a purge, knew that even elders of sensitive conscience would raise no objection now, not for so slight a cause as herself, who could not repay. She continued to focus on the empty screen, wishing a weapon in hand, one last chance, perceiving her enemies more than Ruil alone.

There was another stirring, from a quarter she had not expected. She did look. It was old Moth, who had been an ornament in Council for years, representative of little Eft-sept of the Tern, silent whatever happened, siding with any majority, sleeping through many a session.

"There has been no vote," Moth said.

"But there was," said Eron. "Moth, you must have been napping." There was laughter, obedient, from all Eron's partisans, and it had many voices.

Suddenly Eldest rose, Lian, leaning on the rail. He was not the joke that Moth was. There was quiet. "There was no vote," he repeated. No one laughed. "Evidently, Thel, you have counted your numbers and decided a vote of the full Council would be superfluous." Lian looked toward Raen, blear-eyed, his face working to focus. "Raen a Sul hant Meth-maren. My apologies and condolences, from the Family."

"Sit down, Eldest," said Eron.

The old man briefly pressed Moth's hand, and Moth left her place and descended the steps toward the center where Raen stood. She had difficulty with her robes and the steps, and tottered as she walked. There was displeasure voiced, but no one moved to help or to stop her.

"Procedures," Moth said over the speakers, when she had gained the floor and faced them. "There are procedures. You have not followed them."

"I will tell you something," said Eldest from his place above. He activated his microphone. "It's a dangerous precedent, this destruction of a House, this . . . assumption of consent. I've lived since the first ship came into the Reach, and I'll tell you this: I saw early that men couldn't live here without being corrupted."

"Sit down," someone shouted at him.

"The hives," Eldest said, "had a wealth to be taken; but humanity and the hive-mind weren't compatible. A probe came down on Cerdin; it came into red-hive possession, the crew held captive, such of them as survived. *Celia* probe. The hives gained knowledge. There was *Delia,* then, that got through. Back in human space there was talk about sterilizing Cerdin before the plague could spread. But suddenly the hives changed their attitude. They wanted trade, wanted us, wanted—one ship, they said: one hive for humans, and the Reach set aside for themselves."

There was sullen silence. Moth touched Raen's sleeve, pressed her wrist with a soft-fleshed hand. Someone else started to his feet, a Delt; Yls Ren-barant stopped him. The silence continued, deadly. Lian looked about him, uncertainly, and pursed his lips.

"We tricked them." Lian's voice, quavering, resumed. "We brought in human eggs and the equipment to handle them. Half a billion eggs, all ready to grow. And we set up where this building stands, and we set up our labs and we started breeding while our one ship made its trade runs and the others of us who had skill at communication developed agreements with the hives." His voice grew stronger. "Now do you suppose, fellow Councillors, that the hives didn't know by then what we were about? Of course they saw. But the human animal is a mystery to them, and we kept it that way. They saw a hive-structure. They saw an increasing number of young and a growing social order which well-agreed with their own pattern. We planned it that way. They still had no idea what a non-collective intelligence was, or what it could do. Just one large hive, this of ours, all one mind. They knew better, perhaps, in theory. But the pattern of their own thinking wouldn't let them interpret what they saw.

"When they began to learn, we frightened them with our differences. Frightened them most with the concept of dying. They locked into our chemistry and understood the process, worked out a cure for old age. They had finally gained the dimmest notion, you see, of what our individuality *is*. The hives are millions of years old. Do you reckon why the majat were worried about our dying? Because among majat, there are only four persons . . . red, green, gold, and blue. Those are their units of individuality. These *persons* have worked out how to deal with each other over millions of years. They're accustomed to stability, to memory, to eternity. How could they deal with a series of short-lived humans? So they cured death . . . for some of us, for those of us fortunate enough to be born Kontrin. The beta generations, the product of our cargo of eggs . . . they go on dying at the human rate, but we live forever. Economic ruin, if there were many of us. So even we Kontrin kill each other off from time to time. The majat used to find that shocking.

"But now things will change, won't they? You've gotten red-hive Warriors to kill Kontrin; blue-hive has admitted a human. Things change. Now the majat have taken another vast leap of understanding. And one of the four entities which has lived on Cerdin for millions of years—is on the verge of extinction. Not beyond recall: majat have more respect for life than we do, after their fashion. But you persuaded them to kill an immortal intelligence, knowingly. Several of them. And one day you may live to see the reward of that. Thanks to majat science, some of you may live to see it.

"Seven hundred years we've thrived here and across the Reach. The lot of you have all you could possibly need. The betas take care of the labor and the trade; and the betas, the betas, dear friends, discovered the best thing of all, discovered what the hives really prize: they trade in humanity, altered humanity, gene-tampered humanity, humanity that can't reproduce itself, that self-destructs at forty, for economic convenience. So even the betas don't have to do physical labor; they just breed azi and balance supply and demand. And the barrier to the Outside holds firm, so that the whole Reach and all it produces is ours—including the betas and the azi. None of us tries the barrier.

"Ever been out that far, to the edge? I have. In seven hundred years a man has time to do everything of interest. Ugly worlds. Nothing like Cerdin. But we've established hives that far out, extensions of our four entities here . . . or whole new personalities. Has anyone ever asked them? We've entered into a strange new relationship with our alien hosts; we've become intimately involved in their reproductive process . . . indispensable to them. Without metals, majat could never have left Cerdin. They have no eyes to see the stars, just their own sun, their own sun-warmed earth. But we've changed that. Even majat don't have to work much, not the way they used to seven hundred years ago. But they thrive. And their numbers increase. And back here at Alpha, this Council, this wise . . . expert Council . . . makes ultimate decisions about population levels, and how many of us can be born, and where; and how many betas; and where betas can be licensed to produce azi, and when azi levels have to be reduced. Humanity's brain, are we not, doing for our kind what the queens do for the hives? And in that process, we've grown *different,* my young friends.

"I was here. I was here from the beginning, and I've watched the change. I'm from Outside. I remember. You . . . you've studied this in your tapes, you young ones of a century or so, you Council newcomers. I'm an old man and I'm delaying things. You think you know it all, having been born here, in the Reach, in a new age you think an old Outsider can't understand. But I'm going to go on telling you, because you need to remember it. Because the majat will tell you that a hive that has lost its memory, that has . . . unMinded itself . . . is headed for extinction.

"Do you know that no ship from Outside has ever tried to reach Cerdin? Ever, since *Delia?* We're quarantined. They're all around us, Outside. Human space. These few little stars . . . are an island in a human sea. But you don't see them trying to come in. Ever wonder why?

"They don't want the majat, my friends. They want what the majat produce, the chitin-jewels, the biotics, the softwares. Humans from Outside meet the betas and the azi at Istra station, and they will pay for those goods, pay whatever they must. They cost us little and Outsiders value them beyond price. But they don't want the majat. They don't want hives in their space.

"And above all, they don't want us. Alpha Hydri, the Serpent's Eye. Offlimits by treaty. And no one wants in. No one wants in."

"Get to the point," Eron said.

Slowly Lian turned, and stared at Eron. There was quiet, anticipation. And suddenly outcries erupted, people throwing themselves from seats. A bolt flew from Moth's hand to Eron, and the man fell. Raen flung herself to the back wall, expecting more fire, eyes scanning wildly for weapons on the other side.

"When you practice assassination," Lian said, while Moth held the weapon on Eron's friend Yls, "recall that Moth and I are oldest."

Yls died. Men and women screamed and tried to bolt their seats. Moth continued to fire. There were bodies everywhere, on the floor, draped over seats, over the rail, in the aisles. At last she stopped, and the half of the Council that remained alive huddled against the door.

"Resume your seats," Lian said.

Slowly, cowed, they did so. Moth still had her weapon in hand.

"Now," said Lian, "the matter of a vote."

Someone was sick. The stench of burning was in the hall. Raen clenched her arms about her and shivered.

"Raen a Sul hant Meth-maren," Lian said.

"Sir."

"You may go. I think that it would be advisable to leave Cerdin and seek some House in obscurity. You have outlived all your enemies. Count that fortune enough for a lifetime. I don't think it wise that you shelter with another House on Cerdin; you could too easily become a cause, and the Family has seen enough of that."

"Sir," she began to protest.

"There's no reason to detain you for proceedings. The vote is only a formality. Kethiuy is gone; that is a fact over which Council has no control. You broke the Pact and involved majat. The ones principally involved are dead; their influence is ended. Your own judgment in what you've done was that of a child, and under compulsion. You refuse guardianship; I daresay you are competent to survive without it. So I charge you this, Raen a Sul: avoid majat hereafter. You are given all the privileges of majority, and if you cross Council's notice again, it will be under those conditions. You are free to go, with that understanding. I suggest Meron. Council liaison there will be sympathetic. I have an old estate there that you can use. You won't be without friends or advice."

"I don't need it."

It was out of bitterness she said it. She saw Lian's mouth go to a taut line, and reckoned that she should not have refused; but it was not in her nature to bend. She looked on Moth, looked on Eldest, and turned, walked, with difficulty, to the door and her freedom.

She did not stop, nor look back, nor shed the tears that urged at her. They dried quickly. She knew the passages from the Old Hall at Alpha to the beta City. She carried nothing, but the clothes she had been given and the identity on her hand.

Leave Cerdin: she would, for there was nothing on Cerdin she wanted.

10

THE BETAS OF THE City were shocked, alarmed that a Kontrin appeared alone among them, with bodyguards. Perhaps they had some apprehension of trouble, having heard of the decimation of Kontrin Houses, and of blue-hive, and therefore feared to involve themselves in her affairs; but they had no means to refuse.

She bought medical care, and drugs for the pain; she slept a time in a public lodging, and recovered herself. She bought clothing and weapons, and engaged a shuttle up to station, where she hired a ship with the credit of the Family—the most extravagant she could find. She was moody and the beta crew avoided her.

That was the first journey.

It brought her to Meron. She did not take Eldest's offer, but bought a house and lived there on the endless credit which the chitin-pattern of her right hand signified. There were Halds onworld: her interest pricked at that . . . Pol and Morn; she stirred to care again. Plotting their assassinations and guarding against her own occupied her time . . . until Pol and Morn turned up boldly on her doorstep, and Pol swept her a mocking courtesy.

Pol Hald. She had passed her sixteenth birthday; he was unchanged, whatever age he really was. He stared her up and down and she looked at him, and at Morn, who stood at his shoulder; and she realized with a chill that her gun was on safety in its belt-clip; she could not possibly be quick enough.

"Your operation is entirely too elaborate," Pol said, grinning at her. "But well-thought, little Meth-maren. I applaud your zeal . . . and your precocious cleverness. Please call them off."

She fairly shook with rage, but fear chilled her mind to clarity. Of a sudden she saw the reaction to take with this man, and grinned. "I shall," she said. "Thank you for the courtesy, Pol Hald."

"What self-possession you have, Meth-maren."

"Shall I leave Meron?"

"Stay," he said, and laughed, with a flourish of his chitined hand. "You have what Ruil never had: a sense of balance. I know neither of us would be safe under those terms. There'd be a new plot by suppertime."

She regarded them through slit lids. "Then you leave Meron."

He laughed outright, brushed past her, into her home. Morn followed.

She thumbed the safety off her gun and stared at them, watching their hands. Pol folded his arms and nodded a gesture to his cousin. "Go on," he said, "Morn. You've no interests here."

Morn surveyed her up and down, his gaunt face untouched by any emotion. Without a word he strode to the door and closed it behind him.

And Pol settled in the nearest chair and folded his arms, extended his long legs before him. His death's-head face quirked into an engaging smile.

He ate the dinner she served him; they sat across the table from one another: he made a proposal which she declined, and laughed rather regretfully when she did so. Pol's humor was infamous, and infectious; and he hazarded his life on it now. She refrained from poisoning him; he refrained from using whatever weapons he surely carried on his person. They laughed at each other, and she bade him good night.

He and she turned up at the same social events thereafter, in the busy winter season of Kontrin society on Meron. They smiled at each other with the warmth of old friends, amused at the comment that caused. But they never met in private.

And eventually there was an attempt on her life.

It happened on Meron, a year after Pol and Morn had taken

themselves elsewhere, in separate directions, Morn to Cerdin and Pol to Andra. It happened in the night, on another Kontrin's estate, a Delt, Col a Helim, who was her current, but not exclusive interest. She was twenty-one. Col died. She did not. None came back from that attempt, but they were azi who had done it, and their past was wiped, their tattoos burned away. She swore off Delts, suspecting something local and involving a rival, and moved and engaged a small estate on Silak.

Word reached her there that Lian had died . . . assassination, and no one knew now how long he would have lived, so the longest human life in the Reach reached no natural conclusion and Kontrin everywhere had been frustrated. The attempted coup was a failure, and the assassins all died miserably, the penalty of failure and the revenge of Kontrin who had considered Lian's long life a talisman of luck, an example of their own immortality.

Moth held Eldest's place, first in Council. The Council thus remained much as it had been, and Raen took no interest in its affairs . . . took no interest in the present for anything political. There was no more Kethiuy, although the nightmares lingered. She was mildly amused in one respect, for she reckoned at last that the attempt on her had been connected to Lian's impending fall; but that had failed, the conspirators (Thel and some lesser Houses) decimated, and matters were settled again. The Family knew where she was at all times, and if she had been of continuing importance to any cause, someone would have attempted to enlist her or to assassinate her in the fear that she belonged to some other cause. Neither happened. The remnant of the House of Thon on Cerdin established itself as the new liaison with the hives. Raen settled again on Meron and, when she heard how Thon had usurped the post with the hives, she pursued vices in considerable variety and nuance and gained a name in Meron society. She was twenty-four.

She had her privileges: those never failed; and she had no lack of anything money could buy. She amused herself, sometimes within Kontrin society and sometimes in moody withdrawal from all contact. She looked on betas and azi with the disdain of her birth, which was natural, and her tedious lifespan, which was (since Lian's assassination) indefinite, and her power, which was among betas as fearsome as it was negligible where she would have desired to apply it.

She had as her current interest Hal a Norn hant Ilit, a remote and

seldom-social member of the House most involved in Meron's bank-
ing; she reckoned he might be a direct relative, and tried to jog his
memory which of his kinsmen Morel a Sul Meth-maren had had for
a lover, but he avowed it was several, and she went frustrated. He
was frustrating in other ways, but he was a useful shelter, and they
had some common interests; few could argue comp theory with him,
or for that matter, cared to: she did, and for all the vast disparity in
their age (he was in his third century) and in outlook, he avowed
himself increasingly infatuated.

She found herself increasingly uncomfortable, and began, as
gently as possible, to break that entanglement, coming out of her
isolation into the society he hated; and part of that society was his
grandnephew Gen.

In all of this, there was a certain leisure.

The order which Moth maintained in Council and in the Reach
was a calm one, and a prosperous one, and no one on Cerdin or off
seemed energetic enough to seek Moth's life: it seemed superfluous,
for no one expected that life to extend much longer. What enemies
Moth had were evidently determined to outwait her, and that meant
a surface peace, whatever built up beneath. Raen reckoned with
Moth in power she might even have gone home to Cerdin, had she
asked. She simply declined to make the request, which required on
the one hand a humility toward Council she had never acquired; and
on the other, faith that Moth would survive long enough for her to
entrench herself among friends: she did not think so. And more
than all other reasons, she simply refused to face the ruin at
Kethiuy; there was nothing there for her.

On Meron, there was.

Then strife erupted among majat on Meron, reds and greens and
blues at odds. Golds took shelter and stayed out of sight. Reds
strayed into the passages of the City on Meron, terrifying betas and
occasioning several deaths in panicked crowds. A Kontrin estate or
two suffered minor damage.

Raen quitted Meron then, having lost the four azi who had served
her the last several years.

The four azi, dying in their sleep, did not suffer. Raen did, of bitter anger. It gave her temporary motivation, settling with the
erstwhile Ilit lover who had let red-hivers into the estate; but that
was arranged with disappointing lack of difficulty; and afterward she
was tormented with doubt, whether Hal Ilit had had choice in the

matter. Blue-hive, she heard, skirmished with the others and re-treated, sealed into its hill again, while reds came and went where they would: Thons came from Cerdin to try to persuade them back into quiet.

There was similar disturbance on Andra, and Raen was there, . . . attempted last of all to contact blue-hive directly, but it evaded her, and sealed itself in, while other hives walked Andran streets with impunity.

She was thirty-four. It had been nineteen years since Kethiuy, since Cerdin.

She began, obsessively, to practice certain skills she had let fall in recent years. She withdrew entirely unto herself, and ceased to mourn for the past.

Even for Kethiuy, which was the last thing she had loved.

She was utterly Kontrin, as Moth was, as Lian had been, as all her elders were. She had come of age.

11

"SHE'S ON KALIND," Pol said.

Moth regarded him and his two kinsmen with placid eyes.

"She can be removed," Morn said.

Moth shook her head. "Not yet."

"Eldest—" Tand leaned on her desk, facing her with a lack of re-spect not uncommon in Halds, not uncommon in his generation. "Blue-hive has been astir on Meron; she was there; and on Andra; she was there; and on Kalind; she is there now. The indications are that she's directly involved, contrary to all conditions and advice. She's broken with all her old contacts."

"She's learned good taste," said Pol. He smiled lazily, leaned back in his chair, folded his slim hands on his belly. "And about time."

Morn fixed him with a burning look. Pol shrugged, made a loose gesture, rose and bowed an ironic goodbye. The door closed behind him.

"She's involved," Tand said.

Moth failed to be excited. Tand finally took the point and stood back, folded his hands behind him, silent as Morn.

"You are trying to urge me to something," Moth said.

"We had thought in your good interests, in those of the Family—there was some urgency."

"You are called here simply to inform me, Tand Hald. Your advice is occasionally of great value. I do listen."

Tand bowed his head, courtesy.

Bastard, she thought. *Eager for advancement however it comes fastest and safest. You hate my guts. And, Morn—yours too.*

"Other observations?" she asked.

"We're waiting," Morn said, "for instructions in the case."

Moth shrugged. "Simply observe. That's all I want."

"Why so much patience with this one?"

Moth shrugged a second time. "She's the last of a House; the daughter of an old, old friend. Maybe it's sentiment."

Morn took that for the irony it was and stopped asking questions.

"Simply watch," she said. "And, Tand—don't provoke anything. Don't create a situation."

Tand took his leave, quietly. Morn followed.

Moth settled in her chair, hands folded, dreaming into the colored lights that flowed in the table surface.

BOOK THREE

1

THERE WAS, in the salon of the *Andra's Jewel,* an unaccustomed silence. Normally the first main-evening of a voyage would have seen the salon crowded with wealthy beta passengers, each smartly turned out in expensive innerworld fashions, tongues soon loosened with drink and the nervousness with which these folk, the wealthy of several worlds, greeted their departure from Kalind station. There were corporation executives and higher supervisors, and a scattering of professionals of various fields dressed to mingle with the rich and idle, estate-holders, of whom there were several.

This night there were drinks poured: azi servants passed busily from table to table, the only movement made. The fashionable people sat fixed in their places, venturing furtive glances across the salon.

They were the elite, the powers and movers of beta society, these folk. But they found themselves suddenly in the regard of another aristocracy altogether.

She was Kontrin. The aquiline face was the type of all the inbred line, male or female, in one of its infinite variations. Her gray cloak and bodysuit and boots were for the street, not the society of the salon, elegant as they were. It was possible that they masked armor . . . more than possible that they concealed weapons. The chitinous implants which covered the back of her right hand were identification beyond any doubt, and the pattern held unlimited credit in intercomp, in any system of the Reach . . . unlimited credit: the money for which wealthy betas strove was only a shadow of such entitlement.

She smiled at them across the room, a cold and cynical gesture, and the elite of the salon of *Andra's Jewel* tried to look elsewhere, tried to pursue their important conversations in low voices and to ignore the reality which sat in that corner of empty tables. Suddenly they were uncomfortable even with the azi servants who passed among them bearing drinks . . . cloned men, decorative creations of their own labs, as they themselves had been spawned wholesale out of the Kontrin's, seven hundred years past. Proximity to the azi became suddenly . . . *comparison.*

The party died early. Couples and groups drifted out, which movement became a general and hasty flow toward the doors.

Kont' Raen a Sul watched them go, and in cynical humor, turned and met the eyes of the azi servant who stood nearest. Slowly all movement of the azi in the salon ceased. The servant stood, held in that gaze.

"Do you play Sej?" she asked.

The azi nodded fearfully. Sej was an amusement common throughout the Reach, in lower and rougher places. It was a dicing game, half chance and some part skill.

"Find the pieces."

The azi, pale of face, went among his companions and found one who had the set. He activated the gaming function of the table for score-keeping, and laid the three wands and the pair of dice on the table.

"Sit down," said Kont' Raen.

He did so, sweating. He was young, several years advanced into the service for which he existed. He had been engineered for pleasing appearance and for intelligence, to serve the passengers. He had no education beyond that duty, save what rumor fed him and what he observed of the betas who passed through the salon. The smooth courtesy which he had deepstudied in his training gave him now the means to function. Other azi stood about, stricken by his misfortune, morbidly curious.

"What's your name?" she asked.

"Jim," he said. It was the one choice of his life, the one thing he had personally decided, out of a range of names which belonged to azi. Only azi used it, and a few of the crew. He was vastly disturbed at his loss of anonymity.

"What stakes?" she asked, gathering up the wands.

He stared at her. He had nothing, being property of the line, but his name and his existence.

She looked down and rolled the wands between her hands, the one glittering with chitin, and infinite power. "It will be a long voyage. I shall be bored. Suppose that we make wager not on one game, but on the tally of games." She laid the wands down under her right hand. "If you win, I'll buy you free of Andra Lines and give you ten thousand credits for every game you've won. Ten rounds an evening, as many evenings as there are in my voyage. But you must win the series to collect: it's only on the total of games, our wager."

He blinked, the sweat running into his eyes. Freedom and wealth: he could live out his life unthreatened, even in idleness. It was a prize beyond calculation, and not the sort of luck any azi had. He swallowed hard and reckoned what kind of wager he might have to return.

"But if I win," she continued, "I shall buy your contract for myself." She smiled suddenly, a bleak and dead smile. "Play to win, Jim."

She offered him first cast. He took up the wands. The azi in the salon settled silently, watching.

He lost the first evening, four to six.

2

A SMALL, TENSE COMPANY gathered in the stateroom of the ASPAK Corporation executive. There were other such gatherings, private parties. The salon was still under occupation on this third evening. No one ventured there any longer save during the day. There remained available of course the lower deck lounge, where the second-class passengers gathered; but they were not willing to descend to that society, not under the circumstances. Their collective pride had suffered enough.

"Maybe she's going to Andra," someone suggested. "A short trip . . . perhaps some bizarre humor . . ."

The Andran executive looked distressed at that idea. Kontrin never travelled commercial; they engaged ships of their own, a class of luxury unimaginable to the society of *Andra's Jewel,* and separate. Impatience, near destination . . . even the possibility of assassins and the need to get offworld by the first available ship: the surmise made sense. But Andran affairs did not want a Kontrin feud: there was trouble enough without that. This one . . . this Kontrin, did things no Kontrin had ever done, and might do others as unpredictable. Worse, the name Raen a Sul stirred at some vague memory, seldom as names were ever exchanged between Kontrin and men . . . *Men* . . . *Beta* was not a term men used of themselves.

This one had been on Andra, and might be returning. Majat were where they ought not to be, and suddenly Kontrin were among them. Until lately it had been possible to ignore Kontrin doings entirely; a man could live years and not so much as see one; and now one came into their midst.

"There's a rumor—" someone else said, and cleared her throat, "there's a rumor there's a majat aboard."

Another swore, and there was a moment's silence, nervous glances. It was possible. Majat travelled, rarely, but they travelled. If it were so, it would be somewhere isolate, sinking into dormancy for the duration of the flight. Majat parted from the hive became disoriented, dangerous: this one would have awakened long enough to have performed its mission, whatever it was, and to secure passage home—function assigned it by the hive. So long, it might remain sane, having clear purpose and a goal in sight. Thereafter, it must sleep, awakening only in proximity to its hive.

There were horror tales of majat awakening prematurely on a ship; and majat horror tales were current on Andra, on Kalind, on Meron, unreasoning actions, killings of humans. But the commercial lines could no more refuse a majat than they could have refused the Kontrin. It was a question of ownership, of the origins of power in the Reach, and some questions it was not good to raise.

Silence rested heavily on the gathering, which sat uncomfortably on thinly padded furniture in an anteroom designed for smaller companies. Ice rattled in glasses. The executive cleared his throat.

"Kontrin don't travel alone," he said. "There are always bodyguards. Where are they?"

"Maybe they're . . . some of us," a Kalinder suggested. "I'd be careful what I said."

No one moved. No one looked at anyone else. No Kontrin had ever done such a thing as this one had done: they feared assassination obsessively, guarding the immortality which distinguished their class as surely as did the chitin-patterns. That was another

cause by which men found it difficult to accept the presence of a
Kontrin, for her lifespan was to theirs far longer than theirs was to
that of the azi they created. Men were likewise designated for mor-
tality, as surely as the Kontrin had engineered themselves otherwise,
and kept that gift from others. It was the calculated economy of the
Reach. Only the owners continued. Men were to the Kontrin . . . a
renewable resource.

Someone proposed more drinks. They played loud music and
talked in whispers, only to those they knew well, and eventually this
party too died.

There were other gatherings in days after, in small number, by
twos and by threes. Some stayed entirely in their staterooms, fearing
the nameless threat of meetings in the corridors, unnerved by what
was happening on worlds throughout the Reach. If there was a
majat aboard, no one wanted to find it.

The game continued in the salon. Jim's luck improved. He was
winning, thirty-seven to thirty-three. The other azi's eyes followed
the fall of the wands and the dice as if their own fortunes were
hazarded there.

The next evening the balance tilted again, forty to forty.

3

ANDRA'S JEWEL jumped and made slow progress to Andra station.
Ten grateful first-class passengers disembarked and the Kontrin did
not. The majority of lower-deck passengers left; more arrived, short-
termers, for Jin, and three first-class, bound for Meron. The game in
the salon stood at eighty-four and eighty-six.

The *Jewel* crept outward in real-space, for Jin; again for Sitan and
the barrenness of Orthan's moons; made jump, for glittering Meron.
Such passengers who remained, initiates of the original company,
were dismayed that the Kontrin did not leave at Meron: there had
even been wagers on it. The occupation of the salon continued unin-
terrupted.

The score stood at two hundred forty-two to two hundred forty-
eight.

"Do you want to retire?" Kont' Raen asked when the game stood
even. "I've had my enjoyment of this. I give you the chance."

Jim shook his head. He had fought his way this far. Hope existed in him; he had never held much hope, until now.

Kont' Raen laughed and won the next hand.

"You should have taken it," an azi said to Jim that night. "Kontrin don't sell their azi when they're done with them. They terminate them, whatever their age. It's their law."

Jim shrugged. He had heard so already. Everyone had had to tell him so. He worked the dice in his clenched hand and sat down on the matting of the azi quarters. He cast them again and again obsessively, trying the combinations as if some magic could change them. He no longer had duties on the ship. The Kontrin had marked his fatigue and bought him free of duties. He was no longer subject to ration: if he wanted more than his meals, he did not have to rely on tips to buy that extra. He seldom chose to go beyond ration, all the same, save once or twice when he had been far ahead and his appetite improved. He cast the dice now, against some vague superstition formed of these empty days. He played himself, to test his run of luck.

He could not have quit, the game unfinished, could not go back to the others, to being one of them, and exist without knowing what he had given up. He would always think that he might have been free and rich. That would always torment him. The Kontrin had sensed this, and therefore she had laughed. Even he could understand the irony.

4

ANDRA'S JEWEL reached Silak and docked. *Ship will continue to Istra,* the message flashed to the three passengers who should have disembarked there with the others, to seek connections further. So grand a ship as *Andra's Jewel* did not make out-planet runs with her staterooms empty. But the passengers who had packed, unpacked, with the desperate fear that they would do better to disembark anyway and seek other transportation, however long they had to wait. A few more passengers boarded. The *Jewel* voyaged out, ghostly in her emptiness.

"It's the Kontrin," the ITAK envoy whispered to his wife. "She's going to Istra."

The woman, his partner-in-office, said nothing, but glanced anxiously at the intercom and its blank screen, as if this might be carried to other ears.

"What other answer?" The Istran shaped the words with his lips, soundlessly. "And why would they come in person? In *person,* after all?"

The woman regarded him in dread. Their mission to Meron, dismal failure, had been calamity enough. It was their misfortune that they had chosen the *Jewel* for their intermediate link to Silak— tempted by the one brief extravagance of their lives, compensation for their humiliation on Meron. They were executives in a world corporation; they had attempted to travel a few days in the grand style of their innerworld counterparts, once, *once,* to enjoy such things, foreseeing ruin awaiting them on Istra. "We should have gotten off this ship at Silak," she said, "while we had the chance. There's only Pedra now, and no regular lines from there. We should have gotten off. Now it's impossible she wouldn't take notice of it. She surely knows we're Istran."

"I don't see," he said, "how she could be involved with us. I don't. She's from *before* Meron. Unless—while we were stalled on Meron—some message went through to Cerdin. I asked the azi where she boarded. They said Kalind. That's only one jump from Cerdin."

"You shouldn't have asked the azi."

"It was a casual question."

"It was dangerous."

"It was—"

"Hush! not so loud."

They both looked at the intercom, uncomfortable in its cycloptic presence. "It's not live," he said.

"I think she owns this ship," the woman said. "That's why there aren't any guards visible. The whole crew, the azi—"

"That's insane."

"What else, then? What else makes sense?"

He shook his head. Nothing did.

5

THEY REACHED BARREN PEDRA, and took on a straggle of lower-deck passengers, who gaped in awe at the splendor of the accommodations. Nothing the size of the *Jewel* had ever docked at Pedra. There were no upper-deck passengers: one departed here, but none boarded.

The game stood at four hundred eighteen to four hundred twelve. Bets had spread among the free crew. Some of them came and watched as the azi's lead increased to thirteen. It was the widest the game had ever been spread.

"Your luck is incredible," the Kontrin said. "Do you want to quit?"

"I can't," Jim said.

The Kontrin nodded slowly, and ordered drinks for them both.

Andra's Jewel made out from sunless Pedra and jumped again. They were in Istran space, beta Hydri two, snake's-tail, the Outside's contact point with the Reach.

There were, after the disorientation of jump, a handful of days remaining.

The game stood at four hundred fifty-nine to four hundred fifty-one. Midway through the evening it was four hundred sixty-two to four hundred fifty-three, and there was still a deep frown on the face of Kont' Raen. She cast the wands governing aspect of the dice. They turned up star, star, and black. The aspects were marginally favorable. With black involved, she could have declined the hand and cancelled it, passing the wands to Jim for a new throw. She simply declined the first cast of the dice. The azi threw six and she threw twelve: she won the star and it took next star automatically: twenty-four. The azi declined first throw on the deadly black. She threw four; the azi threw twelve. The azi had won black, cancelling his points in the game. A low breath hissed from the gallery.

"Do you concede?" Kont' Raen asked.

Jim shook his head. He was tired; his position in this game was all but hopeless: her score was ninety-eight; his was zero . . . but it was his option, and he never conceded any game, no matter how long and wearing. Neither did she. She inclined her head in respect to his tenacity and yielded him the wands. His control of the hand, should black turn up, afforded him a marginal chance of breaking her score.

And suddenly there was a disturbance at the door.

Two passengers stood there, male and female, betas. The azi of the salon, so long without visitors to serve of evenings, took an instant to react. Then they hurried about preparing chairs and a table for the pair, taking their order for drinks.

The game continued. Jim threw two ships and a star. He won the ships and had twenty; Raen won the star and took game.

"Four hundred fifty-four," she said quietly, "to your four hundred fifty-two."

Jim nodded.

"Take first throw."

He shook his head; one could refuse a courtesy. She gathered up the wands.

A chair moved. One of the passengers was coming over to them. Raen hesitated in her cast and then looked aside in annoyance, the wands still in her hand.

"I am ser Merek Eln," the man said, and gestured back to the woman who had also risen. "Sera Parn Kest, my wife."

Raen inclined her head as if this were of great moment to her. The betas seemed to miss the irony. "Kont' Raen a Sul." And with cold courtesy: "Grace to you both."

"Are you . . . bound for Istra?"

Raen smiled, though coldly. "Is there anything more remote?"

Merek Eln blinked and swallowed. "The ship must surely start its return there. Istra is the edge of the Reach."

"Then that must be where I am bound."

"We . . . are in ITAK, Istran Trade . . ."

". . . Association, Kontrin-licensed. Yes. I'm familiar with the registered corporations."

"We offer our assistance, our—hospitality."

Raen looked him up and down, and sera Kest also. She let the silence continue. "How kind," she said at last. "I've never had such an offer. Perhaps I'll take advantage of it. I don't believe there are other Kontrin on Istra."

"No," Eln said faintly. "Kontrin, if you would care to discuss the matter which brings you here—"

"I don't."

"We might . . . assist you."

"You aren't listening, ser Merek Eln. I assure you, I have no interests in ITAK matters."

"Yet you chose Istra."

"Not I."

The man blinked, confused.

"I didn't divert the ship," Raen said.

"If we can be of service—"

"You've offered me your hospitality. I've said that I shall consider it. For the moment, as you see, I'm engaged. I have four games yet to go this evening. Perhaps you'll care to watch." She turned her back on ser Merek Eln and sera Kest, looked at Jim, who waited quietly. Azi were accustomed to immobility when not pursuing orders. "What do you know of Istra?" she asked him.

"It's a hive world. A contact point with Outside. Their sun is beta Hydri."

"The contact point. I don't recall any Kontrin going there recently. I knew one who did, once. But surely there are some amusements to be had there."

"I don't know," Jim said very faintly, quieter in the presence of the Istrans than he had been since the beginning. "I belong to Andra Lines. My knowledge doesn't extend beyond the range of my ship."

"Do these folk make you nervous? I'll ask them to leave if you like."

"Please, no," Jim said hoarsely. Raen shrugged and made the cast.

It came up three stars. She took first throw. Twelve. Jim made his: two. Raen gathered thirty-six points. Jim took up the wands as if they were venomed, threw three whites. Raen won the dicing and automatically took game.

"Your luck has hit a sudden downward turn," Raen said, gathering up the three wands. She passed them to him. "But there's still margin. We're at four hundred fifty-five to your four hundred sixty-two."

He lost all but the last game, setting the tally at four hundred sixty-three to four hundred fifty-seven. His margin was down to six.

He was sweating profusely. Raen ordered a drink for them each, and Jim took a great swallow of his, all the while staring at a blank corner of the room, meeting no one's eyes.

"These folk do make you uncomfortable," she said. "But if you win—why, then you'll be out among them, free and very wealthy. Perhaps wealthier than they. Do you think of that?"

He took yet another drink and gave no answer. Sweat broke and ran at his temple.

"How many games yet remain?" she asked.

"We dock three days from now."

"With time in the evening for a set?"

He shook his head. This was to his advantage. He still had his lead.

"Twenty games, then." She glanced at the Istrans, gestured them to seats on opposite sides of her table, between him and her. Their faces blanched. There was rage there, and offense. They came, and sat down. "Do you want to play a round for amusement?" she asked Jim.

"I would rather not," he said. "I'm superstitious."

Azi served them, all four. Jim stared at the area of the table between his hands.

"It's been a long voyage," Kont' Raen said. "Yet the society in the salon has been pleasant. What brings you out from Istra and back, seri?"

"Trade," Kest said.

"Ah."

"Kontrin—" Merek Eln said. She looked at him. He moistened his lips and shifted his weight in his chair. "Kontrin, there's been some disturbance on Istra. Matters are still in a state of flux. Doubt-less—doubtless you've had some report of these affairs."

She shrugged. "I've kept much to myself of late. So trade took you off Istra."

There was a hesitation, a decision. Merek Eln went pale, wiped at his face. "The need for funds," he confided. His voice was hardly more than a hoarse whisper. "There has been hardship on Istra. There's been fighting in some places. Sabotage. One has to be care-ful about associations. If you've brought forces—"

"You expect too much of me," Kont' Raen said. "I'm here on holi-day. That is my profession."

This was irony even they understood as such.

They said nothing. Kont' Raen sipped at her drink and finished it. Then she rose and left the table, and Jim excused himself hastily and withdrew among the azi who served.

The thought occurred to him, not for the first time, that Kont' Raen was simply insane.

He thought that if she gave him the chance now to withdraw from the wager, he would take it, serve the ship to the end of his days, content in his fate.

He lost two points of his margin the next evening. The tally stood at four hundred sixty-seven to four hundred sixty-three.

There was no sleep that night. Tomorrow evening was the last round. No one in the azi quarters offered to speak to him. The others sat apart, as if he had a contagion. It was the same when one approached termination. If he won, they would hate him; if he lost, he would only confirm what they believed, the luck that made them what they were. He crouched on his mat in a corner of the compartment, tucked his knees up to his chin and bowed his head, counting the interminable moments of the final hours.

6

JIM WAS AT the table early as usual, waiting with the wands and the dice. The Istrans arrived. Other azi served them, while even beta crew arrived in the salon to watch the last games. The whole ship was shut down to skeleton crew, and those necessary posts were linked in by monitor.

Jim looked at the table surface rather than face the stares of free men who owned his contract, who had come to watch the show. They would not own it after this night, one way or the other.

There were light steps in the corridor, toward the door. He looked up, saw Kont' Raen coming toward him. He rose, of respect, the same ritual as every evening. Azi set drinks on the table, as every evening.

She was seated, and he resumed his chair.

What others did in the room now he neither knew nor cared. She cast the dice for the first throw; he did, and won the right to begin.

He won the first game. She won the next. The sigh of breath was audible all about the salon.

The third game was hers, and the fourth and fifth.

"Rest?" she asked. He wiped at the sweat that gathered on his upper lip and shook his head. He won the sixth and lost the seventh and eighth.

"Four sixty-nine to four sixty-nine," she said. Her eyes glittered with excitement. She ordered ice, and paused for a drink of water. Jim drained his glass and wiped his face with his chilled hand. The cooling did not seem enough in the salon. People were crowded all about them. He asked for another drink, sipped it.

"Your stakes are greater," she said. "I cede first throw."

He accepted the wands. Suddenly he trusted nothing, no generosity of hers. He trusted none present. Of all the bets which had been made on the azi deck, he was sure now how they had been laid. The looks as the Kontrin tore away his lead let that be known . . . who had bet on him, and who against. Some of those against, he had believed liked him.

He cast. Nothing showed but black and white; he declined and she cast: the same. It was a slow game, careful. At twenty-four he threw a black . . . chose to play the throw against her thirty-six, and won not only the pair of ships, but also the black, wiping out his score. His hands began to sweat. He played more conservatively then, built up his score and declined the next black, dreading black in her hand, which did not show. He reached eighty-eight. She held seventy-two, and swept up a trio of stars to take the ninth game.

It stood at four hundred sixty-nine to four hundred seventy, her favor.

"What do you propose if we tie?" she asked.

"An eleventh game," he said hoarsely. Only then did it occur to him that he might have proposed cancellation of bets. She nodded, accepting him at his word. He must win tenth to force an eleventh.

She gathered up the wands. The living chitin on the back of her hand shone like jewels. The wands spilled across the table, white, white, white.

Game, for the winner.

She offered him the dice. She led; the courtesy was mandated by the custom of the game. His hand was sweating; he wiped it on his chest, took the dice again, and cast: six.

She took up the cubes for her own turn, threw.

Seven.

"Game," she said.

There was silence. Then those in the room cheered . . . save the azi, who faded back, reminded that escape was not for their kind. Jim blinked, and fought for breath. He began to shiver and could not stop.

Kont' Raen gathered up the wands and, one by one, broke them. Then she leaned back in her chair and slowly finished her drink. Quiet was restored in the room. Officers and azi remembered that they had duties elsewhere. Only the Istran couple remained.

"Out," she said.

The couple hesitated, indignant, determined for a moment to stand their ground. Then they thought better of it and left. The door closed. Jim stared at the table. An azi never looked directly at anyone.

There was long silence.

"Finish your drink," she said. He did so; he had wanted it, and had not known whether he dared. "I thank you," she said quietly. "You have relieved my boredom, and few have ever done that."

He looked up at her, suicidal in his mood. He had been pushed far. The same desperation which had kept him from withdrawing from the game still possessed him.

"You could have dropped out," she reminded him.

"I could have won."

"Of course."

He took a last swallow from his glass, mostly icemelt, and set it down. The thought occurred to him again that the Kontrin was quite, quite mad, and that out of whim she might order his termination when they docked. She evidently travelled alone. Perhaps she preferred it that way. He was lost in the motivations of Kontrin. He had been created to serve the ships of Andra Lines. He knew nothing else.

She walked over and took the bottle from the Istrans' table, examined the label critically and poured again, for him and for her. The incongruity of the action made him sure that she was mad. There should have been fresh glasses, no ice. He winced inwardly, and realized that such concerns now were ridiculous. He drank; she did, in bizarre celebration.

"None of them," she said, with a shrug at all the empty tables and chairs, the memories of departed passengers, "none of them could dice with a Kontrin. Not one." She grinned and laughed, and the grin faded to a solemn expression. She lifted the glass to him, ironic salute. "Your contract is already purchased. Ever borne arms?"

He shook his head, appalled. He had never touched a weapon, seldom even seen one.

She laughed and set the glass down.

And rose.

"Come," she said.

Later, high in the upper decks and the luxury of the Kontrin's staterooms, it came to what he thought it might.

BOOK FOUR

1

"COMMERCIAL," MOTH MUTTERED, and steepled her wrinkled hands, staring at them to the exclusion of the several heads of Houses who surrounded her. She laughed softly, contemplating the reports of chaos strewn in a line across the Reach.

"I fear," said Cen Moran, "I lack your perception of humor in the matter. This involves Istra, and the hives, and the surviving Methmaren. I see nothing whatsoever of humor affordable in the combination."

"Kill her," said Ros Hald.

Moth turned a chill stare on him, and he fell silent. "Why? For trespass? I don't recall that visiting Istra is grounds for such extreme measures."

"It's a sensitive area, Istra."

"Yes. Isn't it."

The Hald broke eye contact. Moth did not miss that fact, but glanced instead at Moran and the others, raised querulous brows. "I think some Kontrin presence there might be salutary, provided it's discreet and sensible. The Meth-maren's presence is usually quiet toward non-Kontrin."

"A hive-world," said Moran, "another hive-world, and critical."

"The only hive-world," said Moth, "without Kontrin permanently resident. We've barred ourselves from that . . . sensitive . . . contact point, at least by custom. Depressing as Istra is reputed to be, I suspect we simply lack enthusiasm for the necessary privations. But majat don't seem to mind being there, do they? In my long memory, only Lian had the interest to visit the place after the beta City was set down there—and that was very long ago. Maybe we should reconsider. Maybe we've created a blind spot in our intelligence. Reports from Istra are scant. Perhaps a Kontrin should be there. It surely couldn't hurt their economy."

"But," said Kahn a Beln, *"this* Kontrin, Eldest? There's been trouble across the Reach. And the Meth-maren, of the hive-masters —of *that* House—the simplest prediction would tell us. . . ."

"We will let her alone," Moth said.

"If it were put to a vote," said Moran, "that sentiment would not carry. Thon would be the logical choice, trustworthy. The Meth-maren, no."

Moth looked at him steadily. A measure would have to be written up formally: some one of them would have to put his name on it as proponent. Someone would have to risk his personal influence and the well-being of his agents. She did not estimate that Moran quite meant it as an ultimatum: he was simply kin to the ineffectual Thons. There were more meaningful, more inflammatory issues on which opposition could rise. When challenge came, if it came in the Council at all, it would not be like this, on a directive for assassination; such things did not make good rallying points. Assassinations were usually managed by House or executive order, quietly and without embarrassments.

"Let her alone," Moth said, "for now."

There was a small and sullen silence at the table. Talk began quietly, drifted to other matters. There were excuses made early, departures in small groups. Moth watched them, and noted who left with whom, and reckoned that not a few of them were plotting her demise.

And after me, she thought with a taut, hateful smile, *let it come.*

She spread upon the table the reports which had occupied the committee, all the various problems with which the Council had to deal: over-breeding of azi, population stresses and economic distress among underemployed betas, turmoil in the hives, killings of greens and the lately-recovered blues by reds and golds on Cerdin. The Thon House, hive-liaisons in the place of Meth-marens, proved ineffectual: the reports skirted that fact and covered truth with verbiage.

And, persistently, reports that reds sought out Kontrin and made gifts, trespassed boundaries, turned up in beta areas.

There was a proposal put forward by the House of Ilit and the econbureau that this surplus be consumed by the modest ship-building industry of Pedra. It gathered support; it was very possible that it would pass. It would alleviate conditions that created discontent on several worlds.

Moth studied it, frowning—remembered to push a button, to summon the young man waiting—and sat leaning her mouth against her curled hand and staring moodishly at the persuasive statistics on the graphs. The Hald entered; she was still pursuing her train of thought, and let him stand, the while she read and gnawed at her finger.

At last she shifted the reports into three stacks, and then into one, and put atop it a dry monograph entitled *Breeding Patterns among the Hives.*

"Commercial," she chuckled again, to the listening walls, and looked up sharply at young Tand Hald. "Kill her, you would say too. I've heard the Hald point of view until my ears ache. You're nothing if not consistent. Where's Morn?"

Tand Hald shrugged, stared at her quite directly. "I'm sure I don't know, Eldest."

"Pol with him?"

"I'm sure I don't know that either. Not when I left him."

"Where did you part with them?"

"Meron." He failed to flinch. The eyes remained steady. "Pol involved himself with amusements there. Morn went his own way; I went mine. No one controls them."

She gazed at him steadily, broke contact after a moment. "You want her taken out."

"I give the best advice I have."

"Why are you so apprehensive of this one subject? Personal grudge?"

"No. Surely your agent who watches your other agents would have turned up any personal bias in this."

She laughed softly at the impertinence. The youngest Hald had been with her too long, too closely. She was not diverted. "But why then? What interference has she ever attempted in Family business? She's never made an economic ripple; she only—*travels,* from time to time."

"Is she your agent?" Tand asked, a question which had taken him five years to ask.

"No," Moth said very softly. "But I protect her as if she were. She is, after a remote fashion. Why do you fear her so, Tand?"

"Because she's atypical. And random. And a survivor. She ought to have grudges. She never exercises them . . . save once, but that was direct retaliation. She never pursues the old ones."

"Ah."

"Now she's chosen a place where there's potential for serious harm. There are Outsiders directly available; there are hives, and no one to watch her, only betas. Her going there has purpose."

"Do you think so? She always seems to proceed by indirection."

"I believe there is reason."

"Perhaps there is. Yet in all these years, she's never reached back to Cerdin."

"It was a mistake to have let her live in the first place."

"The Family has searched for cause against her ever since she left Cerdin. We've found none; she's given none."

"So she's intelligent, and dangerous."

Moth laughed again, and the laughter died and she sorted absently through the reports, shifting them into disorder. "How long do majat live?"

"Eighteen years for the average individual." Tand seemed vaguely annoyed by this extraneity. "Longer for queens."

"No. How long do majat live?"

"The hives are immortal."

"That is the correct answer. How long is that?"

"They calculate—millions of years."

"How long have we been watching them, Tand?"

The young man shifted his weight and his eyes went to the floor and the walls and elsewhere in his impatience. "About—six, seven hundred years."

"How long would a cycle take—in the lifespan of an immortal organism?"

"What kind of cycle? Eldest, I'm afraid I don't see what you're aiming at."

"Yes. We don't, do we? We lose our memories with death. Individually. Our records record . . . only what we once perceived as important, at a given hour, under given circumstances. The Drones remember . . . everything."

Tand shook his head. A sweat had broken out on his face. "I wish you would be clear, Eldest."

"I wish I had a long enough record at hand. Don't you see that things have changed? No, of course not. You're only a third of a century old yourself. I'm only six hundred and a half. And what is that? What is that experience worth? The Pact used to keep the hives out of human affairs. Now reds and golds . . . mingle with us, even with betas. Hives are at war . . . on Cerdin, Meron, Andra, Kalind . . . On Kalind, it's blues and greens against red. On Andra, and Cerdin, it's blues and greens against red and gold. On Meron, it's blues against reds and greens, and gold is in hiding."

"And Istra—"

"One can't predict, can one?"

"I don't understand what you're trying to say, Eldest."

"Until you do—spread the word among the Houses that Moth still has her faculties. That killing me would be very unwise."

"The matter," Tand said tentatively, "the matter is Raen a Sul, Eldest."

"Yes, it is, isn't it?" Moth shook her head. Blinked. At nigh seven hundred, the brain grew unreliable, too full of information. There were syntheses which verged on prophecy, cross-connections too full of subtle intervening data. Her hands shook uncontrollably with the effort of tracing down these interloping items. Self-analysis. Of all processes, that was hardest, to know why the data interconnected. Her eyes hurt. Her hands could not feel the papers they handled. She became aware that Tand had been speaking further.

"Go away," she said abruptly.

He went.

She watched him go, without doubt now: her death was planned.

2

THE AZI HAD settled finally, his world redefined. He slept as if the luxury of the upper deck staterooms were no novelty at all. Raen gathered herself up quietly, slipped past the safety web which shrouded the wide bed, and stretched, beginning now to think of departure, of the disposition of personal items scattered through the suite during the months of voyaging.

Now there was the azi . . . help or burden: she had not yet decided which. She had second thoughts of her mad venture, almost changed her mind even on this morning, as often of mornings she had had doubts.

She put it from her mind, refused to think of more than the present day; that was her solution to such thoughts, at least for the hour, at least to pass that tedious time of waiting and solitude. The voyage itself had promised to be unendurable; and it was done; there had even been moments of highest enjoyment, moments worth living, too rare to let finality turn them sour. She refused to let it happen—yawned and stretched in deliberate, self-controlled luxury —went blindly to the console and keyed a double breakfast into the foodservice channel.

A red light blinked back at her at once, Security advisement. Her pulse jolted; she keyed three, which was the channel reserved for ship's emergencies and notices.

MAJAT PASSENGER HAS AWAKENED. PLEASE VACATE VICINITY OF SECTOR ✕31.

On schedule—alarm to the ship, none to her. She punched in communications. "This is 512. I advise you take extraordinary care in emergency in 31. This is not a Worker. Please acknowledge."

They did so. She cut them off, rubbed her eyes and sought the shower, her social duty fulfilled.

The touch of warm water and the smell of soap: some things even the prospect of eternity could not diminish. Water slid over a body which bore only faint scars for all that was past, spare of flesh despite all her public self-indulgences. She endured heat enough to make her heart speed, generating a cloud of comfortable steam within the cabinet, combed her hair and punched the dry circulation into operation.

Dry, combed, composed, she hauled a sheet out of storage, wound into it and ventured the chill air of the outer rooms, back to the console with a new object in mind.

Jim's papers were on the desk. She flicked through them, keyed in ship's store with a few requests for display. Samples in simulacrum flashed onto the screen, accurate representation of his body-type with one and another suit. She indicated approval for several and put them on her account, selected a travelling case from the same source, along with an assortment of necessary personal items and a few of jewelry.

Doing so amused her. She anticipated his delight. But after the screens went dark and the only pleasant necessity of the morning had been cared for, she sat still on the bench and faced the prospect of Istra itself, of other things, in a sudden dark mood which had some origin in a morning headache.

Perhaps it was overmuch of drink the night before. She had certainly overindulged.

Perhaps it was the azi, who had a melancholy about him which touched strongly at her own.

She bestirred herself finally and dressed . . . plain, beige garments, close-fitting. And, which she had not done on the ship, she put on the sleeve-armor, which was simple ostentation. Light, jewel-toned chitin strung on the lightest of filaments, it ran from the living jewels of her right hand to her collar: the beauty of it pleased her, and the day wanted some ceremony, after such long voyaging.

She laughed bitterly, staring back at the replacement of her fortunes, who slept, still oblivious, and thought her all-powerful. Where it regarded a ship like *Andra's Jewel,* this was surely so.

There were several cloaks among her belongings. She took out the beige one, and intended to put it on, to hide the sleeve armor, as it would hide the weapons she carried constantly when she left the stateroom. But it went back into the locker, the beige cloak; she fingered another, that was blue, white-bordered, forbidden.

Even to have it was defiance of the Family. In almost two decades no one had worn that Color.

She did now, in the consciousness of isolation—quiet, furtive defiance; let some beta make inquiry, let some description and name be sent back to Council: at least let it be accurate, so that had they missed all other signals, they might read this one, clear beyond all doubt. She shrugged it on, fastened it, looked back again at the azi.

Jim had worked himself into the farthest corner of the large bed, into the angle of the two walls, limbs tucked, fetal position. He had done it before, also in sleep. It was somewhat disconcerting, that defensive tactic; she had thought he had relaxed beyond it.

"Wake up," she called sharply. "Jim. Wake up."

He moved, disorganized for the moment, then untucked and sat up within the webbing. He rubbed at his eyes, wincing at what was likely a headache to match hers. He looked strangely lost, as if he had misplaced something essential this morning, perhaps himself.

He wanted time, she decided. She paid him no further attention, reckoning that the best thing. He stirred out after a moment, gathered up his clothes from the floor and went to the bath. There was long running of water, then the hum of the shower fans.

Cleanly, Raen thought with approval. She keyed in the Operations channel and sank into a comfortable chair to wait, feet propped, listening to chatter, watching the screen with the mild interest of one who had been herself many times at the controls of a ship on station approach. The meticulous procedures and precautions of the big commercial liner were typically beta, fussy and over-cautious . . . but neither was putting a ship of this size into station berth a process forgiving of little errors. They would spend an amazing amount of time working in, nothing left to visual estimation.

Channel five afforded view of their destination: this was what she had been looking to see. There was the faint dot of the station, due to grow rapidly larger over the next few hours . . . and Istra, a bluish disc as yet without definition. On the upper quarter screen, filtered, was beta Hydri itself, the Serpent's Tail, a malevolent brilliance which forecast less than paradise on Istra's surface.

Two major continents, two ports onworld, a great deal of desert covering those two continents. The weather patterns of Istra bestowed rain in a serpentine belt, low on one continent and coastally on the other, storms breaking on an incredible mountain ridge which created wetlands coastward, and one of the most regrettable desolations of the Reach on the far side. The rainfall patterns never varied, not during all human occupancy. Such life as Istra supported before humans and majat came had never ascended to sapience . . . and such as dimly knew better had retreated from the vicinity of majat and humans both.

She had deepstudied Istra, and knew it with what information the tapes had to give. It was not populous. The onworld industry was agriculture, and that was sufficient for self-support: the Family had never thought it wise to turn its most prosperous face to the Outside. The world was merely support for the station, that was the real Istra: the agglomeration of docks and warehouses swinging in orbit about Istra was the largest man-made structure in the Reach, the channel for all trade which passed in and out.

It was a sight worth seeing if one were out this far. She meant to do so. But it was also true that facilities at this famous station were primitive and that ships other than freighters did not come here. It was actually possible to strand oneself in such a place, if she let the *Jewel* go.

She went bleakly sober, staring at the screen with greater and greater conviction that she should stay aboard the *Jewel,* ride her home again to the heart of the Reach, where a Kontrin belonged. Other acts of irritation she had committed, but this was something of quite different aspect. She had accomplished part of her purpose simply by coming this far.

The Family knew by now where she was; it was impossible that they had not noticed.

An infinite lifespan, and enforced idleness, enforced uselessness, enforced solitude: it was a torment in which any variance was momentous, in which the prospect of change was paralyzing. It might have taken her. The Family had planned that it should, that finally, it would take her.

Her lips tautened in a hateful smile. She was still sane, a marginal sanity, she reckoned. That she was here—at the Edge—was a triumph of will.

The blue light began to blink in the overhead: room service. She rose and started for the door, remembered that she had not yet clipped her gun to her belt and paused to do so.

It was, after all, only two of the azi, bringing breakfast and the purchases from the store. She admitted them, and stood by the open door while they set breakfast on the table and laid the packages on the bench, a considerable stack of them.

To take such a breakfast, from uncontrolled sources . . . was a calculated risk, a roll of the dice with advantageous odds here in the *Jewel*'s closed environment; but stakes all the same greater than she had hazarded in the salon. Accepting the packages was such a risk. The voyage, unguarded, among strangers, was a monumental one. Or taking an azi such as Jim: the tiny triangle tattooed under his eye was real, the serial number tattooed on his shoulder was likewise, and both faded with age as they should be; that eliminated one possibility . . . but not the chance that someone could have corrupted him with programs involving murder. Such risks provided daily diversion—necessary chances; one regarded them as that or went insane from the stress. One gambled. She smiled as the two bowed, their duties done; and overtipped them extravagantly—another self-indulgence: the delight in their faces gave her vicarious pleasure. She was excited with the purchases she had made for Jim, anxious for his reaction. His melancholy was a challenge . . . simpler, perhaps, and more accessible than her own.

"Jim," she called, "come out here."

He came, half-dressed in his own uniform, his hair a little disordered, his skin still flushed from the heat of the shower. She offered the packages to him, and he was somewhat overwhelmed, it seemed, with the abundance of things.

He sat down and looked through the smaller packages, fingered the plastic-wrapped clothing and the fine suede boots, the traveling case. One small box held a watch, a very expensive one. He touched the face of it, closed the box again and set it aside. No smile touched his face, no hint of pleasure, but rather blankness . . . bewilderment.

"They ought to fit," she said, when he failed of the happiness she had hoped for. She shrugged, defeated, finding him a greater challenge than she had thought. "Breakfast is cooling. Hurry up."

He came to the table then, stood waiting for her to sit down. His precise courtesy irritated her, for it was mechanical; but she said nothing, and took her place, let him adjust her chair. He sat down after, gathered up his fork after she had picked up hers, and took his first bite only after she did. He ate without once looking at her.

Still, she persuaded herself, he was remarkably adaptable. Limited sensitivity, the betas insisted of the azi they created, justifying what might otherwise have seemed abuses. She had not understood that when she was a child: there had been Lia, who had loved her; and she had loved Lia. But it was true that azi did not react to things in the way of born-men, and that there were, among them, no more Lias, never one that she had found.

Genetically determined insensitivity? she wondered, staring at Jim. She refused to believe it. Kontrin geneticists had never worked in terms so ill-defined as the ego and the emotions: and, Meth-maren, she knew the labs better than most. No, there had to be specific biological changes, unless betas knew something Kontrin did not, and she refused to believe that: there had to be something, some single, simple alteration, unaided by majat.

Less sensitivity to physical pain? She could conceive how that might be done, and it would have psychological consequences . . . advantageous, within limits. The biological self-destruct inbuilt in azi evidenced some beta expertise with gene-tampering.

Jim intrigued her suddenly, in that monomaniac way that she filled her days, even important ones, with distractions. She found herself thinking of home, and of comforts, and of Lia's human warmth; and ordinarily she would have stopped herself at this point, dead-stopped, but that there was a distance possible this day, in this place, and she felt, suddenly, that life owed her something of comfort, some last self-indulgence, some . . .

And there the thoughts *did* stop. She turned them cold, and made the question merely intellectual, and useful, the matter of gaining knowledge. Jim was a puzzle, one fit for the time—not easy. She had the strange realization that they were a puzzle she had never wondered about, the azi—a presence too useful and ordinary to question; as she wore clothing, and never perceived the technical skills involved in its making, until she had chanced to desire a cloak made, and had stirred herself to visit a place that might manage it. She had discovered by that, a marvelous workshop of threads and colors and machines, and an old beta who handmade things for the joy of them, who found pleasure in the chance to work with rare majat silk. There was behind the production of the cloth an entire chain of ancient arts, which had quite awed her—at distance: there were gifts and gifts, and hers was not creative.

It was that manner of insight with the azi, had been so from the first night of the game, although it was only now she realized why the game had mattered: she had filled her time with it, and gained occupation—anaesthetic for the mind, such occupations, a near-at-hand focus, a work of art to analyze and understand.

The highest one, perhaps. Weaving, sculpting, the composing of poetry—what more than this, that Kontrin left betas to practice? They made men.

His face was surely not unique: there would be others identical to him, at various ages, scattered across the vicinity of Andra. They would be high types, as he was: technicians, house-officers, supervisors, foremen, guards, entertainers—the latter a euphemism on jaded Meron, where anything could be done; a great many of his doubles were likely majat azi, for majat prized cleverness. That he was also pleasant decoration to an establishment would not occur to the majat, whose eyes could not determine that, but it obviously occurred to Andra Lines. All the serving-azi were of that very expensive class, although no two of them were alike. Obviously they were to please the passengers in capacities outside the salon, and Jim seemed to have had some experience of such duties. It was wasteful, as the elaborate decor of the ship was wasteful and extravagant, to settle the most sensitive and capable of azi to tasks far beneath their mental capacity. But that was typical of beta-ish ostentation: if one could pay, one bought and displayed, even if it was completely senseless.

Jim finished his breakfast and sat, staring at the plate between his hands, probably unsure what to do next, but looking distressingly like a machine out of program.

Many, many azi *were* machinelike, incapable of even basic function when diverted from their precise series of duties, or taken from the specific house or factory to which they belonged. A few even went catatonic and had to be terminated if they could not be shocked out of it and retrained. But Jim, had he won the wager, could have passed for beta . . . save for the tattoo; he was capable of living on his own: he was of that order, as mentally alert as any born-man.

Lia had been such.

Jim looked up finally, perhaps conscious of her concentration on him. There was again that sadness . . . the same that she had met in the night, a deep and unreachable melancholy, the same that had faced her mirrorwise across the gaming table: suspicion, perhaps, that some games were not for winning, even if they had to be played out.

"You don't ask questions," she said.

He still did not.

"We're going to Istra," she said.

"I'll leave with you, then."

That sounded like a question. She realized the drift of his previous thoughts, and leaned back, still studying him. "Yes. You should be well-accustomed to traveling, oughtn't you? Haven't you ever wanted to go downworld? I should think you might have had some curiosity about the ports this ship touches."

He nodded, with an infinitesimal brightening of the eyes.

"You can buy," she said, "whatever you like. My resources ceased to amuse me . . . long ago. I pass the curse on to you: anything you want, any extravagance. There would have been a limit to your funds had you won. But with me, there's none. There are hazards to my company; there are compensations too. If there's anything on this ship you've ever wanted to have, you're free to buy it."

That only seemed to confuse him. He had seen betas come and go, richly dressed, ordering fine food and indulging in ship-board pleasures: the limit of his experience in avarice, no doubt. Any beta so invited could have imagined something at once.

"Why don't you go change again?" she suggested. "You don't belong in ship's uniform any longer. See how the clothes suit you. Then you might think about packing. We'll be docked by noon. I have some business to attend, but when it's done, then we'll amuse ourselves, have a look at the world, commit a few extravagances, see if there's not some society to disarrange. Go on, go on with you."

He looked no less confused, but he rose from table and turned to the bench to sort through the packaged clothing. He spilled a stack onto the floor, gathered it up again, only to spill another, clumsiness that was not like him. He knelt and collected everything into groups, hesitating in his movements, finally made his selections and restored order. The sight disturbed her, hit her like a blow to the stomach. Azi. Motor confusion, brought on by too much strangeness, too many changes at once. She held her tongue. A sticking-point in the clockwork: it was like that. Intervention would make it worse.

She thought of Lia, and pushed Lia out of her mind.

He went off with his armful of packages, into the bedroom.

She became aware of subdued chatter from the viewer, and rose to cut it off. Depression returned the more forcefully, the more she tried to ignore it.

I could apply to Cerdin, she thought. *I could beg Moth and Council for shelter. I could go on living, among Kontrin, home again. All I have to do is bow to Council.*

That was always, she reckoned, all it required. And she would not, not now.

She started about her own packing, opening lockers and chests in search of forgotten items.

The room lights flared red suddenly, the whole suite bathed in the warning glow.

"Sera?" Jim was out of the bath in an instant, his voice plaintive with alarm.

Raen crossed the room in four strides and punched in the emergency channel, foreknowing.

MAJAT PASSENGER, the screen read, NOW MOVING. SECTION 50 PLEASE SECURE YOUR DOORS AND REMAIN INSIDE. PLEASE CALL STATION 3 IF YOU FEEL YOU NEED ASSISTANCE.

She punched 3. "Security, this is 512. I've noticed your alarm. Would you kindly key us out? Thank you."

Room light went normal white again. Jim still hovered in the doorway, looking frightened.

She checked the gun, clipped it again to her belt beneath her cloak. "Majat hibernate in flight," she told him. "They shed when they wake. The skin's still soft. Instinct—inevitably drives them for daylight when they've shed; the gravitational arrangement on this ship, you see, the upper decks . . . no attack, just natural behavior. Best just to let it wander. It's slightly deaf in this state; the auditory palps are soft . . . eyes none too keen either. Not to be trifled with. I'm going out to see to it. You can stay here if you like. Not many folk care to be around them."

"Do you want me to come?"

It was not enthusiasm, but willingness. She detected no panic, and nodded. "If you'll make no move without advice. The hazard is minor."

"You and the majat—are together?"

"A hazard of my company. I warned you. Their vicinity affects some people. I hope you're immune."

She opened the door and went out into the corridor, where the lights were still red.

Jim followed before the door shut. "Lock it," she said, pleased that he had come. "Always lock things behind me."

The sweat of fear was already glistening on his face, but he punched the lock into operation and stayed with her as she headed down the corridor.

3

CORRIDOR 50 WAS NEXT the lifts and the emergency shafts. Raen reckoned well enough how a blind majat could have arrived on fifth level: tunnels were natural for it.

And it was there, huddled against a section-door at the farther end of the corridor, a tall hulk of folded limbs and fantastical chitinous protuberances. It glistened in the red light, slick with new skin, bewildered by the barriers that had closed before it.

"Quite blind to most of its surroundings," she said to Jim, and the majat's palps were not all that soft. It caught sound and turned, mandibles moving in great agitation. It was a Warrior, hatchling-naked and weaponless.

"Stand here by the corner," Raen said to Jim. "Step round it if it turns ugly. Never try a long run: no human can outrace a Warrior. Its vision, you see, is entirely thermal, and dependent on contrasts of heat; put something cold and solid between yourself and it, and it's lost you. It doesn't see this corridor in anything like our vision: it sees us, maybe . . . or places where metal is warmed by underlying machinery, or by the touch of a hand. Never touch a wall or a surface with your bare skin if you're trying to elude one. And they not only detect scent: they read it."

The auditory palps still moved, perceiving sound, but at this range, perhaps, unable to distinguish it. Seated, it suddenly heaved itself up on two leathery legs, towering against the overhead. It boomed a warning note.

Raen walked forward slowly, flung back her cloak, held up both her hands, backs outward.

Air sucked in, an audible gust.

"Kontrin," it said in deep harmonies. "Blue-hive Kontrin."

"Blue-hive Warrior." She spoke distinctly, a little loudly, for its sake.

"Yes," it sighed, blowing air from its chambers. "Yess." Auditory palps swept decisively forward, like a human relaxing to listen. It lowered its erect body, forelimbs tucked, the whole eloquent of vast relief, trust. There was pathos in the action, sense-deprived as the Warrior was. Something welled up in her, a feeling she had pursued from world to world and not captured until now.

"I knew that a blue had taken this ship," she said. "I came."

It started forward in evident intent to touch, stopped abruptly. Air pulsed in and out, thumping with the force of its expulsion. The sound became words. "Other. Other. Other."

She realized the fix of its dimmed vision and looked back, where Jim waited by the corner.

"Only an azi, Warrior. Mine, my-hive. Don't be concerned for it."

It hesitated, then stalked up to her, bowed itself, seeking touch. She lifted both her hands to its scent-patches. It absorbed this. Then it bowed further, and in a gesture very like a human kiss, opened its mandibles wide and touched the false chelae to her lips. The venomed spike was very close, the jaws gaping on either side. The wrong taste would snap them shut on reflex, and unlike another Warrior, she had no chitinous defense but the sleeve-armor. Yet the taste was sweet; it gently received taste from her.

"No resolution," it said. "From? From?"

"Cerdin," she said. "Once."

"Queen." The analysis proceeded in its body, and it drew back, mandibles clashing in distress. "I taste familiarity. I taste danger."

"I am Raen a Sul. Raen a Sul hant Meth-maren."

It went rigid. Even the mandibles ceased to move. A Warrior alone, it comprehended only Warrior-memories, whatever the complexities its body might carry for others to read.

"Danger," it concluded helplessly. Auditory palps swung forward and back. "Recently waked." It gave warning of its own disorganization, still trusting, but it retreated. The mandibles began to work again in visible distress.

"Warrior, you have reached Istra. Is this not the place for which blue-hive intended you?"

"Yesss." It scuttled farther back from her, into the corner next the door. "Forbidden. Forbidden. Forbidden."

She stayed where she was. Warriors were often laconic and disjointed in conversation, but this one seemed mortally confused. It crouched down, limbs tucked; and cornered, it might spring at the least advance. "Warrior," she said, "I have helped you. If I were not aboard, this ship might have been—stopped. An accident might have happened to you-unit in your sleep. This was not the case. Before you were hatched, I was in blue-hive Cerdin, within the hive. You are Kalind blue, but is there no memory in Kalind, of Meth-marens? Before you left Cerdin, you knew us, Meth-maren-hive, hive-friends. There was a hill, a lake by a place called Kethiuy. We spoke—for all human hives."

"Warrior," it reminded her; it could not be expected to Remember. But the auditory palps were strained forward, and the mandibles worked rapidly. "Meth-maren hive. Meth-maren. Meth-maren. Kethiuy. Hive-friends. First-humans, Meth-marens. Yessss. Warrior-memory holds Meth-marens."

"Yes," she said. She held out her hands, offering touch, should it accept. There was no queen to advise Warrior, no Drones to Remember for it: she had it snared, almost, almost, and tried not to betray the anxiety in her. It had no means to know how other blues had eluded her. It was going to Istra, as blues had attempted other worlds; but this one, this sending would get through. *She* saw to it, though blue-hive elsewhere had fled her and met disaster, had voyaged and never wakened, or perished in ambush. This one lived, at the one world where she had a chance of protecting it.

At the one world where there was no one of the Family to stop her or forbid her access to the hives.

"Warrior. You were sent to Istra. True?"

"True."

"Our purposes coincide, it may be. Tell me. Why have you come here? What message do you carry?"

It held its silence, thinking, perhaps. It was a new generation, this Warrior; eighteen years was the time of a new generation for its kind . . . all across the Reach, a new generation of blue-hive, quiet within its separate hills—blues withdrawn, while greens came to the labs managed by Thons, performed as always, abided by the Pact under Thon direction.

Until last year.

"Why have you come?" Raen asked.

It eased forward again, wary. The fix of her head was not toward her, but beyond. It turned the head then, rotating it on its circular joints. "Azi. Meth-maren azi."

It wanted touch. Majat called it Grouping, the need to be emotionally sure of others. Jim remained where she had left him, red-dyed in the light. "My azi," Raen confirmed, her heart beating rapidly. "Jim. Jim, come to me, slowly."

He could break and run. She stood in Warrior's way, and perhaps, only perhaps she could restrain Warrior from the kill if Jim set him off. But Jim left his corner and came, stopped at yet a little distance, as if suddenly paralyzed. Warrior shifted forward, the matter of three strides that Raen could not match, and leaned over him.

Jim had simply shut his eyes in panic. Raen reached him, caught his arm, shocked him out of it. "Touch," she told him. "You must touch it." And when he did not move with propriety, reaching instead to the thorax, Raen took his right hand in hers, guided it between the jaws to Warrior's offered scent-patches. The huge Warrior, only minimally sane, bent lower, jaws wide, touched false chelae to Jim's lips, taking taste as well as scent. Jim's face broke out in sweat: this too Warrior tasted, sweeping it from his brow with the delicate bristles of the false chelae.

"Trust it," Raen whispered into his ear, yet gripping his arm. "Stand still, stand still; blues will never harm you once this Warrior has reported on Istra. It can't recognize faces, but it knows the taste now. Maybe it can even distinguish you from your duplicates; I'd imagine it can."

She let go. Warrior had perceptibly calmed. It touched at Jim, touched her.

"Blue-hive," it murmured, deep baritone. And then with a distressing waving of its palps: "Danger."

"There is danger everywhere for blues." Raen offered her right hand to its mandibles, willful hazard, comforting gesture. "Hive-friend. Do you also bear taste of reds? Of Kethiuy? Of killing?"

Mandibles clashed as her hand withdrew; jaws snicked, strongly enough to decapitate human or majat. "Killing," it moaned from its chambers, deep harmony. "Red-hive, killings, yess."

"I was there, on Cerdin, when reds killed blues. Does Kalind blue remember that? Messengers went out from Cerdin then. Surely some got through. Some must have lived."

"Not-clear. Drone-function."

"But you know Cerdin."

"Cerdin." It sucked air and expelled it softly. "Yess. Cerdin. First-hive. This-unit does not make full understanding. This-unit will report. Blue queen of Istra will interpret. Queen will understand."

"Surely she will."

"This-unit will not see Kalind again. This-unit is cut off. I can carry this message no farther than the Istran queen. Then I must un-Mind."

"Perhaps the Istran queen will take you instead, Warrior, and change that instruction."

"This-unit hopes."

"This-unit also hopes, Warrior."

Palps caressed her face with great tenderness. Truly neuter, Warrior had no concept of any function but duty; yet majat units could feel some sentiment on their own, and Warriors were—very slightly —egocentric.

She laid her hand on its forelimb. "What brings you here? What message, Warrior? Answer me."

The great armored head rotated in that gesture that had so many nuances to majat vision. "This-unit does not know; I taste of *revenge,* Kethiuy-queen."

It was complex, then, locked within its body-chemistry; it gave her Warrior-reading only, and the Warrior-mind conceived it as revenge. A chill ran over her skin, an echo of things past.

"I have known you before, Warrior."

"Warrior memory," it confirmed, and touched at her, touched at them both. "Meth-maren. Yesss. Not all Kontrin are friends. Trust you. Trust you, Kethiuy-queen."

A message had gotten through, eighteen, nineteen years ago. Warrior was with her. She touched it, her hand trembling.

"We will be docking soon, Warrior. You must secure yourself for your own protection, and not trouble these beta humans. They are no harm, no harm to you."

"Yes," it agreed. It reared up and looked about, head rotating half this way and half that. "Lost," it complained. "Human-hive. Lost."

"Come," she bade it, and brought it to a security panel, took its right chela and touched it to the emergency grip. It clenched it, secure then as a human safely belted. "You must stay here, Warrior. Let your skin dry. You've come high enough. Hold and wait, and harm no human who doesn't threaten you. I'll come for you when it's time."

"Lost. This-unit must find Istra blue."

She stroked the sensitive side-palps, reckoning what a complex and fearful task Warrior faced, with no sun overhead, encased in one cold metal structure after another on its way. Majat did not easily comprehend that it was not all one sun and all one world. It had entrusted itself to betas for hire, hoping it was given right directions, set on the right ship; and blue messengers faced other obstacles, for Kontrin discouraged their traveling, and accidents befell one after the other. "I will guide you," she told it. "Stay. Wait for me."

"Blue-hive," it breathed, bowed under the pleasurable caress. Jaws clashed. "I wait. Yesss."

"My-chamber is twelfth door beyond the turning-left, as you face."

"This-unit guards."

"Yes," she agreed, touched the palps and drew back. The halls were cold; its processes were slow: it was all too willing now to sink down and rest. She thought of bidding it instead to her own suite, but there was Jim, who stood against the wall in a seeming state of shock. She soothed it a last time with her hand, turned away and took Jim with her, trusting it would be safe; indeed, no one would likely venture that hall, and if someone would have harmed it, of those aboard, that would have been done while it slept, helpless— not now.

This messenger would get through.

Is this the best action? the Mother of Cerdin had asked. Among majat there were no children, only eggs, and adults. Mother had asked a human for advice, and a child had answered: Mother had not known.

It was wise that humans had been forbidden the hive, direct access to queens, to Drones, to the Mind. She abhorred now what she was doing, imprinting Warrior, while it was unadvised by any queen.

That imprint would enter Istran blues, as truth, as true as Warrior's legitimate message.

It was her key to the hives.

4

JIM EXITED THE BATH, whiter than he had been. He had lost the breakfast, and decided on another prolonged bath. Now, wrapped in a bathsheet, he flung himself belly-down on the wide bed and showed no disposition to move.

Raen bent over him, touched his damp shoulders. "You're sure you're all right? You didn't let it scratch you, did you?"

"All right," he echoed indistinctly. She decided that he was, and that the kindest thing she could do at the moment was to let him lie. He was still overheated from the water. She pulled a corner of the bedclothes loose and flung over him, shrugged and walked back to her own business.

She packed, settling everything with precision into her several cases—scuffed and battered from much use, that luggage—but it contained so well the things she would not give up, from world to world. Most that she had bought on the ship she thought of leaving; and then she decided otherwise and simply jammed things in the more tightly: Istra did not promise their equal.

To all of it she added the fifth and sixth cases, the deepstudy apparatus and her precious tapes; she never trusted a strange apparatus, and the tapes—the tapes she kept much beyond their usefulness for casual knowledge, some for pleasure, some for sentiment, a few for reference. And there were half a dozen that Council would be aghast to know existed in duplicate; but Hal Ilit had admitted her within his security, and never seen beyond his own self-indulgence, his own vanity, not even in dying. She counted the tapes through, making sure everything was in its slot, nothing lost, nothing left to assumption.

And she would have taken the refuge deepstudy offered for an hour now, having finished all else: it was the best antidote for unpleasantness. But Jim was there, and she did not mean to make the Ilit's mistake: under deepstudy, one was utterly helpless, and she would not, would never accept sinking into that state in another's presence, even an azi's. She paced the suite in boredom, and finally, sure beyond doubt that there remained nothing to do, she sat down and keyed in the viewer, one of the entertainment channels.

Beta dramas, trivial and depressing . . . worse, when one knew the deliberate psych-sets which had gone into training their lab-born ancestors: work to succeed, succeed to be idle, consume, consume, consume, consumption is status. It worked, economically: on it, the entire economy of the Reach thrived; but it made excruciatingly boring drama. She keyed in docking operations, and found more interest simply in watching the station spin nearer, the abstract shift of light and shadow across its planes.

She heard a sound from the other room. Jim was up and about. She listened for him to head for the bath again in distress, but he did not, and she decided that he had recovered. She heard a great deal of walking back and forth, the crumbling of plastics, and finally the click of a suitcase closing. She looked round the side of the chair and saw him, dressed in conservative street clothes, setting his case beside her several.

He could indeed have been beta, or even Kontrin: he was tall. But he was a little too fair; and there was the minute tattoo beneath the right eye.

"You look very fine, Jim."

He glanced down, seeming embarrassed. "I thank you, sera."

"Formalities are hardly appropriate in private." She spun the chair about from the viewer and looked up at him. "You're all right, then."

He nodded. "I'm sorry," he said almost inaudibly.

"You didn't panic; you stood your ground. Sit down."

He did so, on the bench against the wall, still slightly pale.

"Meth-maren," she said, "is not a well-loved name among Kontrin. And sooner or later someone will make an attempt on my life." She opened her right hand, palm down. "The chitin grafted there is blue-hive; blue-hive and the Meth-marens met a common misfortune two decades ago. Warrior and I have something in common, you see. And listen to me: I once had a few azi in my employ. Somehow a gate was left unlocked and red-hive majat got in. I sleep lightly. The azi didn't. The room was no pretty sight, I may tell you. But an azi who would walk with me out there into the hall . . . might have been of some use to me that night."

"On the ship—" He always spoke in a hushed voice, and the more so now. "We have security procedures. I understand them."

"Do they teach you about self-defense?"

A slight shake of the head.

"They just tell you about locks and accesses and fire procedures."

A diffident nod.

"Well, that's far better than nothing. Hear this: you must guard my belongings and things that I'll use and places that I'll come back to, with far more care than you use guarding me. I take care of myself, you see, and most of my enemies wouldn't go for a head-on attack on me if there were an easier way; no, they'd go for something I'd use, or for an unlocked door. You understand what I'm talking about."

"Yes, sera."

"We're docking in an hour or so. You could save confusion by getting a baggage cart up here. I really don't think azi are going to be safe coming up here, not past Warrior out there. But it wouldn't hurt you, not if you let it touch you and identify, you understand. No more than it would me. You have the nerve for it?"

He nodded.

"Jim, perhaps we may stay together a long time."

He stood up, stopped. "Nineteen years," he said. And when she gave him a puzzled frown: "I'm twenty-one," he said, with the faintest quirk of a smile.

Azi humor. He would live to forty. A feeling came on her the like of which only the blues had stirred in many years. She recalled Lia, and the gentle azi of her childhood: their dead faces returned with a shock; and the slaughter, and the burning . . . She flinched from it. "I value loyalty," she said, turning away.

He was gone for a considerable time. She began to pace the room, realized that she was doing it and stopped, thought of going after him, hated to show her anxiety among betas.

At last the blue light winked in the overhead and she hurried to open the door, stood back to admit him and the cart.

"No trouble?" she asked him. Jim shook his head with a little touch of self-satisfaction and began at once putting the baggage on.

He finished, and settled, lacking anything else to do; she sat, watching their approach to station. Their berth was in sight; the station was by now a seemingly stationary sprawl extending off the screen on both sides, an amazing structure, as vast as rumor promised.

And ships, ships of remarkable design, linked to their berths—freighters, as bizarre in shape as they needed to be, never landing, only needing the capability to link to station umbilicals and grapples; the only standard of construction was the docking mechanism, the same dimensions from the tiniest personal craft to the most massive liner.

A ship was easing out as they came in, slowly, slowly, an aged freighter. The symbols it bore were unlike any sigil or company emblem in Raen's memory; and then she realized it for the round Sol emblem. A thrill went through her.

An Outsider ship.

A visitor from beyond the Reach. It drifted like a dream image, passed them, vanished into the *Jewel*'s own shadow.

"Outsider," she said aloud. "Jim, look, look—the third one at berth is the same design."

Jim said nothing, but he regarded the image intently, with awe on his face.

"The Edge," Raen said. "We've reached the Edge."

5

MEREK ELN'S HANDS TREMBLED. He folded his arms and paced, and looked from time to time at Parn Kest.

"We'd better call in," he said. "There's time enough."

"With a majat involved—" she objected. "A majat! How long can the thing have been aboard."

"It's with *her*. Has to be." He looked toward the door with an inward shudder, thinking of the majat stalking the corridors at liberty, half-sane from its dormancy. The Kontrin had at least calmed the creature: the emergency channel had said so, and thanked her, whether or not the Kontrin cared for anyone's gratitude. But worse could go wrong than had. They had been long away from Istra, half a year removed from the situation there, long removed from the last message.

He stepped suddenly to the console.

"Merek," Parn said, rising, and caught his arm. Sweat stood on her face; it did on his. Her hand fell away. She said nothing. Their cover no longer served to protect them. There was no more guarantee of safety, even in coming home.

He sat down at the console and keyed in the communications channel. Communications was fully occupied with the flow of docking instructions; a message would have to go Priority, at high cost.

Communications wanted financial information beyond ordinary credit; it accepted a string of numbers and codes to bounce back through worldbank, and finally a chain of numbers which was the destination of the message, ITAK company representative on-station.

GO, it flashed.

Merek keyed response. NOTIFY MAIN OFFICE MERON MISSION INBOUND. URGENT ITAK ON STATION MEET US AT GATE WITH SECURITY. AWAIT REPLY WITH DEEP DISTRESS.

There was the necessary long delay.

"You shouldn't have mentioned Meron," Parn said at his shoulder. "You shouldn't have. Not on a public channel."

"Do you want to do this?"

"I wouldn't have called."

"And there wouldn't have been anyone to meet us but maybe— maybe some of the office staff; and maybe things have changed on the station. I want our own security out there."

He mopped at his face, recalling codes. DEEP: that was trouble; and DISTRESS at the end of any message meant majat. He dared not talk of Kontrin. One had no idea where their agents might be placed.

ITAK REPRESENTATIVE WILL BE AT GATE, the reply flashed back. DEEP DISTRESS UNDERSTOOD. OUR APOLO-GIES.

It was the right code, neatly delivered. Merek bit at his lip and keyed receipt of the message.

ITAK took care of its people, if ITAK had the chance to move first. And if other messages had been sent, from the Kontrin or an-other agency, surely it was best to have broken cover and asked for help.

Parn took his hand in hers, put her arm about his shoulders. He was not sure that he had done the right thing; Parn herself had disagreed. But if some message had gone ahead, if the ship had even done something so innocent as flash its tiny passenger list ahead, then it was necessary to be sure that among those gathered to meet the *Jewel,* ITAK would be chiefest.

6

"WARRIOR," Raen called softly.

It stirred, let go its hold on the emergency grip.

"Warrior, we are docked now. It's Raen Meth-maren." She came and touched it, and it must touch in return, and examine Jim as well, swift gestures.

"Yes," it said, having Grouped.

"Jim." Raen gestured at the nearby lift. Jim maneuvered the bag-gage cart in, pressed himself against the inside wall as Warrior eased in, and Raen followed.

The doors sealed, and the lift moved. The air grew very close very quickly with the sealed system and the big majat's breathing. Warrior smelled of something dry and strange, like old paper. The chitin, still wet-looking from shedding, was dry now; where Warrior had broken his old shell, the ship's crew might find a treasure-trove . . . none of the Drone-jewels, of course, but material which still had value in ornament: so the hive paid a bonus on its passage. Warrior regarded them both, mildly distressed as the lift reoriented itself; the great head rotated quizzically: compound eyes made moiré patterns under the light, shifting bands of color buried in jewel-shard armor.

It was beautiful. Raen stroked its palps to soothe it, and softly it sang for her, Warrior-song.

"Hear it?" Raen asked, looking at Jim. "The hives are full of such sound. Humans rarely hear it."

Again the lift shifted itself to a new alignment, hissed to a stop. The doors opened for them. Azi on duty fled back, giving them and their tall companion whatever room they wanted.

There was the hatch, and a wafting of the cold, strange air of Istra station, dark spaces and glaring lights. Crew waited to bid them farewell, a changeless formality: so they had surely wished every passenger departing over the long voyage; but there was the strained look of dementia in their eyes and behind their smiles. *Andra's Jewel* could go home now, to safe and friendly space, to ordinary passengers, and her staterooms would fill again with beta-folk, who never thought of Kontrin or majat save at distance.

Raen lingered to shake hands with each, and laughed. Their hands were moist and cold, and their fingers avoided the chitin on her hand where they could.

"Safe voyage," she wished them one and all.

"Safe voyage," Warrior breathed, incapable of humor.

No one offered to help them down the ramp. Jim managed the baggage, struggling with the cart which they had tacitly appropriated. They boarded the conveyer and rode it down.

There at the bottom of the ramp stood the Istran pair, inside the security barriers, with a clutch of business types and three others who might be azi, but not domestics: guards. Raen moved her hand within her cloak, rested it by her gun, calculating which she might remove first if she had to . . . simple reflex. Her hand rested comfortably there.

The moving ramp delivered them down, and there was view of a drab, businesslike vastness, none of the chrome and glitter of Meron, none of the growing plants of Kalind, or the cosmopolitan grandeur of Cerdin station. This station wasted nothing on display, no expensive shielded viewports. It was all dark machinery and automata, bare joinings and cables and every service-point in sight and reach of hands. It was a trade-station, not for the delight of tourists, but for the businesslike reception of freight. Conveyers laced overhead; transport chutes and dark corridors led away into narrow confinements; azi moved here and there, drab, gray-clad men, unsmiling in their fixation on duty.

Raen inhaled the grimness of it and looked leftward, third berth down, hoping for exotic sights of Outsiders, but all docks looked alike, vast ramps, dwarfing humans, places shrouded in tangles of lines and obscured by machinery. A few human figures moved there, too far to distinguish, tantalizing in their possibilities. And she could not delay to investigate them.

"Lost," Warrior complained, touching nervously at her. The air was cold, almost cold enough to make breath frost. Warrior was almost blind in such a place, and would grow rapidly sluggish.

And the Istrans came forward, further distressing it. Raen reached lefthanded to comfort it, and gave Merek Eln a forbidding stare.

"I'd keep my distance," she said.

Ser Merek Eln did stop, with all his companions. His face was ashen. He looked at the tall majat and at her, and swallowed thickly.

"My party is here," he said. "We have a shuttle engaged. Would you consider joining us on our trip down, Kont' Raen? I . . . would still like to talk with you."

She was frankly amazed. This little man, this beta, came offering favors, and had the courage to approach a majat doing it. "My companions would make that rather crowded, ser."

"We have accommodation enough, if you would."

"Beta," Warrior intoned. "Beta human." It moved forward in one stride, to touch the strange human who offered it favors, and Raen put up her hand at once, touched a sensitive auditory palp, restraining Warrior. It endured this indignity, fretting.

Merek Eln had not fled. It was possibly the worst moment of his life, but he stood still. Her respect for him markedly increased.

"Ser," she said, "our presence here must be very important to you personally."

"Please," he said in a low voice. "Please. Now. The station is not a secure place to be standing in the open. ITAK can offer you security. We can talk on the way down. It's urgent."

All her instincts rebelled at this: it was dangerous, ridiculously dangerous, to accept local entanglements without looking into all sides of the matter.

But she nodded, and walked with them. Jim followed. Warrior stalked beside, statuary in slow motion, trying to hold to human pace.

Their course took them along the dock, nearer and nearer the Outsider berth.

Raen tried not even to glance much that way: it distracted her from the general survey of the area, which her eyes made constantly, nervously. But there were Outsiders; she knew they must be such, by their strange clothing and their business near that berth.

"Are such onworld too?" she asked. "Do they come downworld?"

"There's a ground-based trade mission," Kest said.

That cheered her. She could bear it no longer, and stopped and stared at a group of men near them on the dock . . . plainly dressed, doing azi-work. She wondered whether they were true men or what they were. They stopped their work and stood upright and gaped . . . more at the majat, surely, than at her.

From Outside. From the wide, free Outside, where men existed such as Kontrin had once been. Until now, Outsiders had seen only the shadows of Kontrin; she wondered if they knew—what betas were, or if they had the least comprehension of Kontrin, or realized what she was.

"Sera," Eln said anxiously. "Please. Please."

She turned from the strangers, reckoning the open places about them, the chance of ambush. Warrior touched her anxiously, seeking reassurance. She followed the Eln-Kests at what pace they wanted to set, uncertain whether they were evading possible assassins or walking among them.

BOOK FIVE

1

"THE OLD WOMAN HAS something in mind," Tand said. "I don't like it."

The elder Hald walked a space with his grandnephew, paused to pull a dead bloom from the nightflower. Neighboring leaves shrank at the touch and remained furled a moment, then relaxed. "Something concrete?"

"Hive-reports. Stacks of them. Statistics. She may be aiming something at Thon. I don't know. I can't determine."

The elder looked about at Tand, his heart laboring with the heavy persistence of dread. Tand was outside the informed circles of the movement. There were many things of which Tand remained ignorant: must. Where Tand stood, it was not good that he know . . . near as he was to the old woman's hand. If the blow fell, all that he knew could be in Moth's hands in hours. "What kind of statistics? Involving azi?"

"Among others. She's asking for more data on Istra. She's . . . amused by the Meth-maren. So she gives out. But here's the matter: she muttered something after the committee left. About the Meth-maren serving her interests . . . conscious or unconscious on the Meth-maren's part, I don't know. I asked her flatly was the Meth-maren her agent. She denied it and then hedged with that."

The Hald dropped the dry petals, his pulse no calmer. "The Meth-maren is becoming a persistent irritant."

"Another attempt on her—might be advisable."

The Hald pulled off a frond. Others furled tightly, remained so, twice offended. He began to strip the soft part off the skeleton of the veins. It left a sharp smell in the air. "Tand, go back to the Old Hall. You shouldn't stay here tonight."

"Now?"

"Now."

One of Tand's virtues was his adaptability. The Hald pulled another frond and stripped it, trusting that there would not be the least hesitation in Tand, from the garden walk to the front gate to the City. He heard him walk away, a door close.

His steps would be covered, cloaked in innocence . . . a supposed venture in the City; and back to Alpha, and Old Hall. There were those who would readily lie for him.

The Hald wiped his hand and walked the other path, up to other levels of the Hald residence at Ehlvillon, to eastwing, to other resources.

A pattern was shaping.

On Istra . . . things had long been safe from Council inspection. Communications had been carefully channeled through Meron, screened thoroughly before transmission farther.

He walked the halls of paneling and stone, into the shielded area of the house comp, leaned above it and sent a message that consisted of banalities. There was no acknowledgment at the other end.

But three hours later, a little late for callers, an aircraft set down on the Hald grounds, ruffling the waters of the ornamental pond.

The Hald went out to meet it, and walked arm in arm with the man who had come in, paused by the pool in the dark, fed the sleepy old mudsnake which denned there. It gulped down bits of bread, being the omnivore it was, its double-hinged jaws opening and clamping again into a fat sullenness.

"Nigh as old as the house," the Hald said of it.

Arl Ren-barant stood with folded arms. The Hald stood up and the mudsnake snapped, then levered itself off the bank and eased into the black waters, making a little wake as it curled away.

"Some old business," said the Hald, "has surfaced again. I'm beginning to think it never left at all. We've been very careless in yielding to Eldest's wishes in this case. I'm less and less convinced it's a matter of whim with her."

"The Meth-maren?" Ren-barant frowned and shook his head.

"Not so easy to do it now. She's completely random, a nuisance. If it were really worth the risk—"

The Hald looked at him sharply. "Random. So what happened on Meron?"

"A personal quarrel, left over from the first attempt. Gen and Hal have become a cause with the Ilits. It was unfortunate."

"And on Kalind."

"Hive-matter, but she wasn't in it. Blues have settled again. Reds seem to be content enough."

"Yes. The Meth-maren's gone. Meron's damaged and Kalind isn't unscathed. Attention rests where it doesn't suit us. The old hive-master's talent . . . Arl, we have an enemy. A very dangerous one."

"She hardly made a secret of her going to Istra. Why make so much commotion of it, if she's not as mad as we've reckoned? A private ship could have reached there in a direct jump. She could have had time to work . . ."

"The whole Council noticed, didn't they? It was bizarre enough that it caught the curiosity of the whole Council. Attention focused where we don't need it focused at all."

Ren-barant's face was stark, his arms tightly clenched. "Cold sane, you think."

"As you and I are. As Moth is. I have news, Arl. There was a majat on that liner when it left Kalind. We haven't discovered yet how far it went, whether all the way with her or whether it got off earlier."

"Blue messenger?"

"We don't know yet. Blue or green is a good bet."

Ren-barant swore. "Thon was supposed to have that cut off."

"Majat paid the passage," the Hald said. "Betas can't tell them apart. The Meth-maren boarded at the last moment . . . special shuttle, a great deal of noise about it. We knew about her very quickly. Use of her credit was obvious, at least the size of the transaction and the recipient, which was Andra Lines, through one of their sub-agents. But the majat paid in jewels, cash transaction, freighted up dormant and inconspicuous . . . a special payment to someone, I'll warrant. Cash. No direct record to our banks. No tracing. We still can't be sure how much was actually paid: probably a great deal went into the left hand while the right was making records; but the Meth-maren was right there, using vast amounts of credit, very visible. We didn't find out about the majat until our agents started asking questions among departing passengers. Betas won't volunteer that kind of gossip. But the whole operation, that a hive could bypass our surveillance and do it so completely, so long—"

"The Thons do nothing. Maybe we'd better ask some questions about the quality of that support."

"She's Meth-maren; the Thon hive-masters have no influence with the blues. And Council can vote Thon the post; they can't make them competent in it. Anyone can handle reds. The test is whether Thon can control the blues. I think Thon is beyond the level of their competency, for all their assurances to us. The Meth-maren's running escort for majat; she outwitted Thon, and she's made Council look toward Istra. The old woman, Arl, the old woman is collecting statistics; she's taking interest again; there's a chance she's taken interest for longer than we've known."

The Ren-barant hissed softly between his teeth.

"There's more," the Hald said. "The old woman dropped a word about the Meth-maren being—*useful*. Useful. And that with her sudden preoccupation with statistics. Istran statistics. The Pedra bill is coming up. We'd better be ready, before the old woman hits us with a public surprise. Istra's vulnerable."

"Someone had better get out there, then."

"I've moved on that days ago." And at the Ren-barant's sudden, apprehensive stare. "*That* matter is on its way to being solved. It's not the Meth-maren I'm talking about."

"Yes," the Ren-barant said after a moment. "I can see that."

"Tand's next to her. He stays, no breath of doubt near him. The organization has to be firmed up, made ready on the instant. You know the program. You know the contacts. I put it on you. I daren't. I've gone as far as I can."

The Ren-barant nodded grimly. They began to part company. Suddenly the Ren-barant stopped in his tracks and looked back. "There's more than one way for Moth to use the Meth-maren. To provoke enemies into following the wrong lead."

Ros Hald stared at him, finally nodded. It was the kind of convolution of which Moth had long proved capable. "We've counted on time to take care of our problems. That's been a very serious mistake. Both of them have to be cared for—simultaneously."

The mudsnake surfaced again, hopeful. The Hald tossed it the rest of the morsel: sullen jaws snapped. It waited for more. None came. It slipped away again under the black waters and rippled away.

2

THE ISTRAN SHUTTLE was an appalling relic. There was little enough concession to comfort in the station, but there was less in the tight confines of the vessel which would take them down to surface. Only the upholstery was new, a token attempt at renovation. Raen surveyed the machinery with some curiosity, glanced critically into the cockpit, where pilot and co-pilot were checking charts and bickering.

The Istrans had settled in, all nine of them, Merek Eln and Parn Kest, the several business types and their azi guard. Warrior had taken up position in the rear of the aisle, the only space sufficient for its comfort and that of the betas. It closed both chelae about the braces of the rearmost seats, quite secure, and froze into the statue-like patience of its kind.

Jim came up the ramp, and after some little perplexity, secured the whole carrier into storage behind the Eln-Kest's modest luggage, . . . forced the door closed. Raen let him take his seat first, next the sealed viewport, then settled in after, opposite Merek Eln, and fastened the belts. Her pulse raced, considering the company they kept and the museum-piece in which they were about to hurtle into atmosphere.

"This is quite remarkable," she said to Jim, thinking that Meron in all its decadent and hazardous entertainments had never offered anything quite like Istran transport.

Jim looked less elated with the experience, but his eyes flickered with interest over all the strangeness, . . . not fear, but a feverish intensity, as if he were attempting to absorb everything at once and deal with it. His hands trembled so when he adjusted his belts that he had trouble joining them.

The co-pilot stopped the argument with the pilot long enough to come back and check the door seal, went forward again. The pilot gave warning. The vessel disengaged from its lock and went through the stomach-wrenching sequence of intermittent weightlessness and reorientation under power as they threaded their way out of their berth. The noise, unbaffled, was incredible.

"Kontrin," Merek Eln shouted, leaning in his seat.

"Explanations?" Raen asked.

"We are very grateful—"

"Please. Just the explanation."

Merek Eln swallowed heavily. They were in complete weightlessness, their slight wallowing swiftly corrected. The noise died away save for the circulation fans. Istra showed crescent-shaped on the forward screen, more than filling it; the station showed on the aft screen. They were falling into the world's night side, as Raen judged it.

"We are very glad you decided to accept transport with us," Eln said. "We are quite concerned for your safety at Istra, onstation and onworld. There's been some difficulty, some disturbance. Perhaps you have heard."

Raen shrugged. There were rumors of unrest, here and elsewhere, of crises; of things more serious . . . she earnestly wished she knew.

"You were," Merek Eln said, "perhaps sent here for that reason."

She made a slight gesture of the eyes back toward Warrior. "You might ask it concerning its motives."

That struck a moment of silence.

"Kontrin," said sera Kest, leaning forward from the seat behind. "For whatever reasons you've come here—you must realize there's a hazard. The station is too wide, too difficult to monitor. In Newhope, on Istra, at least we can provide you security."

"Sera—are we being abducted?"

The faces about her were suddenly stark with apprehension.

"Kontrin," said Merek Eln, "you are being humorous; we wish we could persuade you to consider seriously what hazards are possible here."

"Ser, sera, so long as you persist in trying to tell me only fragments of the situation, I see no reason to take a serious tone with you. You've been out to Meron. You're coming home. Your domestic problems are evidently serious and violent, but your manner indicates to me that you would much rather I were not here."

There was a considerable space of silence. Fear was thick in the air.

"There has been some violence," said one of the others. "The station is particularly vulnerable to sabotage and such acts. We fear it. We have sent appeals. None were answered."

"The Family ignored them. Is that your meaning?"

"Yes," said another after a moment.

"That is remarkable, seri. And what agency do you suspect to be the source of your difficulty?"

No one answered.

"Dare I guess," said Raen, "that you suspect that the source of your troubles *is* the Family?"

There was yet no answer, only the evidence of perspiration on beta faces.

"Or the hives?"

No one moved. Not an eye blinked.

"You would not be advised to take any action against me, seri. The Family is not monolithic. Quite the contrary. Be reassured: I am ignorant; you can try to deceive me. What brought the two of you to Meron?"

"We—have loans outstanding from MIMAK there. We hoped for some material assistance . . ."

"We hoped," Parn Kest interrupted brusquely, "to establish inner-worlds contacts—to help us past this wall of silence. We need relief . . . in taxes, in trade; we were ignored, appeal after appeal. And we hoped to work out a temporary agreement with MIMAK, against the hope of some relief. Grain. Grain and food. Kontrin—we're supporting farms and estates which can't possibly make profit. We're at a crisis. We were given license for increase in population, our own and azi, and the figures doubled our own. We thought future adjustment would take care of that. But the crisis is on us, and no one listens. Majat absorb some of the excess. That market is all that keeps us from economic collapse. But food . . . food for all that population . . . And the day we can't feed the hives . . . Kont' Raen, agriculture and azi are our livelihood. Newhope and Newport and the station . . . and the majat . . . derive their food from the estates; but it's consumed by the azi who work them. There are workers enough to cover the estates' needs four times over. There's panic out there. The estates are armed camps."

"We were told when we came in," Eln said in a faint voice, "that

ITAK has been able to confiscate azi off some of the smaller estates. But there's no way to take them by force from the larger. We can't legally dispose of those contracts, by sale or by termination. There has to be Kontrin—"

"—license for transfer or adjustment," Raen finished. "Or for termination without medical cause. I know our policies rather thoroughly, ser Eln."

"We can't get the licenses."

"And therefore you can't export and you can't terminate."

"Or feed them indefinitely, Kontrin. Or feed them. The economics of the farms insist on a certain number of azi to the allotted land area. Someone . . . *erred*."

Eln's lips trembled, having said so. It was for a beta, great daring.

"And the occasion for violence against the station?"

"It hasn't happened yet," one of the others said.

"But you fear that it will. Why?"

"The corporations are blamed for the situation on the estates. Estate-owners are hardly able to comprehend any other—at fault."

There was another silence, deep and long.

"You'll be glad to know, seri, that there are means to get a message off this world, one that would be heard on Cerdin. I might do it. But there are solutions short of that. Perhaps better ones." She thought then of Jim, and laid a hand on his knee, leaning toward him. "You are hearing things which aren't for retelling . . . to anyone."

"I will not," he said, and she believed him, for he looked as if he earnestly wanted to be deaf to this. She turned back to Eln and Kest.

"What measures," she asked them, "*have* the corporations taken?"

No one wanted to meet her eyes, not those two, nor their companions.

"Is there starvation?" she asked.

"We are importing," one of the others said at last, a small, flat voice.

Raen looked at him, slowly took his meaning. "Standard channels of trade?"

"All according to license. Foodstuffs are one of the permitted—"

"I know the regulations. You're getting your grain from Outside trade. Outsiders."

"We've held off rationing. We've kept the peace. We're able to feed everyone."

"We've tried to find other alternatives," Merek Eln said. "We can't find surplus anywhere within the Reach. We can't get it from Inside. We've tried, Kont' Raen."

"Your trip to Meron."

"Part of it, yes. That. A failure."

"Ser Eln, there's one obvious question. If you're buying Outsider grain . . . what do you use to pay for it?"

It was a question perhaps rash to ask, on a beta vessel, surrounded by them, in descent to a wholly beta world.

"Majat," one of the others said hoarsely, with a nervous shift of the eyes in Warrior's direction. "Majat jewels. Softwares."

"Kontrin-directed?"

"We—pad out what the Cerdin labs send. Add to the shipments."

"Kontrin-directed?"

"Our own doing," the man beside him said. "Kontrin, it's not forbidden. Other hive-worlds do it."

"I know it's legal; don't cite me regulations."

"We appealed for help. We still abide by the law. We would do nothing that's not according to the law."

According to the law . . . and disruptive of the entire trade balance if done on a large scale: the value of the jewels and the other majat goods was upheld by deliberate scarcity.

"You're giving majat goods to Outsiders to feed a world," Raen said softly. "And what do majat get? Grain? Azi? You have that arrangement with them?"

"Our population," sera Kest said faintly, "even now is not *large*—compared to inner worlds. It's only large for our capacity to produce. Our trade is azi. We hope for Kontrin understanding. For licenses to export."

"And the hives assist you in this crisis—sufficient to feed all the excess of your own population, and the excess of azi, and themselves. Your prices to the majat for grain and azi must be exorbitant, sera Kest."

"They—need the grain. They don't object."

"Do you know," Raen said, ever so softly, "I somehow believe you, sera Kest."

There was a sudden stomach-wrenching shift as the shuttle powered into entry alignment. They were downward bound now, and the majat moved, boomed a protest at this unaccustomed sensation; then it froze again, to the relief of the betas and the guard azi.

"We're doing an unusual entry," Raen observed, feeling the angle.
"We don't cross the High Range. Bad weather."

She looked at the beta who had said that, and for that moment her pulse quickened—a sense that, indeed, she had to accept their truths for the time. She said nothing more, scanning faces.

They were coming in still nightside, at a steeper angle than was going to be comfortable for any reason. There might be quite a bit of buffeting. Jim, unaccustomed to landings even of the best kind, was already looking gray. So were the Eln-Kests.

Two corporations: ITAK onworld and ISPAK, the station and power corporation overhead. ISPAK was a Kontrin agency, that should be in direct link with Cerdin. So were all stations. They were too sensitive, holding all a world's licensed defense; and in any situation of contest, ISPAK could shut Istra down, depriving it of power. With any choice for a base of operations, ITAK onworld was not the best one, not unless the stakes were about to go very high indeed.

No licenses, no answer to appeals: the link to Cerdin should have had an answer through their own station. No relief from taxes; other worlds had such adjustments, in the presence of Kontrin. Universal credit was skimmed directly off the tax; majat were covered after the same fashion as Kontrin when they dealt through Kontrin credit; but they could, because they were producers of goods, trade directly in cash, which Kontrin in effect could not. Throughout the system, through the network of stations and intercomp, the constant-transmission arteries which linked all the Reach, there were complex formulae of adjustment and licensing, the whole system held in exact and delicate balance. A world could not function without that continual flow of information through station, to Cerdin.

Only Istra was supporting a burden it could not bear, while inner worlds as well were swollen with increased populations, with no agricultural surpluses anywhere to be had. Council turned a deaf ear to protests, after readjusting population on a world where arable land was scarce.

And the azi-cycle from lab to contract was eighteen years, less for majat-sale.

Nineteen years, and Council had closed its eyes, deafened itself to protests, talked vaguely about new industry. Population pressure was allowed to build, after seven hundred years of licensed precision, every force in meticulous balance.

She watched the screen for a time, the back of her right hand to her lips, the chitin rough against them.

Blue-hive, blue-hive messenger, hives in direct trade with betas—and a world drowning in azi, as all the Reach was beginning to feel the pressure—a forecast for other worlds, while Council turned a deaf ear to cries for help.

Moth still ruled. That had to be true, that Moth still dominated Council. The Reach would have quaked at Moth's demise.

What ARE you doing? she wondered toward Moth.

And put on a smile like putting on a new garment . . . and looked toward ser Eln and sera Kest, enjoying their unease at that shift of mood. "I seem to recall that you invited me to be your guest. Suppose that I accept."

"You are welcome," Kest said hoarsely.

"I shall take the spirit of your hospitality . . . but not as a free gift. My tastes can be very extravagant. I shall pay my own charges. I should expect no private person to bear with me, no private person nor even ITAK. Please permit this."

"You are very kind," said ser Eln, looking vastly relieved.

They began to feel their descent. The shuttle, in atmosphere, rode like something wounded, and the engines struggled to slow them, cutting in with jolting bursts. Eventually they reached a reasonable airspeed, and the port shields went back. It was pitch black outside, and lightning flared. They hit turbulence which dampened even Raen's enthusiasm for the uncommon, and dropped through, amazingly close to the ground.

A landing-field glowed, blue-lit, and abruptly they were on it, jolting down to a halt on great blasts of the engines.

They were down, undamaged, moving ponderously up to the terminal, a long on-ground process. Raen looked at Jim, who slowly unclenched his fingers from the armrests and drew an extended breath. She grinned at him, and he looked happier, the while the shuttle rocked over the uneven surface. "Luggage," she said softly. "You might as well see to it. And when we're among others, don't for the life of you let someone at it unwatched."

He nodded and scrambled up past her, while one of the guard azi began to see to the Eln-Kests' baggage.

The shuttle pulled finally up to their land berth, and met the exit tube. The pilot and co-pilot, their dispute evidently resolved, left controls and unlatched the exit.

Raen arose, finding the others waiting for her, and glanced back at Warrior, who remained immobile. Cold air flooded in from the exit, and Warrior turned its head hopefully.

"Go first," Raen bade the Istran seri and their azi. They did so in some haste; and Jim pulled the luggage carrier out after the ITAK azi. Raen lifted her right hand and beckoned Warrior to follow her out; the ship's officers scrambled back into the cockpit and hastily closed their door.

The party began to sort themselves into order in the exit tube, the ITAK folk and their armed azi keeping ahead. Raen walked with Jim and Warrior, whose strides were apparent slow motion beside those of humans.

Customs officials were waiting at the end: incredibly, they only stared stupidly at Warrior still coming and proceeded to hold up the ITAK men, stopping the whole party, with Warrior fretting and humming distress. The Eln-Kests and the others began at once producing cards for the agents, who bore ISPAK badges.

It was bizarre. Raen stared at the uniformed officials for the space of a breath, then thrust her way to them, motioned for the Eln-Kests to move on. There were stunned looks from the officials, even outrage. She made a fist of her right hand and held that in their view.

There was no recognition for an instant: a Kontrin wearing House Color, and a majat Warrior, and these betas simply stared. Of a sudden they began to yield, melted aside, vying for obscurity. "Move!" Raen said to the others, ordering azi, betas and majat with equal rudeness; her nerves were taut-strung; public places were never to her liking, and the dullness of these folk bewildered her.

They entered the concourse, a place surprisingly trafficked . . . AIRPORT, a sign advised, pointing elsewhere, which might explain some of the traffic; a sign advised of a scheduled flight to Newport weekly, and a board displayed scheduled flights to Upcoast, but few walkers had any luggage. It was the stores, Raen decided, the shopping facilities, which might be the major ones for the beta City here. Everywhere the ITAK emblem was prominently displayed, the letters encircled; undercorporations advertising goods and services and selling from small sample-shops all bore the ITAK symbol somewhere on their signs. The faint aroma from restaurants, their busy tables, gave no hint of a world on the brink of rationing and starvation. The goods were on a par with Andra, and nothing indicated scarcity.

Betas, crowds of betas, and nowhere did panic start in that horde. Adults and rare children stared at them and at Warrior . . . stared long and hard, it might be, but there was no panic at such presence. It was insane, that on this world a majat Warrior could be so ignored; or a Kontrin, evident by Color.

They were not sure, she thought suddenly. Downworlders. No one of them had *seen* a Kontrin. They perhaps suspected, but they did not *ex*pect, and they were not in a position, these short-lived betas, to recognize a Color banned in innerworlds for two decades. It was even possible that they did not know the Houses by name; they had no reason to: no beta of Istra had to deal with them.

But a majat needed no recognition. Betas elsewhere had died in panic, trampling each other . . . until majat in the streets became ordinary. She had heard that this had happened in places she had left.

Her nape-hairs prickled with an uncommon sense of a whole world amiss. She scanned the displays they passed, the garish advertising that denied economic doom, but most of all she regarded the crowds, free-walking and those standing by counters who turned to look at them.

The hands, the hands: that was her continual worry. And she could not see behind her.

"I read blue-hive," Warrior intoned suddenly. "I must contact."

"Where?" Raen asked. "Explain. Where are you looking? Is there a heat-sign?"

It stopped, froze. Mandibles suddenly worked with frenzied rapidity, and auditory palps swept back, deafening it, like a human stopping his ears. Raen whirled to the fix of its gaze, heard a solitary human shriek taken up by others.

Warriors.

They poured forward out of an intersecting corridor, a dozen of them, almost on them, and the sound they shrilled entered human range, agony to the ears. Blue Warrior moved, scuttled for a counter, and the attackers pursued with blinding speed, more pouring out from another hall, overturning displays of clothing. Men screamed, dashed to the floor by the rush, trying to escape the shop.

Raen had her gun in hand . . . did not even recall drawing; and put a shot where it counted, into the neural complex of the leading Warrior, whirled and took another. She stumbled in her retreat, hit a solid wall, stood there braced and firing.

Reds. Hate improved her aim. Her mind was utterly cold. Three

went down, and others swarmed the counter where betas and Warrior scattered in panic. She fired into the attackers and swung left,
following Warrior's darting form, into several reds. She took out
one, another. Warrior leaped on the third and rolled with it in a tangle of limbs, a squalling of resonance chambers. Raen caught movement out of the tail of her eye and whirled and fired, no longer
alone: the azi guards had decided to back her. Betas had lifted no
hand against majat, dared not, by their psych-set; but humans were
dead out on the floor. One body was almost decapitated by majat
jaws. Blood slicked the polished flooring in great smears where
majat feet had slipped. Other humans were bitten.

Surviving reds tried to Group; her fire prevented it. She saw other
majat crowded in the corner down at the turning, Grouped and
thinking. Not reds; they would have come into it. The reds which
survived were confused. Azi fire crippled them; Raen sighted with
better knowledge of anatomy and finished the job. Blue Warrior was
up, excited.

Then came the flare of a weapon from the farther group, several
of them. Warrior went down, limbs threshing, air droning from resonance chambers.

"Stop them!" Raen shouted at the azi. The majat charged, ran
into their concentrated fire: five, six, seven of them downed. One
scuttled off, slipping on the floor, a limb damaged. Two shielded
that retreat with their own bodies. They were the sacrifices. Raen
took one. The azi butchered the other with their fire.

They were alone, then. Humans lay tangled with dead majat. She
looked about her, at majat still convulsing in death-throes: those
would go on for some minutes . . . there was no intelligence behind
it. Merek Eln and Parn Kest were down, along with their companions from ITAK, and one of the guard azi. Bystanders were dead. A
siren began to sound. It was already too late for the victims of bite:
they had long since stopped breathing.

Blue Warrior still moved. She left the wall and the two living azi
guards and went out into the center of the bloody floor, where Warrior lay, in a seeping of clear majat fluids. She held out her hand and
it knew her.

Air sucked into the chambers. Auditory palps extended, trembling.

"Taste," it begged of her.

"Reds didn't get it," she said. "We took them all."

"Yesss."

Someone cried out, down the corridor. More tall shapes had entered, moving in haste: she flung up her hand, forbidding the azi to fire.

"Blues have come," she said. Warrior attempted to rise, but had no control of its limbs. She gave it room, and the blues scattered human medical personnel and what security forces had arrived. They crossed the last interval cautiously, stiff and sidling, until Raen showed her right hand, and they recognized her for blue-hive Kontrin.

Then they came in a rush. Some went at once to the fallen reds, taking taste, booming to each other in majat language, and two bent over Warrior.

Taste passed, long and complex, the mandibles of living and dying locked. Then the first Warrior drew back, seeming disoriented. The second took taste, in that strange semblance of a kiss. Other blues came. Somewhere a human wept, audibly. Medical personnel tried quietly to drag victims away from the area. Raen stood still. A third, a fourth Warrior bent over the fallen Kalind blue. The message was being distributed as far as Warrior's fluids could suffice.

The fifth one breathed something in majat language; Warrior sighed an answer. Then the Istran blue's jaws closed, and Warrior's head rolled free.

"Kontrin," another intoned, facing her.

"I am Raen Meth-maren. Tell your Mother so, Warrior. This-unit was from Kalind. Mother will know. Can you reach your hill safely from here?"

"Yesss. Must go now. Haste."

It turned away. Separate Warriors gathered up the head and body of Warrior, lest other hives read any portion of its message. Grouped, they turned and scuttled out.

Two remained.

One came forward, Istran blue, auditory palps extended in sign of peaceful approach. It bowed itself and opened its mandibles. It was Istra's gift, the fifth Warrior, the one who had tasted and killed. In a sense, it *was* Warrior: the thread continued.

Raen touched its scent-patches, accepted and gave taste in the majat kiss. It backed, disturbed as Warrior had been disturbed; but it had Warrior's knowledge of her, and Grouped, with a delicate touch of the chelae.

"Meth-maren," it breathed. Its fellow came forward, and likewise desired taste; Raen gave it, and saw distress in the working of mandibles and the flutter of palps. It resolved its conflict after a moment, touched at her.

They were hers. They followed, as she crossed the littered floor. The two guard azi were still standing against the wall; no one had claimed them, and they seemed in a state of shock. They had lost their employers. They had failed. Merek Eln and Parn Kest were dead, both bitten. One of the businessmen was decapitated; the others had been bitten. So had the third guard azi, and a number of bystanders.

The luggage carrier had been thrust back into a recess beyond the counter. Raen walked that way, and found Jim, jammed within that recess, sitting with his knees tucked up and both hands clutching a gun set upon them. His face was white; his teeth chattered; he had the gun braced and stable.

Guarding the luggage, as she had told him.

For an instant she hesitated, not knowing what he might do; but he did not fire . . . likely could not fire. She approached him quietly and disengaged the gun from his hands, realized Warrior's presence at her shoulder and bade it and its companion stay back. She knelt, put her hand on Jim's rigid arm.

"We need to get out of here. Come on, Jim."

He nodded. Out of near-catatonia, it was a wonder that he could do that much. She patted his shoulder and waited, and he wiped at his face and began to make small movements toward rising, shaking convulsively.

She thought then of the other two azi, who had been in the shuttle with them, who had heard what was said. She flung herself to her feet and pushed past Warrior, past the counter.

The two azi stared at her; they had not moved. But by now Security police, betas ITAK-badged, had arrived on the scene, and some of them started gingerly forward.

"You," she said, rounding on the two azi, "belong to me. Is that clear? I'm transferring your contract. The formalities will be taken care of. You say nothing . . . *nothing,* hear me? I'm buying you out only because I don't like terminating azi."

The two seemed to believe her. She turned then and faced the police, who had hesitated at a safe distance—the majat were still near her—and now started forward again.

"There's been enough commotion," she said, turning toward them her hand, that, with her cloak, was identification enough. "This was a hive-matter and that's enough said. It's settled." She walked to Merek Eln's body, bent and took from his pocket the identity card she had seen at customs. There was, as she had expected, an address. It seemed to be in an ITAK executive district. "I want some manner of transport for myself, three azi, our baggage and two Warriors at once; and an armed officer or two for escort, thank you."

Possibly they thought that this had to go through channels; they stood still a moment. But then the senior gave orders to one of the officers, who left, running.

"Chances are," Raen said, "that the matter is confined to the hives; but you'll kindly call and put this number under immediate surveillance. And you can escort us to that vehicle."

The officer looked at the ID, made a call on his belt unit, . . . would have retained the card, but that Raen held out her hand and insisted. She turned, pocketing it, and gestured to the two guard azi to take charge of the baggage. Jim was leaning on the counter, seeming to have recovered himself, although he was still shaken. She returned the gun to him and he hastily put it in his pocket, missing the opening several times in his agitation. He walked well enough. Warrior and companion stalked along with them, and the shop personnel and the terminal employees and others who had reason to be in the cordoned area stared at them uneasily as they sought the door.

"The car will be there," the senior officer said. "There's an executive from the Board coming out to meet you, Kontrin; we're profoundly embarrassed—"

"My sincere regrets for the next of kin. I want a list of the names and citizen numbers and relatives of those killed. There will be compensation and burial expenses. Relay the information to that address. As for the executive, I'm more interested in settling myself at the moment. There's another call I want you to make. I understand there's an Outsider trade mission in the City. I want someone from that mission . . . I don't care who . . . at that address as quickly as possible."

"Sera—"

"I wouldn't advise you to consult with ITAK on it. Or to fail to do it."

Outer doors opened. She heard the officer behind her speaking urgently on the matter through his belt unit; it would be relayed. An

ITAK police personnel transport waited outside, armored officers with rifles ringed about it. Raen kept her hand near her own weapon, trusting no one.

It took time to load baggage in, to have the azi and the two majat settled in the available space in the rear of the transport. "We can find a car," an officer said; Raen shook her head. She did not trust being separated from her belongings. She still feared majat, a sniping shot; their vision could hardly tell one human from another, but they were stirred enough not to care for such niceties.

The majat must go in last. Warrior fretted, nervous at so many humans it must not touch. Raen touched the sensitive palps, held it attentive an instant. "You must not touch the azi in the vehicle, Warrior. Must not frighten them. Trust. Be very still. You-unit tell the other Warrior so."

It boomed answer, protest, perhaps; but it boarded, its partner with it. The officer slammed the door. Raen hurried round and flung herself in beside the driver. A man slammed the door. She set her drawn gun comfortably on her knee in plain sight as they moved out, watching the shadows of the pillars as they whipped past the terminal entry for the exit ramp.

They were clear. She gave the officer driving the address she wanted and relaxed slightly, trying not to think of Warrior and its companion and the azi in the rear, behind the partition, and what misery they were severally undergoing, two Warriors forbidden to touch and three azi pent up with majat in near darkness.

Night-time city whisked past, lines of domes marching out into dark interstices of wild land, asterisk-city, mostly sealed or underground. The flavor of the air was coppery and unpleasant. The stormclouds boiled above them, frequent with lightnings, and a spattering of rain hit the windshields and windows, fragmenting the lights. Then they were underground again, locked into the subway track, whisking in behind a big public carrier. Raen hated these systems, this projectile-fashion passage through public areas; but it was, perhaps, the safest means of travel this night.

Majat hives did not have communication equipment—no links with station—but majat had been ready for them: red-hive, with ambush prepared. Humans had participated in it almost certainly.

And more than Warrior had died: two beta envoys were gone, two who had been in prolonged contact with a Kontrin, who had perhaps talked too much.

She was not about to trust ITAK. She doubted, at least, that they would move against her openly: it might be—if they knew she was alone, that there was not behind her an entire Kontrin sept and House—

But one bluffed. It was all, in fact, that Kontrin had ever been able to do among betas, in one sense—for the armed ships that rested solely in Kontrin hands were inevitably far away when one might need them; but the ships did exist. So did the intimate knowledge of the psych-sets with which the original beta culture had been created. So did the power to license and embargo, to adjust birth quotas, to readjust any economic fact of a beta's existence, individually or by class.

The beta beside her did not attempt friendliness, did not speak, did not acknowledge her: stark fear. She had seen the reaction elsewhere. She remembered the port, the salon of the ship . . . reckoned what her coming might mean to Istra, which had not seen Kontrin onworld in centuries, many beta lifespans; the veil jerked rudely aside, a whole world subjected to what she had done to the folk of *Andra's Jewel.*

In her present mood, her hand clenched and sweating on the grip of the gun, with the reaction of the ambush finally overtaking her, she little cared.

3

THE CAR DISENGAGED from the tube-system and nosed up the ramp into a residential circle. It was an area of lighted paving, with space for greenery—or something similar—in the center. A high wall encircled them, gates 41, 42, 43 . . . the rain-spattered windshield showed the glare of more lights, vehicles clustered at the area of 47. A guard let them through the open gate; they eased up the curved drive. Floodlights from the cars had the grounds in garish clarity: twisted tree-forms, dappled trunks and tufts of tiny leaves. The garden was all rocks and spiky plantings, and the house was a white, tiered structure, contiguous with the neighboring houses, so that the whole would form a cantilevered ring, like one vast apartment, each groundlevel with its own walled garden. The driver wove past two obstructing vehicles and stopped the car before a well-lit entry, a portico with uniformed officers aswarm about the door.

Raen opened the door and stepped out, spattered by raindrops whipped in under the portico, and waited while the driver and another officer opened the rear doors. They retreated in haste, and Warrior one and Warrior two climbed out, grooming themselves in evident distaste. Jim followed, and the two guard azi . . . unharmed, Raen was glad to see.

"Jim," she said. "You two. Get the luggage out and put it inside the house." She looked then to the officers on the porch and those with her. "Are there occupants?"

"The house has been shut for half a year, Kontrin." A man in civilian clothes edged forward among the others . . . dark-haired, overweight, balding. There was a woman with him, likewise civilian, matched in age, and in corpulence. "Hela Dain," she said. "My husband Elan Prosserty, vice-presidents on the board."

"ITAK is vastly sorry," the man said, "for this reception. Our profound apologies. If we had known you were without sufficient guard . . . You're not injured, Kontrin."

"No." She recalled the gun and slipped it back into its place beneath the cloak. "I'm a guest of the Eln-Kests. Posthumously. I regret the circumstances, but I'll take the hospitality nonetheless. If one of your security people will lodge himself at the front gate . . . outside, if you will . . . to discourage the most obvious intruders, I'll take care of the rest. Kindly come inside. I requested another presence here; have they arrived?"

The Dain-Prossertys made shift to follow her in the wake she cut through the crowd of police and armored guards, into the house, with its stale air and mustiness. Agents were inside likewise, and another group, conspicuous for their white faces and their bizarre dress, four of them.

Outsiders, indeed.

"Kontrin," Hela Dain said with careful deference. "The senior of the trade organization, ser Ab Tallen, and his escort."

Armed. She did not miss that. Tallen was gray-haired, thin, aging. There was one of his young men of strange type, a physiognomy exotic in the Reach. She put out her hand, and Tallen took it without flinching—smiling, his eyes unreadable, cold . . . real. No Kontrin had devised the psych-set behind that face.

"Kont' Raen a Sul hant Meth-maren," she said. *"The* Meth-maren. A social courtesy, ser Tallen. How kind of you to come."

Tallen did not flinch, though she reckoned the summons as delivered by the police had had no option in it. "An opportunity," he said, "which we were not about to refuse. The fabled Kontrin company."

"The Family, ser. The company has set its mark on things, but those days are past." The Outsider's ignorance dazed her; she was pricked by curiosity, but it was not the time or place, not with betas at her elbow. She turned away, made a nod of courtesy toward the ITAK executives. "How kind of you all to come. I trust the little difficulty has settled itself and that it will stay settled. Would you kindly rid me of this commotion of police, seri? Extend them my thanks. I trust my communication lines are free of devices and such. I trust they have been making sure of that. I shall trust that this is the case. I don't have to tell you how distressed I would be to discover something had slipped their notice. Then I would have to carry on some very *high* inquiries, seri. But I am sure that no one would let such a thing happen."

Fear was stark in their faces. "No," Dain assured her at once. "No," her husband echoed.

"Of course not," she said very softly, put a hand on each of their arms as she turned them for the hall, dismissing them. "I thank you very much . . . *very much* for disarranging yourselves to come out here on such a night. Convey to the board my thanks for their concern, my sorrow for the Eln-Kests and for the damage at the port. And if one of you will contact me tomorrow, I will be very pleased to make that gratitude more substantial; you've done very kindly by me tonight. Such attention to duty should be rewarded. You personally, seri. Would you be very sure of the guards you set at the gate, of their dependability? I always like to know who is accountable. I shall be through with these folk in very short order. Merely a courtesy. I do thank you."

They let themselves be put into the hall; Raen turned back then, hearing them quietly ordering police out. There was a sudden disturbance; she looked back: the majat were in, stalking back through the house, on their own security check.

She regarded the man Ab Tallen, gave a deprecating shrug. "I shall be staying, ser. I wanted to be sure your mission was informed of that fact. And I shall welcome the chance to talk with you at leisure, as soon as matters are stable here."

"You're of the government, Kont' Raen—"

"Kont' Raen is sufficient address, ser. Kontrin *are* the government, and the population. And is your mission permanent here?"

"We understood that our presence onworld had official—"

"Of course it does. ITAK is competent to extend such an invitation. I have no plans to interfere with that. In fact, I'm quite pleased by it." It was truth, and she let a bright smile to the surface, a conscious weapon. "If I had not asked to see you, you would have had to wonder whether I knew of your presence and how I regarded it. I've told you both beyond possibility of misunderstanding. Now we can both rest tranquil tonight. I'm extremely tired. It's been a very long flight. Will you favor me with a call tomorrow?"

This man was not so easily confused as the Dain-Prossertys. He gave a self-possessed and slight nod of the head, smiled his official smile. "Gladly, Kont' Raen."

She offered her hand. "How many Outsiders are on Istra?"

His hand had grasped hers. There was a very slight reaction at that question. "A varying number." He withdrew the hand in smooth courtesy. "About twenty-two today. Four went up to station at the first of the week. We do come and go with some frequency: our usefulness as trade liaison depends on that freedom."

"I would expect that, ser Tallen. I assure you I've no plans to interfere. Do make the call tomorrow."

"Without fail."

"Ser." She gave a nod of courtesy, dismissal. Tallen read it, returned it with the same thoughtfulness, gathered his small company, and left; the others not without paying their courtesy likewise . . . not guard-types, then. She stared after them with some curiosity as to precisely how authority was ordered among Outsiders, and what strange worlds had sent them, and how much they truly understood.

The police had vacated; there was the sound of cars pulling away outside. The Dain-Prossertys had disappeared. She walked into the hall, the door open on the rain on one side, Jim and the two guard-azi with the baggage on the other. The majat stalked up behind her from another doorway, and stopped, sat down, waiting.

She drew a breath and looked about her, at the house and the azi. It was a comfortable place: execrable taste in furnishings . . . it gave her a little pang of regret for the Eln-Kests, for in its beta-ish way it had a certain warmth, less beauty than Kontrin style, but a feeling of habitation, all the same.

"Stay now, Kontrin-queen?"

She looked at the Warrior who had spoken, the smaller of the two. "Yes. My-hive, this place." She looked at Jim, at the new azi. "You have names, you two?"

"Max," one volunteered; "Merry," the other. They were not doubles. Max was dark-haired and Merry was pale blond, Max brown-eyed and Merry blue. But the heavy-bodied build was the same, the stature the same, the square-jawed faces of the same expression. The eyes told most of them . . . calm, cold, stolid now that their existence was re-ordered. They could recognize threats; they were likely compulsive about locks and security; they would fight with great passion once the holder of their contracts identified the enemy.

"You two will take direction from Jim as well as from me," she told them. "And identify yourselves to the majat: Jim, show them. Warrior, be careful with these azi."

The two Warriors shifted forward in slow-motion, met Jim; auditory palps flicked forward in interest at his taste, Kalind blue's memory. Max and Merry had to be shown, but they bore the close touch of mandibles with more fortitude than betas would have shown: perhaps the ride enclosed with the majat had frightened all the fear out of them.

"That's well done," she said. "There's not a majat won't know you hereafter; you understand that. —Luggage goes upstairs, mine does; the other can go to some room at the back: Jim, see to it. You two help him; and then check out the place and make sure doors are locked and systems aren't rigged in any way." She wiped a finger through the dust on a hall table, rubbed it away. "Seals aren't very efficient. Be thorough. And mind, Kontrin azi have license to fire on any threat: *any* threat, even Kontrin. Go on, go on with you."

They went. She looked at the two majat, who alone remained.

"You remember me," she said.

"Kethiuy-queen," said the larger, inclining its head to her.

That was Warrior's mind.

"Hive-friend," she said. "I brought you Kalind blue, brought Kalind hive's message. Can you read it?"

"Revenge."

"I am blue-hive," she said. "Meth-maren of Cerdin, first-hive.

What is the state of things here, Warrior-mind? How did reds know us?"

"Many reds, redsss, redsss. Go here, go there. Redss. Goldss. I kill."

"How did reds know us?"

"Men tell them. Redss pushhh. Much push. I defend, defend. The betas give us grain, azi, much. Grow."

"How did you know to come to the port, Warrior?"

"Mother sendss. I killed red; red tastes of mission, seeks blue, seeks port-direction. I reported and Mother sent me, quick, quick, too late."

It was the collective *I*. *I* could be any number of individuals.

"But," she said, "you received Kalind blue's message."

"Yesss."

"This-unit," said the other, "is Kethiuy-queen's messenger. Send now. Send."

"Thank Mother," she told it. "Yes. Go."

It scuttled doorward with disturbing rapidity, a rattle of spurred feet on the tiles—was gone, into the dark.

"This-unit," intoned the other, the larger, "guards."

"This-hive is grateful." Raen touched the offered head, stroked the sensitive palps, elicited a humming of pleasure from Warrior. She ceased; it edged away, then stalked out into the rain—no inconvenience for Warrior, rather pleasure: it would walk the grounds tirelessly, needing no sleep, a security system of excellent sensitivity.

She closed and locked the front door, let go a breath of relief. The baggage had disappeared; she heard Jim's voice upstairs, giving orders.

The temperature was uncomfortably high. She wandered through the reception room and the dining room and located the house comp, found it already activated. That was likely the doing of the police, but the potential hazard worried her. With proper staff she would have insisted on a checkout; as it was, she stripped off her cloak and set to work herself, searching for the most likely forms of tampering, first visually and then otherwise. At last she keyed in the air-conditioning.

Failing immediate catastrophe, feeling the waft of cold air from the ducts, she sat down, assured that she could see the door in the reflection of the screen, and ran through the standard house programs from the list conveniently posted by the terminal . . . called up a floor plan, found the usual security system, passive alarm, nothing of personal hazard: betas would not dare.

Then she keyed in citycomp, pulled Merek Eln's ID from her belt and started inquiries. The deaths were already recorded: someone's extreme efficiency. The property reverted to ITAK; the Eln-Kests had not used their license-for-one-child, and while Parn Kest had living relatives, they were not entitled: the house had been in Eln's name. A keyed request purchased the property entire, on her credit.

Human officials, she reflected, might be mildly surprised when citycomp and ITAK records turned that up in the morning. And Parn Kest's effects . . . Merek Eln's too . . . could be shipped to the relatives as soon as it was certain there was no information to be had from them. It was the least courtesy due.

Max and Merry came noisily downstairs, rambled about the lower floor and the garage looking for security faults, finally reported negative.

She turned and looked at them. They seemed tired—might be hungry as well. "Inventory shows canned goods in the kitchen stores. Azi quarters are out across the garden, kitchen out there too. Does that suit you?"

They nodded placidly. She sent them away, and began reckoning time-changes. She and Jim had missed lunch and, she figured, supper, by several hours.

That accounted for some of the tremor in her muscles, she decided, and wandered off to join Max and Merry in their search of kitchen storage. Warrior could make do with sugared water, a treat it would actually relish; Warrior would also, with its peculiar capacities, assure that they were not poisoned.

4

JIM ATE, sparingly and in silence, and showed some relief. It was the first meal he had kept down all day. She noted a shadow about his eyes and a distracted look, much as the crew of the *Jewel* had had at the last.

Notwithstanding, he would have cleared the dishes after . . . his own notion or unbreakable habit, she was not certain. "Leave it," she said. He would not have come upstairs with her, but she stopped and told him to.

Second door to the right atop the stairs, the main bedroom: Jim had set everything there, a delightful room even to a Kontrin's eye, airy furniture, all white and pale green. There was a huge skylight, a bubble rain-spotted and showing the lightnings overhead.

"Dangerous," she said, and not because of the lightnings.

"There are shields," he offered, indicating a switch.

"Leave it. We wouldn't be safe from a Kontrin assassin, but we probably will from the talent Istra could summon on short notice. Let's only hope none of the Family has been energetic enough to precede me here. Where's your luggage?"

"Hall," he said faintly.

"Well, bring it in."

He did so, and set about unpacking his own things with a general air of distress. She recalled him in the terminal, frozen, with the gun locked in his hands. The remarkable thing was that he had had the inclination to seize it in the first place . . . the dead guard, she reckoned, and opportunity and sheer desperation.

He finished, put his case in the closet and stood there by the door, facing her.

"Are you all right?" she asked. "Warrior's outside. Nothing will get past it. No reason to worry on that account."

He nodded slowly, in that perplexed manner he had when he was out of his depth.

"That skylight—doesn't bother you, does it?" The thought struck her that it might, for he was not accustomed to worlds and weather.

He shook his head in the same fashion.

She put her hand on his shoulder, a gesture of comfort as much as other feeling; he touched her in return, and she looked into his face this time cold sober, in stark light. The tattoo was evident. The eyes . . . remained distracted, perplexed. The expression was lacking.

His hand fell when she did not respond, and even then the expression did not vary. He was capable of physical pleasure—more than capable. He felt—at least approval or the lack of it. He suffered shocks . . . and tried to go on responding, as now, when a beta or Kontrin would have acknowledged distress.

"You did well," she said deliberately, watched the response, a little touch of relief.

Limited sensitivity. Suspicion washed over her, answers she did not want. He made appropriate responses, human responses, answered to affection. Some azi could not; likely Max and Merry were too dull for it. But even Jim, she thought suddenly, did not react to stress as a born-man might. She touched him; he touched her. But the responses might as easily be simple tropisms, like turning the face to sunlight, or extending cold hands to warmth. To be approved was better than to be disapproved.

Lia too. Even Lia. Not love, but programs. Psych-sets, less skillfully done than the betas' own.

Beta revenge, she thought, sick to the heart of her. *A grand joke, that we all learn to love them when we're children.*

She hated, for that moment, thoroughly, and touched Jim's face and did not let it show.

And when she was lying with the azi's warmth against her, in Merek Eln's huge bed, she found him—all illusions laid aside—simply a comfortable presence. He was more at ease with her than he had been the first night, an incredible single night ago, on the *Jewel;* he persisted in seeking closeness to her, even deep in sleep, and the fact touched her. Perhaps, whatever he felt, she was his security; and whatever his limitations, he was there, alive—full of, if not genuine humanity, at least comfortable tropisms . . . someone to talk to, a mind off which her thoughts could reflect, a solidity in the dark.

It stopped here; everything stopped here, at the Edge. She lay on her back staring up, her arm intertwined with Jim's. The storm had passed and the stars were clear in the skylight: Achernar's burning eye and all, all the other little lights. The loneliness of the Reach oppressed her as it never had. The day crowded in on her, the Outsider ship ghosting past them in the morning, the presence of them in the house.

What's out there, she wondered, *where men never changed? Or do we all . . . change?*

Perspective shifted treacherously, as if the sky were downward, and she jerked. Jim half-wakened, stirred. "Hush," she said. "Sleep." And he did so, his head against her, seeking warmth.

Tropism.

We created the betas, built all their beliefs; but they refused to live as we made them: they had to have the azi. They created them; they cripple them, to make themselves whole by comparison. Of what did we rob the betas?

Of what they take from the azi?

She rubbed at Jim's shoulder and wakened him deliberately. He blinked at her in the starlight. "Jim, was there another azi on the *Jewel,* more than one, perhaps, that you would have liked to have here with you?"

He blinked rapidly, perplexed. "No."

"Are you trying to protect them?"

"No."

"There was none, no friend, no—companion, male or female?"

"No."

She considered that desolation a moment, that was as great as her own. "Enemy?"

"No."

"You were, what, four years on that ship, and never had either friend or enemy?"

"No." A placid no, a calm and quiet no, a little puzzled.

She took it for truth, and smoothed his hair aside as Lia had done with her when she was a child, in Kethiuy.

She at least . . . had enemies left.

Jim—had nothing. He and the majat azi, the naked creatures moving with will-o'-the-wisp lights through the tunnels of the hive—were full brothers, no more nor less human.

"I am blue-hive," she whispered to him, moved to things she had never said to any human. "Of the four selves of majat . . . the gentlest, but majat for all that. Sul sept is dead; Meth-maren House is dead. Assassins. I'm blue-hive. That's what I have left.

"There was an old man . . . seven hundred years old. He'd seen Istra, seen the Edge, where Kontrin won't go. Majat came here to live, long ago, but Kontrin wouldn't, only he. And I." She traced the line of his arm, pleased by its angularity, mentally elsewhere. "Nineteen years ago some limits were readjusted; and do you know, they've never been redone. Someone's taken great care that all that not be redone.

"Nineteen years. I've lived on every hive-world of the Reach. I've caused the Family a minimum of difficulty. Not from love, not from love, you understand. Ah, no. There's an old woman in Council. Her name is Moth. She's not dictator in name, but she is. And she doesn't trouble me. She does the nothing she always preferred. And the things let loose nineteen years ago—have all come of age.

"The Houses are waiting. Waiting all this time. Moth will die, one of these days. Then the scramble for power, as the Reach has never seen it."

"Sera—"

"Dangerous listening, yes. Don't call me that. And you have sense enough to keep quiet, don't you? The azi down in the azi quarters . . . are not to be trusted. Never confide in them. Even Warrior knows the difference, knowing you were with me before they were. No, trust Warrior if ever you must trust anything; it can't tell your face from that of any other human, but hail it blue-hive and give it taste or touch, it or any blue. I'll show you tomorrow, show you how to tell the hive-markings apart. You must learn that and show Max and Merry. And if there's ever any doubt of a majat, kill it. I mean it. Death is a minor thing to them. Warrior—always comes back. Only humans don't."

"Why—" From Jim, question was a rarity. "Why did they attack us at the port?"

"I don't know. I think they wanted Warrior."

"Why?"

"Two questions in sequence. Delightful. You're recovering your balance."

"Sera?"

"Raen." She struck him lightly with her fist, an excess of hope. "My name is Raen; call me Raen. You can manage that. You were entirely wasted on the *Jewel*. Handling of arms: everything that pair downstairs can do; and anything else, anything else. You can learn it. You're not incapable of learning. Go back to sleep."

He did not, but lay to this side and that, and finally settled again when she rested her head against his shoulder.

Security.

That, she reckoned, was somewhat mutual.

BOOK SIX

1

THE MOTHER OF Istra blue took taste, and heaved herself back, mandibles working. Drones soothed Her, singing in their high voices. She ceased, for a moment, to produce new lives.

"Other-hive." She breathed, and the walls of the Chamber vibrated with the low sound. "Blue-hive. Blue-hive Kontrin. Methmaren of Cerdin. Kethiuy."

The Drones moved closer, touched. She bowed and offered taste to the foremost, and it to the next, while She gave to a third. Like the motion of wind through grass it passed, and the song grew in its wake. An impulse extraordinarily powerful went out from them; and all through the Hill, activity slowed. Workers and Warriors turned wherever they were, oriented themselves to the Chamber.

In the egg-chamber, frightened Workers, sensing vague alarm, began building a seal for the shafts. Theirs was the only activity.

Mother lowered Her head and reached out for the reporting Warrior yet again; and Warrior, knowing fear of Mother for the first time in its existence, locked a second time into Mother's chemistry, suffering the reactions of Her body as the messages swirled through Her fluids.

Others crowded close, seeking understanding.

They could not interpret fully. Each understood after its own kind.

There was impression of a flow of chemistry which had begun many cycles ago, a tiny taste of Cerdin, homeworld. The Mind Remembered. There had been a small hill. The memory went back before there were humans, salt-tasting, quick-perishing; before the

little lake had filled; before the hill itself had stood. There were
ages, and depths. The Mind reeled in ecstasy, the reinforcement of
this ancient memory. There were partings, queens born of eggs ship-
sent, hives hurled out to the unseen stars, over distances the Mind
comprehended only when majat eyes beheld a new heat source in
the heavens, different in pattern and timing and intensity, only when
majat calculations reckoned angles and distances and an impression
of complexities beyond the comprehension of the Mind, mysticism
alien to majat processes.

Vastness, and dark, and cold.

Where the Mind was not.

Death.

At last the Mind had something by which to comprehend death,
and finitude of worlds, and time before and after itself. It staggered
in such comprehensions, and embraced abstracts.

Finite time, as humans measured it, suddenly acquired meaning.

The Mind understood.

Kalind-mind. There was dazzling taste of it, which had tasted of
Andra, and of Meron, which had tasted of Cerdin, a wave starting at
Cerdin and rippling outward: violence, and enmity. Destruction.
Cerdin. Destruction.

The motion in the hive utterly ceased. Even the egg-tenders froze,
paralyzed in the enormity of the vision.

Growth since. Growth, denying death.

Mind reached outward, where there was no contact, for the distances were too far, and synthesis was impossible. There was only
the longing, a stirring in the chemistries of the hive.

"Hazard," a Warrior complained, having tasted Kontrin presence,
and the slaughter of blues, the murders of messengers.

It could comprehend nothing more; but the hive closed the more
tightly.

"She—" Mother began, interpreting across the barriers of type,
which was queen-function, while chemistries meshed on other levels,
"she is Meth-maren hive. She *is* the hive. She is Kethiuy. Her
Workers are late-come, gathered from strange hives. Azi. She tastes
of danger, yess. Great hazard, but not hostile to blues. She preserved
us the messenger of Kalind. She was on Meron, and Andra; her taste
is in those memories. She was *within* the Hill on Cerdin. She has
patterned with Warriors, against majat, against humans. Istra-reds

. . . taste of hate of her. Cerdin-taste runs in red-memory, taste of humans and death of blues. Great slaughter. Yess. But the entity Raen Meth-maren is blue-hive Kontrin. She has been part of the Mind of Cerdin."

"Queen-threat," a Warrior ventured.

The Drones sang otherwise, Remembering. The Mother of Cerdin blue-hive lived in Kalind blue's message. There was a song that was Kethiuy, and death, abundant death, the beginning of changes, premature.

"Meth-maren," Mother recalled, feeding into the Mind. "First-human. Hive-friend."

Then the message possessed Her, and She poured into the Drones a deep and abiding anger. The Mind reached. Its parts were far-flung, scattered across the invisible gulfs of stars, of time, which had never been of significance. The space existed. Time existed. There was no synthesis possible.

The Drones moved, laved Mother with their palps, increasingly disturbed. They rotated leftward, and Mother also moved, drawing from Warriors and Foragers far-ranging on the surface—orienting to the rising sun, not alpha, but beta Hydri, beholding this in the darkness of the Hill.

The Drones searched Memory, rotated farther, seeking resolution. Full circle they came, locked again on the Istran sun. Workers reoriented; Warriors moved.

The circling began again, slow and ponderous. Seldom did Mother move at all. Now twice more the entire hive shifted prime direction, and settled.

A Warrior felt Mother's summons and sought touch. It locked into Mother's chemistry and quivered its entire length in the strength of the message it felt. It turned and ran, breaking from the Dance.

A Worker approached, received taste, and likewise fled, frantically contacting others as it went.

The Dance fragmented. Workers and Warriors scattered in a frenzy in all directions.

The Drones continued to sing, a broken song, and dissonant. Mother produced no egg. A strange fluid poured from Her mandibles, and the Workers gathered it and passed to the egg-tenders, who sang together in consternation.

2

THE HOUSE-COMP's memory held a flood of messages: those from the Dain-Prossertys, who had lost no time; anxious inquiries from the ITAK board in general; from ISPAK, a courteous greeting and regrets that she had not stayed in the station; from the police, a requested list of casualties and next of kin; from forward ITAK businesses, offers of services and gifts.

Raen dealt with some of them: a formal message of condolences to the next-of-kin, with authorization for funeral expenses and the sum of ten thousand credits to each bereaved, to be handled through ITAK; to the board, general salutations; to the Dain-Prossertys a suggestion that any particular license they desired might be favorably considered, and suggesting discretion in the matter.

She ordered printout of further messages and ignored what might be incoming for the time, choosing a leisurely breakfast with Jim, the while Max and Merry ate in the azi quarters, and Warrior enjoyed a liquid delicacy in the garden—barely visible, Warrior's post, a shady nook amongst the rocks and spiky plants, a surprise for any intruders.

A little time she reckoned she might spend in resting; but postponing meetings with ITAK had hazard, for these folk might act irrationally if they grew too nervous.

There was also the chance that elements of the Family had agents here: more than possible, even that there could have been someone to precede her. In the *Jewel*'s slow voyage there was time for that.

She toyed with the idea of sending Council a salutation from Istra, after two decades of silence and obedience. The hubris of it struck her humor.

But Moth needed no straws added to the weight under which she already tottered. Raen found it not in her present interest to add anything to the instabilities, to aggravate the little tremors which were beginning to run through the Reach. Kontrin could act against her on Istra; but they would not like to, would shudder at the idea of pursuing a feud in the witness of betas, and very much more so here at the window on Outside. No, she thought, there would be for her only the delicate matter of assassination . . . and Moth, as ever, would act on the side of inaction, entropy personified.

No such message would go, she decided, finishing her morning tea. Let them discover the extent of their problem. For herself—she had them; and they had yet to discover it . . . had a place whereon to stand, and, she thought to herself, a curiosity colder and more remote than all her enemies' ambition: to comprehend this little ball of yarn the while she pulled it apart.

To know the betas and the azi and all the shadows the Kontrin cast on the walls of their confinement.

Jim had finished his breakfast, and sat, hands on the table, staring between them at the empty plate. The azi invisibility mode. If he did not move, his calculation seemed to be, then she would cease to notice him and he could not possibly bother her. The amazing thing was that it so often worked. She had seen azi do such things all her life, that purposeful melting into the furnishings of a room, and she had never noticed, until she persisted in sitting at table with one, until she relied on one for company, and conversation, and more than that.

It is something, she thought, *to begin to see.*

She pushed back from the table without a word, seeking her own invisibility, and went off to the computer.

The printout had grown very long during breakfast. She tore it off and scanned it, found overtures from some of the great agricultural cooperatives within ITAK—suggesting urgent and private consultations. Word had indeed spread. Some messages were from ITAK on the other continent, imaginatively called West: that was the Newport operation; simple courtesies, those. Another had come from ISPAK, inviting her up for what it called an urgent conference. A message from ITAK on East acknowledged with gratitude the one she had sent before breakfast and urged her to entertain a board meeting at some convenient time; the signature was one ser Dain, president, and of a sudden she smiled, recalling sera Dain and her husband . . . betas too, had their Family, and she reckoned well how the connections might run in ITAK. Small benefit, then, from corrupting Prosserty: Dain was the name to watch.

And finally there was the one she had hoped for, a courteous greeting from ser Tallen of the trade mission, recalling the night's summons and leaving a number where he might be reached: the address was that of a city guest house . . . considering Newhope, probably the only guest house.

She keyed the same message to all but Tallen. NOTED. I AM PRESENTLY ARRANGING MY SCHEDULE. THANK YOU. R.S.M.-m.

To Tallen: AT TWO, MY RESIDENCE, A BRIEF MEETING. RAEN A SUL.

She cleared that with the police at the gate, lest there be misunderstandings; and reckoned that it would be relayed to ITAK proper.

And a brief call to ITAK registry, bypassing automatic processes: Max and Merry were legally transferred, even offered as a company courtesy; she declined the latter, and paid the modest valuation of the contracts.

Supply: she arranged that, through several local companies . . . ordered items from groceries to hardware in prodigious quantity, notwithstanding borderline shortages. Fruit, grain, and sugar were in unusual proportion on that list . . . distressing, to any curious ITAK agent who investigated.

To the nine neighbors of Executive Circle 4, the same message, sent under the serpent-sigil of the Family: TO MY NEIGHBORS: WITH EXTREME REGRET I MUST STATE THAT AN ATTEMPT ON MY LIFE MAKES NECESSARY CERTAIN DEFENSIVE MEASURES. THIS CIRCLE MAY BE SUBJECT TO HAZARDOUS VISITORS AND ACTIONS ON THE PART OF MY AGENTS MAY NECESSITATE SUDDEN INCURSIONS INTO NEIGHBORING RESIDENCES. I REFUSE RESPONSIBILITY FOR LIVES AND PROPERTY UNDER THESE CIRCUMSTANCES. IF, HOWEVER, YOU WISH TO RELOCATE FOR THE DURATION OF MY STAY ON ISTRA, I SHALL BE HAPPY EITHER TO PURCHASE YOUR RESIDENCE OR TO RENT IT, WITH OR WITHOUT FURNISHINGS. I SHALL MEET ANY REASONABLE PRICE OR RENT WITHOUT ARGUMENT AND OFFER TO BEAR ALL EXPENSES OF TEMPORARY OR PERMANENT RELOCATION IN A COMPARABLE CIRCLE, PLUS 5,000 CREDITS GENERAL COMPENSATION FOR THE INCONVENIENCE. KONT' RAEN A SUL HANT METH-MAREN, AT 47. RESPONSE EXPECTED.

Then she settled back, shut her eyes and rested for a few moments

. . . set herself forward then, having begun the sequences in her mind.

Kontrin-codes. Kontrin had set up worldcomp and intercomp, and maintained both. There were beta accesses, in a hierarchy of authorizations; there were many more reserved to Kontrin, and some restricted to specific Houses, to those who worked directly with specific aspects of the central computers at Alpha—with the trade banks or the labs or the other separate agencies, which met in Council: the democracy of the Family, the secrecy that kept certain functions for certain Houses, making Council necessary. Meth-marens had had somewhat to do with establishing Alphacomp in the very beginning—in matters of abstract theory and majat logic, the mathematics of the partitioned hive-mind: translation capacity, biocomp, and the dull mechanics of warehousing and hive-trade; but Ilit had had the abstract interest in economics.

Merely to enter worldcomp or even intercomp, and to touch information of betas' private lives . . . any Kontrin could do that. Trade information was hardly more difficult, for any who knew the very simple codes: locations of food-stuffs, ships in port, licenses and applications for license. It was all very statistical and dull and few Kontrin without direct responsibility for a House's affairs would bestir themselves to care what volume of grain went into a city.

She did. Hal Ilit had realized, perhaps, the extent of her theft from him; perhaps this shame as much as the other had prompted him to turn on her. Certainly it was shame that had prompted him to try to deal with her on his own, a man never experienced in violence.

He had been in most regards, an excellent teacher.

And the Eln-Kests, according to the statistics on record, had not been lying.

There was a periodic clatter in the next room, the rattle of dishes. Jim was probably at the height of happiness, doing what his training prepared him to do. It irritated her. She ordinarily carried on some operations in her mind, and could not to her usual extent, whether through preoccupation or because of the extraneous noise: she posted them to the auxiliary screens and checked them visually.

The rattle of dishes stopped. There was silence for a time. Then it began again, this time the moving of chairs and objects, a great deal of pacing about between.

She threw down the stylus, swore, rose and stalked back to the main rooms. Jim was there, replacing a bit of sculpture on the reception hall table.

"The noise," she said, "is bothering me. I'm trying to work."

He waved a hand at the rooms about him, which were, she saw now, clean, dusted, well-ordered. *Approve,* his look asked, and killed all her anger. It was his whole reason for existence on the *Jewel.*

It was his whole reason for existence anywhere.

She let go her breath and shook her head.

"I beg pardon," he said, in that always-subdued voice.

"Take a few hours off, will you?"

"Yes, sera."

He made no move to go; he expected her to walk away, she realized, being the one with a place to go. She thought of him at breakfast, absolutely still, mental null . . . agony, she thought. It was what the Family had tried to do with her. She could not bear watching it.

"I've a deepstudy unit upstairs," she said. "You know how to use it?"

"Yes, sera."

"If you can't remember, I'm going to make a tape that says nothing but *Raen.* Come on. Come upstairs. I'll see whether you know what you're doing with it."

She led the way; he followed. In the bedroom she gestured at the closet where her baggage was stored, and he pulled the unit out, while she located the 'bin bottle in her cosmetics kit and shook out a single capsule.

He set it up properly, although he seemed puzzled by some of the details of it: units varied. She watched him attach the several leads, and those were right. She gave him the pill, and he swallowed it without water.

"Recreation," she said, and sorted through the second, the brown case, that held the tapes. "You're always free to use the unit. I wish you would, in fact. Any white tape is perfectly all right for you." She looked at him, who sat waiting, looking at her, and reckoned that no azi was capable of going beyond instructions: she had never known one to, not even Lia. Psych-set. They simply could not. "You don't touch the black ones. Understood? If I hand you a black one, that's one thing, but not on your own. You follow that?"

"Yes," he said.

They were black ones that she chose, Kontrin-made. The longest was an artistic piece, participant-drama: a little cultural improvement would not be amiss, she thought. And the short one was *Istra*. She put them in the slot. "You know this machine, do you? You understand the hazards? Make sure the repeat-function never adds up to more than two hours."

He nodded. His eyes were beginning to dilate with the drug. He was not fit for conversation—fumbled after the switch, in token of this. She pushed it for him.

There was delay enough for him to compose himself. He settled back, folded his arms across his belly, eyes glassy. Then the machine began to activate, and it was as if every nerve in his body were severed: the whole body went limp. It was time to leave; the machine was a nuisance without the drug, and she never liked to look at someone undergoing the process—it was not a particularly pretty sight, mouth slack, muscles occasionally twitching to suggestion. She double-checked the timer to be sure: there was a repeat function, that could be turned to suicide—dehydration, a slow death as pleasant or as terrible as the tape in question; it was not engaged, and she turned her back on him and left, closed the door on the unit and its human appendage.

Every tape she had had since she was fifteen was in that box, and some she had recovered in duplicate for sentiment's sake. *If he knew them all,* she thought wistfully, *he might be me.* And then she laughed, to think of things that were not in the tapes, the ugly things, the bitter things.

The laugh died. She leaned against the rail of the stairs and reckoned another thing, that she should not have meddled at all, that she should ravel at other knots that had importance, and let this one alone.

No more than the hives, she thought, and went downstairs.

3

AB TALLEN BROUGHT a different pair with him . . . an older woman named Mara Chung and a middle-aged man named Ben Orrin. Warrior was nervous with their presence: what Warrior could not touch made it entirely nervous, and the police had liked Warrior no better, having the duty of escorting the Outsiders to the safety of the house.

Max served drinks: Jim was still upstairs, and Raen was content with that, for Max managed well enough, playing house-azi. She sipped at hers and watched the Outsiders' eyes, what things drew them, what things seemed of interest.

Max himself was, it seemed. Ser Orrin was injudicious enough to stare at him directly, glanced abruptly at some point on the glass he held when he realized it.

Raen smiled, caught Max's eye and with a flick of hers, dismissed him to neutrality somewhere behind her. She looked at her guests. "Seri," she murmured, with a gesture of the glass. "Your welcome. Your profound welcome. Be at ease. I plan no traps. I know what you've been doing on Istra. It's of no moment to me. Probably others of the Family find it temporarily convenient. A measure which has prevented difficulties here. How could the Reach complain of that?"

"If you would be clear, Kont' Raen—what interests you do serve, forgive me. We might be on firmer footing."

"Ser Tallen, I am not being subtle at the moment. I am here. I don't choose to see anything of the transactions you've made with Istra. Pursuing that would be of no profit to me, and a great deal of inconvenience. Some interests in the Family would be pleased with what you're doing; others would be outraged; Council would debate it and the outcome would be uncertain, but perhaps unfavorable. Myself, I don't care. The hives are fed. That's a great benefit. Azi aren't starved. That's another. It makes Istra liveable, and I'm living on Istra. Plain?"

There was long silence. Tallen took a drink and stared at her, long and directly. "Do you represent someone?"

"I'm Meth-maren. Some used to call us hive-masters; it's a term we've always disliked, but it's descriptive. That's what I represent, though some dispute it."

"You control the majat?"

She shook her head. "No one—controls the majat. Anyone who tells you he does . . . lies. I'm an intermediary. An interpreter."

" 'Though some dispute it,' you said."

"There are factions in the Family, seri, as aforesaid. You might hear others disputing everything I say. You'll have to make up your own mind, weighing your own risks. I've called you here, for one thing, simply to lay all things out in open question, so that you don't have to ask ITAK questions that are much easier to ask of me directly. You had to wonder how much secrecy you needed use with certain items of trade; you could have wasted a great deal of energy attempting to conceal a fact which is of no importance to me. I consider it courtesy to tell you."

"Your manners are very direct, Kont' Raen. And yet you don't say a word of why you've come."

"No, ser. I don't intend to." She lowered her eyes and took a drink, diminishing the harshness of that refusal, glanced up again. "I confess to a lively curiosity about you—about the Outside. How many worlds are there?"

"Above fifty around the human stars."

"Fifty . . . and non-human? Have you found other such?"

Tallen's eyes broke contact, and disappointed her, even, it seemed, with regret to do so. "A restricted matter, Kont' Raen."

She inclined her head, turned the glass in her hand, let the melting ice continue spinning, frowned—thinking on Outside, and on the ship at station, Outbound.

"We are concerned," Tallen said, "that the Reach remain stable."

"I do not doubt." She regarded him and his companions, male and female. "I doubt that I can answer your questions either."

"Do you invite them?" And when she shrugged: "Who governs? Who decides policies? Do majat or humans dominate here?"

"Moth governs; the Council decides; majat and humans are separate by nature."

"Yet you interpret."

"I interpret."

"And remain separate?"

"That, ser," she answered, having lost her self-possession for the second time, "remains a question." She frowned. "But there remains one more matter, seri, for which I asked you here. And I shall ask it and hope for the plain truth: among the bargains that you have made with concerns inside the Reach—is there any breach of quarantine? You're not—providing exit for any citizens of the Reach? You've not agreed to do so in future?"

They were disturbed by this, as they might be.

"No," Tallen said.

"Again, my personal position is one of complete disregard. No. Not complete. I would," she said with a shrug and a smile, "be personally interested. I would be very interested to see what's over the Edge. But this is not the case. There is no exit."

"None. It would not be tolerated, Kont' Raen, much as it is regrettable."

"I am satisfied, then. That was the one item which troubled me. You've answered me. I think that I believe you. All our business for my part is done. Perhaps a social meeting when there's leisure for it."

"It would be a pleasure, Kont' Raen."

She inclined her head, set her glass aside, giving them the excuse to the same.

There were formalities, shaking of hands, parting courtesies: she went personally to the door and made sure that Warrior did not approach them as they entered their car and closed the doors.

"Max," she said, "see to the gate out there. Make sure our security is intact."

He was over-zealous; he went without more than his sunvisor, and she frowned over it, for Istra's sun was no kinder than Cerdin's. New azi. Anxious and over-anxious to please. It was worse in its way than dealing with housecomp.

The car reached the gate and exited; Max saw to the closing and walked back, Warrior gliding along at a little distance, keeping a critical majat eye on all that passed.

Max entered, sought more instruction. "Just protect yourself when you go out, after this," she said peevishly, and dismissed him. She was depressed by the encounter, had hoped otherwise, and logically could not say why.

She closed and sealed the door, blinking somewhat from the change of light, from the portico to the inner hall—looked up, for Jim was on the stairs, watching her.

He looked yet a little abstracted; deepstudy did that to one. And he had been upstairs longer than the tape had run . . . asleep, perhaps. It was a common reaction.

"You didn't repeat it, did you?" she asked, thinking of Max's excessive zeal, concerned for that.

"I listened aloud for several times."

"You were supposed to enjoy it."

"I thought I was supposed to learn it." He shrugged from the stare she gave him for that, glanced down briefly, a flinching. "Is there something I can do now?"

She shook her head, and went back to her work.

The supplies arrived: Jim went out with Max and Merry to fend off Warrior while they were unloaded; it evidently was managed without incident, for she heard nothing of it. Six of the neighbors called, advising that they were indeed seeking shelter elsewhere; three were silent, and calls to them raised no human answer, only housecomp. There were several more calls from various sources, including ITAK and ISPAK.

For the most part there was no sound in the house at all, not a stirring from Jim, wherever he was and whatever he did to pass the time. He appeared at last, prepared supper, shared it with her in silence and vanished again. She would have spoken with him at dinner, but she was preoccupied with the recollection of her work with the comp net, and with the hazard of dipping as she did into intercomp; it was nothing to touch lightly, a taut-strung web which could radiate alarms if jostled too severely. She did not need abstract discussion with an azi to unhinge her thought.

He was there after midnight, when she came to bed, and even then she was not in a mood for conversation; he sensed this, evidently, and did not attempt it. But the work was almost done, and she could, for a time, let it go.

She did so; he obliged, cheerfully, and seemed content.

4

She went down alone in the morning, letting Jim sleep while he would; and the fear that some urgent message, some calamity, some profound change in circumstances might be waiting in the housecomp's memory, sent her stumbling down to check on it before her eyes were fully open.

Only the same sort of message that had been coming in during the last day and night. She scanned the message-function a second time, refusing to believe in her continued safety, and finally accepted that this was so—pushed her hair out of her eyes and wandered off to the kitchen to make a cup of coffee: Outsider-luxuries, cheaper here than in innerworlds, for all the threat of famine. Istra was not backward where it regarded what was obtained from Outsider trade.

She drank her breakfast standing up, staring glaze-eyed at the garden through the kitchen's long slit window, thinking even then that the house had far too many windows, too many accesses, and that the walls were a good deal too low to serve even against human intruders: they masked what went on outside and close to them, and were no defense, only a delay.

The rising of beta Hydri gave a wan light at this hour—wan by reason of the shaded glass. The light rimmed the walls, the edge of the azi-quarters which showed a gleam of interior light, and over the wall, far distant, showed a vague impression of the domes of another arm of the City, with brush and grassland intervening: another hazard. Within the walls was deep shadow. The light frosted edges of rocks, of hastate-leaved plants, of the garden's few trees, which were gnarled and twisted and looked dead until one realized that the limp strings which hung along the limbs were leaves. A vine which ran among the rocks like a brown snarl of old cable by day had miraculously spread leaves for the dawn. Other things likewise had leafed out or bloomed, for the one brief period of moderate light and coolness. By day the garden reverted to reality. It was much like Cerdin. The Eln-Kests had had an eye for gardens, for Istran beauty, declining to import showy exotics from Kalind, which would have died, neglected: these thrived. It was a quality of subtle taste unsuspected in folk whose front-room decor was as it was. Raen thought of the green-and-white bedroom, and the subtlety of that, and reckoned that the same mind must have planned both, a character unlike what she knew of betas.

A large shadow appeared in the window, stopping her heart; it was Warrior—at least majat, wanting in. She opened the door, hand on the gun she had in her pocket, but it was in truth only Warrior, who sat down on the floor and preened itself of dew.

A little sugar-water more than satisfied it; it sang for her while it drank, and she stroked the auditory palps very softly in thanks for this.

"Others come," it said then.

"Other blues? How do you know so, Warrior?"

It boomed a note of majat language. "Mind," it translated, probably approximating.

"Is blue-hive not far, then?"

It shifted, never ceasing to drink, into a new orientation. "There."

It faced down-arm from residence circle 4.

"Come that way," it informed her, then reoriented half about. "Blue-hive there, our-hill."

They would come an eighth of the way round the asterisk-city and up the wild interstice to the garden wall. And majat runners could cover that ground very quickly.

"When?"

It stopped drinking and measured with its body the future angle of the sun, a profound bow toward the far evening. Late, then. Twilight.

"This-hive hopes you remain with us, Warrior."

It began drinking again. "This-unit likes sweet. Good, Kethiuy-queen."

She laughed soundlessly. "Good, Warrior." She touched it, eliciting a hum of pleasure, and went about her business. Warrior would of course do what the hive determined, immune to bribery, but Warrior would at least give its little unit of resistance to being removed, as valid a unit of the Mind as any other.

And the hive was reacting. She went about her work, schooling herself to concentration, but burning with an inner fire all the same: the hive . . . had heard her, regarded her. The approach through Kalind Warrior had had its imprint.

It was there again, the contact which she had lost. Nearly twenty years, and many attempts, and this one had taken: she had allies, the power of the hives.

All possibilities shifted hereafter. Being here, at the Edge, was no longer a protracted act of suicide, a high refuge, a place where enemies could not so easily follow: the circular character of events struck her suddenly and amazed her with her own predictability. She had run, a second time, for the hive.

It was time to attack.

5

HOUSE RECORDS HAD indicated a vehicle in the garage: systems in it seemed up and operable. Max and Merry both, by their papers, had some skill in that regard. "Go out," she said, "and check it out by eye; I'm not inclined to trust housecomp's word on it."

They went. Citybank provided an atlas in printout. A sorrowfully thin atlas it proved to be, only a few pages thick, for an entire inhabited world. Newhope and Newport were *the* two cities, Newport seeming a very small place indeed; and the town of Upcoast was the other major concentration of population, only an administrative and warehousing area for the northern estates. The rest of the population was dotted all over the map, in the rain-belts, on farms and pumping stations and farms which served as depots on the lacery of unpaved roads. Over most of the land surface of Istra was nothing but blankness, designated Uninhabited. There was the spectacular upsurge of the High Range on East; and an extremely wide expanse of marsh southward on West, marked Hazard, which given the habit of Istran nomenclature, might be the name of the place as well as its character. Small numbers were written beside the dots that were farms . . . 2, 6, 7, and those in black; and by depots and by the cities, likewise, but ranging up to 15,896 at Newhope.

Population, she realized. A world so sparse that they must give population in the outback by twos and threes.

In the several pages of the atlas, three were city-maps, and they were all of the pattern of Newhope. The city was simplicity itself: an eight-armed star with business and residential circles dotted along its arms and with wedges between wistfully titled Park . . . Park doubtless being the ambition. Reality was outside, over the garden wall, a sun-baked tangle of weeds and native trees which could not have known human attention in centuries. Newhope must have had ambitions once, in the days of its birth . . . ambition, but no Kontrin presence to aid it: no relief from taxes, no Kontrin funds feeding back into its economy, for beautification, luxury, art.

Most of the building-circles were warehouses: the two arms of the city nearest the Port were entirely that. There were local factories, mostly locally consumed equipment for agriculture, light arms, clothing, food processing. There were services and their administrations; worker-apartments for the ordinary run of betas; midclass apartments and some residential circles for the midclass well-to-do; and one arm was all elite residence-circles, like circle 4, which this house occupied. The highest ITAK officials lodged in circle 1, the lowest in 10. And the guest house was second circle of the eighth arm: the Outsider-mission's residency, while ITAK offices were dead center, zero-circle.

Useful to know.

There was a closing of doors upstairs. She heard footfalls, soft, wandering here and there. She punched time: the morning was well along.

The reflection in the dead screen showed her Jim standing in the doorway, and she pushed with her foot, turned the chair nearly full about.

"You certainly had your sleep this morning," she said cheerfully.

"No, sera."

She let go her breath, let pass the *sera*. "What, then? You weren't meddling with the tapes, were you?"

"I didn't remember them well. I tried them again."

"For enjoyment. I thought you would enjoy them. Maybe learn something."

"I'm trying to learn them, sera."

She shook her head. "Don't try beyond convenience. I only meant to give you something to fill your time."

"What will you want for lunch, sera?"

"Raen. I don't care. Make something. I've a little more to do here. I'll be through in half an hour. We should have staff here. You shouldn't have to serve as cook."

"I helped in galley sometimes," he said.

She did not answer that. Jim strayed out again. Warrior met him: she saw the encounter reflected when she had turned about again, and almost turned back to intervene. But to her gratification she saw Jim touch Warrior of his own accord and suffer no distress of it. Warrior sang softly, hive-song, that was strange in the human rooms; it trailed after Jim as he went kitchenward.

"Sugar-water," she heard from the kitchen, a deep harmony of majat tones, and afterward a contented humming.

The car functioned, with no problems. Raen watched the short street flow past the tinted windows and settled back with a deep breath. Merry drove, seeming happy with the opportunity. Max and Warrior, minutely instructed regarding each other as well as intruders, were guarding the house and grounds; but Jim she would not leave behind, to the mercy of chance and Max's skill at defense. Jim sat in the back seat of the Eln-Kests' fine vehicle, watching the scenery, she saw when she looked back, with a look of complete absorption.

Doing very well with this much strangeness about him, she

reckoned of him. *Doing very well, considering.* She smiled at him slightly, then gave her attention forward, for the car dipped suddenly for the downramp to the subway and Merry needed an address.

"D-branch circle 5," she said, the while Merry took them smoothly onto the track for Center.

The program went in. The car gathered speed, entering the central track.

Something wrong whipped past the window on Merry's side. Raen twisted in the seat, saw an impression of stilt-limbed walkers along the transparent-walled footpath that ran beside the tracks.

Tunnels. Natural to majat, easy as the wildland interstices. But there were beta walkers too, and no sign of panic.

"Merry. Do majat have free access here? Do they just come and go as they please?"

"Yes," he said.

She thought of calling the house and warning Max; but Max and Warrior had already been stringently warned. There was no good adding a piece of information that Max would already know. The danger was always there, had been. She settled forward again, arms folded, scanning the broad tube, the lights of which flicked past them faster and faster.

"Majat make free of all Newhope, then, and betas just bear with it, do they?"

"Yes, sera."

"They work directly for betas?" She found amazement, even resentment, that majat would do so.

"Some places they do. Factories, mostly."

"So no one at the Port found a Warrior's presence unusual. Everyone's gotten used to it. How long, Merry, how long has this been going on?"

The azi kept his eyes on the tracks ahead, his squarish face taut, as if the subject were an intensely uncomfortable one. "Half a year. . . . There was panic at first. No more. Hives don't bother people. Humans walk one side, majat the other, down the walkways. There are heat-signs."

Redsss, redsss, Warrior had tried to tell her. *Go here, go there. Redss pushhh.*

"What hive, Merry? One more than others?"

"I don't know, sera. I never understood there was a difference to be seen, until you showed me. I'll watch." His brow was creased with worry. Not so slow-witted, this azi. "Humans don't like them in the city, but they come anyway."

Raen bit at her lip, braced as the car went through a maneuver, scanned other majat on the walkway. They whipped into the great hub of Central and changed tracks at a leisurely pace. There were human walkers here, swathed in cloaks and anonymous in the sun-suits which Istra's bright outdoors made advisable; and by twos, there were armored police . . . ITAK security: everything here was ITAK.

They whipped out again on another tangent. D, the signs read.

More majat walkers.

Majat, casually coming and going in a daily contact with betas . . . with minds-who-died. Once majat had fled such contact, unable to bear it, even for the contacts which gave them azi, insisting to work only through Kontrin. Death had once worried majat—azi-deaths, no, as majat deaths were nothing—but betas they had always perceived as individual intelligences, and they had fled beta presence in horror, unable to manage the concepts which disrupted all majat understanding.

Now they walked familiarly with minds-who-died, unaffrighted.

And that sent a shiver over her skin, a suspicion of understanding.

D-track carried them along at increasing velocity; they took the through-track until the lights blurred past in a stream.

And suddenly they whisked over to slow-track, braking, gliding for the D circle 5 ramp. Merry took over manual as they disengaged, delivered them up into a shaded circle free of traffic and pedestrians, a vast area ringed by a pillared overhang of many stories—which must outwardly seem one of those enormous domes. The summit was a tinted shield which admitted light enough to glare down into the center of the well of pillars.

They drove deep beneath the overhang, and to the main entry, where transparent doors and white walls lent a cold austerity to the offices. LABOR REGISTRY, the neat letters proclaimed, 50-D, ITAK.

It was the beginning of understandings, at least. Raen contemplated it with apprehensions, reckoned whether she wanted to leave the azi both in the car or not, and decided against.

"Merry, I don't think we'll be bothered here. It's going to be hot;

I'm sorry, but stay in the car and keep the doors locked and the windows sealed. Don't create trouble, but if it happens, shoot if you have to: I want this car here when I come out. You call Max every ten minutes and make sure things are all right at the house, but no conversation, understand?"

"Yes."

She climbed out and beckoned to Jim, who joined her on the walk and lagged a decorous half-pace behind as she started for the doors. She dropped a step and he caught up, walked with her into the foyer.

The offices were unnaturally still, desks vacant, halls empty. The air-conditioning was excessive, and the air held a strange taint, a combination of office-smells and antiseptic.

"Is this place going to bother you?" she asked of Jim, worried for that, but she reckoned hazards even of leaving him here at the door.

He shook his head very faintly. She looked about, saw a light on in an office down the corridor from the reception area. She walked that way, slowly, her footsteps and Jim's loud in the deserted building.

A man occupied the office—had heard their coming evidently and risen. It was modern, but untidy; the desk was stacked high with work. DIRECTOR, the sign by the door declared.

"Ser," Raen said. He surveyed them both, blinked, all at once seemed to take the full situation into account, for his face went from ruddy to pale; a Kontrin in Color, a man in impeccable innerworlds dress and with an azi-mark on his cheek.

"Sera."

"I understand," Raen said, "that there are numerous personnel to be contracted."

"We have available contracts, yes, sera."

"Numerous contracts. I'd like a full tour, ser—"

"Itavvy," he breathed.

"Itavvy. A tour of the whole facility, ser."

The smallish beta, graying, balding . . . looked utterly distressed. "The office—I've responsibility—"

"It really doesn't look as if you're overwhelmed with visitors. The whole facility, ser, floor by floor, the whole process, so long as it amuses me."

Itavvy nodded, reached for the communications switch on the

desk. Raen stepped across the interval and put out her chitined hand, shook her head slowly. "No. You can guide us, I'm sure. Softly. Quietly. With minimum disturbance to the ordinary routine of the building. Do you object, ser?"

6

THE LABOR REGISTRY was a maze of curving corridors, all white, all the same. Lifts designated sub-basements down to the fifth level; Raen recalled as many as twenty stories above ground, although the lifts in this area only went to the seventh: she recalled the overhang. They passed row on row of halls, a great deal of seemingly pointless walking with ser Itavvy in the lead. There were doors, neat letters: LIBRARY: COMP I: LEVEL I: RED CARDS ONLY.

She made no sense of it, had no idea in fact what she was seeking, save that in this building was what should have been a thriving industry, and in the front of it were empty desks and silent halls.

Itavvy paused at last at a lift and showed them in, took them to third level, into other identical halls, places at least populated. Gray-suited techs stared at the intrusion of such visitors and stopped dead in their tracks, staring. White-suited azi, distinguishable by their tattoos, stepped from their path and then resumed their cleaning and their pushing of carts.

Itavvy led them farther.

"I'm tired of walking aimlessly," Raen said. "What do you propose to show us on this level? More doors?"

"The available contracts, sera."

Raen walked along in silence, scanning doors and labels, searching for something of information. Periodically corridors branched off from theirs, always on the right. Inevitably those corridors ended at the same interval, closed off by heavy security doors. RED CARD ONLY, the signs said.

She stopped, gestured toward the latest of them. "What's there, ser Itavvy?"

"General retention," Itavvy said, looking uncomfortable. "If sera will, please, there are more comfortable areas—"

"Unlock this one. I'd like to see."

Itavvy unhappily preceded them down the short corridor, produced his card and unlocked the door.

A second door lay beyond, similarly locked: they three stood within the narrow intervening space as the outer door boomed and sealed with a resounding noise of locks. Then Itavvy used his card on the second, and a wave of tainted air met them, a vastness of glaring lights and gray concrete, a web of catwalks.

The scent was again that of antiseptic, compounded this time with something else. Itavvy would too obviously have been glad to close the door with that brief look, but Raen walked stubbornly ahead, moving Itavvy out before her—no beta would have the chance to slam a door at her back—and looked about her.

Concrete, damp with antiseptic, and the stench of humanity and sewage.

Pits. Brightly lit doorless pits, a bit of matting and one human in each, like larvae bestowed in chambered comb. Five paces by five, if that; no doors, no halls between the cells . . . only the grid of catwalks above, with machinery to move them, with an extended process of ladders which could, only if lowered, afford the occupants exit, and that only a few at a time.

The whole stretched out of view around the curve of the building and far, far, across before them. Their steps echoed fearsomely on the steel grids. Faces looked up at them, only mildly curious.

Raen looked the full sweep of it, sickened, deliberately inhaled the stench.

"Are contracts on these available?"

"For onworld use, sera."

"No export license."

"No, sera."

"I understand that a great number of azi have been confiscated from estates. But the contracts on those azi would be entangled. Where are they housed? Among these?"

"There are facilities in the country."

"As elaborate as these?"

Itavvy said nothing. Raen calculated for herself what manner of facilities could be constructed in the sparsely populated countryside, in haste, by a pressured corporation-government. These facilities must be luxurious by comparison.

"Yet all of these," she said, "are warehoused. Is that the right word?"

"Essentially," Itavvy whispered.

"Are you still producing azi at the same rate?"

"Sera, if only you would inquire with ITAK Central—I'm sure I don't know the reasons of things."

"You're quite satisfactory, ser Itavvy. Answer the question. I assure you of your safety to do so."

"I don't know of any authorization for change. I'm not over Embryonics. That's another administration, round the other side, 51. Labor doesn't get them until the sixth year. We haven't had any less of that age coming in. I don't think . . . I don't think there can be any change. The order was to produce."

"Origin of that order?"

"Kontrin licensing, sera." The answer was a hoarse whisper. "Originally—we appealed for a moderate increase. The order came back quadrupled."

"In spite of the fact that there existed no Kontrin license to dispose of them when they reached eighteen. The export quota wasn't changed."

"We . . . trusted, sera, that the license would be granted when the time came. We've applied, sera. We've even applied for permission to terminate. We can't do that either. The estates—were all crowded above their limits. They're supposed to turn them back after a year, for training. But now—now they're running their operations primarily to feed their own workers . . . and they're panicked, refusing to give them up, the permanent workers and the temporaries." Itavvy wiped at his face. "They divert food—to maintain the work force and it doesn't get to the depots. Our food. The station's food. ISPAK has threatened a power cutoff if the estates go on holding out, but ITAK has—reasoned with ISPAK. It wouldn't stop the estate-holders. They have their own collectors, their own power. And they won't give up the azi."

"Are the holders organized?"

The beta shook his head. "They're just outbackers. Blind, hardheaded outbackers. They hold the azi because they're manpower; and they're a means to hold out by human labor if ISPAK follows through with its threat. Always . . . always the farms were a part of the process; azi went out there in the finishing of their training and shifted back again, those that would be contracted for specialized work—good for the azi, good for the farms. But now, sera, the estates have been threatening to break out of the corporation."

"Hardly sounds as if these holders are blind, ser Itavvy . . . if it comes to a fight, they've the manpower."

"Azi."

"You don't think they'd fight."

Beta deference robbed her of an honest answer. Itavvy swallowed whatever he would have said; but he looked as if he would have disputed it.

"It hardly sounds as if they're without communication on the issue," Raen said, "since they're all doing alike. Aren't they?"

"I wouldn't know, sera."

"Only on East, or is West also afflicted?"

Itavvy moistened his lips. "I think it's general."

"Without organization. Without a plan to keep themselves from starving."

"There's already been work toward new irrigation. The river . . . that supplies Newhope . . . is threatened. They expand—"

"Unlicensed."

"Unlicensed, sera. ITAK protests, but again—we can do nothing. They feud among themselves. They fight for land and water. There are—" He mopped at the back of his neck. "Maybe two and three holders get together. And azi . . . muddle up out there. They're trading, these holders."

"Trading?"

"With each other. Goods. Azi. Moving them from place to place."

"You know so?"

"Police say so. Azi are more on some farms than we put there."

Raen looked over all the cells, as far as the eye could see. "Weapons?"

"Holders have always had them."

She walked forward, slowly, the little boxes shifting past. The ceiling weighed upon the senses. There was only gray and black and the white glare of light, no color but the shades of humanity, all gray-clothed.

"Why," she asked suddenly, "are they walled off one from the other? Security?"

"Each is specifically trained. Contact at random would make it more difficult to assure specificity."

"And you get them at six years? Is it different from this, the young ones?"

The beta did not answer. At last he gave a vague shrug.

"Show me," Raen said.

Itavvy started walking, around the curve. New vistas of cells presented themselves. The complex seemed endless. No walls were discernible, no limits, save a core where many catwalks converged, a vast concrete darkness against the floodlights.

"Do they ever leave this place?" Raen asked as they walked above the cells, provoking occasional curious stares from those below. "Don't they want for exercise?"

"There are facilities," the beta said, "by shifts."

"And factories. They work in the city factories?"

"Those trained for it." Perhaps Itavvy detected an edge to her voice. His grew defensive. "Six hours in the factories, two at exercise, two at deepstudy, then rest. We do the best we can under crowded circumstances, sera."

"And the infants?"

"Azi care for them."

"By shifts. Six hours on, two of exercise?"

"Yes, sera."

Their steps measured the metal catwalk another length. "But you're not sending these out to the estates anymore. You're more and more crowded week by week, and you're not able to move them."

"We do what we can, sera."

They reached the core, and the lift. Itavvy used his card to open the door, and they stepped in. SEVEN, Itavvy pushed, and the lift shot up with heart-dragging rapidity, set them out on that level with a crashing of locks and doors, echoes in vastness.

It was otherwise silent.

All these levels, she began to understand, all these levels were the same, endless cubicles, floor after floor, the same. Seven above ground. Five below. And there was silence. All that space, all those cells, all that humanity, and there was nowhere a voice, nowhere an outcry.

Itavvy led the way out onto the catwalk. Raen looked down. These were all small children, six, seven years. The faces upturned held mild curiosity, no more. There were no games, no occupations. They sat or lay on their mats. Same gray coveralls, same shaven heads, same grave faces. At this age, one could not even tell their sex.

None cried, none laughed.

"God," she breathed, gripping the rail. Itavvy had stopped. She suddenly wanted out. She looked back. Jim stood at the rail, looking down. She wanted him out of this place, now, quickly.

"Is there a door out on this level?" she asked, perfectly controlled. Itavvy indicated the way ahead with a gesture. Raen walked at his unhurried pace, hearing Jim following.

"What's the average contract price?" she asked.

"Two thousand."

"You can't produce them for anything near that cost."

"No," said Itavvy. "We can't."

It was a long walk. There was nothing to fill the silence. She would not hurry, would not betray her reaction, disturbing betas whose interests were involved in this operation, stirring apprehensions. Nor would she turn and look at Jim. She did not want to.

They reached a door like the one on third—passed that and its mate into sterile halls and light and clean air. She breathed, breathed deeply. "I've seen what I came to see," she said. "Thank you, ser Itavvy. Suppose now we go back to your office."

He hesitated, as if he thought of asking a question; and did not. They rode the lift to main, and walked the long distance back to the front offices, all in silence. Itavvy had the air of a worried man. Raen let him fret.

And when they three stood once again in the beta's office, with the door closed: "I have an estate," Raen said, "ridiculously understaffed. And a security problem, which affords me no amusement at all. How many contracts are available here?"

Itavvy's face underwent a series of changes. "Surely enough to fill all your needs, Kontrin."

"The corporation does reward its people according to the profits their divisions show, doesn't it? All these empty desks . . . this isn't a local holiday, is it?"

"No, sera."

Raen settled into a chair and Itavvy seated himself at his desk. Raen gestured to Jim, and he took the one beside her.

"So," she said. "And the number of contracts available for guard personnel, azi only?"

The beta consulted the computer. "Sufficient, sera."

"The exact number, please."

"Two thousand forty-eight, sera, nineteen hundred eighty-two males, rest females; nineteen hundred four under thirty years, rest above."

"Counting confiscated azi, or are these on the premises?"

"On the premises."

"A very large number."

"Not proportionately, sera."

"Who usually absorbed them?"

"Corporation offices. Estate-holders . . . it's wild land out there."

"So a great number of those tangled contracts in custody in the country . . . would be guard-trained, wouldn't they?"

"A certain number, yes, sera."

Itavvy's eyes were feverish; his lips trembled. He murmured his words. Raen reckoned the man, at last nodded.

"I'll buy," she said, "all two thousand forty-eight. I also want sun-suits and sidearms. I trust an establishment which sends out guards sends them out equipped to work."

He moistened his lips. "Yes, sera, although some buyers have their own uniforms or equipment."

"You'll manage." She rose, walked about the office, to Itavvy's extreme nervousness, the while she looked at the manuals on the counter by the comp unit. She looked up a number, memorized it, turned and smiled faintly. "I'll take the others as fast as you can train them. Those tangled contracts . . . if you'll check tomorrow, you'll find the matter cleared and the contracts salable. I trust you can quietly transfer azi from there to here as spaces become available."

"Sera—"

"The children, ser Itavvy. However do you substitute for—human contact? Do tapes supply it all?"

Itavvy wiped at his lips. "At every minute stage of development . . . deepstudy tapes, yes, sera. The number of individuals, the economics . . . it would be virtually impossible for a private individual to have the time, the access to thousands of programs developed over centuries to accomplish this—"

"Eighteen years to maturity. No way to speed that process, is there?"

"For some purposes—they leave before eighteen."

"Majat azi."

"Yes."

"And moving them out without programming—as they are—"

"Chaos. Severe personality derangements."

She said nothing to that, only looked at him, at Jim, back again. "And more than the two thousand forty-eight . . . how long does it take for training? On what scale can it be done?"

"Minimally . . . a few days." Itavvy shuffled the papers spread across his desk, an action which gave him excuse to look elsewhere. "All channels could be turned to the same tapestudy—easier than doing it otherwise. But the legalities—the questions that would be raised on this world—they'd have to be moved, shipped, and IS-PAK—"

"You know, ser Itavvy, that your loyalty is to ITAK. But ITAK is a Kontrin creation. You are aware then of a—higher morality. If I were to give you a certain—favor, if I were to ask your silence in return for that, and certain further cooperations, you would realize that this was not disloyalty to ITAK, but loyalty to the source of ITAK's very license to function."

The beta wiped at his face and nodded, the papers forgotten, his eyes fever-bright. He looked at her now. There was no possibility of divided attention.

"I'm creating an establishment," she said very softly, "a permanent Kontrin presence, do you see? And such an establishment needs personnel. When this process is complete, when the training is accomplished as I wish, then I shall still need reliable personnel at other levels."

"Yes, sera," he breathed.

"The great estates, you see, these powers with their massed forces of azi—this thing which you so earnestly insist has no organization —could be handled without bloodshed, by superior force. Peace would come to Istra. You see what a cause you serve. A solution, a solution, ser, which would well serve ITAK. You realize that I have power to license, being in fact the total Kontrin presence: I can authorize export on the levels you need. I'm prepared to do so, to rescue this whole operation, if I receive the necessary cooperation from certain key individuals."

The man was trembling, visibly. He could not control his hands. "I am not, then, to contact my superiors."

She shook her head slowly. "Not if you plan to enjoy your life, ser. I am extremely cautious about security."

"You have my utmost cooperation."

She smiled bleakly, having found again the measure of betas. "Indeed, ser, thank you. Now, there's an old farm on B-branch, just outside the city, registered to a new owner, one ser Isan Tel. You'll manage to find some azi of managerial function, the best: its housecomp has instructions for them. Can you find such azi?"

Itavvy nodded.

"Excellent. All you can spare of them, and all of the guard-azi but two hundred males that I want transferred to my own estate . . . go to the establishment of Isan Tel. Provisioned and equipped. Can you do it?"

"We—can, yes."

She shook her head. "No plural. You. *You* will tend every detail personally. The rumor, if it escapes, will tell me precisely who let it escape; and if there is fault in the training—I need not say how I would react to that, ser. You would be quite, quite dead. On the other hand, you can become a very wealthy man . . . wealthy and secure. In addition to the other contracts, I want half a dozen domestics to my address; and ser Tel's estate will need a good thirty to care for the guard-azi. Possible?"

Itavvy nodded.

"Ser Itavvy, after today, an identity will be established, one ser Merek Sed. He will be a very wealthy man, with properties on several worlds, with trade license, and an account in intercomp, a number I shall give you. You will be that individual. He will be a creator of art. I shall purchase art for the decoration of my house . . . and so will ser Isan Tel. Be discreet at first, ser Itavvy. Too ostentatious a display of your new wealth would raise fatal questions. But if you are clever—Merek Sed can retire in great comfort. You have family, ser Itavvy?"

He nodded again, breathing with difficulty. "Wife. A daughter."

"They also can be built into Merek Sed's identity. Untraceable. Only you and I know how he was born. Once off Istra, utterly safe. I will put your wife and daughter into those records too, and give you their new citizen numbers . . . at a price."

"What—price?"

"Loyalty. To me. Discretion. Absolute." She tore off a sheet from a notepad and picked up a pen, wrote three numbers. "The first is a number by which you can contact me. Do so tomorrow. The second is the citizen number of ser Merek Sed. The third is an account number which will provide you an earnest of things to come. Use only cash-machines, no credit purchases . . . don't patronize the same store repeatedly. Create no patterns and don't let others know how much your fortunes have improved. Recall that if you're suspected, the consequences to me are mere annoyance; to you . . . rather more serious. For your family also. I can defend myself from my annoyances. But I fear that they would devour others, ser Itavvy." She held up the paper.

He took it.

"The delivery," she said, "of the guards for my house . . . today?"

"Yes."

"And all equipage with them?"

"Yes. That can be arranged. We have warehouse access."

"And the transfer of the azi to the Tel estate?"

"Will begin today, sera. I could suggest an abbreviated training, if only the use of arms is required, and not specialized security—"

"Hastening the program?"

"Hastening it by half, Kontrin."

"Acceptable."

"If the authorizations to clear the papers on the others could be given—"

"Not from this terminal, ser, but if you'll check after your delivery to my house, number 47A, if you'll kindly make a note of that, you may find that certain problems have vanished. And the Tel estate access is South Road number 3. You have all that?"

"Yes, sera."

She smiled. "Thank you, ser Itavvy. Payment will clear at delivery. And a further matter: should you ever notice on your house-comp a call from ser Tel in person . . . check the Sed account at once. There'll be passage for Sed and family, to ISPAK and elsewhere. It would be wise at that point to use it. I do take care of my agents, ser, if it's ever necessary."

"Sera," he breathed.

"We're agreed, then." She rose, offered her chitin-sheathed hand with deliberation, knowing how betas hated contact with it. Itavvy took it with gingerly pressure, rising.

"Jim," she said softly then, drew him with her, out of the office.

And in the foyer she looked back. Itavvy had not come out of his office . . . would not perhaps, for a small space. She took Jim's arm. "All right?" she asked.

Jim nodded. Upset, she thought, how not? But he showed no signs of worse disturbance. She pressed his arm, let it go, led the way to the door.

The car still waited. She looked right and left, walked out into the heat. The filtered light coming down the huge well to the pavement was not screened enough: the ventilation was insufficient. When they reached the car, Merry opened the door with a look of vast relief and started the air-conditioning at once. He was drenched with sweat, his blond hair plastered about his face.

"Everything all right?" she asked, letting Jim in.

"At the house . . . quiet. No trouble."

Raen closed the door, looked back yet again at Jim. He looked none the worse for the experience, even here, where he might have given way in private. He seemed quite composed, quite—she thought with disturbance—as composed as the faces which had looked up at them from the cells, silent, incapable of tears.

"Center," she directed Merry, settling forward in her seat again and folding her arms about her. "We're going to pay another call. ITAK's due one."

7

IT WAS VERY LIKE the Labor Registry, the circle which was the heart of ITAK: it was only wider, taller, and perhaps deeper underground.

The Center drew a great deal of traffic, cars prowling the circle-drive . . . probably every car in East, every car on the continent resorted here regularly, in a city where everyone but the higher ITAK officials must rely on public transport. A space was available in front of the main doors, probably vacant because it was restricted; Raen directed and Merry eased into it, parked, let them out and locked the doors.

She and Jim were actually well into the building before the reaction set in among the betas. It began with shocked stares. Word apparently flashed then throughout the building, for by the time she reached the main hall, with its central glass sculpture, there was a delegation to meet her, minor executives anxious to escort her upstairs where, she was assured, the Board was hastily assembling to meet her.

She cast a glance at the sculpture, which ascended in a complex shaft to a light-well all its own, and took advantage of beta Hydri's glare to illumine colors and forms all the way down. "Lovely," she murmured, and looked at the betas. "Local, seri?"

Heads nodded. Anxious gestures tried to urge her elsewhere, hallward. She shrugged and went with them, Jim treading softly in her wake, playing at invisibility. No one spoke to him, no one acknowledged his presence: the tattoo let them know what he was despite his dress. Bodyguard, they would think him, not knowing his harmlessness, and therefore he served the function well. Betas crowded about them, one babbling on about the glass-artist, an Upcoast factor's son.

They entered the lift, rode it to the uppermost floors, entered directly from it a suite of offices the splendor of which equalled many an establishment on Andra, and a second crowd waited to greet the visitor: division heads, secretaries, minor officials, a chattering succession of introductions.

Raen smiled perfunctorily, reckoning those who might be worth recalling, met the Dain-Prossertys again, and ser Dain himself, the president, and two more Dains high on the staff. The inner office was opened, revealing chairs arranged about a vast hollow table, and the ITAK emblem blazoned on the wall like the Kontrin symbol in Council.

Illusions, illusions. She smiled to herself, and brought Jim in with her, offered him a seat at the table beside her, offending them all. Azi women appeared, to take requests for drinks. She ordered for herself and Jim, the same that he had ordered on-ship, and leaned back, waiting, while betas took their seats and made their orders and hissing whispers tried to solve the problem of a disturbed seating arrangement. A chair was brought in. The first drinks arrived: Raen's, Jim's, president Dain's and the Dain-Prossertys'.

Raen sipped at hers and studied them all, who had to wait on theirs. The serving-azi hastened breathlessly . . . decorative, Raen thought, eyeing the young women with a critic's cold eyes, reckoning whether they were homebred or foreign, and whether they were equally to the taste of the beta women on the board.

Foreign, she decided. Mixed as populations were in the Reach, seven hundred years had brought some definition among azi, whose generations were short and subject to brief fads. These had the look of Meron's carnival decadence, long-limbed, elegant, sloe-eyed.

The last drinks appeared; the azi took themselves hence very quickly. Raen still mused the question of beta psych-sets, looked at Dain, who was murmuring some courtesy to her, and nudged herself out of her analysis to look on him as a man, plump, nearly bald, eyes full of anxiety. She kept seeing labs, and the Registry's gray honeycomb of cells.

"Ser Enis Dain," she said. "I recall your message." She smiled and regarded the others. "It's very kind of you to disarrange your schedules. I'll take very little of your time."

"Kont' Raen Meth-maren, we're very honored by your visit."

She nodded. "Thank you. Your people have been very cooperative. I've appreciated that. I know that my presence is a disturbance. And you're doubtless wanting to ask me questions; let me save you time and effort. You'd like to know if my coming is going to disturb your operations here, and most of all whether the seri Eln-Kest, personally lamented, had anything to do with bringing me here."

There was disturbance in their faces. They were not apparently accustomed to such directness. She sipped at her drink and three others did so by reflex.

"I know your difficulties here," she said. "And I know other details, and I shall not confide in any until I am sure what other agency arranged that reception of my party at the port, thank you."

"Sera," said Dain senior, "Kontrin—the hives—the hives are beyond our influence, beyond our power to restrain. We apologize profoundly for the incidence, but it was a hive matter."

She frowned darkly. This casting back of the Kontrin's eternal answer for majat intrusions had, on the lips of a beta, suspicion of irony. For a moment she readjusted her estimate of ser Dain's craft, and then, staring at his chin, which wobbled with anxiety, dismissed her suspicions of subtlety. "A hive matter. If so, ser, majat have come into possession of communications equipment—modified for their handling. Or how else would they have informed themselves? Tell me that, seri. How did they know we were coming?"

Dain made a helpless gesture. "The information was widespread."

"Public broadcast?" The notion appalled her.

"ITAK general channels," Dain answered faintly.

She waved her hand in disgust, dismissing the matter. "Trust that I shall find my own way and provide my own security. If you have any policy of allowing majat to walk freely in and out of ITAK agencies . . . revise it."

"We have protested—"

"If majat object to being evicted, mention my name and invoke the Pact. If you can't move them . . . Well, but you've let matters go too far, haven't you? They're all over the city."

"They've done no harm. They—"

"If you will believe me, seri, hive matters and Kontrin affairs are better avoided. And while I remind myself of it . . . since you're un-accustomed to the protocols of Kontrin presence . . . a bit of advice in self-protection. Houses have their differences. We all do. And if another Kontrin arrives here, your safest action is to inform me at once and stay neutral. Such a visitor would correctly assume that I have agents among you and that I have personal interests in protect-ing the world of Istra. A friend would of course treat you well—an enemy . . . if I were removed . . . could be very disruptive in his search for my agents, who would disrupt in their turn. . . . You do see your hazard, seri. I don't think Istra could easily bear that sort of thing.

"As for the benefits of my presence, you'll see them very soon. You want licenses; I understand that some Kontrin somewhere has blocked all your appeals. I shall expect, in fact, that any opposition who turns up here will probably be that agency, do you see, seri? I can grant those licenses. I've already begun to purchase . . . extrav-agantly . . . items which will permit me to live in comfort and safety, of course to the aid of your tax balance and the security and prosperity of the company. Council on Cerdin hasn't received your appeals; you've been cut off deliberately; and if it goes on, your economy will collapse. I shall take immediate steps to improve mat-ters. And I do imagine that that action will turn up enemies—mu-tual enemies—very quickly."

"Kontrin," said ser Dain, hard-breathing. "In no wise was the at-tack on your person of our doing. There is no one in ITAK who would desire—"

"You can only speak your hopes, ser Dain, not certainties. I'll look to myself. Simply afford me your cooperation."

"Our utmost cooperation."

She gave them her almost-best smile. "Then I thank you, seri. I've found possibilities in Istra, a change from the ordinary. I'd like to travel a bit. An aircraft—"

"Your safety—"

"Trust me. An aircraft would be very useful. Armed, if you feel it necessary."

"We'll provide it," Dain said; the man at his left confirmed his uncertain look with a nod.

"I'll furnish my own security about my property; I'd appreciate ITAK security temporarily about the aircraft allotted to my use. All these things of course are not gifts: they'll be credited against ITAK's taxes. Kontrin presence is never financially disadvantageous, seri."

"We are enormously concerned—" This was sera Ren Milin, head of Agriculture, "enormously concerned for your personal safety. Dissidents and saboteurs are presently confined to attacks on depots, but one more deranged than the rest . . ."

"I do appreciate your concern. You have heavy arms . . . for onworld security . . . surely. I'd appreciate it if a goodly number were delivered to my estate, say, sufficient for a thousand men."

Faces went uniformly stark with shock.

"Precaution, you see, against dissidents, saboteurs, and deranged persons. If it's generally known that we're armed, ITAK being so inclined to general broadcast channels, there will be less temptation. I certainly hope not to use them. But you wouldn't like the consequences of a Kontrin killed here . . . by your own locals. No. You'd be surprised how even Houses at odds with mine would look on that: the Family . . . would be forced to make a very strong answer to that. The facts of policy. Kindly see that the arms arrive. They're quite safe in my hands. My security, after all, is yours. And enough, enough unpleasantness. I'm quite delighted by your courtesy. I'll extend you my own hospitality as soon as I'm decently settled and housed. If there's entertainment to be had, I'd appreciate knowing. I suffer from boredom. I do hope there's some society here."

The pallor did not entirely depart. They murmured courtesies, professed themselves honored and delighted by the prospect of her company socially. She laughed softly.

"And Outsiders!" she exclaimed ingenuously. "Seri, I saw an Outsider ship up at station . . . an ordinary sight for you, surely, but profoundly exciting for one from innerworlds. I've met these folk, had some chance to talk with them. Do you include them in your society?"

That brought silence, a moment of awkwardness.

"It could be arranged," sera Dain said.

"Excellent." Raen finished her drink and set it aside.

"We'll be pleased to provide what we can in all respects," ser Dain managed to say. "Would you care for another drink, Kont' Raen?"

"No, thank you." She gathered herself up and waited for Jim, deliberately slipped her hand within his arm. "I'm quite content with your courtesy. Very pleased. Thank you so much. And don't worry about what I shall uncover. I know that you've been driven to unusual methods, unusual sources. I give you warning that I know . . . and I shall refrain from seeing what perhaps shades your license. The maintenance of order here under trying circumstances is a tribute to your ingenuity. I don't find fault, seri. And do forgive me. My next call will be entirely social, I assure you."

Men moved to reach the door, to open it for her. She smiled at them one and all and walked out, with Jim beside her, in a crowd of security agents who made turmoil in the outer offices.

The agents, armored police, and Dain senior himself insisted on staying with them, in the lift and out into the foyer. She lingered there an instant, with the crowd milling about, looked up to the glass sculpture.

"Find me the artist's address," she said to Dain. "Send it to me this evening. Would you do that?"

"Honored," he said. "Honored to do so."

She walked on. The crowds broke and closed.

"You would find interest, perhaps," ser Dain rambled on, while the police in advance of them pushed folk from before the doors to clear passage, "in an example I have in my own house, if you would do me the honor to—"

Shadows moved beyond the tinted-glass doors, out beneath the pillars, about the car . . . too-tall shadows, fantastical.

"*Sera,*" Jim protested.

Under her cloak she drew her gun, but ser Dain put out his hand, not touching—offering caution. "The police will move them. Please, sera!"

Raen paid him no heed, stayed with the rush of the agents and the police as they burst outside.

Greens. Warriors. They swarmed about the entrance, about the car. "Away!" a policeman shouted at them. "Move away!"

Auditory palps flicked out, back, refusal to listen. The majat did move back somewhat, averaging a line, a group.

"Green-hive!" Raen shouted at them, seeing the beginning formation. She brought her hand out into the open, gun and all. Auditory palps came forward, half. At her right was the car; Merry surely still had the doors locked. "Jim," she said. "Jim, get in the car. Get in."

"Blue," green leader intoned. "Blue-hive Kontrin."

"I'm Raen Meth-maren. What are greens doing in a beta City?"

"Hive-massster." There was more than one voice to that, and an ominous clicking from the others. They began to shift position, edging to the sides.

"Watch out!" Raen yelled, and fired as the greens skittered this way and that. Green leader went down squalling. Some leapt. She whirled and fired, careless of bystanders, took others. Police and security began firing, with Dain screaming orders, his voice drowned in bystanders' panic.

Then the greens broke and ran, with blinding rapidity, across the pavings, down into the subway ramp, down into tunnels, elsewhere.

Dying majat scraped frenetically on the concrete, limbs twitching. Humans babbled and sobbed. Raen looked back and saw Jim by the car, on his feet and all right; Dain, surrounded by security personnel, looked ill.

"Better find out if the rest of the building is secure," Raen said to one of the police. Another, armor-protected, was being dragged from the body of a dead majat; safe, he lay convulsing in shock. Someone was leaning over against the side of a column, vomiting. Two victims were decapitated. Raen looked away, fixed Dain with a stare. "This comes of trifling with the hives, ser. You see its consequences."

"Not our choosing. They come. They come, and we can't put them out. They—"

"They feed this world. They buy the grain. Don't they?"

"We can't put them out of the city." Dain's face poured sweat; his hands fluttered as he sought a handkerchief, and mopped at his pallid skin. For an instant Raen thought the aging beta might die on the spot, and so, evidently, did the guards, who moved to support him.

"I believe you, ser Dain," Raen assured him, moved to pity. "Leave them to me. Lock them out of your buildings; use locks, everywhere, ser Dain. Install security doors. Bars on windows. I can't stress strongly enough your danger. I know them. Believe me in this."

Dain answered nothing. His plump face was stark with terror.

Merry had the car doors open. She waved an angry gesture at Jim, who scrambled in and flung himself into the back seat. She settled into the front, clipped her gun to her belt, slammed the door. "Home," she told Merry. And then with a sharp look at the azi: "Can you?"

Merry was white with shock. She imagined what it must have been for him, with majat swarming all about the car, only glass between him and majat jaws. He managed to get the car down the ramp and engaged to the track, keyed in the com-unit. "Max," he said hoarsely, "Max, it's all right. We're clear of them now."

She heard Max answer, reporting all secure elsewhere.

She looked back then. Jim was sitting in the back seat with his hands clasped before his mouth, eyes distracted. "I had my gun," he said. "I had it in my pocket. I had it in my pocket."

"Practice on still targets first," she said. "Not majat."

He drew a more stable breath, composed himself, azi-calm. The car lurched slightly, having found the home-track, gathered speed.

Out the back window she saw a group of majat along the walkway . . . the same or others; there was no knowing.

She faced forward again, wiped at her lips. She found herself sweating, shaken. The car whipped along too fast now for hazard: no passers-by could define them at their speed. The lights became a flickering blur.

No majat troubled the A4 ramp. And at the house there was no evidence of difficulty. Raen relaxed in her seat, glad, for once, of the sight of the beta police on guard at the gate. There was a truck at a neighbor's: the furnishings were being removed. She regarded that bleakly, turned her head again as their own gate opened for them.

Merry took the car slowly up the drive, stopped under the portico and let them out, drove on to put the car in the garage, round the drive and under.

Warrior arrived around the corner of the house, through the narrow front-back access, Raen squinted in the light, anxious about any majat at the moment.

And Max opened the front door, let them both into the shade and coolness of the inner hall. "You're all right, sera?"

"All right," she confirmed. "Don't worry about it. Merry will tell you how it was."

Warrior stalked in, palps twitching.

"Do you scent greens?" Raen asked. "Greens attacked us. We killed some. They killed humans."

"Greensss." Warrior touched her nervously, calmed as she put her hand to its scent-patches, informing it. "Greenss make shift. Reds-golds-greens now. Weakest, greens. Easy to kill. Listen to red-Mind."

"Who listens, Warrior?"

"Always there. Warrior-Mind, redsss. I am apart. I am Warrior blue. Good you killed greens. Run away greens? Report?"

"Yes."

"Good?"

"They know I'm here now. Let them tell that to their hive."

"Good," Warrior concluded. "Good they taste this, Kethiuy-queen. Yess."

And it touched and stalked back outside.

Jim was standing over against the wall, his face strained. Raen touched his arm. "Go rest," she said.

And when he had wandered off to his own devices, she drew a deep breath, heard Merry coming in the side door—looked at Max. "No trouble at all while I was gone?"

He shook his head.

"A cold drink, would you?" She walked into the other room, on into the back of the house, toward the comp center.

Messages. The bank was full of them. The screen was flashing, as it would with an urgency.

She keyed in. The screen flipped half a dozen into her vision in rapid sequence. URGENT, most said. CALL DAIN.

One was different. I AM HERE, it said simply. P.R.H.

Pol.

She sat down, stricken.

BOOK SEVEN

1

MORE REPORTS. Chaos multiplied, even on Cerdin.

Moth regarded the stacks of printouts with a shiver, and then smiled, a faint and febrile smile.

She looked up at Tand.

"Have you made any progress toward the Istran statistics?"

"They're there, Eldest. Third stack."

She reached for them, suffered a fluttering of her hand which scattered them across the table: too little sleep, too little rest lately. She drew a few slow breaths, reached again to bring the papers closer. Tand gathered them and stacked them, laid them directly before her. It embarrassed and angered her.

"Doubtless," she said, "there are observations in some quarters that the old woman is failing."

From Tand there was silence.

She brushed through the papers, picked up the cup on the table deliberately to demonstrate the steadiness of her right hand . . . managed not to spill it, took a drink, set it down again firmly, her heart beating hard. "Get out," she said to Tand, having achieved the tiny triumph.

Tand started to go. She heard him hesitate. "Eldest," he said, and came back.

Near her.

"Eldest—"

"I'm not in want of anything."

"I hear rumors, Eldest." Tand sank on his knee at the arm of her chair; her heart lurched, so near he was. He looked up into her face, with an earnestness surprising in this man . . . excellent miming.

"Listen to me, Eldest. Perhaps . . . perhaps there comes a time that one ought to quit, that one could let go, let things pass quietly. Always there was Lian or Lian's kin; and now there's you; and is it necessary that things pass this time by your death?"

Bewilderment fell on her at this bizarre maneuver of Tand Hald; and within her robes, her left hand held a gun a span's remove from his chest. Perhaps he knew; but his expression was innocent and desperately earnest. "And always," she whispered in her age-broken voice, "always I have survived the purges, Tand. Is it now? Do you bring me warning?"

The last question was irony. Her finger almost pulled the trigger, but he showed no apprehension of it. "Resign from Council," he urged her. "Eldest, resign. Now. Pass it on. You're feeling your years; you're tired; I see it . . . so tired. But you could step aside and enjoy years yet, in quiet, in peace. Haven't you earned that?"

She breathed a laugh, for this was indeed a strange turn from a Hald. "But we're immortal," she whispered. "Tand, perhaps I shall cheat them and not die . . . ever."

"Only if you resign."

The urgency in his voice was plain warning. Perhaps, perhaps, she thought, the young Hald had actually conceived some softheartedness toward her. Perhaps all these years together had meant something.

Resign Council; and let the records fall under more critical eyes. Resign Council; and let one of their choice have his hand to things.

No.

She gave a thin sigh, staring into Tand's dark and earnest eyes. "It's a long time since Council functioned without someone's direction. Who would take Eldest's place? The Lind? He's not the man for this age. It would all come undone. He'd not last the month. Who'd follow him? The Brin? She'd be no better."

"You can't hold on forever."

She bit at her dry lips, and even yet the gun was on its target. "Perhaps," she said, allowing tremor to her voice, "perhaps I should take some thought in that direction. I was so long, so many, many years at Lian's side before he passed; I think that I've managed rather well, have I not, Tand?"

"Yes, Eldest . . . *very* well."

"And power passed smoothly at Lian's death because I had been so long at his side. My hands were at the controls of things as often as his; and even his assassination couldn't wrench things out of order . . . because I was there. Because I knew all his systems and where all the necessary matters were stored. Resign . . . no. No. That would create chaos. And there are things I know—" Her voice sank to the faintest of whispers, "things I know that are life and death to the Family. My death by violence—or by accident—would be calamity. But perhaps it's time I began to let things go. Maybe you're right. I should take a partner, a co-regent."

Tand's eyes flickered with startlement.

"As I was with Lian . . . toward the last. I shall take a co-regent, whoever presents the strongest face and the most solid backing. I shall let Council choose."

She watched the confusion mount, and kept a smile from her face.

"Young Tand," she whispered, "that is what I shall do." She waved her right hand, dismissing him; he seemed never to have realized where her left one was, or if he did, he had good nerves. He rose, gray and grim as iron now, all his polish gone. "I shall send out a message," she said, "convoking Council for tomorrow. You must carry it. You'll be my courier."

"Shall I tell the elders why?"

"No," she said, knowing that she would be disobeyed. "I'll present them the idea myself. Then they can have their time to choose. The transition of power," she said, boring with sudden concentration into Tand's dark eyes, "is always a problem in empires. Those which learn how to make the transfer smoothly . . . live. In general chaos who knows *who* might die?"

Tand stood still a moment. Moth gave him time to consider the matter. Then she waved her hand a second time, dismissing him. His departure was as deliberate and graceful as usual, although she reckoned what disturbance she had created in him.

And, alone, Moth bowed her head against her hands, trembling. The trembling became a laugh, and she leaned back in her chair in a sprawl, hands clasped across her middle.

Not many rulers had been privileged to be entertained by the wars of their own successions, she reckoned; and the humor of seeing the Hald and their minions blinking in the light with their cover ripped away, publicly *invited* to contend for power, while she still lived . . . That was worth laughter.

Her assassination had been prepared, imminent. Tand's action was puzzling . . . some strange affliction of sentiment, perhaps, or even an offer relayed from the others; and with straight-faced humor she had returned the offer doubled. Of course they would kill her as soon as their choice was well-entrenched in power . . . but time . . . *time* was the important thing.

She grinned to herself, and the grin faded as she gathered up the falsified Istran reports, stacked them with the others.

The Meth-maren would have need of time.

To leave this place, Cerdin and Council and all of them, and have such a place as the old Houses had been, old friends, dead friends—that was the only retirement for which Moth yearned, to find again what had died long ago, those who had built—instead of those who used.

But one of the folders was the Meth-maren's, and Moth opened the record, stared morosely at the woman the child had become.

The data was random and the cross-connections inexplicable, and her old age grew toward mysticism, the only sanity . . . too much knowledge, too wide a pattern.

Lian also must have seen. He had complained of visions, toward the last, weakness which had encouraged assassins, and hastened his death.

He had died riveted in one of those visions, trembling and frothing, a horror that left no laughter at all in Moth.

She had had to do it.

"Eggs," Lian had cried in his dying, "eggs . . . eggs . . . eggs . . . eggs," as if recalling the beta children, the poor orphaned creatures, the parentless generation—the thousands growing up too soon, cared for en masse, assembly-lined into adulthood, men and women at ten, to care for others, and others . . . to bear natural children at permission, as they did all things at permission, forever. *Give them luxury,* Lian had said once. *Corrupt them, and we shall always control them. Teach them about work and rewards, and reward them with idleness and ambition. So we will always manage them.*

So betas, seeking idleness, created azi.

Eggs . . . eggs . . . eggs . . . eggs.

Eggs of eggs.

Moth shuddered, reliving the fissioning generations who had spawned all reality in the Reach.

Seven hundred years. From one world to many worlds, a rate of growth no longer controlled.

Eggs.

Potential.

I am the last, Moth thought, *who was once human. The last with humanity as it once was. Even the Meth-maren is not that.*

Least of all . . . that.

Eggs making eggs.

Family, she thought, and thought of an old saying about absolute power, and absolute corruption.

Only the azi, she thought, *lack power.*

The azi are the only innocents.

2

POL HALD SAT DOWN, propped his slim legs on a table, folded his hands and looked about him with a shrug of amusement.

Raen took the drink that Jim served her and leaned back, stared balefully as Pol accepted his and looked Jim up and down, drawing the obvious conclusions. Jim glanced down, an azi-reaction to such attention.

"Thank you, Jim," Raen said softly. For a very little she would have asked Jim to sit down and stay, but Pol was another matter than the ITAK board . . . cruel when he wished to be; and he often wished to be.

Jim vanished silently into the next room. Warrior did not. The majat sat in the corner next to the curio table, rigidly motionless as a piece of furniture.

"Beta-ish," Pol observed of the decor, of the whole house in general, a flourish of his hand. "You've a bizarre taste, Meth-maren. But the azi shows some discrimination."

"What are you doing here?"

Pol laughed, a deep and appealing chuckle. "It's been eighteen years since we shared a supper, Meth-maren. I had a mad impulse for another invitation."

"A far trip for little reward. Does Ros Hald's table not suffice?"

He had pricked at her. She flicked it back doubled, won a slight annoyance of him. That gaunt face had not changed with the years; he had reached that long stage where he would not. She added up numbers and reckoned at least over seventy. Experience. The gap was narrowed, but not by much.

"I've followed you for years," he said. "You're the only Meth-maren who ever amused me."

"You've done so very quietly, then. Did the Hald send you?"

"I came." He grinned. "You have a marvelous sense of humor. But your style of travel gave me ample time to catch up with you." He drank deeply and looked up again, set the glass down. "You know you've set things astir."

She shrugged.

"They'll kill you," Pol said.

"They?"

"Not I, Meth-maren."

"So why are you here?" she asked, mouth twisted in sarcasm. "To stand in the way?"

He made a loose gesture, looked at her from half-lidded eyes. "Meth-maren, I am jealous. You outdid me." He laughed outright. "I've studied to annoy Council for years, but I'll swear you've surpassed me, and so young, too. You know what you're doing here?"

She said nothing.

"I think you do," he said. "But it's time to call it off."

"Take yourself back to Cerdin, Pol Hald."

"I didn't come from Cerdin. I heard. I was willing to come out here. You're my personal superstition, you see. I don't want to see you go under. Get out of here. Now. To the other side of the Reach. They'll understand the gesture."

She rose. "Warrior," she said.

Warrior came to life, mandibles clashing, and reared up to its full height. Pol froze, looking at it.

"Warrior, tell me, of what hive is this Kontrin?"

"Green-hive," Warrior said, and boomed a note of majat language. "Green-hive Kontrin."

Pol moved his chitined right hand, a flippant gesture that was a satire of himself. "Am I to blame for the choice of hive? It's Meth-maren labs that set the patterns, that reserved blue for chosen friends . . . of which we were not."

"Indeed you were not."

Pol rose, walked to the window, walked back again, within reach of Warrior, deliberate bravado. "You're far beyond the limits. Do you know . . . do you understand what deep water you're into?"

"That my House died for others' ambitions? That something was set up two decades ago and no one has stopped it? How are they keeping it from Moth? Or are they?"

Pol's dark eyes flicked aside to Warrior, back to her. "I grow nervous when you become specific. I hope you'll consider carefully before you make any irrevocable moves."

"I learned, Hald. You taught me a lesson once. I've always held a remote affection for you on that account. No rancor. We said once we amused each other. Will you answer me now?"

He made a shrug of both hands. "I'm not in good favor among Halds. How could I know the answers you want?"

"But what you know you won't tell me."

"Moth has not long to live. That I know. For the rest of what I know: the Halds are your enemies . . . nothing personal, understand. The Halds want what Thel reached for."

"And no one has undone what Eron Thel did."

Pol made a gesture of helplessness. "I don't know; I don't know. I protest: I am not in their confidence."

It was possibly true. Raen kept watching the hands and the eyes, lest a weapon materialize. "I appreciate your concern, Pol."

"If you'd take my advice, get out of here . . . clear over to the far side, they would understand, Raen a Sul. They'd read that as a clear signal. Capitulation. Who cares? You'll outlive them if you guard your life. Running now is your only protection. My ship is onworld. I'd take you there. The Family wouldn't harm you. The Halds may not take me into their intimate confidence, but neither will they come at me."

She started to laugh, and saw Pol's face different from how she had ever known it, drawn and tense . . . no laughter, for one of a few times in his irreverent life.

"Go away," she said very softly. "Get yourself to that safety, Pol Hald. You'll survive."

He said nothing for a moment, looked doubtful. "What is it you have in mind?"

She did laugh. "I wonder, Pol Hald, if you don't surpass me after all. Maybe they did send you."

"I think you'll hear from the Family soon enough."

"Will I? Where's Morn, Pol?"

He shrugged. "I don't know. Cerdin, maybe. Or near these regions. It could be Morn. Or Tand. Or one of the Ren-barants. Or maybe none of them. When Moth falls, they'll pull your privileges, and then you'll be deaf, dumb and blind, grounded on Istra."

"Moth's on my side, is she?"

"She has been. I don't know who it will be. Truth. I started from innerworlds when I was sure where you'd gone . . . when I knew for certain it wasn't a cover. Morn headed the other way. Tand moved inworlds, even earlier than that. He's likely with Moth. I'm handing you things that would break the Reach wide open if you called Moth."

"You're challenging me to do that?"

Again a shrug, a hint of mockery. "I'm betting the old woman knows a good part of it already."

"Or that it's already too late? It would take eight days for the shockwave to reach us."

"Possible," he said. "But not my reason."

"Then you believe I don't want the break right now. You could be mistaken."

Pol said nothing.

"You don't plan," Raen said in a hard voice, "to be setting up on Istra."

"I've a problem," Pol said. "If I go back, I'll be called in; and if I run alone . . . they'll know I heard something here that made it advisable. I've put myself in difficulty on your account, Meth-maren."

"If I believed any of it."

Pol made another of his elaborate gestures of offense. "I protest. I shall go back to my ship and wait until you think things over in a clearer mind. Someone else will come, mark me."

"Ah, I don't doubt that much. And help would be convenient. But likewise I remember the front porch at Kethiuy. You knew. You knew when you were talking to me. Didn't you?"

A profound sobriety came on Pol's face. He lowered his eyes, raised them steadily. "I knew, yes. And I left, with the rest of the Halds, before the attack. Revenge, Meth-maren, involving another generation. It had nothing to do with you."

"Now it does."

He had no answer for that. Neither did he flinch.

"This one's mine," she said. "I always had profound respect for your intelligence, Pol Hald. You were in Hald councils before I was born. You were alive when the Meth-marens split, Sul from Ruil. You have contacts I don't. You've access to Cerdin. You've been staying alive and embarrassing Council twice my whole lifespan. You knew, back in Kethiuy. You're telling me now that you don't figure precisely what's in others' minds?"

Pol drew a long breath, nodded slowly, looking down. "The plan was, you understand, to break out of the Reach. That was Thel's idea. To build. To breed. And it's all here on Istra, isn't it? You've put it together for yourself."

"Enough to take it apart."

"They'll kill you for sure. They'll drag Moth down and kill you before they let you expose their operation."

"Their."

"Their. I'm not in favor. I go my own way. As you do. I'll run when the time comes. I'll stay, while the mood takes me. Only you won't have that luxury. Is it worth this much, your vendetta?"

"It's beyond argument."

He looked at Warrior, stared into the faceted eyes, glanced back with a faint touch of revulsion. "Hive-masters. It's that, isn't it? Ruil Meth-maren tried to use the hives. And Thel wanted to use them. Look where that took us."

"No one," she said, *"uses* the hives. Hive-master was a Ruil word. Sul never used it. And Thon's still playing that dangerous game. Are red-hivers out again on Cerdin?"

"They make gifts to all the old contacts."

Warrior's palps flicked nervously. "Pact," it said.

Pol glanced that way in apprehension.

"Do you not understand the danger?" Raen asked him. "The hives don't have anything to gain . . . nothing Hald could want out of the exchange."

"Azi," Pol said. "They ask for more azi. For more land. More grain."

"Hives grow," said Warrior. "Hives here—grow."

Raen looked on Warrior. Truth. It was clear truth. It fit with all the knowledge elsewhere gathered.

"Don't you understand?" she appealed to Pol. "Doesn't Council? Who talked first of this expansion? Thel, Ruil . . . or red-hive?"

"Thel claimed unique partnership, claimed that even Drones could be brought into partnership with humans."

Her heart beat very fast. She laid her hand on one of Warrior's auditory palps, stroked it gently, gently. "O Pol. Don't they realize? Drones are the Memory. Humans can't touch that."

Pol shrugged, and yet his dark eyes were quick with worry. "The Meth-marens are dead. The hive-masters are dead, all but you. And Council doesn't have access to you, does it? Moth's kept saying that you were important."

"I'm flattered," she said hoarsely. "Hive-masters. Ruil deluded themselves. There were never hive-masters. They listened to the hives. Get out of here. Take your ship. Tell them they're all mad. I'll give you reasons enough to tell them."

He shook his head. "I wouldn't live to get there. And they wouldn't listen. Can't. It's gone too far. Moth will be dead by the time I could get there. Eight days, message-time or ship-time, at quickest. I couldn't—couldn't get there in time."

"And someone's on his way here."

"There's no way not."

Pol was talking clear sense. She continued to soothe Warrior, aware it was recording, aware of the nervous tremor of the palp against her hand. She felt it calm at last. "There are extensions of ITAK on the other continent. Are there blues with the other city, Warrior?"

"Yess. All hives, red, gold, green, blue. New-port."

"Same-Mind, Warrior?"

"Same-Mind."

"No queen."

"Warriorss. Workerss. From this-Hill."

She looked at Pol. "Suppose that I trusted you. Suppose that I asked you to do me a small favor. Have you your own staff?"

"Twelve azi. The ship is mine. My entire estate. I'm mobile. In these times it seems wise."

"I haven't an establishment on the other continent."

"You plan to take me out of the way."

"You can take West and be sure of the situation there in the matter of a day or two."

"You may not have that much time. They'll stop you. I mean that."

"Then it's wise that I cultivate *you,* isn't it? If they pull my authorizations you'll still have yours, won't you, Pol Hald?"

"You have a dazzling mutability. You'd rely on me?"

"One does what one must."

"You'd have my neck in the jaws with no compunction, wouldn't you?"

"I'm figuring you started from innerworlds first and farthest out. So there's a little time yet. You can do me that small service and still have time to run. And I'd run far, Pol. I would, in your place."

All posing fell aside. He stared at her. "I've told you something. I wish I understood the extent of it."

"The Halds should have asked my help. Or Moth should have. If they'd asked, I might have come." She gave Warrior's auditory palp a light brush, and Warrior turned its head, reacted in slight pleasure. "It's good to see you, Pol. I'd not say that of any of the rest of the Family, I assure you. My old acquaintances no longer interest me. The Family . . . no longer interests me. I've found here what you've been searching for all your life."

"And what do you take that to be, Raen a Sul?"

"The Edge. That which limits us."

"You don't have Ros Hald's ambitions."

She laughed, which was no laughter. "Mine are yours. To push until it gives. Here's the stopping-place. Beware red-hive. You understand me?"

"You have disquieted me."

"You never liked peace."

"What shall I look for in West?"

"Guard-azi. Buy up those you can. Ship them to East, to the Labor Registry. Arms as well."

"You're planning civil war."

She smiled again. "Tell the estate-holders in West . . . and ITAK there . . . to prepare for storm."

"How can I, when I don't know what you have in mind?"

"It's your choice. Go or stay."

"I know my choices, youngster."

"You'd better get yourself clear of this house, in any case. There'll be blue-hive thick about here in a little while, and that hand of yours is no guarantee of friendship. Get out of Newhope, in either direction you choose."

He put on a long face. "I'd thought of dinner, alas; and more things after."

"Later, Pol Hald. I confess you tempt me."

A twinkle danced in his eye, a favorite pose. "Then I'm not without hope. Alas, you've your azi for consolation, and I'm not without my own. Sad, is it not?"

"The time will come."

He bowed his head.

"You know my call number. It never changes."

"You know mine."

"Betas on Istra," she said, "have played the same dangerous game as Hald and Thon. Red-hive gives them gifts. I'll warrant red-hive walks where it will in West."

"I've no skill with majat."

"Keep it that way. Refuse to be approached. Shoot on the least excuse."

"Hazard," Warrior broke in, coming to life again. "Green-hive Drone, take care: danger. Red-hive kills humans, many, many, many. You are not green-hive Mind. No synthesis. None."

"What's it saying?" Pol asked. "I can never make sense of them."

"Perfect sense. It knows you're naïve of majat, and it warns you that without hive-friendship, green-hive chitin is no protection to you, even from greens. Red-hive and even greens have learned to kill intelligences. Red-hive has learned to make agreements with minds-that-die, and no longer has trouble with death. What's more . . . they've learned to *lie*. Consider the hive-Mind, Pol; consider that those who lie to majat have to be unMinded. But they can lie to humans without it . . . a profound discovery. Red-hive has gone as far from morality as majat can go. Hald and Thel and Thon helped . . . or otherwise. Get out of here. You've not much time. Be careful at the port. Are you armed?"

He moved his hands delicately. "Of course."

She offered her hand, warily; he took it, with a wry smile.

"I'll give you West," he said, letting go her hand. "Is that all you want?"

She grinned. "I'll be content with that." And soberly: "Keep within reach of your ship, Pol. It's life."

He took his leave, let himself out. In a moment she heard a car start and ease down the drive. She went to housecomp to open the gate, did so, picked him up briefly on remote. He cleared the gate and she closed it.

Warrior came, hovered at her shoulder. "This-unit heard things of other hives. Redsss. Trouble."

"This-unit is concerned, Warrior. This-unit begins to think that the hives know more than you've told me."

It drew back, jaws clicking. "Red-hive. Red-hive is—" It gave a booming and shrill of majat language. "No human word, Kontrin-queen. Long, long this red-hive, gold-hive—" Again the combination of sound, discord. "Red-hive is full of human-words: push-push-eggs-more-more."

"Expansion. They want expansion. Growth."

Warrior tried to assimilate that. It surely knew the words; they did not satisfy it.

"Synthesis," it said finally. "Red-hive messengers come. Many, many. Red-hive—easy, easy that messengers come. Kontrin permit. Goldss, yes. Greens, sometimes. Many, many, no blues."

"I know. But Kalind blue reached you. What did it tell you?"

"Kethiuy-queen . . . many, many, many messengers, reds, golds, greens. No blues. Blues have rested, not part of push-push-push. No synthesis. Now blue messenger. We taste Cerdin-Mind."

"Warrior. What was the message?"

"Revenge," Warrior said, which was the essence of Kalind blue. And suddenly auditory palps flicked left. "Hear. Others."

She shook her head. "I can't hear, Warrior. Human range is small."

It was listening. "Blues, they say. Blues. They are coming. Many-many. Goodbye, Kethiuy-queen."

And it fled.

3

THE SUN WAS almost below the horizon; it was no longer necessary to wear cloaks or sunsuits or to fear for the eyes. And the garden was alive with majat.

Raen kept Jim by her, constantly, and Max and Merry as well, not trusting the nervous Warriors. She walked the garden, making sure that Warriors saw their presence clearly, to realize that they justly belonged there.

And suddenly others were there, rag-muffled figures, swarming over the back garden wall among the Warriors; and other majat accompanied them, smaller, with smaller jaws: Workers, a horde of them.

Ragged human figures came to her and sought touch with febrile hands and eyes visored even at dusk, and their movements were strange, nervous. One and several others unmasked, sought mouth-touch with Jim and Max and Merry and danced away from their vicinity when Raen bade them go.

"What are they?" Jim asked, horror in his voice.

"Don't worry for them," Raen said. "They belong to the majat. They have majat habits." And seeing how all three azi reacted to their majat counterparts: "Blue-hive azi, go in, go inside the building, seek low-level and settle there."

"Yes," they said together, song-toned, and with that mad-blind fix of hive-azi stares. They scampered off, to seek the basement of the house, the dark places where they would be most at home.

Workers set to work without asking, began to pry up stones with their jaws, began to dig, through the pavings, into the moist earth.

And suddenly there was a buzz from the front gate.

Raen swore, waded off through the crowd of Warriors, beckoning Jim and Max and Merry to come with her. "Warrior," she shouted at the nearest. "Keep all majat out of sight behind the house. No enemies. No danger. Just stay here." And to Max and Merry: "Get down by the gate. I imagine that's the new azi coming in. You're in charge of them. See they don't wander loose. Get them in strict order and check them off against the invoice, by numbers, visually."

They hurried off at a run. She went inside with Jim as her shadow, unsealed the gate from the comp center when she saw the trucks by remote: they bore the Labor Registry designation. She kept watching, while the trucks disgorged azi and supplies, while Merry and Max called off numbers and ranged the men in groups of ten. The men stood; the boxes formed a square in the front garden. As each truck emptied, it pulled out, and when the last vehicle cleared the gate, Raen closed it and set the alarm again.

"They'll not like the majat at all," Raen said. "Jim, go find one of the quieter Warriors and ask it to come to the front of the house with you—alone. Better they see one before they see all of them."

He nodded and went. Raen put the outside lights on and went out the front door, walked out into the midst of the orderly groups, two hundred six men, by tens.

Max and Merry were checking numbers as she had said, a process the brighter lights made easier. Each was read, not by the stencil on the coveralls, but by the tattoo on the shoulder; and each man passed was directed into military order over by the portico. Neat, precise, the team of Max and Merry; and the two hundred were minds precisely like theirs . . . all too precisely, having come from the same tapes.

Every figure stiffened, looked houseward. Raen glanced and saw Jim with his unlikely shadow slow-stepping along in close company. "There are many such here," Raen said before panic could take hold. "*I* hold your contracts. I tell you that you're very safe with these particular majat. They'll help you in your duties, which are to protect this house. Understood?"

Each head inclined, the fix of their eyes now on her. Two hundred men. In the group were many who were duplicates, twin, triplet, quadruplet sets, alike even to age. There were two more Maxes and another Merry. They would accept. They would accept her and the majat as they would accept anything which held their contracts. It was their psych-set. Like Max and Merry, they fought only when they were directed, only when their contract-holder identified an enemy. But for their own lives, they would scarcely put up resistance. Did not. Until things were clear to them, they were docile. Warrior exercised curiosity about them, stalked down near them. They bore this: their contract-holder was present to instruct them if instructions were to be given.

Guard-function.

Specificity, Itavvy had called it.

"Warrior," she said, "come." And when it had joined her, with Jim shadowing it, she soothed it with a touch and kept it by her, an act of mercy.

The process continued. But by one man both Max and Merry delayed, looked closely at the mark, disputed. "Sera," Max called.

The man bolted. Warrior moved. "No!" Raen yelled, but Warrior was deaf to that, auditory palps laid back, a blur of motion. Azi scattered.

But it was Max and Merry who had the fugitive; Raen raced through the chaotic midst, calmed the anxious Warrior. Jim stayed with her. Other azi stayed about, sober-faced, stunned, perhaps, that one of their number had done violence.

The azi in Max's grip stopped fighting, gazed past Raen's shoulder and surely understood what he had narrowly escaped. He was a man like the others, shave-headed, gray-clad, a number stenciled on his coverall; but Merry pulled back the cloth from his shoulder and showed the tattoo as if there were something amiss.

"It's too dark, sera," Merry said. "Papers say twenty-nine, but the mark's bright."

The man's eyes shifted back to Raen, a face rigid with terror.

Such things had been done . . . a beta highly bribed, promised protection. "I'd believe a fluke of the dye," Raen said softly. "But not an azi who'd break and run. Who sent you?"

He gave no answer, but wrenched to free himself.

"Not an assassin," Raen said, though the hate in that face gave her pause to think so. "Betas don't go for that. Or—" she added, for the expression was nigh to madness, "maybe not beta at all. Are you?"

"He's little," Merry said, "for guard-type."

That was so too.

A smile took her, sudden surety. "Outsider. One of Tallen's folk."

It hit to the mark. The pale eyes shifted from hers.

"O man," she said softly. "To go to that extent . . . or did you know what you were getting into when you set that mark on yourself?"

There was no more resistance, none. In that moment she felt a touch of pity, seeing the young Outsider's desperation. Twenty-nine. He did not look that.

"What's your name?" she asked him.

"Tom Mundy."

"You *are* Tallen's. Easier with him, Max. I doubt he's here to do murder. I rather well think he realizes he's made a mistake. And I wonder if we haven't swept up something utterly by chance. Haven't we, Tom Mundy?"

"Let me go."

"Let him go, Max. But," she added at once as the young Outsider braced himself for escape, "you'll not make it across the City like that, Tom Mundy."

He looked as if he were on the brink of madness. Some shred of sense held him to listen.

"I'll *send* you to Tallen," she said, "without asking you a thing. But if you'd like a drink and a place to sit down, while my people finish checking things out, it would be more convenient for us."

"Outsider-human," Warrior murmured in mingled tones.

The Outsider began to weep, tears running down his face; and would have sat down where he was, but that Jim and Merry took him in hand and led him up to the porch, to the door.

4

THERE WAS AT LEAST for the time, quiet in the house—stirrings in the back, noises in the basement, but nothing visible in the main room.

And the azi who had been Tom Mundy sat on the couch clutching a drink in his hands and staring at the floor.

"I would like," Raen said softly, "one simple question answered, if you would." Jim was by her, and she indicated a place by her; Jim sat down, settled back with a disapproving look.

Mundy slowly lifted his head, apprehension on his face.

"How," Raen asked, "did you find yourself in such circumstances? Did you come to spy on me? Or did someone put you there?"

He said nothing.

"All right," she said. "I won't insist. But I'm guessing it looked like a means for information. And you made a mistake. A real azi number, real papers, guard-status: a spy could pick up a great deal of information that way, and no one would shut an azi away from communications equipment. I'd guess you make regular reports to Tallen, because no one would suspect you'd do such a thing. But it went wrong, I'm guessing."

He swallowed heavily. "You said that I could go."

"The car's being brought. Max and one of the others will deliver you to Tallen's doorstep—a surprise to him, perhaps. How long were you in those pits?"

"I don't know," he said hoarsely. "I don't know."

"You didn't plan coming here, then." She read the man's apprehensions and leaned back, shrugged off the question. "You'll get to Tallen alive, don't fear that. You'll come to no harm. How long have you been working on this world?"

Again an avoidance of her eyes.

"There are more of you," she said. "Aren't there?"

She obtained a distraught stare.

"Probably," she said, "I've bought more than one of you and haven't detected it. I own every guard-azi contract available on this continent. I'd sort you out if I could. You've been standing guard in ITAK establishments, gathering information, passing it along to Tallen. Of no possible concern to me. Actually I favor the enterprise. That's why I'm making a present of you to him. I'd advise you, though, if you know of others in that group, you tell me. There are others, aren't there?"

He took a drink, said nothing.

"Did you know what you were getting into?"

He wiped at his face and leaned his head on his hand, answer enough.

"Tell Tallen," she said, "I'll pull his men out if he'll give me the necessary numbers. I doubt you know them."

"I don't," he said.

"How did you end up in the Registry?"

"Took—took the place of an azi the majat killed. Tattoo . . . papers . . . a transport guard. Then the depots shut down. Company stopped operating. Been there—been there—"

"A long time."

He nodded.

A born-man, subjected to tapes and isolation. She regarded him pitifully. "And of course Tallen couldn't buy you out. An Outsider couldn't. Even knowing the numbers, he couldn't retrieve you. Did anyone think of that, before you let that number be tattooed on?"

"It was thought of."

"Do you fear us that much?" she asked softly. He avoided her eyes. "You do well to," she said, answering her own question. "And you know us. You've seen. You've been there. Bear your report, Tom Mundy. You'll do well never to appear again in the Reach. If not for the strict quotas of export, you might have been—"

Her heart skipped a beat. She laughed aloud, and Tom Mundy looked at her in terror.

"Azi," she laughed. "Istra's primary export. Shipped everywhere." And then with apprehension, she looked on Jim.

"I am azi," Jim said, his own calm slightly ruffled. "Sera, I *am* azi."

She laid a hand on his arm. "There's no doubt. There's no doubt,

Jim." There was the sound of a motor at the door. "That will be the car. Come along, ser Mundy."

Tom Mundy put the drink aside, preceded her to the door in evident anxiety. She followed out under the portico, where Max had the car waiting, Max standing by it.

"Max, seize him," Raen said.

Mundy sprang to escape; Max was as quick as the order, and fetched him up against the car, rolled with him to the pavement. Majat were at hand, Warriors. Jim himself made to interfere, but Raen put out a hand, restraining him.

Mundy struggled and cursed. Max shouted for human help, and several more azi arrived on the run.

It needed a struggle. "Don't harm him," Raen called out, when it began to look as if that would be the case; Mundy fought like a man demented, and it took a number of azi to put him down. Cords were searched up, all with a great deal of confusion. A shooting, Raen decided, watching the process, would have been far simpler; as it was the police at the gate wanted to intrude: she saw their lights down the drive, but the gate would keep them out, and she reckoned they would fret, but they would not dare climb a wall to investigate.

Mundy was held, finally, hands bound. He cursed and screamed until he was breathless, and lay heaving on the pavement. Max and another gathered him to his feet, and Raen stepped back as he spat at her.

"I'll keep my word," she said, "eventually. Don't try me, Tom Mundy. The worst thing I could do is send you back. Isn't it?"

He stopped fighting then.

"How long have you been infiltrating?" she asked. "How many years?"

"I don't know. Would it make sense I'd know? I don't."

"Keep him under guard, Max. Don't take your eyes off him. One of the basement storerooms ought to be adequate. He won't *want* loose down there. Constant watch. See to it."

They drew him into the house, and through it. Raen lingered, looked at the disturbed Warriors, whose mandibles clicked with nervousness. "Wrong-hive," she explained in terms they would understand. "Not enemy, not friend, wrong-hive. We will isolate that-unit. Pass this information. Warrior must guard that-unit."

They spent a moment analyzing those concepts, which were alien to the hive. A stranger should be ejected, not detained.

"That-unit will report if it escapes. We will let it go when it's good that it report."

"Yesss," they said together, comprehending, and themselves filed into the house, nightmare shapes in the Eln-Kests' hallway.

She started to go in, realized Jim was not with her, and turned back, saw him standing by the car, saw the blank horror on his face. She came back, took his hand. From inside the house came a scream of hysteria. She slipped her hand up to Jim's elbow; decided to walk round the long way, beneath the portico, past the corner, within the walkway to the back, where there was quiet.

"I *am* azi," Jim said.

She pressed his arm the more tightly. "I know so. I know so, Jim. Don't distress yourself. It's been a long, hard day."

She felt the tremor, wordless upset.

"The fall of the dice," she said, "was a fortunate thing for me. But what a place you've come to."

"I am azi."

"You do very well at it."

She walked with him out the arch into the back garden, into chaos, where guard-azi tried to set their supplies in order, where nervous Warriors stalked among humans and touched one and the other. It was pitiful that the azi did not object, that they simply stopped and endured, as no betas would have done, although they were surely afraid. Raen moved among them, sorted Warriors away from humans, nodded to Merry, who began hastily to motion his men into the shelter of the azi quarters. There was no hesitation among them.

The doors closed. Thereafter majat ruled in the garden, and majat azi scampered out the back door, naked, having shed their sun-protections, with their mad eyes and their cheerful grins, their ready acceptance of the touches of Workers and Warriors. They had come to help, and plunged quite happily into the excavations underway in the garden.

"They'll want feeding," Raen said. "They're our responsibility. Jim, go locate the domestics. Have them cook up enough for the whole lot. The majat azi will prefer boiled grain. There look to be about fifty of them."

Jim murmured agreement, and went, tired and shaken as he was. She watched him at the azi quarters gather up the six in question, watched him shepherd them across to the house, fending away the persistent majat azi. He managed. He managed well. She was able, for a moment, to relax . . . lingered, gazing on the shadow-forms of majat, the blue lights of the azi winking eerily in the shadowed places of the garden, where the tunnel was deepening.

"Worker," she said when one passed near her, "how far will the tunnel go?"

"Blue-hive," it said, which was answer, not inanity. A chill went over her skin. She surmised suddenly that there were tunnels begun elsewhere, an arm of the hive reached out into the city.

Mother accepted; Mother had ordered. The hive reached out to embrace them and protect. She wrapped her arms about her, found the lights shimmering in her vision.

There was a freshness in the air, of moisture and evening. A little drop fell on her arm and she looked up, at a sky mostly clouded. There was another rain coming. It would hardly trouble the majat, or their azi.

She wandered inside finally, as domestic azi came out, bearing foodstuffs, hastening for fear of the majat, to the kitchens in the azi quarters.

One remained in the house kitchen, under Jim's direction, preparing a different meal. "Thank you," Raen said to them both; she would have eaten azi porridge without compunction, so tired she was; but she was glad when a good dinner was set before her and Jim took his place at the end of the table.

The hive was about her. The song began. She could hear it in the house, illusory and soft as the rainfall, as old dreams.

Then she thought of the basement, and the cup hesitated at her lips; she drank, and began reckoning of other things.

Of Itavvy, and promises; of Pol Hald; of Tallen.

Of the Family.

There were messages upon messages. Comp spat them out in inane profusion; and she sat and searched them, the while thunder rumbled overhead.

One was ser Dain. MY HUMBLEST APOLOGIES. THE ARTIST IS SER TOL ERRIN, 1028D UPCOAST. There was more, mostly babble. She rubbed her eyes, took a sip of coffee, and entered worldcomp to pull a citizen number, to link it with another program.

One was Pol Hald. NEWPORT IS DISMAL. MY SUFFERING IS EXTREME. REJOICE.

She drank more coffee, sinking into the rhythms of the majat song which ran through the house, nerved herself for intercomp. The dataflow never stopped, world to station, station to station, station to world, jumping information like ships from point to point. Data launched could not be recalled.

She called up the prepared program regarding contracts, and export quotas, the oft-denied permits.

GRANTED, she entered, to all of them.

In an hour the board would be jammed with queries, chaos, the deadlock broken. Cerdin would not know it for eight days.

She called up the city guest house, and drew a sleepy outsider out of bed. "Call Tallen," she said, using her own image and direct voice, which she had not used on Istra.

Tallen appeared quickly, his person disordered, his face flushed. "Kont' Raen," he said.

"I've an azi," she said, "who knows you. His name was Tom Mundy."

Tallen started to speak, changed his mind. Whatever of sleep there was about him vanished.

"He's not harmed," she said. "Won't be. But I want to know how long this has been going on, ser Tallen. I want an answer. How much and how many and how far?"

"I'll meet with you."

She shook her head. "Just a plain answer, ser. Monitored or not. How far has the net spread itself?"

"I have no desire to discuss this long-distance."

"Shall I ask Mundy?"

Tallen's face went stark. "You'll do as you please, I imagine. The trade mission—"

"Is under Reach law. Kontrin law. I do as I please, yes. He's safe for the moment. I'll give him back to you, so you needn't do anything rash. I merely advise you that you've done a very unwise thing, ser. Give me those numbers and I'll do what I can to sort things out for you; you understand me. I can act where you can't. I'm willing to do so . . . . a matter of humanity. Give me the numbers."

Tallen broke contact.

She had feared so. She shook her head, swallowed down a stricture in her throat with a mouthful of cooling coffee, finally turned housecomp over to automatic.

She drank the rest of the coffee, grimacing at the taste, followed it with half a measure of liquor, and sat listening to the thunder.

"Sera," Jim said, startling her. She glanced at the doorway.

"Go to bed," she told him. "What about the azi downstairs? Settled?"

He nodded.

"Go on," she said. "Go rest. You've done what you can."

He was not willing to leave; he did so, and she listened as his footsteps went upstairs. She sat still a moment, listening to the hive-song, then rose and went downstairs, into the dark territory of the basement.

Majat-azi gathered about her. She bade them away, suffered with more patience the touch of Workers and Warriors. There was a door guarded by Warriors. She opened it, and two guard-azi rose to their feet, from the chairs inside. The third huddled in the corner, on a mat of blankets.

"I've spoken with Tallen," she said. "He's very upset. Is there anything I can get for your comfort?"

A jerk of the head, refusal. He would not look at her face. They had taken the cords off him. There was the double guard to restrain him.

"You were a transport guard. Were you sensible enough to understand that what you're seeing on this world is not the usual, that things have gone vastly amiss?"

Still he would say nothing, which in his place, was the wiser course.

She sank down, rested her arms across her knees, stared at him. "I'll hazard a guess, ser 113-489-6798, that all you've done has been a failure: that Tallen would have known *me* had it succeeded. You've scattered azi off this world, if at all, only to have the embargo stall them, if not here, on Pedra, on Jin. And do you know where they'll be? In cases similar to your own. You entered that facility when the depots were closed . . . about half a year ago. What do you think will become of those stalled there for years, as some are—two years already, for some? What do you think will come out of that? You think they'll be sane? I doubt it. And how many azi have access to transmission of messages via intercomp? None, ser. You've thrown men away. Like yourself."

Eyes fixed on hers, hollow, in a shaven skull. Thin hands clasped knees against his chest. He would never, she thought, be the man he would have been. Youth, cast away in such a venture. More than one of them. He might break. Most would, if majat asked the questions. But she much doubted that he knew anything beyond himself.

"Majat," she said, "killed the azi you replaced. Was that a hazard, running the depots?"

"They're all over," he said hoarsely. "Farms—armed camps for fear of them."

Cold settled on her at that. She nodded. "Ever see them in the open?"

"Once. Far across the fields. We drove out of it, fast as we could."

"What do you suppose they would do?"

"There'd been trucks lost. They'd find the trucks. Nothing else."

She nodded slowly. "It fits, ser Mundy. It does fit. Thank you. Rest now. Get some sleep. You'll not be bothered. And I'll get you back to Tallen in one piece if you'll stay in this room. Please don't try my guards. A scratch from a majat is as deadly as a bite. But they won't come into this room."

She rose, left, walked out among the Warriors. The door closed behind her. She singled out one of the larger ones, touched it, soothed it. "Warrior, many azi, many, in blue-hive? Weapons?"

"Yes."

"The hives have taken azi, taken food?"

There was a working of mandibles, a little disturbance at this question. "Take, yesss. Red-hive takes, goldss take, greens take, blue-hive, yessss. Store much, much. Mother says *take, keep, prevent other-hives.*"

"Warrior, has blue-hive killed humans?"

"No. Take azi. Keep."

"Many azi."

"Many," Warrior agreed.

5

JIM SAT ON THE BED, massaged his temples, tried to still the pounding in his skull. *Never panic; never panic. Stop. Think. Thinking is good service. It is good to serve well.*

He seldom recalled the tapes verbatim. The thoughts were simply there, inwoven. This night he remembered, and struggled to remember. He was unbearably tired. Strange sights, everything strange —he trembled with the burden of it.

The other Kontrin had gone, that at least, away around the world; but the majat would not go, nor this flood of azi. He remained unique: he sensed this, clung to it.

He had *here,* and the others did not. He had this room, this place he shared with her, and the others did not.

He rose finally, and went through all the appropriate actions, born-man motions, for although the *Jewel* had rigid rules about cleanliness, there had been no facilities such as these, even in upper decks. He showered, coated himself liberally with soap, once, twice, three times . . . in sheer enjoyment of the fragrance, so unlike the bitter detergent that had come automatically through the azi-deck system, stinging eyes and noses. He worked very hard at his personal appearance: he understood it for duty to *her,* to match all these fine things she had, the use of which she gave him; and *she* was the measure of all the wide world through which she drew him. He had seen rich men, powerful men, in absolute terror of her; and majat who feared her and majat who obeyed her; and another Kontrin who treated her carefully; and he himself was closest to her, an importance as heady as wine. On the ship he had been terrified by the reaction of others to her; he had not known how it would be to live on the other side of it, shielded within it.

He was *in* the house, and others were not. He had seen new things, the details of which were still a muddle to him, most even without words to call them or recall them, without comparisons to which to join them, only some that her tapes had given him. He had been with her in places far more important than even those powerful rich men had been, that society which drifted through the salon of the *Jewel,* offering snippets of their lives to his confused inspection, a stream dark before and dark after. He had gone out, into that unimaginable width in which born-men lived, and *she* was there, so that he was never lost.

He had stood back over the pens, which he had half-forgotten, as all that time before the *Jewel* was confused in his memory, hard to touch from the present, for it had been so empty, so void of detail. Today he had looked down, as he had looked down in earlier times, and known that he was not on his way back from exercise, to return again to the pens and the half-world of the tapes breathing through his mind. This time he had come to look, and to walk away again, at *her* back, until the stink purged itself into clean air and light. There was no fear of that place again, forever.

She prevented.

She was there, in the night, in the dark, when his dreams were of being alone, within the walls, and only the white glare of spotlights above the tangled webs of metal, the catwalks . . . when one huddled in the corner, because the walls were at least some touch, somewhere to put one's back and feel comforted. On the azi-deck everyone slept close, trying to gain this feeling, and the worst thing was being Out, and no one willing to touch. Being Out had been the most terrible part of the long voyage here, when he had borne the Kontrin like a mark on him, and no one had dared come near him. But she did . . . and more than that, more even than the few passengers who had engaged him for a night or even a short voyage, several with impulses to generosity and one that he tried never to remember . . . she stayed. The rich folk had let him touch, had shown him impressions of experiences and luxury and other things forever beyond an azi's reach; each time he would believe for a while in the existence of such things, in comfort beyond the blind nestlings-together on the azi-deck. *Love,* they would say; but then the rich folk would go their way, and his contract rested with the ship forever, where the only lasting warmth was that of all azi, whatever one could gain by doing one's work and going to the mats at night In with everyone, nestled close.

Then there was Raen. There was Raen, who was all these things, and who had his contract, and who was therefore forever.

Warm from the shower he lay down between the cool sheets, and thought of her, and stared at the clouds which flickered lightnings over the dome, at rain, that spotted the dome and fractured the lightnings in runnels.

He had no liking for thunder. He had never had, from the first that he had worked his year in Andra's fields, before the *Jewel*. He liked it no better now. Nonsense ran through his head, fragments of deepstudy. He recited them silently, shuddering at the lightnings.

> *To some eyes, colors are invisible;*
> *To others, the invisible has many colors.*
> *And both are true. And both are not.*
> *And one is false. And neither is.*

He squeezed shut his eyes, and saw majat; and the horrid naked azi, the bearers of blue lights; and an azi who was no azi, but a born-man who had gone mad in the pens, listening to azi-tapes. The lights above the pens had never flickered; sounds were rare, and all meaningful.

The lightning flung everything stark white; the thunder followed, deafening. He jumped, and lay still again, his heart pounding. Again it happened. He was ready this time, and did not flinch overmuch. He would not have her to know that he was afraid.

She delayed coming. That disturbed him more than the thunder.

He slept finally, of sheer exhaustion.

He wakened at a noise in the room, that was above the faint humming of the majat. Raen was there; and she did not go to the bath as she had on the nights before, but moved about fully dressed, gathering things quietly together.

"I'm awake," he said, so that she would not think she had to be quiet.

She came to the bed and sat down, reached for his hand as he sat up, held it. The jewels on the back of hers glittered cold and colorless in the almost-dark. Rain still spattered the dome, gently now, and the lightnings only rarely flickered.

"I'm leaving the house," she said softly. "A short trip, and back again. You're safest here on this one."

"No," he protested at once, and his heart beat painfully, for *no* was not a permitted word. He would have made haste to disengage himself from the sheets, to gather his own belongings as she was gathering hers.

She held his arm firmly and shook her head. "I need you here. You've skills necessary to run this house. What would Max do without you to tell him what to do? What would the others do who depend on his orders? You're not afraid of the majat. You can manage them, better than some Kontrin."

He was enormously flattered by this, however much he was shaking at the thought. He knew that it was truth, for she said it.

"Where are you going?" he asked.

"A question? You amaze me, Jim."

"Sera?"

"And you must spoil it in the same breath." She smoothed his hair from his face, which was a touch infinitely kind, taking away the sting of her disappointment in him. "I daren't answer your question, understand? But call the Tel estate if you must contact me. Ask comp for Isan Tel. Can you do that?"

He nodded.

"But you do that only in extreme emergency," she said. "You understand that?"

He nodded. "I'll help you pack," he offered.

She did not forbid him that. He gathered himself out of bed, reached for a robe against the chill of the air-conditioning. She turned the lights on, and he wrapped the robe about himself, pushed the hair out of his eyes and sought the single brown case she asked for.

In truth she did not pack much; and that encouraged him, that most of her belongings would remain here, and she would come back for them, for him. He was shivering violently, neatly rearranging the things she threw in haphazardly.

"There's no reason to be upset," she said sharply. "There's no cause. You can manage the house. You can trust Max to keep order outside, and you can manage the inside."

"Who's going with you?" he asked, thinking of that suddenly, chilled to think of her alone with new azi, strange azi.

"Merry and a good number of the new guards. They'll serve. We're taking Mundy, too. You won't have to worry about him. We'll be back before anything can develop."

He did not like it. He could not say so. He watched her take another, heavier cloak from the closet. She left her blue one. "These azi," he said, "these—*strange* azi—"

"Majat azi."

"How can I talk to them?" he exclaimed, choked with revulsion at the thought of them.

"They speak. They understand words. They'll stay with the majat. They *are* majat, after a fashion. They'll fight well if they must. Let the majat deal with their own azi; tell Warrior what you want them to do."

"I can't recognize which is which."

"No matter with majat. Any Warrior is Warrior. Give it taste and talk to it; it'll respond. You're not going to freeze on me, are you? You won't do that."

He shook his head emphatically.

She clicked her case shut. "The car's ready downstairs. Go back to bed. I'm sorry. I know you want to go. But it's as I said: you're more useful here."

She started away.

"*Raen.*" He forced the word. His face flushed with the effort.

She looked back. He was ashamed of himself. His face was hot and he had no control of his lips and he was sick at his stomach for reasons he could not clearly analyze, only that one felt so when one went against Right.

"A wonder," she murmured, and came back and kissed him on the mouth. He hardly felt it, the sickness was so great. Then she left, hurrying down the stairs, carrying her own luggage because he had not thought in time to offer. He went after her, down the stairs barefoot . . . stood useless in the downstairs hall as she hastened out into the rainy dark with a scattering of other azi.

Majat were there, hovering near the car with a great deal of booming and humming to each other. Max was there; Merry was driving. There were vehicles that did not belong to the house, trucks which the other azi boarded, carrying their rifles. Merry turned the car for the gate and the trucks followed.

Max looked at him. He thrust his hands into the pockets of his bathrobe and looked nervously about. "Everything goes on as usual," he told Max. "Guard the house." And he went inside then, closed the door after him, . . . saw huge shapes deep in the shadows, the far reaches of the hall, heard sounds below.

He was alone with them. He crossed the hall toward the stairs and one stirred, that could have been a piece of furniture. It clicked at him.

"Be still," he told it, shuddering. "Keep away!"

It withdrew from him, and he fled up the stairs, darted into the safety of the bedroom.

One had gotten in. He saw the moving shadow, froze as it skittered near him, touched him. "Out!" he cried at it. "Go out!"

It left, clicking nervously. He felt after the light switch, trembling, fearing the dark, the emptiness. The room leapt into stark white and green. He closed the door on the dark of the hall, locked it. There were noises downstairs, scrapings of furniture, and deeper still, at the foundations. He did not want to know what happened there, in that dark, in that place where the strange azi were lodged.

He was human, and they were not.

And yet the same labs had produced them. The tapes . . . were the difference. He had heard the man Itavvy say so: that in only a matter of days an azi could be diverted from one function to another. A born-man put in the pens had come out shattered by the experience.

I am not real, he thought suddenly, as he had never thought in his life. *I am only those tapes.*

And then he wiped at his eyes, for tears blinded him, and he went into the bath and was sick, protractedly, weeping and vomiting in alternation until he had thrown up all his supper and was too weak to gather himself off the floor.

When he could, when he regained control of his limbs, he bathed repeatedly in disgust, and finally, wrapped in towels, tucked up in a knot in the empty bed, shivering his way through what remained of the night.

6

THE FREIGHT-SHUTTLE bulked large on the apron, a dismal half-ovoid on spider legs, glistening with the rain, that puddled and pocked the ill-repaired field and reflected back the floodlights.

There were guards, a station just inside the fence. Raen ordered the car to the very barrier and received the expected challenge. "Open," she radioed back, curt and sharp. "Kontrin authorization. And hurry about it."

She had her apprehensions. There could be delays; there could be complications; ITAK could prove recalcitrant at this point. The azi with her were untried, all but Merry. As for Mundy, in the truck behind . . . she reckoned well what he would do if he could.

The gates swung open. "Go," she told Merry.

Her own aircraft, guarded by ITAK, was at the other end of the port. She ignored it, as she had always intended to ignore it, simply giving ITAK a convenient target for sabotage if they wished one.

It was the shuttle she wanted. Beta police and a handful of guard-azi were not sufficient to stop her, if her own azi kept their wits about them.

Shuttle-struts loomed up in the windshield. Merry braked and half-turned, and the truck did so too, hard beside them. Raen contacted the station again. "Have the shuttle drop the lift," she ordered. There were guards pelting across the apron toward them, but her own azi were out of the truck, forming a hedge of rifles, and that advance slowed abruptly.

Evidently the call went through. The shuttle's freight lift lowered with a groaning of hydraulics that drowned other sound, a vast column with an open side, lighted within.

"Crew is not aboard," she heard over the radio. "Only ground watch. We can't take off. We're not licensed—"

"Merry," she said, ignoring the rest of it. "Get a squad aboard and take controls. Have them call crew and ground service to get this thing off, and take no argument about it. Shoot as last resort. . . . move! My azi," she said into the microphone, "will board. No resistance and there'll be no damage."

Merry had bailed out of the car and gathered the nearest squad. She opened the door, the gun in one hand, microphone in the other. Other figures exited the truck, dragging one who resisted: Mundy; stilt-limbed ones followed. The police line disordered itself, steadied.

"Kontrin," a voice said over the radio, "please. We are willing to cooperate."

Rain blew in the open door of the car, drenched her, slanted down across the floodlights, hazing the stalemated lines. Mundy fought and cursed, disturbing the momentary silence: nuisance, nothing more. Police would not move for so slight a cause, not against a Kontrin; policy would work on higher levels.

There was a sound of machinery inside the open cargo lift: the lights were extinguished . . . Merry's orders. They would make no targets.

Shadows passed the car: the three Warriors skittered over the wet pavement and into the lift, following their own sight, that cared nothing for darkness.

No one moved. An inestimable time later she heard Merry's voice over the radio advising her they had the ship.

She left the car. "By squads," she shouted. "Board!"

She went with the first, that drew Mundy along with them—reached the dark security of the lift. Mundy screamed at the police, a voice swiftly muffled again. The next ten started their retreat.

"Be still," she said, annoyed by continued struggles from the Outsider. "They'll do nothing for you. Don't try my patience."

The last squad was coming in, rifles still directed at the police. Her attention was fixed on that. And suddenly there was another truck coming. She expelled a long breath of tension, held it again as the truck scattered bewildered police, as it came straight for the cargo lift and jolted up within, rain-wet and loud, the azi with her dodging it. More of her men poured from it, dragging prisoners.

Tallen. They had got him, and all his folk. She found her heart able to beat stably again, and shouted orders as the truck backed out again. It almost clipped the hatch, missed. The azi driver bailed out while it was still moving and raced for the hatch, pelted aboard.

She hit the close-switch, and the lift jolted up, taking them up, while the ITAK police gazed at the diminishing view of them. Just at total dark, she hit the lights, and looked over the azi and the Warriors and the shaken prisoners.

"Ser Tallen," she said, and nodded toward Tom Mundy, who had no joy to see his own people. Pity took her, for Mundy turned his face away as far as he could, and when she bade Tallen released to see to him, Mundy wanted only to turn away, a shaven ghost in gray.

"You're going home," she said to Tallen. She had no time for other things. She gave brief orders to an older azi, setting him in charge, and set herself in the personnel lift, rode it up to more immediate problems.

A nervous pointing of weapons welcomed her above; she waved them aside and looked past Merry to the watch crew, who huddled under the threat of guns, away from controls, in the small passenger compartment.

"Kontrin," the officer-in-charge said, and rose: the azi let him. He was, she noted, ISPAK, not ITAK. "We've done everything requested."

"Thank you. Come forward, ser, and run me some instrument checks; I suppose that you can do that, until the crew shows."

The ISPAK beta wiped at his face and came with her, well-guarded, showed her the functioning of the board; it was exceedingly simple, lacking a number of convenient automations. Outside, there was the ministration of ground-service. That, she reflected, simply had to be trusted: one simply minimized the chances.

She settled into the nearest of the cushions, folded her arms and closed her eyes as the first touch of dawn began to show, for she was robbed of sleep this night, and she reckoned that this frightened beta would hardly risk anything with so many armed azi at her back.

Then crew arrived, with a flurry of distressed calls to the bridge; they were no more relaxed by the time they had negotiated the personnel lift, past the azi below and the Warriors with them, and into the upper level to the welcome of Merry's armed squad.

"Just do your job," Raen advised them. They settled in, speaking only in fragments and that when they must. "We're not scheduled," was the captain's only protest. "We may not have a berth up there."

"We'll get one," Raen said. She reached for the com switch herself, requested lift clearance, obtained it, priority. If traffic was in the way, it would be diverted or aborted. The shuttle's engines were in function; it settled earthward as its stilts drew in, and engaged its moving-gear, trundled ponderously out toward the lifting area.

"Merry," she asked of the passenger area. "All right back there?"

"Yes, sera."

"Have Tallen up after lift. Strict security on the rest."

They were entering position, wings extruding, gathering speed. Then wings locked, and they made their run. "Use the handholds," she remembered to snap at the azi still standing, and they left the ground, under heart-dragging acceleration.

Pol, she thought in that vulnerable moment, Pol was on-world, ship-based—could down a shuttle if he would, if she had guessed wrong; and there was ISPAK to contend with. She doubted then, whether she should not have gone back to ISPAK at once, taken it first, instead of delaying on-world.

But there was also blue-hive. Principally, there was blue-hive.

They passed the worst of lift, launched on an angled ascent that would carry them at last to intercept with station. The deck would slant for the duration. "Rest," she bade the standing azi, lest they tire, "half at a time. Sit down." They settled, by their own way of choosing, but all kept weapons ready, and held to the safety grips, for the sensation of flight was new to them.

The lift had activated: she saw the indication on the board, and left her cushion, negotiated her way back to it.

Tallen. An armed azi escorted the man, and waited while he caught the handhold and exited the lift . . . no pleasant sensation, the personnel lift during flight, and the man was old—not as Kontrin aged, Raen thought sorrowfully, but as betas did. It was sad to understand.

"Apologies, ser," she welcomed him. "Are your folk all right?"

"Our rooms raided, ourselves handled as we were——"

"Apologies," she said in a cold voice. "But no regrets. You're off Istra. You're alive. Be grateful, ser."

"What's going on?"

"There are very private affairs of the Reach involved here, ser Outsider." She gestured him into the corner by the passenger compartment, where they could stand more comfortably, and waited until he had braced himself. "Listen to me: you were not well-advised to have cut off my warning. You've Mundy back; you've information, for what it's worth. But you've killed the others. You understand that. It's too late for them. Listen to me now, and save something. Your spies have not been effective, have they?"

"I don't know what you're talking about."

"You do, ser. You do. And the only protection you have is myself, ser. The betas surely can't offer you any, whatever their assurances to the contrary."

"Betas."

"Betas. Beta generation. The children of the labs, ser. The plastic civilization."

"The eggs." Comprehension came to his eyes. "The children of the eggs."

"They're set up to obey. We've conditioned them to that. Do you understand the pattern you see now? Your spies haven't helped you. You've dropped them into the vast dark, ser, and they're gone, swallowed up in the Reach."

"These——" he looked about him at the guards. "These creatures——"

"Don't," she said, offended. "Don't misname them. The azi are quite as human as the betas, ser. And unlike the betas, they're quite aware they're programmed. They've no illusions, but they deserve respect."

"And you go on creating them. You've pushed a world to the breaking point. Why?"

"I think you suspect, ser Tallen; and yet you go on feeding them. No more. No more."

"Be clear, Kont' Raen."

"You've understood. You've been gathering all the majat goods we and the betas can sell you, swallowing them up, shipping them out. Warehousing them—against a time of shortage, if you've been wise, taking what you could get while you could get it. But to do that, you've been doing the worst thing you could have done. You've been feeding the force that means to expand out of the Reach. And worse, ser, much worse—you've been feeding the hives. This generation for industrialization, the next for the real move. And you've fed it."

He turned a shade yet paler than he had been. "What do you propose, Kont' Raen?"

"Shut down. Shut down trade for a few years. Now. The Reach can't support these numbers. The movement will collapse under its own weight."

"What's your profit in telling us?"

"Call it internal politics."

"It's mad. How do we know what authority you have to do this?"

She lifted a hand toward the azi. "You see it. I could have handled this otherwise. I could have pulled licenses. But that wouldn't have told you why. I am telling you now. I mean what I say, ser: that your continued trade is supplying a force that will try to break out of the Reach. That a few years of deprivation will destroy that hope and make a point to them. We're not without our vulnerabilities. Yours is the need for what we alone supply. But you've been oversupplied in these last few years. You can survive a time of shut-down. I assure you you can't come in and *take* these things: trying to take them would destroy the source of them . . . or worse things . . ." She looked directly into his eyes. "You would stand where we do, and be what we are."

"How can I carry a report to my authorities based on one person's word? There's another of your people on Istra. We've heard. This could be an attempt to prevent our contacting—"

"Ah, he'd tell you differently, perhaps. Or perhaps he'd shrug and say do as pleased you. *His* reasons you'd not understand at all."

"You play games with us. Or maybe you have other motives."

"Invade us. Come in with your ships. Fire on betas and innocent azi, break through to Cerdin and take all that we have. Then where will you be? The hives won't deal with minds-that-die; no, they'll lead you in directions you don't anticipate. I give you a hive-master's advice, ser, that I've withheld from others. Is it not so, that your desperation is because you need us? Your technology relies on what we produce? And do we not serve well? You're safe, because we know well what we do. Now a hive-master says: stop, wait, danger, and you take it for deception."

"Get my agents out."

She shook her head. "It's too late. I've given you warning. A decade or two, ser. An azi generation. A time of silence. Believe me now. We'll get you to your ships. A chance to run, to get out of here with what lives I can give you."

He stared at her. The ship was already coming into release from Istra's gravity, and there was a feeling of instability. She beckoned him toward the lift.

"Believe me," she said. "It's the only gift I can give. And whatever you do, you'd best get down to your people, ser Tallen. They'll wonder. They'll need your advice. See it's the right advice. My men will let you free, and you'll do what you please on that dock."

Tallen gave her a hard and long look, and sought the lift; the guard went with him.

Raen hand-over-handed her way back to the cushion, scanned instruments, looked at the crew. "Put us next the Outsider ships. If we need to clear a berth, we'll do that."

The captain nodded, and she settled, arms folded, with station communications beginning to hurl frantic questions at them.

7

"IT'S SETTLED," the Ren-barant said.

The Hald looked about him in the swirl of brightly clad heads of septs and Houses, and at the Thel, the Delt, the Ilit and others of the inner circle. Here were the key votes, the heads of various factions. They went armed into Council, remembering Moth, remembering another day. Ros Hald felt more than a touch of fear.

"I don't trust the old woman," the Ilit said. "I won't feel easy until this is past." His eyes darted left and right, his voice lowered. "This could as easily be a way to identify us, eliminate the opposition. We could go the way the others did, even yet."

"No," Ros Hald said fiercely. "No. Easiest of all if she gives over the keys we need. She'll do that. She's buying living time and she knows it."

"Then she knows other things too," said the Delt.

Hald thought of that, as he had thought of it a hundred times, and saw no other course. The others were filing into the Council chamber. He nodded to his companions and went.

The seats were filled, one by one, with nervous men and women, heirs of the last purge.

Doubtless there were many weapons concealed now, within robes of Color of House and sept.

But when Moth entered, and all those present rose in respect—even the Hald and his faction rose, because respect cost nothing—she had Tand for her support and seemed incredibly frail. Before now, she had doddered somewhat; now she had difficulty even lifting her head to speak before Council.

"I don't trust this," the Ren-barant whispered, fell silent at the press of the Hald's hand.

"I have come to a difficult decision," Moth began, and rambled on about the weight of empire and the changes in the Council, which had cast more and more weight on First Seat, which had made of her the dictator she avowed she would not be, that none of them had meant to be.

Her voice faltered and faded often. The Council listened with rare patience, though none of this was at all surprising, for Tand and rumor had spread her intent throughout the Family, even into factions which would not have been powerful enough to have their own spies. There could not be a representative present that did not know the meaning of this meeting.

She spoke of the hives, ramblings of which they were even yet patient.

And suddenly she began to laugh, so that more than one hand in the hall felt after a weapon and her life hung on a thread; but her own two hands were in sight, and one had to wonder who her agents were and where they might be positioned.

"The hives, my friends, my cousins—the hives have come asking and offering now, have they? And the hive-masters divided on the question, and now they're gone. I'm tired. I am tired, cousins. I see what you don't see, what no one else is old enough to see, and no one cares to see." She looked about, blinking in the glare of lights, and Ros Hald tensed, wondering about weapons. "Vote," she said. "You've come here ready, have you not, already prepared, not waiting on me? Not waiting for long debate? You've been ready for years. So vote. I'm going to my chambers. Tell me which of you will share responsibility for the Family. I'll accept your choice."

There was a murmur, and silence; she looked about at them, perhaps surprised by that silence, that was a touch of awe. And in that
silence, Moth turned off the microphone, and walked up the steps
among them, slowly, on Tand's arm, in profound stillness.

Ros Hald rose. So did Ren-barant, and Ilit, and Serat and Dessen
and all the many, many others. For a moment, at the top of the
stairs, Moth stopped, seeming to realize the gesture, and yet did not
turn to see. She walked out, and the door closed. The standing heads
of House and sept sank down again into seats. The silence continued
a moment.

Next-eldest rose and declared the matter at hand, the nomination
of one to stand by Moth, successor to Moth's knowledge and position. The dictatorship which had become fact without acknowledgment under Lian's last years, became acknowledged fact now,
with Moth's request for a legal heir.

Ren-barant rose to put forward the name of Ros Hald.

There was no name put in opposition. A few frowned, huddled together. Ros Hald marked them with his eyes, the next group that
would try for power in the Family, the next that needed watching.
Four Colors were not represented today; four Houses were in
mourning. The opposition had no leaders.

"The vote," next-eldest asked.

The signs flashed to the board. No opposition, seven abstentions,
four absent.

It was fact.

A cheer went up from Council, raucous and harsh after the long
silence.

8

THE SHUTTLE DOCKED, jolted into lock next to one of the Outsider
vessels. The azi caught at support, and one fell—shame-faced,
recovered his footing. "All right, all right," Raen comforted him,
touching his shoulder, never taking her eyes from the crew. "Squad
two, stay with this ship and keep your guns aimed at the crew. They
may try to trick you; you're quite innocent of some maneuvers, fresh

as you are from Registry. Don't reason. Just shoot if they touch anything on that control panel."

"Yes, sera," said the squad leader, who had seen service before. The crew stayed frozen. She gathered up Merry and squad one and rode the overcrowded lift down to the lock, where the other squads and the Warriors stood guard over the Outsiders.

They were free of restraint, Tallen and his folk, huddled in a corner with the guns of eighty-odd azi to advise them against rashness. Raen beckoned them to her and they came, cautiously, across the dark cavern of the hold. One of their own men had Mundy in hand, had him calmed, had restored him to a fragile human dignity, and Mundy glared at her with hate: no matter to her. He was neither help nor harm.

"We're going out," she said to Tallen. "Ser, there's one of your ships beside us and its hatch is open. We've warned them. When you're aboard, take my advice and pull all Outsider ships from station as quickly as you can undock. Run for it."

Tallen's seamed face betrayed disturbance, as it betrayed little. "That far, is it?"

"I've risked considerable to get you here. I've given you free what you spent men to learn. Believe *me,* ser, because from the agents the Reach has swallowed you'll *never* hear. If it's clear they're not azi, they'll perish as assassins, one by one. It's our natural assumption. I'll give you as much time as I can to get clear of station. But don't expect too much, ser."

Merry was by the switch. She signalled. He opened up to the ramp.

It was as she remembered the dock, vast and shadowy and cold, an ugly place. Security agents and armored ISPAK police ringed the area. She walked out, her own azi about her, rifles slung hip-level from the shoulder. She wore no Color, but plain beige, no sleeve-armor. It was likely that they knew with whom they had to deal, all the same, for all the terseness of the messages she had returned their anxious inquiries.

Next to them, the Outsider ship waited. "Go," she told Tallen, whose group followed. "Get over there, before something breaks loose here."

He delayed. She saw in surprise that he offered his hand, publicly. "Kont' Raen," he said, "can *we* help *you?*"

"No," she said, shaken by the realization of finality. Her eyes went to the Outsider's ramp, the lighted interior.

To go with them, to see, to know—

Their duty forbade. And so did something she vaguely conceived as her own. She found tears starting from her eyes, that were utterly unaccustomed.

"Just get out of here," she said, breaking the grip. "And believe me."

He apparently did, for he walked away quickly then, and his people with him, as quickly as could not be called a run. They reached the ramp, rode it up. The hatch sealed after.

Raen folded her arms within her cloak, the one hand still holding her gun, and stared at the ISPAK security force, which her own azi faced with lowered weapons. Breath frosted in the icy air.

"Sera," one called to her. "ISPAK board has asked to see you. Please. We will escort you."

"I will see them here," she said, "on the dock."

There was consternation among them. Several in civilian dress consulted with each other and one made a call on his belt unit. Raen stood still, shivering with the chill and the lack of sleep, while they proposed debate.

She was too tired. She could not bear the standing any longer. Her legs were shaking under her. "Stand your ground," she bade the azi. "Fire only if fired upon. Tell them I'll come down when the board arrives. Watch them carefully."

And quietly she withdrew, leaving Merry in charge on the dock, trusting his sense and experience. In the new azi she had little confidence; they would not break, perhaps, if it came to a fire fight, but they would die in their tracks quite as uselessly.

She touched the Warriors who hovered in the hatchway, calming them. "We wait," she said, and went on to the lift, to the bridge, to the security of the unit which guarded the crew and the comfort of a place to sit.

Likely, she thought, *they'll arrive at the dock now, now that I've come all this way up.*

They did not. She reached past the frozen crew and punched in station operations, listened to the chatter, that at the moment was frantic. Outsider ships were disengaging from dock one after the other, necessitating adjustments, three, four of them, five, six. She grinned, and listened further, watched them on the screens as they came within view, every Outsider in the Reach kiting outward in a developing formation.

Going home.

A new note intruded, another accent in station chatter. She detected agitation in beta voices.

She pirated their long-scan, and froze, heart pounding as she saw the speed of the incoming dot, and its bearing.

She keyed outside broadcast. "Merry! Withdraw. Withdraw everyone into the ship at once."

The dot advanced steadily, ominous by its speed near a station, cutting across approach lanes.

They would not have sent any common ship, not if it were in their power to liberate a warship for the purpose. Swift and deadly, one of the never-seen Family warships: Istra station was in panic.

And the Outsider ships were freighters, likely unarmed.

"Sera!" Merry's voice came over the intercom. "We're aboard!"

A light indicated hatch-operation.

"Back off," Raen said to the beta captain. "Undock us and get us out of here."

He stared into the aperture of her handgun and hastened about it, giving low-voiced orders to his men.

"Drop us into station-shadow," Raen said. "And get us down, fast."

The captain kept an eye to the incoming ship, that had not yet decreased speed. Station chatter came, one-sided—ISPAK informing the incoming pilot the cluster formation was Outsider, that no one understood why.

For the first time there was deviation in the invader's course, a veering toward the freighters.

The shuttle drifted free now, powering out of a sudden, in shadow.

"Put us in his view," Raen ordered. The captain turned them and did so, crossing lanes, but nothing around the station was moving, only themselves, the freighters, and the incomer.

Raen took deep breaths, wondering whether she should have gambled everything, a mad assault on station central, to seize ISPAK . . . trusting the warship would not fire.

It fired now. Outsiders must not have heeded orders to stop. She picked it up visually, swore under her breath; the Outsiders returned fire: one of that helpless flock had some kind of weapon. It was a mistake. The next shot was real.

She punched in numbers, snatched a microphone. "Kontrin ship! This is the Meth-maren. You're forbidden station."

The invader fired no more shots. He was, perhaps, aware of another mote on his screens; he changed course, leaving pursuit of Outsiders.

"It's coming for us!" a beta hissed.

Raen scanned positions, theirs, the warship's, the station's, the world. In her ear another channel babbled converse with the invader. *Shuttle* . . . she heard. *One onworld . . . one aloft . . . Plead with you . . .*

"Sera," the captain moaned.

"It can't land," she said. "Head us for Istra."

They applied thrust and tumbled, applied a stabilizing burst and started their run.

"Shadow!" Raen ordered, and they veered into it, shielded by station's body, at least for the instant.

"We can't do it," someone said. "Sera, please—"

"Do what it can't do," she said. "Dive for it." Her elbow was on the rest; she leaned her hand against her lips, found it cold and shaking. There was nothing to do but ride it through. The calculation had been marginal, an unfamiliar ship, a wallowing mote of a shuttle, diving nearly headlong for Istra's deep.

Metal sang; instruments jumped and lights on the board flicked red, then green again. "That was fire," Raen commented, swallowing heavily. A voice in her ear was pleading with the invader. The shuttle's approach-curve graph was flashing panic.

They hit atmosphere. Warning telltales began flashing; a siren began a scream and someone killed it.

"We're not going to make it," the captain said between his teeth. He was working desperately, trying to engage a failed system. "Wings won't extend." The co-pilot took over the effort with admirable coolness, trying again to reset the fouled system.

"Pull in and try again," Raen said. The beta hit retract, waited, lips moving, hit the sequence again. Of a sudden the lights greened, the recalcitrant wings began to spread, and the betas cried aloud with joy.

"Get us down, blast you!" Raen shouted at them, and the ship angled, heart-dragging stress, every board flashing panic.

They hit a roughness of air, rumbling as if they were rolling over stone, but the lights started winking again to green.

"Shall we die?" an azi asked of his squad leader.

"It seems not yet," squad-leader answered.

Raen fought laughter, that was hysteria, and she knew it. She clung to the armrest and listened to the static that filled her ear, stared with mad fixation on the hands of the terrified betas and on the screens.

Pol, she kept thinking, *Pol, Pol, Pol, blast you, another lesson.*

Or it was for him also, too late.

9

"So it's you," Moth said, leaned back in her chair, wrapped in her robes. She stared up at Ros Hald, with Tand; and the Ren-barant, the Ilit. "It's Halds, is it?"

"Council's choice," Ros Hald said.

Moth gave a twisted smile. She had seen the four vacant seats, action taken before she had even announced her intent. "Of course you are," she said, and did not let much of the sarcasm through. "You're welcome, very welcome beside me, Ros Hald. Tand, go find some of the staff. We should offer hospitality to my partner-in-rule."

Tand went. Ros Hald kept watching her nervously. That amused her. "What," she asked, "do you imagine I've let you be chosen . . . to arrange your assassination, to behead the opposition?"

Of course it occurred to him, to all of them. They would all be armed.

"But I was sincere," she said. "I shall be turning more and more affairs into your hands."

"Access," he said, "to all records."

You've managed that all along, she thought, smiling. *Bastard!*

"And," he said, "to all levels of command, all the codes."

She swept a hand at the room, the control panels, the records. The hand shook. She was perpetually amazed by her own body. She had been young—so very long; but flesh in this last age turned traitor, caused hands to shake, voice to tremble, joints to stiffen. She could not make a firm gesture, even now. "There," she said.

And fired.

The Hald fell, the Ilit; the Ren-barant fired and burned her arm, and she burned him, to the heart. Tand appeared in the doorway, hung there, mouth open.

And died.

"Stupid," she muttered, beginning then to feel the pain. The stench was terrible. She felt of her own arm, feeling damage; but the right one had not been the strong one, not for a long time.

Azi servants crept in finally. "Clear this out," she said. Her jaw trembled. She closed the door when they had gone, and locked it. There was food secreted about, an old woman's senile habit; there was wine, bottles of it; there was the comp center.

She sat, rocking with the pain of her wound, smiling to herself without mirth.

10

THE GROUND WAS COMING up fast and the air was full of burning. They broke through haze and came in over bleak land, desert. It was not what the display showed on the screen; the ship's computer was fouled. The sweating betas labored over the board, retaining control over the ship, jolting them with bursts of the braking engines. There was no knowing where they were; cloud and panic had obscured that. They might yet land.

And all at once a mountain wall loomed up in front of them, vast beyond reason.

"Blast!" Raen shouted. "Altitude, will you?"

"That's the High Range," one of the betas said. "The winds—the winds—the shuttle's not built for it, Kontrin."

"We're on the way home, we're over East, blast you: take us up and get over it!"

The deck slanted. They were launching themselves for what altitude they could gain for that sky-reaching ridge. A beta cursed softly, and wept. The High Range loomed up, snow-crowned. Jagged peaks thrust up above the clouds which wreathed them. The mad thought came to Raen that if one must die, this was at least a thing worth seeing—that such a glorious thing existed, uncultivated by Kontrin, who hungered after new things: hers.

Istra, the High Range, the desert—all explored, all possessed, in this mad instant of ripping across the world.

The azi were silent, frozen in their places. The crew worked frantically, sighted their slot in that oncoming wall and aimed for it, the lowest way, between two peaks.

"No!" Raen cried, reckoning the winds that must howl down that funnel. She hit the captain's arm and pointed, a place where needle-spires thrust against the sky—cursed and insisted, having flown more worlds than earthbound betas knew. He veered, tried it, through turbulence that jolted them. Needles reared up in the screens. Someone screamed.

They went over, whipped over that needled ridge and sucked down a slope that wrung outcries from born-men and azi, down-drafted, hurtling down a vast rock face and outward. She saw spires in the slot they had not taken, reckoned with a wrench at the stomach what they had narrowly done.

"Controls aren't responding," the captain muttered. "Something's jammed up."

"Take what you can," Raen said.

The man asked help; the co-pilot lent a hand, muttered something about hydraulics. Raen set her lips and stayed still the while the frantic crew tried their strength and their wits. The rocks flew under them, turned to gold and gray-green, and ahead, the white-hot flare that was water under beta Hydri's light, serpentine, the River, and horizon-wide, the Sea.

Poor chance they had if they were carried out into *that* maelstrom of Istran storms, of endless water, and glare.

The captain made the right decision: retros jolted them, and they began losing airspeed with such abruptness it felt as if they were halting midair. "Hold on," she shouted at the azi, trying not to think of belowdecks, nigh a hundred men without safety harness. The engines continued to slam at them in short bursts, until they were lumbering along at a wallowing pace and dropping by sickening lurches.

Beyond recall now, with the controls locked up.

"Merry," Raen called to below, "brace up hard down there; we're going to belly in if we're lucky."

Another lurch downward, with alternate trees and grassland before them, with sometime bursts of the engines to give them more glide, and wrestlings by manual at the attitude controls.

Hills sprang up in their path. *We'll not make it,* Raen thought, for the betas were at the end of their resources; and then the jolt of braking engines nigh took the breath out of them and they lumbered into a tilt, feathered with the attitude jets.

She braced then, for they were committed beyond recall, and the valley walls were right in front of them. The engines jolted, one and then the other, compensating for a damaged wing.

The nose kept up. Raen watched the land hurtle toward them, waiting for the contact; it hit, slewed—the straps cut in. Then the nose flew up, slammed down, and somebody hurtled past Raen on his way to the control panel. Another hit her in the back. A gun discharged.

And she remained conscious through impact, with azi bodies before her and about her, while sirens screamed and the shriek of metal testified what was happening below. She cursed through it, watching horrified as the azi in front of her bled his life out on the control panel and the betas screamed. The worse horror was that the azi did not.

And when the ship was still—when it was evident that the feared fire had not taken place, and the shriek of metal had died—there was still no outcry from the azi. Two of the betas were unconscious, a half dozen of the azi so. Raen gathered herself up on the sloping deck and looked about her. Azi faces surrounded her, calm, bewildered. The betas cursed and wept.

"We can manual this lock," Merry's voice came over the intercom. "Sera? Sera?"

She answered, looked at the betas, who had begun working at the emergency chute. Hot air and glare flooded the opened hatchway. Merry, down below, was attempting his own solution. Fire still remained a possibility.

"Get supplies," she said. "All the emergency kits." They were not going to be adequate for so many men. She opened a locker and found at least a reserve of sunsuits, lingered to put one on the while azi clambered out, and slid down—her own men, she thanked her foresight, with such clothing, and with weapons. Her own suit was in her luggage, and one of the azi had brought it, but at the moment she had no idea where it was . . . cared nothing.

Injured azi moved themselves; the betas she left to betas, and made the slide to safety, into the arms of her azi below, steadied herself and looked about: the hold chute was deployed, and men were exiting there. She staggered across the grass, angry that her knees so betrayed her, found Merry, whose battered face wept blood along a scraped cheek. "The hold—many dead?"

"Six. Some bad, sera."

So few hours, from the null of the pens, and to die, after eighteen years of preparing. She drew a deep breath and forced it out again. "Get them all out." She sat down on the grass where she was, head bowed against her knees, pulled up the sunsuit hood, adjusted her gloves, small, weary movements. They had to get clear of the ship. The ship was a target. They had to move. She shut her eyes a moment and oriented herself, slipped the visor to a more comfortable place on her nose, adjusted up the cloth about her lower face, as anonymous as the azi.

Warriors living-chained down from the hatch, hale and whole. She called to them and rose, bared a hand to identify herself. They came, humming and booming in distress at their experience, offered touch. "Life-fluids," they kept saying, alarmed by the deaths.

"Watch," she said, gesturing at all that empty horizon of fields, thinking of raided depots and murdered azi. "Let no majat come on us."

"Yess," they agreed, and hovered never far away.

An azi brought her luggage, her battered brown case, and she laughed with the touch of hysteria for that, extracted her kit of lotions and medicines and jammed those in her side pocket, cast the rest away.

The azi were all out, she reckoned. She walked among them, saw that Merry had taken her at her word, for the dead lay in a group, half a dozen not counting the one above, on the bridge; and a little apart from them were four with disabling injuries; and apart from them was a large group of wounded; and a group which bore virtually none. She looked back that course again, suddenly understanding how they were grouped, that the wounded, huddled together, simply waited, knotted up as she had seen Jim do when he was disturbed.

Waiting termination.

She cast about in distress, reckoned what would be the lot of any left in beta care. "We carry those that can't walk," she told Merry, and cursed the luck, and her softness, and turned it to curses at the hale ones, ordering the emergency litters, ordering packs made, until men were hurrying about like a disturbed hive.

And the beta captain limped to her . . . she recognized the graying brows through the mask. "Stay with the ship," he urged her.

"Stay yourself." Her head throbbed and the sun beat through the cloth; she forced herself to gentle language. "Take your chances here, ser. Kontrin feud. Stay out of it."

And seeing her own folk ready, she shouted hoarse orders and bade them move.

North.

Toward Newhope, toward any place with a computer link.

11

MORN HALD PACED the office of the ISPAK station command, waited, settled again at the console.

Such resources as the Family had at its command he called into use; a code number summoned what vessels waited at Meron, and long as it would take for the message to run via intercomp, as long as it would take those ships to reach Istra—they were as good as on their way.

He relied on the Hald for that.

The Meth-maren had provided the overt provocation the Movement needed, the chaos she had wrought at station, that elevated the matter above a feud of Houses. Panicked Outsiders were running, refusing all appeals to return—had *fired* on a Kontrin vessel. Morn's thin hands were emphatic on the keys, violent with rage.

His witness, under *his* witness the Meth-maren had managed such a thing; and he was stung in his pride. Outsiders were involved. He had hesitated between destroying them and not; and the thought of embroiling himself with that while the Meth-maren found herself escape and weapons—for that he had pulled away, to his prime target, to the dangerous one. There was no knowing in what she had her hand, where her agents were placed by now.

Revenge: she had never sought it, in all the long years, had wended her insouciant way from dissipation to withdrawal, and retaliated for only present injuries. The Family had tolerated her occasional provocations, which were mild, and seldom; and her life, which crossed none; and her style, which was palest imitation of Pol's.

Morn read the comp records and cursed, realizing the extent of what she had wrought in so few days: the azi programs disrupted, export authorizations granted, winning the allegiance of ITAK, which was therefore no longer reliable—she knew, she *knew*, and Outsiders, perhaps not the first to do so, were scattering for safety in their own space. News of that belonged in the hands of the Movement before it reached Council: he sent it, via Meron, under Istrancode, which would be intercepted.

So she might have launched instructions to Meron, to Andra, to whatever places an agent might have become established over two decades. They had worked to prevent it, had found no agent of the Meth-maren in all the years of their observation; and that, considering what she had done on Istra, disturbed all his confidence.

Betas hovered distressedly in the background of the command center, as yet simply dazed by the passage of events—betas who had learned to avoid his anger. But any of them—any of them—could be hers. His own azi stood among them, armored and armed, discouraging rashness.

To disentangle a Kontrin from a world was no easy matter. It was one which he did not, in any fashion, relish. His own style was more subtle, and quieter.

He put in a second call to Pol, waited the reasonable time for it to have relayed wherever he was lodged, and for Pol to have responded. He kept at it, sat with his chitined hand pressed against his lips, staring balefully at the flickering screen.

SALUTATIONS, the answer came back.

He punched in vocal, his own face instead of the Kontrin serpent that masked his other communications; Pol's came through on his screen, mirror-wise, but Pol's was smiling.

"Don't be light with me, cousin," Morn said. "Where are you?"

"Newport."

"She's been here," Morn said. "Was here to meet me, as you were not."

Pol's face went sober. He quirked a brow, looked offended. "I confess myself surprised. A meeting, then, not productive."

"Where is she based?"

"Newhope. You've not been clear. What happened?"

"She cleared in a shuttle and station picks up nothing."

"Careless, Morn."

Morn gave a cold stare to the set's eye, suffered Pol's humor as he had suffered it patiently for years. "I'm holding station, cousin, and I'll explain in detail later why *you* should have taken that precaution. It may not please you to learn. Get after her. I'd trade posts with you, but I trust you haven't been idle in your hours here."

He had sobered Pol somewhat. "Yes," Pol said. "I'll find her. Enough?"

"Enough," Morn said.

BOOK EIGHT

1

Jim WENT ABOUT the day's routines, trying to find in them reason for activity. He had washed, dressed immaculately, seen to a general cleaning for what rooms of the house were free of majat. But the sound of them filled the house, and what jobs could occupy the mind were soon done, and the day was empty. One frightened domestic azi held command of the kitchen, and together they prepared the day's meals on schedule, two useless creatures, for Jim found himself with no appetite and likely the other azi did not either, only that it was routine, and maintenance of their health was dutiful, so that they both ate.

There was supper, finally, with no cessation of the frenetic hurryings in the garden, the movements at the foundations. Night would come. He did not want to think on that.

"Meth-maren."

A Warrior invaded the doorway, and the domestic scrambled from the table over against the wall, throwing a dish to the floor in his panic. "Be still," Jim said harshly, rising. "Your contract is here and the majat won't hurt you."

And when it came farther, seeking taste and touch, he gave it. "Meth-maren azi," it identified him. "Jimmm. This-unit seeks Meth-maren queen."

"She's not here," he told it, forcing himself to steadiness for the touch of the chelae, the second brush at his lips, between the great jaws. He shuddered in spite of himself, but the conviction that it would not, after all, harm him, made it bearable—more than that, for she was gone, and the majat at least were something connected with her. He touched Warrior as he had seen her do, and calmed it.

"Need Meth-maren," it insisted. "Need. Need. Urgent."

"I don't know where she is," he said. "She left. She said she would come back soon. I don't know."

It rushed away, through the door to the garden, damaging the doorframe in its haste. Jim followed it past the demoralized house-azi, looked out into the ravaged back garden where a deepening pit delved into the earth, where the neighbor's wall had been undermined. Guard-azi stood their posts faithfully, but as close to the azi quarters door as they might. He went out past the excavation, past the guards—sought Max, and having located him in the azi quarters, told him of Warrior's request, not knowing what he ought to have answered.

"We must stay here as we were told," Max concluded, his squarish face grimly set, and there was in his eyes a hint of disapproval for the azi who suggested a violation of those instructions. Jim caught it and bit off an answer, turned and hesitated in the door, irresolution gnawing at him with a persistence that made his belly hurt. The hive wanted: Raen would have been disturbed at an urgent message from the hive. She needed to know.

And he was charged simply to keep the house in order.

That was not, now, what she needed. The look that had been in her eyes when she left him had been one of worry, anxiousness, he thought wretchedly, because she must leave him in charge, *him* who could not understand the half of what he ought.

He looked back, shivering. "Max," he said.

The big guard-azi waited. "Orders?" Max asked, that being the way Raen had arranged things.

"I'm going upstairs. You're in charge down here."

"She said you were to work."

"She said I was to take care of things. I'm going upstairs. I have something to do for her. You're in charge down here. That's the order I'm giving you. I'm responsible. I'll admit to it."

Max inclined his head, accepting, and Jim strode back the way he had come, across the devastation of the garden, past the domestic azi in the kitchen, who was mopping up the broken dish—past the comp center, the screens of which flashed with messages which waited on Raen. The walls vibrated with song. Warriors hulked here and there in the dark places of the hall. A majat-azi scampered out of the farther doors, female, naked, bearing a blue light that glowed feebly in the shadow. She grinned and trailed fingers across his shoulder as she passed, and he shuddered at the madness in that laughing face. A male followed, younger than left the pens to any other service, and the same wildness was in his eyes. A whole stream of them began to pour up from the basement with a Worker behind them, fluting orders for haste.

He fled in horror, lest he be swept up with them by accident, herded with them into the dark pit outside. He ran the stairs, hurled himself into the bedroom, saw it safely vacant and locked the doors.

It was a moment before he could unknot his clenched hands and arms and straighten. One part of him did not want to go farther . . . would rather seek the corner of the room and tuck up there and cease.

Like the lower azi, when they reached the limit of their functions.

Raen needed more than that. This tall, gaunt Kontrin had come, and talked with her, and she had been distressed: the strange born-man azi had distressed her further. He understood that there were connections he could not comprehend, that perhaps she was somewhere with *him,* who was of her kind—and that in hazardous things an azi of his training was useless.

Keep the house in order.

It was far from what she needed, but it was the limit of his function. He had seen betas, who could make up what to do: Kontrin, whose function he could not conceive, but who simply *knew.* He had seen the pens and knew himself.

Dimly he realized that if Raen were lost, he would be terminated: someone had told him that they did not pass on their azi; but he failed to take alarm at that. He thought should that happen, he would simply sit down and wait for termination, out of interest in other things, without further use. There was an unfamiliar tightness in his throat that had bided there most of the day, a tenseness that would not go away.

Be calm, old tapes echoed in his mind. *Calm is always good. When you cannot be calm, you are useless. A useless azi is nothing. Turn off all disturbance. Instruction will come. You are blameless if you are calm and waiting for instruction.*

Next came the punishment, if he let the emotion well up, the in-built nausea. He was shaking, torn between the tightness in his throat and the sickness which heaved at his stomach, and knew that if he let the one go, the other would follow. He had no time for this. He fought down the hysteria with a simple exercise of self-distraction, refusing to think in the direction of his feelings. *Calm, calm, calm is good. Good is happy. Happy is useful. Good azi are always useful.*

He busied himself at once, taking the deepstudy unit out of the closet, opening the case with the tapes. *Calm, calm, calm,* he insisted to himself, for his hand shook as he deliberately chose the tapes with the black cases, the forbidden ones. The disobedience increased the pain in his stomach. *For her,* he kept telling himself; and, *Good azi are always useful,* playing one tape against the other. If he had what was in her tapes he would know what she knew; if he knew what she knew, he would understand what to do.

He propped up a divider from the case, contrived a way to brace the stack which he made in the play-slot, for they were far more than the machine was designed to hold. Focus the mind, concentrate only on the physical action: that was the means to keep calm in crisis. Never mind where the action was tending; it was only necessary to do, until all was done.

He prepared the machine. He prepared the chair, throwing over it a blanket for padding; last of all he prepared himself, stripped completely, smoothed the blanket so that there would be not the least wrinkle to crease his skin during the long collapse, and found the pill bottle where he had left it last, in the bath. He sat down then, with the pill clenched in his teeth, attached the leads. Last of all he drew the edges of the blanket over himself and swallowed the pill, waiting for the numbness to begin.

I shall change, he thought, and panic rose in him, for he had always liked the individual he was, and this was self-murder.

He felt the haziness begin, bade himself goodbye, and threw the switch—composed his arms loosely at his sides and leaned back, waiting.

The machine cycled in.

He was not unconscious; he was hyperconscious, but not of things around him—gripped and shaken by the alienness that poured in.

Attitudes. Information. Contradictions. The minds of immortals, the creators of the Reach. He absorbed until body began to scream out distantly to mind that there was hazard, and went on absorbing.

He could not want to stop, save in the small pauses where instruction ceased. Then he would try to scream for help. But he was not truly conscious, and body would not respond at all. The stream began again, and volition ceased.

2

"METH-MAREN," Mother intoned, distraught. "Find, find this queen." Workers soothed Her; Drones sang their dismay. There was/had been impression of separation, the hive-consciousness that had been established for a time stretched thin, soaring as in flight.

Then disaster.

Workers labored, frantically. The hive reached out and sought Meth-maren hive, one with it. Workers died in the stress, jaws worn away, bodies exhausted, and the husks were caught up and carried away as the work boiled forward. Azi fell beneath their burdens and drank and rested and staggered back to their work, to die there.

There was in the hive the frightened taste of a green scout, who had fallen to Warriors. Disorientation was in its hive also, the memory of Meth-marens of ages past, before the sun had risen at such an angle and the world had changed colors.

And it in turn had tasted the minds of golds, who tasted of reds, whose fierceness now had a taint of hesitancy, less push and more of fear.

"Kill," the Warrior portion of blue-Mind urged. "Restore health. Kill the unhealthy."

Drones sang of memory, and the balance of the hive shifted toward Warrior-thoughts and shifted back again to Mother, as She wrenched it to Herself, fierceness greater than theirs, for it embraced eggs, survival.

BUILD, the command went out, and the Workers hastened in frenzy.

3

THEY HUDDLED, an exhausted group, in the shade of a hedge. Raen slipped fingers under her visor and wiped sweat from her eyes, withdrew them, adjusted the rim to a new place and grimaced it back to the old. The hood of her sunsuit was back, the gloves off, the sleeves unfastened to the elbow; toward evening as it was, still the heat lingered as the residue of a furnace. The suits that saved from burn, ventilated as they were by majat-silk insets, left the skin sticky with perspiration, clung with every movement. A dead azi's rifle was on her knees, weight on sore muscles; she had food and a canteen from the emergency stores and would not drink, tormenting herself with the thought of it—supplies meant for ten, and a cluster of thirsty men about her: neither did others drink, being azi, and waiting. The wounded bore their wounds, and the insects, without a sound: it was only surprise could get an outcry from them, and there was none of that. They knew what the situation was. They were the lighter by two they had started with, the worst-wounded; the bearers had been glad, and she did not delude herself otherwise. In that day she had reconsidered her mercy, and gazed at two others as bad, and at the grasslands endless about them, and she had almost turned the gun on them. Instead she had given them a sip of water, that compounded the idiocy, and the same to the bearers: for herself and the others there was only the chance to moisten mouths and spit it back, and no one defied instructions.

She was, however long ago, of Cerdin, and Cerdin's sun was no kinder; she was, for the rest, accustomed to exercise, and most of these were not. She had Merry by her, poor Merry, his lips as cracked as hers felt, his face bruised as well as scraped; she trusted him more than the others, these babes new from the pens. Merry helped, used his wits; the others obeyed.

There was a stirring, a shrilling; they snatched rifles up nervously, but it was one Warrior, their own, that bore a white rag tied on a forelimb so that the azi could tell it. It ran low, scuttled up waving its palps and seeking scent.

"Here," Raen said, turning her hand to it. It came, offered taste, the sweet fluids of its own body, and it was welcome. She touched the scent-patches, soothed it, for it had been moving hard, and air pulsed from the chambers so it had difficulty with human speech.

"Mennn. Humannsss. Human-hive."

She gave a great breath of relief. Every face was turned toward it, faces suddenly touched with hope. She caressed the quivering palps. "Warrior, good, very good. Where are other Warriors?"

"Watching men."

"Far?"

It quivered slowly. Not far, then. "We leave the wounded and five to help them," she said. "We'll come back for you injured when we've gotten transport. I say so. Understood?"

Heads inclined, all together.

"Come on," she told Merry. "Choose those to stay and let's move."

Warrior moved ahead of their concealment, a black shape in the starlight. Likely Warrior was screaming orders; human ears could not pick it up. In a moment all three came back to the hedgerow, clicking with excitement.

"Guardss," Warrior said, with two neat bows in the appropriate directions: majat vision in the cool of night could hardly miss a human.

"No majat," Raen asked.

"Humanss. Human-hive."

Fifty men were, in the last twos, grouping behind her. Lights showed ahead, floodlights about the fields, the farmyard. An azi barracks showed light from the windows; the farm house had the same, windows barred, proof against majat.

"Door's nothing," she said to Merry. "A burn will take it. Azi won't fight if we can get the betas first."

"Take the guards out," Merry said. "Three men each, no mistakes. I'll take one."

She shook her head. "Stay by me at the door. I'll get it, ten men with me take the house, twenty round the side door. You get down by that porch and take any charge starts out the door of the barracks."

"Understood," Merry said, and orders passed, quick and terse, by units.

"No firing unless fired on," Raen said, and took the nearest Warrior by the forelimb. "Warrior: you three stay here. Guard this-place until I call."

"Warrior-function: come," it lamented.

"I order, Meth-maren, hive-friend. Necessary."

"Yess," it sighed.

"I go first," she said, to the distress of Merry and the others, but they said no word of objection. She stood up, gripped her rifle by its body, and started out into the road, dejected, limping. Her eyes, her head still downcast, flicked nervously from one to the other of the guardposts she knew were there, in the hedges.

"Stop!" someone shouted at her.

She did so, looked fecklessly in that direction, with no move of her rifle. "Accident," she said. "Aircraft went down—" and pointed back. The azi came from their concealment, both of them, naïve that they were. "I need help," she said. "I need to call help."

One of them determined to walk with her. The other stayed. She limped on toward the house, toward the door, studying the lay of the place, the situation of windows; the barracks was at her back, the porch before.

And the azi with her went up the steps ahead of her, rang at the door, pressed the housecom button. "Ser?"

Someone passed a window to the door.

"Ser, there's a woman here—"

"Istra shuttle went down," she cried past him. "Survivors. I need to call for help."

The door unlocked, opened. A graying beta stood in it. She slipped inside, leaned against the wall, whipped the rifle up.

"Don't touch the switch, ser. Don't move."

The beta froze, mouth open. The guard-azi did likewise, and in that instant a rush of men pelted across the yard. The guard whirled, found targets, fired in confusion, and the rush that hit the door threw him over, swept the beta against the wall, ringing him with weapons. Her azi kept going, and elsewhere in the house were shots and outcries. "No killing!" she shouted. "Secure the house! Go, I've got him." She held her rifle on the man, and the azi swept after their comrades.

It was a matter of moments then, the frightened family herded together into their own living room, the azi servants, one injured, along with them.

Merry held the front porch. The first shot into the azi barracks had convinced the others. Her men regrouped, meditating that problem.

"Ser," Raen said to the householder, "protect your azi. Call them out unarmed. No one will be hurt."

He did so, standing on the porch with enough rifles about to assure he made no errors. In the house, the family waited, holding to one another, the wife and a young couple that was likely related in some way, with an infant. The baby cried, and they tried to hush it.

And fearfully the farm's azi came out as they were told; she bade Merry and some of the men search the barracks and the azi themselves for weapons.

But most of all was water, food. She gave them permission as quickly as she could, and they drank their fill—brought her a cup, which she received gratefully, and a grimy fistful of dried fruit. She chewed at it and kept the rifle slung hip-level, pocketed some, drank at the water. The householder was allowed to rejoin his family on the chairs in the living room. "Ser," Raen said, "apologies. I told the truth: we've injured among us. I need food, water, transport, and your silence. You're in the midst of a Kontrin matter. —Kont' Raen, seri, with profound apologies. We'll not damage anything if we can help it."

A cluster of beta faces stared back at her, gray with terror, whether for their attack or for what she told them, she was not sure.

"Take what you want," the man said.

The baby started crying. Raen gave the child a glance and the woman gathered it to her; the injured azi touched it and tried to soothe it. Raen took a deep breath for patience and looked at the lot of them. "You've a truck here, some sort of transport?"

Heads nodded.

She went off to the center of the house, hunting comp, located it, a sorry little machine pasted with grocery notices and unexplained call-numbers. She keyed in, called the house in Newhope, the number she had arranged for emergency.

"Jim?" she called. And again: "Jim!"

There was no response.

Her hand began to shake on the board. She clenched it and leaned her mouth against it, considering in her desperation how far she could trust Itavvy or Dain or anyone else in ITAK. "Jim," she said, pleading, and swore.

There was still no response. JIM, she keyed through, to leave a written message, STAND BY. EMERGENCY.

She put the next one through to Isan Tel's estate, where a few managerial azi kept the fiction of a working estate, unsupervised azi and a horde of guards. STAND BY. EMERGENCY. EMERGENCY.

And a third one to the Labor Registry. EMERGENCY, TEL CONTRACT. PLEASE STAND BY.

None used her name. She dared not. She rose and took two of the men with her, walked out past Merry's unit to the road, and up it to the place where they had left the Warriors. They were there, fretting and anxious. "All safe," she told them. To each she gave two pieces of the dried fruit, which they greatly relished. "I need one-unit to stay with me, two for a message," she said.

"Yess," they agreed, speaking together.

"Just tell Mother what's happened. Tell her I'm coming to Newhope, but I'm slow. I need help, blue-hive azi, weapons. Fast."

There was an exchange of tones. "Good," one said. "Go now?"

"Go," she said; and two darted off with eye-blurring speed, lost at once in the night and the hedges. The other remained, shadowed her with slow-motion steps as she and her guards returned to the house.

"Merry," she said, when she had come to his group, where they huddled on the porch, tired men with rifles braced on knees toward the azi barracks. Merry gathered himself up, haggard, the light from the door showing darkly on his wounded cheek, his blond hair plastered with sweat and dust. "One of the two of us," she said hoarsely, "has to get the truck back after those men. You've land-sense. Can you do it? Are you able to? I need you back; I rely on you too much."

Pride shone in the azi's eyes. "I'll get back," he said; she had never imagined such a look of intensity from stolid Merry. It approached passion. Such expression, she saw suddenly, rested not alone in his face, but in those of others. She did not understand it. It had something to do with the tapes, she thought, and yet it was no less real, and disturbed her.

"Truck ought to be in the equipment shed. Watch yourselves, walking around out here. We think we've accounted for everyone. I haven't had time to check comp thoroughly."

"I need three men."

She nodded; Merry singled out his men and left for the side of the house. She stationed Warrior by the side of the porch by the other azi and left them so, limped up the steps and into the house, giving only a glance to the captive betas. Her legs shook under her, adrenalin drained away. She sank down and wiped her face with her hand.

"Get a water-container," she told one of the azi. And to the beta, "ser, is there a key for that vehicle?"

"By the door."

She looked and saw it hanging. "Take that to Merry," she told the azi. "Take a bit of that dried fruit too. There'll be at least some can appreciate it."

The azi gathered up the items and left, came back again; distantly there was a moaning of an engine, that turned off where the road would be: Merry was on his way.

"True that the shuttle crashed?" the beta woman asked.

Raen nodded. "Broken limbs in plenty, sera. And dead. We had a hundred men aboard that ship."

The betas' faces reflected compassion for that.

"I'm sorry," Raen said, "for breaking in. It's necessary. Your names, seri? I'd rate you compensation if it were safe. It's not, at the moment."

"Ny," the man said, nodded at his wife. "Berden. My son and his wife. Grandchild. Kontrin, you can have anything, only so you leave us all right."

"There's majat," the young man said. "We've got to have our defenses whole. Have to, Kontrin."

"I've heard how that is. I've heard how the farms won't give up their azi."

"All the protection we have," Ny said.

Raen looked at them, at the house, recalling the situation of buildings and the fields. "But you could rather well survive in such a place, could you not—producing your own food and power? And ITAK and ISPAK both know it. You don't have to yield up your grain; and they know that too."

"Need it," Ny said. "We need the azi; azi've no desire at all to go back to the pens either. They've lived loose here, lived well, here. We don't turn them back, no, Kontrin. We don't."

It was a bold speech for a beta. It did not offend her. "Indeed," she said, "you've a secure and enviable land here. I'd a notion to destroy your comp at least; but you're not ITAK folk nor ISPAK, are you? You have a map of the area?"

"Comp room," Berden said. "Drawer under the machine."

"I thank you," she said quietly, rose on aching limbs and limped off to the cluttered little room.

The map was there. She sat down before the unit and studied it, found their location conveniently marked, a rough two hundred kilometers south of a major tributary of the River, nearly a thousand from Newhope.

She hesitated a moment, then coded in one of her several male

personas, keyed in a purchase of passage; the program under that
name was already set. One sped to the persona of Merek Sed and
family, a matter of honor. One sped to the real person of one ser
Tol Errin 1028D Upcoast, a worker in glass, with his family, with
offer of an immediate commission on Meron, freighter-passage.

A mad gesture. A whim. Some things were worth saving.

It took an instant of time. She nerved herself again and keyed
Newhope, again on emergency. "Jim!" she snapped, and gave instructions in case any other azi was in hearing, to answer her.

There was nothing. She broke connection quickly.

She sat then with her hand pressed against her mouth, staring at
the board distressedly and trying to reckon now what to do.

She looked about her. There had gathered a quiet ring of surplus
azi, exhausted, sitting on the floor and all about, young faces looking
toward her with anxious eyes.

They all had Merry's look.

4

THERE WERE DREAMS, horrid dreams, and one of them was a
shadow, tall and gaunt, leaning across the light.

It seized and shook, and Jim tore his arm free and cried out, claw-
ing at the leads which were no longer there, trying to free himself of
the nightmare. He had no strength. The grip closed on him and held
him still, and for a time there was only his pulse for reality, a throbbing in his ears and a dull wash of rose across his eyes.

"Wait outside," a voice said above him.

"Dying." The tones were song, deep and sorrowful.

"Wait outside." Harsher now. "Go."

"Stranger," the song mourned. "Stranger, stranger, green-hive."

But it retreated, as far as the door. He could hear it clicking.

Hands caught his face between. "Azi," the male voice said. "Azi,
come back, come back, wake up. Quietly now. Was it suicide? Did
she order you to this?"

The words made sense and then did not. Senses grayed out again,
his whole body numb and heavy. Then there was sharp pain, and he

came back, feeling it, but unable to reckon where the pain was centered.

"He's coming out of it," the voice said. "Stay back. Let him be."

"Green-hive," the other fretted, retreated again, muttering deep notes of distress. He turned his head, opened his mouth to cry to it for help.

"No." A hand covered his mouth, hard. He struggled at that, vision clearing. He knew the face that leaned above him: not simply recognized, but *knew*—

Knew the Halds, and the man Pol, who was dangerous, whose House and sept had clear reason to hate the Meth-marens. He fought the muffling hand, and had no strength in his limbs or his hands, scarcely even the power to lift them.

"Be very still." Pol leaned close, his breath fanning his cheek. "I've talked my way in here, you see. The majat is watching . . . such moves as they have eyes to see. Do you hear me, azi?"

He tried to nod against the hand. He could scarcely breathe; words passed out of sense again.

"I told you to stay downstairs."

"Let him go." Max's voice. Jim struggled back toward the sound, toward understanding. "I shouldn't have let you in."

"But you have. Get the Warrior out of here. Guard the door if you like. Leave me with him."

Max, Jim wanted to say. He murmured something. Max did not answer.

"Get downstairs," Pol Hald said. "Hear me?"

The crack of authority was in his voice. Jim winced at it. Max went. The door closed. Pol Hald rose and locked it, and Jim rolled onto his side, holding the chair arm, fighting to move at all. Pol returned, caught his arms, jerked at him. His head snapped back with a crack: muscle control was gone. He could not even lift it.

"Shuttle's down," Pol said, "but not in either port. Where is she? Come out of it and answer me."

He could not. He tried to shake his head to protest the fact. Pol flung him down, let him alone; steps retreated, came back—he was roughly lifted and a cup held to his lips.

"Drink it, hear? If there's a mind left in you. Was it her order you did this?"

He drank. The water eased his throat. Pol let him back then, and touched wet fingers to his temples. He shut his eyes and drifted, came back again to a faint rattling of plastic.

"Kontrin tapes," Pol muttered. "History. Law. Comp theory—blast! where did she get that one?" He thought that it was safe to rest while the voice railed elsewhere, but suddenly the hands fastened into his toneless limbs again and pressed to the bone. "Why, azi?"

He lay still, looking at Pol, and Pol at him.

"You know me," Pol said. *"Don't you?* You know me."

He blinked, no more than that. It was truth. Pol understood it.

And slowly Pol sank down beside the chair, gripped his arm quite gently. "You're sane. Don't think you can pretend it undid you. I've seen suicides by deepstudy. You're not gone. You're lying there with your teeth shut on everything, but I understand, you hear? You've studied what you ought not. I'm not dealing with an azi, am I? You're something else. How long have you been delving into those particular tapes?"

He answered nothing, and there was knowledge in his mind, memory of the Family, what he could expect of Halds.

"She ordered this? She set you to suicide?"

"Not suicide." The accusation that touched her, stung him. "No. *I.* My choice. To learn."

"And what have you learned, azi?"

"My name is *Jim.*"

"You *have,* haven't you?"

He thought that Pol would kill him. He expected so, but there was nothing he could do about it; he tried to move, and Pol helped instead of hindering, hauled him forward to sit on the edge, put a glass into his hands. He expected water and got juice, gagged on it. "Drink it," Pol snapped at him, and when he had done so, dragged him bodily into the bath and into the shower, turned the water on him. He sank down, too weak to stand, and leaned against the glass.

It was Max who pulled him from it. Max's strong hands lifted him, half-carried him to the bed.

"Pol," he objected. "Where is he?"

"Downstairs." The guard-azi looked at him in anguish. "He came to the gate outside—said *she's* in trouble. What do we do? What orders?"

Max was asking him. He stared at the azi. Nothing made sense. There was only the single word. *She.*

He snatched at his abandoned clothing, looked up suddenly at a move in the open doorway. Pol stood there, a shape among shadows.

"The mind's working now, isn't it? More than these that could be argued into letting the likes of me into the house."

It was. Jim looked reproach at Max, and suddenly realized a gulf between. He did not know what he should and knew more than gave him comfort. His knees went out from under him and he had to lean, caught wildly at the chair.

"You've thrown yourself into shock," Pol said. "The body won't stand that kind of insult; throws metabolism into erratic patterns. Help him, azi."

Max did so, caught him and set him down, grasped his arms. "What do we do?" Max asked of him. "He's not armed. We saw to that." Max tugged and pulled the clothes onto him, shook at his arms. "Warriors are all about. He *can't* do any damage. Can he, Jim? He talks about her, about some trouble. What are we supposed to do? You're to give the orders. What?"

He fought nausea, looked up at the Hald. "The first thing is not to trust him. He's older and wiser than we."

Pol grinned. "You've studied Raen's tapes. Her mind-set. You reckon that, azi? That you *are* her mind-set?"

"The second thing," Jim said, resisting the soft voice that unraveled him, "is to make doubly sure that he isn't armed."

Pol solemnly spread open his hands. "I swear."

"And never believe him." He was shaking, violently. He sat still, conserving the energy he had in him, tried to think past the pains in his joints and the contractions of his stomach. *Blood pressure,* a forgotten tidbit of information surfaced, explaining the intense feeling that his head was bursting. "You think you can take this house. You won't."

The Family would kill him, he thought. If Raen were lost, he would die. If Raen survived, it was possible that she would kill him for what he had done. Neither was important at the moment. The necessity was not to let the Hald get control of the staff.

"Search him again, Max," he said.

Pol bristled. Max approached him with deference—evidence of how little thorough that first search had been; but Pol submitted, and it was done, with great care.

"I'm not alone now," Pol said, the while Max proceeded. "There's another of the Family here. I have to contact the Meth-maren. You understand me. The time has come. He'll be here. He'll not be subtle; he'll not need to be. The whole house is vulnerable."

"Who?" Jim asked.

"Morn. Morn a Ren hant Hald."

That name too he knew. First cousin to Pol. Traveling companion. Experienced in assassination.

"You often appear together," Jim said. "You make jokes. He kills."

Pol's face reacted, to Max's searching or to an azi's presumption. He frowned and nodded slowly. "Morn is nothing to trifle with. You understand that at least. I'll get her out of here. You listen to me, azi."

"Jim."

"I can get her off this world. Elsewhere. Out of the Family's hands. I have a ship waiting at the port. I have to reach her in time."

Jim shook his head slowly.

"You know," Pol said, as Max finished; he brushed distastefully at his clothing. "You know where she is."

"No, ser. You know well she wouldn't tell me."

"She would have established other contacts. Other points. Numbers, records. Names."

"She wouldn't have confided them to me."

"There had to be records."

"Max!" Jim said. "Have Warrior keep a guard about the comp center. Now. Do it! Warrior!"

Max moved, drew his gun: Pol's instant move was stopped cold. The Hald stepped back, then.

And there was a shadow in the door, that filled it, moiré'd eyes that swept them. "This-unit guardsss," it said.

"This stranger," Jim said, "must not go near the comp."

"Understandss. Comp center: many-machine. Sssafe."

Pol's eyes hooded. "You've killed us all. Morn won't hesitate at wiping out this whole house. Do you understand that?"

"I understand it very well. *We're* only azi."

Perhaps Pol caught that sarcasm. He gave him a long and penetrating look. "It's Raen's mind-set," he said. "Male, she's no different."

Jim swallowed at the sickness in his throat. *Calm, calm,* an old tape kept insisting somewhere. And: *Distraction is argument that needs no logic,* another advised him, Kontrin. Pol was skilled in the tactic. Jim painted a smile on his face and tucked a corner of the blanket about him against a tendency to chill, reckoning that what happened would at least be quick, unless Pol or Morn directly laid hands on him. "The staff," he said, "will make you comfortable, ser. But you'll stay away from the computer."

"You realize a direct strike could wipe this house out. That with the stakes I fear she's playing—the Family may not care that betas or a Kontrin die in the process." Pol's mouth twisted as though the words choked him. "I don't care for a few betas or a houseful of azi and majat. But *she's* another matter with me. You hear me. I'll not be taken down by a houseful of azi."

"There are majat."

The Kontrin went stone-faced.

"The staff," Jim repeated, "will make you comfortable in this room. But you'll not leave it."

Pol folded his arms.

"She'll come back," Jim said.

Pol shook his head. "I doubt that she can, azi. The shuttle was never meant for landing elsewhere. She'll die, if she's not dead already."

It undermined his confidence of things. He could not keep that from his face.

"You know," Pol said reasonably, "that she admitted me here herself. She'd never have let an enemy that close to her. You have her mind. You know that better than anyone would. She wouldn't have let me in the door to see the lay of things, if she didn't know that I wasn't the enemy."

"I don't try to think as she does." Jim hugged the blanket about him, stared bleakly at the Hald. "I don't know enough. I only know what she told me, which was to stay and hold this house. You can say what you wish, ser. It may entertain you. It won't make any difference."

Pol cursed him, and Warrior stirred in the doorway.

"Green-hive," Warrior moaned.

"That is another reason," Jim said. "We simply wait for her. Maybe she'll tell me then that I was wrong."

"She's never going to have the chance."

Jim shrugged, tucked his feet up, crosslegged on the bed. "How shall we pass the time, ser? I am passably skilled at Sej."

5

THE QUEASINESS OF DOCKING upset the child. Wes Itavvy hugged her against him, looked at his wife, mute, full of things he should have said. They held Meris between them, clasping her hands, saying nothing. The shuttle made this run nearly empty: they three, a family of five from Upcoast, whose faces were no less worried. The port had been a-bristle with police. IDs were checked, and Itavvy had endured that in terror, expecting at any moment there would be someone who knew his face, who could detect the false numbers, the lies behind the precious tickets.

They had gone through. They had taken almost nothing in baggage, in their haste. There was disaster at their backs. It was palpable, throughout the city, through the subways, where armored police patrolled, with rifles levelled, in shops closed, in newslines censored, broadcasts cancelled.

They had made it through. Station let them dock. The procedure completed itself and the crew unsealed the hatches.

"Come on," he said, feeling his pocket for the authorizations. There was a freighter . . . the tickets advised so . . . it was the best place to go now, no lingering on station. They carried their own baggage off, jostling the Upcoast family in their haste.

Police.

And not police. Armored men with a serpent for an emblem, levelling rifles at them.

"Papers," one said.

Itavvy produced them. For a brief, agonizing moment he thought that they would then be waved on; but the man kept them, checked those likewise of the Upcoast group.

"Both for the *Phoenix*," he said into his com-unit.

"Faces check?" a voice came back.

"No likeness."

Itavvy reached, to have the papers. The faceless man held them, and the others, motioned at them with the rifle. "Waiting room," he said.

"We'll miss our boarding," a youth from Upcoast protested.

"Nothing's leaving," the armored man said.

Azi, Itavvy realized in indignation. No Kontrin, but an azi force was holding them. He opened his mouth to protest: the rifles gestured, and he closed it. Meris started to cry; his wife gathered her up, and he took the burden from her, went after the Upcoasters into the designated waiting area.

DOCK 6, BERTH 9, he could see on the signs outside the clear doors as they were ushered through. Berth 11 was their ship, safety.

From here, past azi guns, there was no reaching it. He looked at the Upcoasters, at his wife, hugged Meris to him. A guard deposited their baggage inside the door and unmasked to search through it, disarranging one and proceeding to the next, putting nothing back.

6

"NOTHING," THE AZI REPORTED, and Morn scowled, folded his arms.

"No more flights," he said, looking at the ISPAK president. "Nothing moves out, no more come up."

"Kont' Morn," the beta breathed, appalled.

He cared little for that. He had no trust at all for ITAK, and believed in ISPAK's loyalty only while guns were on them and in the command center.

And from Pol there was yet no word. Pol was down in Newhope; that much was certain: his ship pulsed out a steady flow of status information, but there were only azi aboard.

The Meth-maren had weapons enough at her disposal if she had linked into ITAK. She had still the resources of the Family with which to buy beta loyalties. And to take those privileges needed Council.

Except by one procedure.

"She's dead," Morn said suddenly, bewildering the beta. "I'll enter in the banks that the Meth-maren's dead. And ISPAK will witness it. Then it'll be true, by the law—do you agree, ser?"

"Yes, Kont' Morn," the man said; as it had been yes, Kont' Pol, and Kont' Raen before that.

"All Kontrin and a world's corporations are sufficient witness."
He glared at the beta to see the reaction to this, and the beta simply
looked frightened. He motioned to the console. "Get ITAK in link.
Use your persuasion."

The man sat down and keyed a message through, the while Morn
leaned above him, one hand on his chair, one on the panel's rim;
and often the man's hands trembled over a letter, but he made no
errors. ITAK protested; NO CHOICE, the ISPAK beta returned. It
was untidy; it fed into intercomp, to be examined and made permanent record. Morn scowled and let it. The records were only as dangerous as Council chose to regard them, and Council—was as Council went. Risks had to be taken.

ITAK complied, under threat, registering protest. *Brave little
betas,* Morn thought, with respect for the Meth-maren's hold on
them. It amused him. He watched the ISPAK beta trembling with
psych-set guilt and that amused him the more. "Move over," he said,
thrust the man out of the way, glared until the man moved far away,
by the door. Then he set his own fingers to the keys, with both
ITAK and ISPAK signatories, coded in his own number . . . and
Pol's: for that he had gained long ago, committed it to memory: he
had taken that precaution, as he tolerated nothing near him he could
not control—save Pol. All a world's Kontrin and the corporations:
the latter, K-codes could forge; but only on Istra did it come down
to so small a body of the Family.

Worldcomp accepted it; it leaped to intercomp. Morn smiled,
which he did rarely.

Officially dead, so far as Istra was concerned; universally dead in
the eight to sixteen days it would take for the message to reach
homeworld and fan out again in intercomp. She could not use her
codes or her credit: they were wiped.

He pushed back from the console, rose, turned to the azi who
waited. "Get the shuttle ready," he said. "My own."

One left. He turned to the ISPAK beta.

And suddenly the comp screens began to flash with alarm.

He was at the panel in an instant, keyed through a query.

No answer returned to him. He sat down and plied the keys, obtained only idiocy. Panic flashed into him. With all the speed he
could manage he K-coded intercomp out-of link, separating it from
the deadness that was Istra.

The cold reached his stomach. Worldbank was wiped. All records,
all finance, *null.*

The Meth-maren's death-notice.

It was keyed to that, and he had done it.

"Kill the power!" he shouted, rounding on the ISPAK beta. "Kill all the power on Istra. Dead, you understand me?"

There was silence. Nothing of the sort had ever been done before, the threat never carried out, the withdrawal of station power from a world.

"Yes, Kontrin," the beta stammered hoarsely. "But how long, how long are we talking about?"

"Until you hear from me to restore it. Shut it down." He turned to the board, keyed a message to his ship, ordering more azi to the command center. "I'm going down," he said to the azi present, to Leo, who was chief of them. The azi looked troubled at that, no more. "There's no more time to spend with this. You know procedures."

Leo nodded. Twenty years Leo had been in his service, the last five as senior. Efficiency and intelligence. There was no beta would get past him, no one who would get near controls. Azi lined the room, thirty of them, armed and armored, impersonal as the majat, and that resemblance was no chance. Beta psych-set was terrified by it. There was no one of them about to make a move under those guns.

He looked about him, saw the screens which monitored the collectors, saw the incredible sight of vanes turning, all at the same time, averting into shadow.

"*We* must have power," the ISPAK beta objected.

"Without dispute," he said. The beta looked abjectly grateful.

Morn ignored him and, gathering two of the azi to accompany him, left the center.

There was a Kontrin ship onworld, Pol's; and Pol remained silent, leaving only azi to report.

It was the first law, in the Family, to trust no one.

7

FIGURES RIPPLED ACROSS the comp screen. Raen saw the sudden dissolution of information and sprang back from it with a curse.

Dead. They had gotten to that, then, to pull her privileges.

And all Kontrin onworld had to agree to it.

Pol, she thought. *You bastard!*

She swore volubly and kept working, fed in the Newhope call number. "Jim," she said. "Jim. Any staff, punch five and answer."

There was no answer.

JIM, she sent, BEWARE POL HALD.

She suddenly found chaos in the machine, nonsense, and finally only house-functions.

"Power's down in the main banks," she said, turning to look at one of the older azi, who attended her shadow-wise, armed, wherever she went in the house. She cut the unit off and walked back into the doorway of the living room, where the Ny-Berdens and their family remained with the house-azi. "Worldcomp's undone," she said, and at their blankly incredulous stares: "Power's going to go soon, I'd imagine. Very soon. You've some collectors here. Is that enough to keep your house running?"

They only stared.

"I hope for your sakes that such is the case," she said, looking about her at the smallish rooms, the hand-done touches, the rough and unstylish furnishings. She turned again and raised her voice to them. "You understand, don't you? Istra's been cut off. Power will be cut. Worldcomp's been dissolved—wiped. No records, no communications, nothing exists any longer."

The ser and sera gathered their son and daughter-in-law and grandchild close about them and continued to stare at her. *Your doing,* their eyes said. She did not argue with them. It was so. Her azi sat still, waiting. The azi belonging to the estate sat outside, ranged in orderly rows in the shade of the azi-quarters, under the guns of her own. There had been need to feed them, to give them at least a little relief from the confinement. Silence prevailed everywhere about the house and grounds.

"Is your local power," Raen asked yet again, "enough for you?"

"If nothing's damaged," ser Ny answered at last, and faintly.

"Confound it, I'm not proposing to harm you. I'd not do that. We'll leave you your cells and your farm machinery. I'm worried about your survival. You understand that?"

They seemed perhaps a little reassured. The child whimpered. The young mother hugged and soothed her.

"Thank you," ser Ny said tautly.

An azi came up beside her, offered a cup of juice, bowed. *Blast, what triggered that impulse?* she wondered, concerned for the azi's stability, for she had not ordered it. She sipped it gratefully all the same. The air-conditioning might not last, not unless the farm collectors could carry it. More than likely it would have to be sacrificed for the farm's more essential machinery, the pumps to irrigate, refrigeration for stored goods.

Distantly there was the sound of an engine.

"Sera!" an azi shouted from the porch. "The truck's back!"

Everyone started to his feet, save the Ny-Berdens and their family: the azi guarding them did not let the guns turn aside. The truck groaned and rumbled its way to the porch. Raen put on her sun visor and took her rifle in hand, walked out to meet it.

It was a wretched sight, the covered vehicle laden with injured, with men bleeding through their bandages or, deep in shock, trying to protect unset bones. Warrior danced about anxiously, scenting life-fluids: "Go, out of the way," Raen bade it. Merry climbed down, and the three he had taken to help him climbed out of the back, exhausted and staggering themselves from the heat. Raen ordered cold water for them, ordered the others to work while Merry and his companions slumped in the shade of the truck.

Willing hands off-loaded the injured into the air-conditioned house, to the bedrooms, the carpeted floors, everywhere there was room. They gave them water, and what medicines they could find in the house. Some were likely dying. All were in great pain, quiet as azi were always quiet, so long as they retained any consciousness of what they were doing. Some moaned, beyond that awareness.

Raen walked back into the living room, where her sunsuit lay over the back of a chair. She looked at the kitchen door, where Merry stood, shadow-eyed and bruised and bloody. "There's no taking them farther," she said hoarsely. "It's too cruel. Some, maybe. Some." She looked at Ny and Berden. "You tell me, seri. What would happen to those men here, in your care? I can terminate the worst or I can leave them—but not for you to do it. You tell me."

"We can manage for them," Ny said. "Want to." He pressed Berden's hand. "Never killed anybody. Don't want anybody killed in this house."

She believed that, by means having nothing to do with logic.

"Are you," Berden asked, "leaving us our own azi?"

She had intended otherwise until that moment. She looked at the beta woman and nodded. "Keep them. Likely you'll need their help yourselves, and probably they're no use in a fight."

The youth stood up, provoking a nervous reaction of his wife and of the armed azi. "I'm coming with," he said. "You're going to the City; you're going to fight. I'm coming with. There's others too. From other farms."

She was bewildered by that, saw his parents and wife almost protest, and not; saw ser Ny nod his head in slow agreement.

"I have the place to hold," Ny said sorrowfully. "But Nes'd go if he wants. Take some of the guard-azi with him, ours. We can spare. Settle with those citymen, and 'bove-worlders."

"You don't understand," Raen protested. "You can't help. It's not ISPAK; it's not ITAK either."

"What, then?" asked the younger Ny, his brow wrinkling. "What are you going to fight, Kontrin?"

It was a good question, better than he might know. Raen looked about her at their refuge, the farm, that might survive the chaos to come . . . looked back at him and shrugged. "Hive-matter. Things that have wanted settling for a long time."

"There's men would go," the young beta insisted. "Farms like ours and big estates too, belly-full with the way ITAK's run us. There's men all over would go to settle this once for all, would go with you, Kontrin."

"No."

"Sera," Merry objected. "This is sense he offers."

"This is the tapes," she said, looked about at all their faces, azi and beta. *"Tapes* . . . you understand that? You owe me nothing. We taped it into your ancestors seven hundred years ago. All your loyalty, all your fear of us, your desire to obey. It's all psych-set. Your azi know where their ideas come from. I'm telling you about yours. You're following a program. Stop, before it ruins you."

There was silence, stark silence, and the young man stood stricken and the young woman held her child close.

"Be free," Raen said. "You've your farm. Let the cities go. I doubt there'll be more azi. These are the last. They'll go at their forty-year. Have children. Never mind the quotas. Have children, and be done with azi and with us."

"It's treason," the older Ny said.

"We created you; is that a reason to die with us? Outsiders have left the Reach, for a time long in *your* terms. The old woman who rules on Cerdin will fall soon, if not already: that they've come for me openly says something of that; and there'll be chaos after. Save what you can. Depend on no one."

"You stay, then," said Berden. "You stay with us, sera."

She looked at the beta in affront, and the gentleness in that woman's face and voice minded her of old Lia; it hurt. "Tapes," she said. "Come on, Merry. Load the truck." She glanced again at the Ny-Berdens. "I'm sorry about taking from you; all I can give you in return is advice. You've the lifetime of these azi to prepare yourselves for years without them, for a time when there'll only be your children to farm the land. And never—*never* meddle with the hives."

The azi gathered themselves, packed up food and water, headed for the waiting truck. Raen turned her back on the betas, pulled on the sunsuit, took up her rifle again, went out down the steps. Warrior hovered there, clicking with anxiety. Merry was tying on containers of extra fuel, a can and a half. "All we have?" she asked; Merry shrugged. "All, sera. I drained it."

Already the azi were boarding, all who could come and many who should not, insisting they were guard-azi and not farmers.·

For them she felt most grief, for men who could imagine nothing more than to come with her. Even some of the farm azi rose and started forward, as if they thought that they were supposed to come, but she ordered them back, and they did not.

Then Merry climbed aboard, waiting on her. She saw two more waiting . . . long-faced, and the back of the truck was jammed; she motioned them into the cab, two more that they could manage, for in the back, men sat three deep, rifles leaned where they could; or stood, leaning on the frame. Heat went up from the ground and the truck in waves.

She squeezed herself in with Merry and the two others, pulled the door shut: no air-conditioning . . . they needed the fuel. There was a last scurrying and scrabbling atop the truck. Warrior was minded to ride for a space, boarded even as Merry put the vehicle in motion and it labored out, swaying and groaning, toward the dirt road.

"Left," Raen said when they reached the branching, directing them toward the River, and abandoned depots and the City.

She had the map, on her knee, and the hope that the vehicle would hold together long enough. She looked at Merry, past the two azi who shared the cab with them. Merry's face was solid and stolid as ever, no sign of dread for what they faced.

How could there be, she wondered, for the likes of them, who knew their own limits, that they were designed and bred for what they did, and did it well?

They had not even the luxury of doubt.

We are outmoded, they and I, she thought, closing her hands about the smooth stock of the rifle. *Appropriate, that we go together.*

BOOK NINE

1

THERE WAS A PRESENCE at the door, beyond the sealed steel. Moth did not let it hasten her, carefully poured wine into the crystal with a steady left hand. The right hung useless. It throbbed, and the fingers were too swollen to bend. She did not look at it. The bandages sufficed; the robes covered it; and she deliberately forced herself to move about, ignoring it.

Something hissed at the door. She caught a flicker from the consoles about the room, a sudden shriek of alarm after. She set the wine down quickly and keyed broadcast to the hall outside.

"Stop it," she snapped. "If you want these systems intact, don't try it."

"She's alive," she heard in the background.

"Eldest," an old voice overrode it, a familiar voice. She tried through the haze of pain to place it. Thon. That was Nel Thon. "Eldest, only your friends are here. Open the doors. Please open the doors."

She said nothing to that.

"Crazy," someone said farther away. "Her mind has gone." Someone hissed that voice to silence.

"No," she answered it. "Quite sane. That you, Nel?"

"Eldest!" The voice overflowed with relief. "Please, open the doors. It's settled, over with. The forces loyal to you have won. Use the intercomp channels and confirm it for yourself."

"Loyal to *me?*" Pain made her voice harsh and she fought to make it even again. "Go back to the hives, Thon. Tell *them* your loyalty."

"Everything is stable, Eldest. Unlock the doors."

"Go your way, Nel Thon. Lord it in Council without me. Try

your own terminals to intercomp. They'll work . . . so far." She drew a deep breath and cared little now how her voice sounded. "That door opens from the inside, cousins. Force it and you'll trigger a wipe."

There was a burst of voices from outside. She could not distinguish words.

"Please," said Nel Thon. "Is there some condition you want? Is there any assurance you want?"

"The same goes," she continued, "for trying to gain access to the banks, dear cousins. My key is fed in with a destruct order. When I go, it goes. Figure your way around *that,* cousins."

There was profound silence outside.

In time a whispering of anguished voices retreated from the area. She left the set on broadcast and settled back again, picked up the goblet and drank, sipped at it slowly, for the wine had to last.

2

THE SHIP WAS THERE, on the field, a sleek, familiar shape too graceful for the ground. Morn took time for a glance, attended to the necessary business of landing: the shuttle was not made for fine maneuvers.

Touchdown. He ignored the field patterns; tower was dead, and there were no lights to relieve the evening haze. He used the moving gear to take the shuttle up to the rear of the starship, out of the track of its armament.

"They answer," the azi at com told him quietly. "They're Hald azi and they're upset."

"Time they responded," Morn said. He began shutdown, closed off systems. "Standard procedures." He looked back through the ship, to the dozen who were with him, armored and armed. Chatter crackled in his left ear: no port control, but the Istra shuttle coming in with thirty more of his men, hard behind him. "Ask where Pol is."

"They say," the com-azi reported back slowly, "that he's gone into the City some time ago, hunting the Meth-maren face to face. They weren't told how he's proceeding, or where."

"Is Sam with him?" Morn asked, for that one of Pol's azi was his most reliable.

"No. It's Sam I'm talking to."

"Tell him to open that ship." Morn rose, ducking the overhead, felt for his gun and gathered up his sun-kit and his rifle. One-unit readied itself to accompany him.

"Sam says," the com-azi called after him, "that he doesn't want to open. He says he's not sure he should."

Morn looked at the com-azi, his breath shortened by temper. "Tell Sam he has no choice," he said, and opened the hatch.

There was a thunder of engines outside, the Istra shuttle coming in. "Have them form up beside this ship," he directed two-unit leader, and rode the extending ladder down: one-unit was quickly at his heels.

He had a prickling at his nape, being in the open, near the terminal building. Betas might occupy that point, that flat roof, ITAK betas, who were likely *hers* to a man, and dangerous. He darted glances to all likely points for snipers, and half-ran the space to Pol's sleek *Moriah,* careless of dignity. Sam was capitulating, lowering the ramp, having come to his senses.

He climbed it with half his escort, stood inside, breathing the cold air of the hatchway. Pol's whole staff gathered there, Sam prominent among them, a sandy-haired azi with a scar at his brow.

"Out of my way," Morn said, and elbowed Sam aside; the others moved, pushed aside by his armored escort. He walked into controls with Sam anxiously struggling his way through after—sat down and read through what there was to read.

There was nothing. He turned around, a frown gathered on his face. "Sam. What kind of operation has he out there? What force is with him?"

The azi ducked his head in distress. "Alone, ser. He went alone."

Morn drew in his breath, eyes flicking over the staff of *Moriah,* finding them far too many: it was likely truth. Guard-azi. Dark-haired Hana, a female azi who was Pol's eccentricity, not even particularly beautiful. Tim, like Sam, Pol's accustomed shadow.

"Where," Morn asked, "is the Meth-maren based? City? ITAK Central?"

"We don't know."

It was truth. Sam was distressed; the whole staff was distraught.

"Stay and hold this ship," Morn directed his own men. "If Pol shows up, tell him to stay here."

A stifling feeling of things wrong assailed him. He thrust his way past them, out, down the ramp again where the other half of one-unit waited. The second shuttle had disgorged its occupants. Thirty more men waited orders.

A long partnership, his with Pol: forty years. They had shared much, had hunted together—and not only in sport. He tolerated Pol's humor and Pol supported his grimmer amusements.

Pol's humor. He looked about him, at dead buildings, at a sky void of traffic, the only sound that of the wind tugging at cloth and the popping of cooling metal. It was not a time or place for an exercise of whim, not even Pol's.

He had sent Pol, in advance of the order which sent him: Pol's humor, to ask this of him.

Pol . . . who avoided Cerdin of late; who avoided many old connections, and the hold at Ehlvillon—and, avowing her tedious, . . . Moth.

He paused, hard-breathing, looking back at *Moriah*. Pol avowed he had no sense of humor. Pol contrived, finally, to disturb his self-possession.

He shouted an order to the azi, stalked off toward the buildings of the terminal. Azi hastened to cluster themselves about him, shielding him with their armor and their bodies; he took this for granted, it being their function, and himself conspicuous for the Color that he wore.

Sun's glare still reflected off windows, but there was more than one window missing, betokening more than a quiet power shutdown here. That drew him, promising some insight into what had happened in the City.

And in the terminal, scattered over the polished floors, there were dead, male and female, young and old.

With live majat.

"Don't fire!" Morn snapped. One stepped lightly toward them, in the doorway. He saw the badges on it: it was a red, that had never been trouble for Hald.

"Kontrin," it moaned, when he held up his fist. "Green-hive."

"Hald. Morn a Ren hant Hald."

Palps swept forward. "Hhhhald. Friend. Giffftss."

He did not like them: he had never liked them. He stood still now with azi rifles about him and was glad of the guns. It stood at safe distance, forelimbs tucked in respect. "Red-hive," he asked it, "you did this, wrecking the port?"

"Meth-maren betas. They stopped the gifftss."

The tone of that chilled the flesh. But one took allies where one could, when family failed. "I'll settle with the Meth-maren for you. I need to locate her base. Her-hive. Understand?"

"Yes. Understand." It shifted forward, and the azi flinched, torn between terror and duty. It extended a forelimb, touched at his chest, and he suffered it, concealing his loathing, reckoning he might have to accept worse than this. "Red-hive knows Meth-maren hive, yes. Blues guard. This-unit will call otherss, many, many, many Warriors, reds, golds, greens, all move. Come kill, yess."

"Yes," he confirmed—did not touch it; that risk was one he did not choose to run, and the Warrior did not offer.

Others moved, to a shrilling command only partially in human hearing. They gathered, out of all the recesses of the terminal, a living sea of chitinous bodies.

"Tunnels," the Warrior said. "Tunnels for beta-machines. Ssub-wayss."

3

THE HOUSE STIRRED and hummed with activity. One could hear it, even in the upper floors, the stir of many feet, the singing of majat voices. Jim sat still in the semi-dark beneath the dome, on the bed, hands loose over his crossed legs, watching the Kontrin who slumped angrily in the chair opposite. They were at a silence, and Jim found that profound relief, for Pol Hald reasoned well, and wounded accurately when he wanted to.

The power was gone, had been for hours; he believed now that it would not return.

There's no more comp, Pol had advised him. *Nothing. If you'd listened earlier, something might have been done. Something still might. Listen to me.*

Jim gave no answers. He could not argue with such a fluency; he could only steadfastly refuse. Max, downstairs, gave him the means to refuse. Warrior, standing faithfully outside, was a guard against which even Pol Hald's reasoning could not prevail.

Newhope's dead, Pol had said. *There's nothing here for her. Only trouble. He's here. Morn's here. He'll be coming, and she'll know that.*

He could not listen to such logic. It made sense.

Below, the majat swarmed and stirred and tugged at foundations.

And in the dome above, the stars began to show in a darkening sky, the majat song to swell louder.

"Does it never stop?" Pol demanded.

Jim shook his head. "Rarely."

Pol hurled himself suddenly to his feet. Jim rose, alarmed. "Relax," Pol said. "I'm tired of sitting."

"Sit down," Jim said, received of Pol a cold and sarcastic look. There was a certain incongruity in the situation.

And abruptly the song fragmented to a shrilling note.

Outside, Warrior dived for the stairs, scuttled away. "Come back!" Jim shouted at it, and jerked from his pocket the gun which he had for his protection, an azi against a Kontrin. Pol saw it, raised both hands and turned his face aside, miming peace.

Jim held the gun in both hands to steady it. "Max!" he shouted, panic hammering in him.

"Please," Pol said fervently. "I'd not be shot by mistake."

Steps tramped up the stairs, not human ones, but spurred feet which caught on the carpet fiber, with the hollow gasp of majat breathing. Warrior loomed up in the doorway again.

"Many, many," it announced. "Trouble."

Jim did not take his eyes off Pol—motioned nervously with the gun, indicated the chair. Pol subsided, his gaunt face anxious.

"Where's Max?" Jim asked of Warrior.

"Down. All down in outside. Warrior-azi, yess. Much danger. Reds, golds, greens are grouping. Blues are here, Jim-unit. Kill this green, take taste to Mother, yesss."

Pol looked for once sober, his hands held in plain sight. "Argue with it, azi."

"Stay still!" Jim tried to control his breathing, tried to reason. "I hold this place," he said. "No, Warrior. This is Raen's. She'll understand it when she comes."

"Queen." Warrior seemed to accept that logic. "Where? Where is Meth-maren queen, Jim?"

"I don't know."

Warrior clicked to itself, edged forward. "Mother wants. Mother sends Warriors out, seek, seek, find. I guard. This-chamber is no good, too high. Come, this-unit guides, down, down, where safety is, good places, deep."

"No," Pol advised softly, alarm in his voice.

"I trust Warrior more. Up, ser. Up. We're going downstairs."

Pol made a gesture of exasperation and rose, and this sudden lack of seriousness in him, Jim watched with the greatest apprehension. Pol sauntered out, past him, and Warrior led them downstairs, Jim last and with the gun at Pol's back.

The center of the house, windowless, was plunged in darkness, blue lights bobbing and flaring on the walls and making strange shadows of their bearers. Majat-azi skipped about them, touching them, Pol as well. The Kontrin cursed them from him, and they laughed and scampered off, taking the light with them.

Other azi remained, in the blackness. "Jim," Max's voice said. "They urged us to come in. Was it right to do? I thought maybe we shouldn't, but they pushed us and kept pushing."

"You did right," Jim said, although in his mind was the horrible possibility of being swept up with the majat-azi, herded deep below. "The Hald is with us. Watch him."

"Tape-fed obstinance," Pol's voice came, outraged, for they laid hands on him. "If you would listen—"

"I won't."

"At least check comp."

Jim hesitated. It ceased to be an attempt to unsettle him, began to seem plain advice. He felt his way aside, into the comp center, shuddered as a majat-azi brushed his shoulder. He caught a slim female arm. "Stay, come," he asked of her, for the light's sake, and took her with him, into the face of the dead machinery, the dark screens.

But paper had fed out, printout, in the machine's dying.

He was stricken, suddenly, with the realization Pol had been urging him to what he should have done. He drew the majat-azi to the machine, tore off the print and laid it on the counter. "Light," he said, "light," and she lent it, leaning on his shoulder with her arm about him. He ignored her and ran through the messages as rapidly as he could read the dim print in azi-light. Most were of no meaning to him; he had known so. Pol might understand, and he knew that Pol would urge him to show them to him: but he dared not, would not. It was useless; the key to these was not in the tapes he had stolen.

JIM, one said plainly. STAND BY. EMERGENCY.

It was not signed. But only one who knew his name could have used a comp board.

Sent before her trouble, perhaps; the possibility hit his stomach like a blow, that she had needed him, and he had been upstairs, unhearing.

"Stay!" he begged of the azi, who had tired of what she did not understand. He caught at her wrist and held her light still upon the paper, ran his eyes over the other messages.

JIM, the last said, BEWARE POL HALD.

He thought to check the time of transmission; it was not on this one, but on the one before . . . an ITAK message . . . One in the night and one in the morning.

He looked up, at a commotion in the doorway, where dancing azi-lights cast Pol Hald and Max and others into a flickering blue visibility.

Alive, his heart beat in him. *Alive, alive, alive.*

And they had let Pol in.

"Is it from her?" Pol asked. *"Is it from her?"*

"Max, get him down to the basement."

Pol resisted; there were azi enough to hold him, though they had trouble moving him. "Please," Jim said sharply, rolling up the precious message, and the struggle ceased. He felt the insistent hands of the majat-azi touching him, wanting something of him. He ignored her, for she was mad. "Please go," he asked of the Kontrin. "Her orders, yes. This house is still hers."

Pol went then, led by the guard-azi. Jim stood still in the dark, conscious of others who remained, majat shapes. All through the house bodies moved, and round about it, a never-ceasing stream.

"Warrior," Jim asked, "Warrior? Raen's alive. She sent a message through the comp before it died. Do you understand?"

"Yess." A shadow scuttled forward. "Kethiuy-queen. Where?"

"I don't know. I don't know that. But she'll come." He looked about him at the shapes in the dark, that flowed steadily toward the front doors. "Where are they going?"

"Tunnels," Warrior answered. "Human-hive tunnels. Reds are moving to attack; golds, greens, all move, seek here, seek Kethiuy-queen. We fight in tunnels."

"They're coming up the subway," Jim breathed.

"Yes. From port. Kontrin leads, green-hive: we taste this presence in reds. This-hive and blue-hive now touch; tunnel is finished. All come. Fight." It sucked air, reached for him, touched nervously and uncertainly he sought to calm it, but Warrior would have none of it. It clicked its jaws and moved on, joining the dark stream of others that flowed toward the doors.

Azi went, majat-azi, bearing blue lights in one hand and weapons in the other, naked and wild. Warriors hastened them on. Jim tried to pass them, almost gathered up in their number, but that he ducked and went the other way, down the hall and down the stairs.

Blue azi-lights were there, hanging from majat fiber, and a draft breathed out of an earth-rimmed pit, the floor much-trampled with muddy feet. Max and the other azi were there in a recess by the stairs, and Pol Hald among them.

Pol rose to his feet, looking up at him on the stairs. Azi surrounded him with weapons. "There's nothing," Pol said, "so dangerous as one who thinks he knows what he's doing. If you had checked comp while it was still alive—when I told you to—you could have contacted her and been of some use."

That was true, and it struck home. "Yes," he admitted freely.

"Still," Pol said, "I could help her."

He shook his head. "No, ser. I won't listen." He sank down where he stood, on the steps. At the bottom a majat-azi huddled, a wretched thing, female, whose hands were torn and bleeding and whose tangled hair and naked body were equally muddied. It was uncommon: never had he seen one so undone. The azi's sides heaved. She seemed ill. Perhaps her termination was on her, for she was not young.

"See to her," he told one of the guard-azi. The man tried; others did, and the woman would take a little water, but sank down again.

And suddenly it occurred to him that it was much quieter than it had been, the house silent: that of all the Workers which had labored hereabouts—not one remained.

The tunnel breathed at them, a breath neither warm nor cold, but damp. And from deep within it, came a humming that was very far and strange.

"Max," Jim said hoarsely. "They've gone for the subways of the city. A red force is coming this way."

Pol sank down with a shake of his head and a deep-voiced curse.

Jim tucked his arms about his knees and wished to go to that null place that had always been there, that he saw some of the guard-azi attain, waiting orders. He could not find it now. Tape-thoughts ran and cycled endlessly, questions open and without neat answers.

He stared at Max and at the Kontrin, at the Kontrin most of all, for in those dark and angry eyes was a mutual understanding. It became quieter finally, that glance, as if some recognition passed between them.

"If you've her mind-set," Pol said, "use it. We're sitting in the most dangerous place in the city."

He looked into the dark and answered out of that mind-set, consciously. "The hive," he said, "is safety."

Pol's retort was short and bitter.

4

ITAVVY ROSE AND WALKED to the door, walked back again and looked at his wife Velin as the infant squirmed and fretted in her arms, taxing her strength. One of the Upcoast women offered a diversion, an attempt to distract the child from her tears. Meris screamed in exhausted misery . . . hunger. The azi outside the glass, with their guns, their faceless sameness, maintained their watch.

"I'll ask again," Itavvy said.

"Don't," Velin pleaded.

"They don't have anger. It isn't in them. There are ways to reason past them. I've dealt—" He stopped, remembered his identity as Merek Sed, who knew little of azi, swallowed convulsively.

"Let me." The gangling young Upcoaster who had spent his time in the corner, sketch-pad on his knee, left his work lying and went to the door, rapped on it.

The azi ignored it. The young artist pushed the door open; rifles immediately lowered at him. "The child's sick," the youth said. "She needs milk. Food. Something."

The azi stood with their guns aimed at him . . . confused, Itavvy thought, in an excess of tension. Presented with crisis. Well-done.

"If you'd call the kitchens," the artist said, "someone would bring food up."

Meris kept crying. The azi hesitated, unnerved, swung the rifle in that direction. Itavvy's heart jumped.

Azi can't understand, he realized. *No children. No tears.*

He edged between, facing the rifle. "Please," he said to the masked face. "She'll be quiet if she's fed."

The azi moved, lifted the rifle, closed the door forcefully. Itavvy shut his eyes, swallowed hard at nausea. The young artist turned, set a hand on his shoulder.

"Sit down," the youth said. "Sit down, ser. Try to quiet her."

He did so. Meris exhausted herself, fell whimpering into sleep. Velin lifted bruised eyes and held her fast.

Then, finally, an azi in ISPAK uniform brought a tray to the door, handed it in, under guard.

Drink, sandwiches, dried fruit. Meris fretted and ceased, given the comfort of a full belly. Itavvy sat and ate because it was something to do.

The identity of Merek Sed would collapse. They were being detained because someone was running checks. Perhaps it had already been proven false. They would die.

Meris too. The azi had no feeling of difference.

He dropped his head into his hands and wept.

5

THE TRUCK LABORED, ground up the slope from the riverbed, picking up dry road in the headlights. Raen threw it to idle at the crest, let what men had gotten off climb on again, the truck sinking on its suspension as it accepted its burden. She read the fuel gauge and the odometer, cast a look at Merry, who opened the door to look out on his side. "They're all aboard," he said.

"Then go back to sleep." She said it for him and the two azi crowded in between them, and eased the truck forward, walking it over ruts that jolted it insanely and wrenched at her sore arms. A thousand kilometers. That was one thing on the map, and quite another as Istrans built roads. The track was only as wide as the truck. The headlights showed ruts and stones, man-high grass on either side of the road, obscuring all view.

A nightmare shape danced into the lights before them, left again: Warrior stayed with them, but the jolting on this stretch was such that it chose to go on its own feet.

By the map, this was the only road. They were on the last of their fuel, that which they had brought in containers, having used the stored power and both main and reserve tanks. They might nurse a kilometer back out of batteries after the fuel ran out. Cab light went on. Merry was checking the map again, counting with his fingers and making obvious conclusions.

"It's six hundred to go," Raen said, "and it pulls too much. We're loaded way beyond limits and we're not going to do it."

"Map shows good road past the depot."

"Easier walking, then." Raen looked to the side as a black body hit the door, scraped and scrambled its way to the roof of the truck. Warrior had decided to ride again. Six hundred kilometers more: easy on a good road with an unburdened truck. As exhausted men would walk it . . . days.

"Could be fuel there," Merry offered.

"One hopes. If we get that far."

"I'll drive again, sera."

"We'll change over at the depot. Rest."

Merry turned the light out. He did not seem to sleep, but he said nothing, and in him, in the two with them—likely in all those men in the rear—there was evident that familiar blankness. They lost themselves in that, and perhaps found refuge.

She had no such. There was a stitch in her back which had been growing worse over the hours, and fighting the steering aggravated it; the right shoulder ached, until finally she chose to let the right hand rest in her lap, however much that tired the left. The jolt of the crash, she reckoned. Pain was something she had long since learned to ignore. A stoppered bottle sat beside her; she moved the right hand to it, flipped the cap with her thumb, took a drink of water, capped it again. It helped keep her awake. She worked a bit of dried fruit from her pocket, bit off a little and sucked at that: the sugar helped too.

The road worsened again, after a little smoothness; she applied both hands for the while, relaxed again when it passed. Imagination constructed a picture of the men in the back, jammed in so that some must constantly stand, or lie on others, whose muscles must cramp and joints stiffen, all jolted cruelly with every hole she could not avoid and every lean and lurch of the turns.

Figures flicked past on the odometer, a red pulse far too slow. The fuel registered lower and lower, most gone now out of the last filling.

Then the road smoothed out on a flat high enough to see no flooding. She kicked them up to a better pace, and Merry came out of his trance and shifted position, causing the other two men to do the same.

"Should be coming up on the depot," she said.

Merry leaned to take a look at the fuel and said nothing.

There was a scraping overhead. A spiny limb extended itself over the windshield. Warrior slid partially down, and Raen swore at that, for they had no margin for delays. It scraped at the glass, insisting on her attention, and at the realization it was urgent her heart began to beat the faster.

She let off the accelerator, coasted, rolled down the window lefthanded. Warrior scrambled off when they slowed enough, paced them, the while the headlights picked out only dusty ruts and high weeds.

"Others," Warrior breathed. "Hear? Hear?"

She could not. She braked, threw the engine to idle, quieter.

"Many," Warrior said. "All around us."

"The depot," Merry said hoarsely. "They've got it." Raen nodded, a sinking feeling in her stomach.

"Get the men out," she said. "They'd better limber up, be ready for it, be ready to dive back in on an instant. Third thorax ring, center; or top collar-ring, if they don't know. Make sure they understand where it counts."

Merry bailed out, staggering, felt his way around to the back. Warrior was dancing in impatience beside the truck. The two men in the cab edged out and followed Merry.

"How far?" Raen asked. Warrior quivered very rapidly. Near, then. She felt the truck lighten of its load, eased off the brake and set it in gear, not to waste precious fuel. Merry's door was open. She left it so; he might need it in a hurry. "Warrior—hear me: you must not fight. You're a messenger. Understand?"

"Yess." It accepted this. It was majat strategy. No heroism, she thought suddenly, not among majat: only function and common sense, expediency to the limit. Warrior was very dangerous at the moment, excited. It paced the slow-moving truck as the men did. "Give message."

"Not yet. I don't want you to go yet."

The road curved, took a small decline, rose again. Then blockish shapes hove up in the starlight, among the distinctive structures of collectors.

The depot. The road went through it, that cluster of buildings that likely spelled ambush. Raen kept the truck rolling, watched the fuel that was registering just slightly: enough to carry them through— maybe.

Then the shrilling of Warriors erupted from the left of the road. She began to feel the jolting of the truck, men climbing aboard in haste. She kept it slow.

"Warrior," she said, "don't answer them."

"Yes," it agreed. "I am very quiet, Kethiuy-queen."

"Can you—" The wheels jerked into a rut and she wrenched it over again. "Can you tell their hive?"

"Goldsss."

That made sense. Golds even on Cerdin had chosen the open places, the fields, avoiding men. Once reds had done so too.

The headlights picked out girders, the frame of a collector, the wall of a weathered building, with barred and broken windows. The light flashed back off jagged glass.

Objects lay in the road, where it widened to include the buildings. Corpses, she realized, avoiding one. Human forms, desiccated by heat and sun, scattered in a pattern of flight from the central building. Another shape hove up, brown metal—the rear of a truck, with open doors.

Merry darted past, running to it, a group of men with him. Her eyes picked out something better: pumps, a fuel delivery in the shadow of the truck, a spidery tantalus with lines intact.

She pulled in, braked, bailed out and ran round to the side; Merry was before her, the nozzle in.

"It needs a pump," he said, anguished; and then flicked a glance up, at the collectors. She had the same thought. "Go," she said to the man nearest. "Should be a switch in the building. It ought to work."

The azi ran. All about them now, the shrilling was ominously louder.

"Golds," Warrior boomed. "Here, here, watch out!" It moved, swiftly, dancing in its anxiety. Fire spat in the building.

"Watch it!" Raen cried, ran for the door of it; Merry was in the same stride with her.

A Warrior sprang out at them; she fired from the hip and crippled it, as Warrior pounced. Two others were on them: azi-fire raked past and took them. Raen clutched the rifle and kicked the door wider, on a dark room and an azi convulsing on the floor, majat-bitten. There were no others; Warrior shouldered past her, and she was sure by that. Merry found the comp, called out, and she punched POWER-ON. Lights came on, inside and out, blinding. . . . local reserve, from the collectors.

"Works!" she heard an azi call from outside. "Works!"

And the shrilling was moving in on them.

"We could use that other truck," Merry said.

"Don't be greedy."

"Less load, better time."

"Try it," Raen said. "Hurry."

He left, running. She walked out after. They were no clearer to majat eyes in the lights than in the dark; but the heat of the lights themselves was an advertisement. The golds knew beyond doubt now, perhaps delayed in the process of Grouping.

Warrior had darted out again; it rose from the corpse of a gold, mandibles clicking. "Other blues," it translated for her. "Both dead. Gold-hive killed blue messengers. Lost. Message in gold-hive now. Bad, Kethiuy-queen, bad thing. This-unit goes now."

"Wait," she said. It would not get through, not with golds ringing them. She bit her lips and kept scanning beyond the lights, reckoning how blind they were to the land outside the circle of them.

And the majat were cut off by the cluster of buildings; that was why there was no rush as yet. Majat sought them visually, and the buildings were between. The group-mind had to be informed, to make nexus.

Quickly now she passed among the azi still outside, touched shoulders, ordered them into the truck with the tank most full. Warrior danced about in her wake, quivering with anxiety, wanting instruction. "You too," she told it. "Get inside, inside the front of the truck, this side, understand? Merry, we may have to give up on the second."

"First is full." Merry snatched the nozzle from the first truck and passed it to another man, who swung the tantalus over to the second. He put the cap on. "We can make it, sera. And if one should break down on the road—"

"I'm putting most of the men in my truck. We'll sort things out if we both get out of here."

"Good, sera. Leave me two men, that's all."

"Get up there and be sure this thing starts," she yelled at him, over a rising in the majat-sound. She hastened then, saw that Warrior had contrived to work its unyielding body into the cab. She slammed the door on it, raced round the back, giving last orders to the men jammed inside, vulnerable with the rear of the truck open to the air. "Get the tanks when we're clear," she shouted at them. "Pick your time and do it."

"Sera!" several cried suddenly.

She looked over her shoulder. A glittering tide swept under the lights and the girders, with speed almost too great for the eye to comprehend.

"Merry!" she screamed, and ran, flung herself into her seat, slammed the door, rolled the window up as she started the motor. It took. She slung the truck back and around, screening Merry for the instant, saw him and his partners dive for the cab and get the doors closed. The truck rocked, and all at once majat were all over them, tearing at the metal and battering at the glass. Some had weapons, and sought targets for their vision.

Merry's truck started moving, lurched forward at full; she hit the accelerator hard behind him. The tantalus ripped loose and raked the majat clinging to the front; Warrior, tucked beside her, squirmed and shrilled in its own language, deafening, itself blind by reason of the glass about it. "Sit still," Raen shouted at it, trying to rake majat against the corner of a building.

Suddenly everything flared with light.

The tanks. One of the men had gotten them. Majat dropped from the truck; rear-mirrors showed an inferno and majat scattering across the face of it, blinded in that maelstrom of heat. Red fire laced in their wake, and open road and grass showed before them, the whole area alight with that burning. Buildings caught, and blazed red.

She sucked in a breath, fought the wheel to keep in Merry's wake, down the road, her own vehicle overladen, but free. A sound pierced her ears, Warrior's shrill voice, passing down into human range. "Kill," Warrior said, seeming satisfied.

The road smoothed out. They began to make time, blind as they were in Merry's dust cloud.

And when the light was out of sight over several hills she punched in the com and raised Merry. "Good work. Are you all right up there?"

"All right," he confirmed.

"Pull off and leave the motor running."

He did so, easing to a comfortable stop. She pulled in behind and ran round the front to open the door for Warrior before it panicked. It disentangled itself, climbed down, grooming itself in distaste, muttering of gold-scent.

"Life-fluids," it said. "Kill many."

"Go now," she bade it. "Tell all you know to Mother. And tell Mother these azi and I are coming to blue-hive's Hill, to the new human-hive nearest it. Let Warriors meet us there."

"Know this place," Warrior confirmed. "Strange azi."

"Tell Mother these things. Go as quickly as you can."

"Yess," it agreed, bowed for taste, that for its kind was the essence of message. She gave it, that gesture very like a kiss, and the majat drew back. "Kethiuy-queen," it said. And strangely: "Sug-ar-water."

It fled then, quickly.

"Sera." Merry came running up behind her; she turned, saw him, saw his partners sorting men from truck to truck.

"We have casualties?"

"Eight dead, no injured."

She grimaced and shook her head. "Leave them," she said, and walked back to supervise, put several men on watch, one to each point, for the headlights showed only grass about, and that not far. The glow was still bright over the hills.

The dead were laid out by the road, neatly: their only ceremony. Units organized themselves, all with dispatch.

"Sera!" a lookout hissed, pointed.

There were lights, blue, floating off across the grass.

"Hive-azi," she exclaimed. "We're near something. Hurry, Merry!"

Everyone ran; men flung themselves into one truck or the other, and Raen dived behind the wheel of her own, slammed the door, passed Merry in moving out: she had the map. The truck, relieved of half its weight, moved with a new freedom.

And suddenly there was the promised paving, where the depot road joined the Great South. Raen slammed on the brakes for the jolt, climbed onto it, spun the wheel over and took to it with a surge of hope.

Behind them, reflected in the mirrors, the fire reached the fields.

6

THE SOUND OF HAMMERING resounded through the halls of ITAK upstairs. Metal sheeting was going into place, barriers to the outside. The hammer-blows echoed even into the nether floors, the levels below. In the absence of air-conditioning and lights, the lower levels assumed a strange character, the luxury of upstairs furnishings crowded into what had been lower offices, fine liquor poured by the lighting of hand-torches.

Enis Dain lifted his glass, example to the others, his board members, their families, and the officials, whoever had been entitled to shelter here. There was still, from above, through the doors still open, the sound of hammering.

Some had fled for the port. Unwise. There was a Kontrin reported there, the Enemy that the Meth-maren had warned them would come. Likely they had met with him, to their sorrow. Dain drank; all drank, the board members, his daughter, who sat by Prosserty—a useless man, Prosserty, Dain had never liked him.

"It's close in here," Prosserty complained. Dain only stared at him, and, remembering the batteries, cut off the handtorch, leaving them only the one set atop the table. He began calculating how long a night it would be.

"About sixteen days of it," he said. "About time for Council to get a message from the Meth-maren. We can last that long. They'll do something. Until then, we last it out. We've comfort enough to do that."

The hammering stopped upstairs.

"They're through up there," Hela Dain said. "They'll be sealing us in now."

Then glass splintered, far above.

And someone screamed.

The lights were out. 117-789-5457 sat tucked in the corner on her mat, mental null. The lights had been out what subjectively seemed long, and the temperature was up. Sounds reached her, but none were ordinary. She knew a little unease at this, wondering if food would come soon, and water, for water no longer came from the tap, and it always had, whatever cubicle she had occupied.

Always the lights had been above, and the air had been tolerable.

But now there was nothing.

Sounds. Sounds without meaning. The quick patter of soft feet. 117-789-5457 untucked and looked up. There was a strange glow in the blackness, blue lights, that wove and bobbed above, not on the catwalks, but on the very rims of the cells. Faces, blue-lighted; naked bodies; wild unkempt hair; these folk squatted on the rim of her own cell, stared down, grinning.

Hands beckoned. Eyes danced in the lights. "Come," they said, voices overlapping. "Come. We help. Come, azi."

She rose, for they reached hands to her, and one leaned down very far, helped by the others, caught her hands and drew her, by all their efforts, up.

117-789-5457 looked about her, balancing on the wall, held by strong, thin hands. Lights wove and bobbed everywhere. Laughter echoed in the silent places. Out of all the cells, azi were drawn.

"Take all azi, young, old, yess," one laughed, and danced away. "Come, come, come, come."

117-789-5457 followed, along the walls, for she had never refused an order. She smiled, for that seemed the way to please these who ordered her.

"There's fire in the city," the voice from downworld continued thinly, azi-calm, and Leo K14-756-4806 listened without looking, taking deeply to heart his instructions, which placed him in charge of station command. Morn depended on him. He listened, and did not waver, although he was distressed for what he heard.

Regarding his own men he could not tell: they kept their masks, that being Morn's general instruction; and he could not read their reactions to the voice from the shuttle, that brought them ill news.

But there was wavering certainly in the ranks of the captive betas, and of the guard-azi who belonged to the station, who stood under levelled rifles, along with the betas.

"We must restore power," the head beta appealed to him. "The city must have it."

"The fires are in every quarter," the impartial voice continued. "We've had no contact with Morn since he entered the terminal. What shall we do, Leo?"

"Wait for orders," Leo answered, looked about the center, at betas and station azi. No one moved. The betas did not dare and the station azi would not, lacking instruction.

"This is *Moriah,*" another azi voice broke in. "We're getting nothing from city communications any longer. Everything's in complete chaos."

"Just stand by your posts," Leo said. There was nothing else to say. He paced back across the command center, arms folded, looked constantly at the betas, challenging them to advance any more ideas of their own.

They did not.

Warriors were back, great bodies shifting through all the rooms of the house, shrilling and booming signals that hurt the ears. Jim ventured the stairs to the turning, met some coming down and flung himself aside, for the Warriors were in haste, and had no inclination to speak. Pol's oath erupted out of the blue-lit depths.

"They're running," the Kontrin said.

"Max," Jim pleaded, at the edge of panic. "Max—"

Max came; all the azi followed, bringing Pol, scrambling up the stairs against the spiny flood of majat down them. Furniture crashed throughout the house, the press of too many bodies. The house boiled with them; the dark rooms hummed with distress and anger.

And the glow of fires shone through the back windows, distant ruddy smoke billowing up.

"They're blind in fire," Pol said. "Some betas have figured one way to fight them."

"Windows," Max said. "Stations."

Azi moved, each rifleman to a window.

"Your blues are beaten," Pol said above the hum of majat-voices. "I'd suggest we get out of here."

Jim shook his head fiercely, strode up the hall to look out the open door, where dark shapes scurried about the front garden. "They're not running, not all of them. They're still going to hold this place."

Max cast a look too, and at him. "I'd suggest we get out there, work ourselves into cover in the rocks. Harder to dislodge us that way."

"I can't say." Jim swallowed heavily. "Do it. I don't think walls can stop them."

"Want advice?"

Jim looked about, back to the wall, at Pol Hald. The gaunt Kontrin stood between his guards, without threat.

"I've some interest in the management of this," Pol said. "The man's right; but occupy those windows with vantage, front and back for screening fire if you need it. And get your own Warriors behind you; your men can't tell blues from reds in the dark."

"It's sense," Max said.

A sound began . . . started with the feeling of pressure in the ears, so that many pressed their hands to them; and then became pain, a shrilling that grated in the bones.

It was all around them. The Warriors in the house retreated into a knot, grouping, booming to each other in panic.

"Warrior!" Jim cried. "Stay!"

They clicked and shrilled in reply, flicking palps this way and that, and majat-azi who had come with them scampered from their vicinity, faces stark with fright. Jim started forward.

"No," Pol exclaimed, reached out to grip his arm. "No, blast it, you're not Meth-maren. Stay back from them."

That too was good advice. He retreated outside with Max, settled in the rocks with a Kontrin of Hald beside them, and shook his head to clear his ears, pressure that would not go away.

We're going to die, he thought, and panicked entirely, for it was a born-man thought, a born-man fear: the tapes had done it to him, prepared him only for this, this sick dread. Max's face was calm. The Kontrin gave him a twisted smile, as if he had read his mind, and mocked him in the fear they shared.

Sound rose about them, madness.

7

THE TRUCK JOLTED, BADLY. Raen caught at the door, rubbed her blurred eyes, looked askance at the azi who, however indifferent a driver, kept the pace, tailing Merry.

"How's the fuel holding?" she asked, leaning to see. It was reserve tank, half full. They were still all right.

And the odometer: ten kilometers from their goal. The lights of the city should have been visible, but she expected none. She folded her arms and sat regarding the sweep of the horizon, finding yet no sight of their goal, nothing in the faint glimmering of dawn, which began to fade the stars.

But there were no stars northward.

She sat up, her heart beating hard against her ribs. She had slept. There was no drowsiness in her now.

"Merry," she said into the com. "Merry. Are you awake up there?"

"Sera?"

"Smoke. Smoke over the city."

"Yes. I see it, sera."

"We're going to pass. Turn's coming up. Stand by. Go round him, Will. We've a little space yet."

Five kilometers. The truck accelerated; Merry dropped back. Four. She started watching on the right, closely, wondering in agony about the accuracy of the maps.

The kilometers ticked off. "Slow down," she said. The driver eased down. There was a stake with an illegible number, a spur, a mere eroded place off the paved road, but trucks had passed it: crushed weeds showed in the dawning.

"Take it," she said. The driver did so, eased them onto it, carefully, while the truck swayed and lurched and weeds whispered against the doors.

They were blind in this place. She would have given much then for Warrior's sight and hearing. Turn after turn took them out of sight of the road, and the only comfort was Merry's vehicle showing in the mirror by her window.

A turning, a descent of the road, a brief climb around the curve of a hill: a weathered cluster of buildings showed before them, a desolate place . . . but someone had been cutting weeds.

Itavvy, she thought, *prosperity on your house.*

Doors opened; men came out, sunsuited, rifles levelled, to meet the trucks. Beside her, Will reached for his own rifle. She gathered up hers, opened the door.

"Isan Tel," she said. "Comp code 579-4645-687."

One man nodded to the others, his rifle lifted out of the line of fire; other weapons were turned away. Sunmasks and visors came off. There were several among them female; several of more clerical look than guard-type, some unarmed.

"I'm your contract," she said. "I can't clear it on comp; you know that. Ask your azi-in-charge: did you not find orders in comp to keep to these buildings and fight only majat that attacked you?"

"That's truth," a man said, quiet voice, quiet manner, minding her of Jim. Faces all about took on a look of great relief, as if their entire world had suddenly settled into order: it had asked much of them until now, that azi alone hold the place. She saw their eyes fixed on her, with that deep calm that did not belong in the situation: contract-loyalty.

"The hives are moving," she said. "Have you had trouble here?"

The manager-azi lifted an arm toward the south, the open fields. "Majat came in. We took a few. They went back again."

She indicated the northeast. "Nothing from that direction."

"No, sera."

She nodded. "You're on blue-hive's doorstep; but they're not human-killers. The others were golds, more than likely. You've already done your proper service, sitting here, guarding blue-hive. I have your contract. We go further now, but only azi that won't freeze or panic."

Their calm was disturbed by talk of blue-hive. She saw the ripple of dismay, turned and waved at Merry. "Out! We're going afoot from here. Any who'll come, any who are able."

Her own azi climbed out, none hesitating, with rifles and what gear they had; weary as they were, she looked on them with some hope. "We're going to fight *for* a hive," she said. "For blue-hive, our own, back in the city. We have to go among them; into it, if we can. Stay, if that's too much for you."

She started walking . . . knew Merry, at least, would join her. He was there, at once, and hardly slower, the others, filthy, sorry-looking men; she looked back, and not one had stayed. The Tel estate azi were on their heels, plain by their clean clothing and their energy. In the rear, the managers and the domestics trailed along, perhaps reckoning now they were safer not to be left in the deserted buildings.

They climbed, pushing aside the high weeds, finding trails overgrown and forgotten in the hills. "Majat trails," she said to Merry. "Abandoned ones."

"Blue-hive?"

"Better be."

Something urged at her hearing. She kept her eyes to the high rocks, the folds of the land.

A majat warning boomed out. She spun left; rifles jerked about, hovered unfired on the person of a Warrior, testament to azi discipline. She turned her fist to it, that stood against the sky.

"Meth-maren," it intoned.

"Warrior, you're too far for my eyes. Come closer."

It shifted forward, a blue beyond doubt. Others appeared out of the rocks, jaws clicking with excitement.

"Here are azi of my-hive," she said. "They've held the valley till now; now they'll fight where needed."

It lowered itself, offered touch and taste, and she took and gave it, moving carefully lest some new azi take alarm. "Good, good," it pronounced then. "Mother sends. Come, come quick, Kethiuy-queen. Bring, bring, bring."

She looked back; none who followed had fled; none offered to go back now. Warrior danced with impatience and she touched Merry's arm and started after it, following the devious ways it led, over stone and through brush.

Suddenly the hive gaped before them, a dark pit, seeming void of defense; but Warriors materialized out of the weeds, the stones of the hills, boiled out from the darkness. She hesitated not at all, hearing their guide boom a response to them; and one Warrior touched her—by that move, one who knew her personally.

"Warrior?" she asked it.

"This-unit guides. Come. Come, bring azi."

Blue lights bobbed in the pit. She went without question toward them, Merry beside her, others close at her heels. The darkness enveloped them, and majat-azi scampered just ahead, wretched creatures who no longer laughed, but stumbled and faltered with exhaustion. Blue light ran chaotically over the walls, showing them the way. Warrior-song shrilled in the dark.

And the majat-azi touched her, urged her on, breathlessly, faster and faster. "Mother," they cried, "Mother, Mother, Mother."

Raen gasped for air and kept moving, stumbling on the uneven floor, catching herself against the rough walls.

All at once the blue lights were not sufficient. Vast darkness breathed about them, and they streamed along the midst of it. A great pale form loomed ahead, that dragged itself painfully before them, huge, filling all the tunnel.

It was Mother, who moved.

Who heaved Herself along the tunnel prepared for Her vast bulk. The walls echoed with Her breathing. About her were small majat who glittered with jewels; and before her moved a dark heaving flood of bodies, dotted with azi-lights.

Majat-language boomed and shrilled in the tunnel, deafening. And, terrible in its volume, came Her voice, which vibrated in the earth.

Raen gathered herself and passed beside that great body, moving faster than ever Mother could. There was room, barely, that she and the men with her could avoid the sweep of Mother's limbs, that struggled with even thrusts to drive Her vast body along, at every rumbling intake of Her breath.

"I am here!" Raen cried.

"Kethiuy-queen," She answered. The great head did not turn, could not; Mother remained fixed upon Her goal.

"Am I welcome, Mother? Where are you going?"

"I go," Mother said simply, and the earth quivered with the moving of Her. Air sucked in again. "I go. Haste. Haste, young queen."

Anxiety overwhelmed her. She increased her pace, moving now among the Drones, whose chittering voices hurt her ears.

Then the Workers, all that vast horde, azi scattered among them; and the strange-jawed egg-tenders, leaving their work, precious eggs abandoned.

She looked back. Mother had almost vanished in the shadows. She saw Merry's bruised face in the faint blue glow, felt the touch of his hand.

"We're going north," she said, comprehension suddenly coming on her, the Workers who had plied the basement, the preparation of a way.

"To fight for them?" Merry asked hoarsely, and glanced back himself, for there were men who still followed. Perhaps they all did; strung out through the tunnel, it was no longer possible to see. Perhaps some collapsed in withdrawal, gone mad from fear; or perhaps training held, and they had no sensible dread.

"I belong," she said, "where this merges."

"Where, sera?"

"Home," she said.

8

A HORDE OF STEPS approached the steel doors, a surge of panicked voices. Moth stirred, lifted her head, although to do so took more strength than she had left to spend on them, who troubled her sleeping and merged with dreams.

"Moth!" A voice came out of the turmoil. She knew this one too, old Moran, and fear trembled in that sound. "Moth! Thon is gone— *gone.* The hive-masters couldn't hold them. They're in the City. Everywhere—"

She touched her microphone, braced before her on the console, beside the wine bottle and her gun. "Then lock your own doors, Moran. Follow my example."

"We need the codes. Moth, do something."

She grinned, her head bobbing slightly with weakness. "But haven't you figured it out yet, Moran? I am."

"The city's in wreckage," the voice from *Moriah* said. "Leo, Leo, we've still had no contact with him. There were majat here. Even they've left, moved elsewhere. He should have been in contact by now."

"Hold the ships," Leo repeated, and looked up at the other azi, his own and the station's. They were exhausted. There had been no food, no off-shift. He thought that he ought to send for something to eat. He was not sure that he had appetite for it.

The betas sat in a knot over to the side of the door. One of them had become ill, holding his heart. He was an older beta. They fed him medicines and he seemed to have recovered somewhat; this was of no concern, for he was not a necessary beta. None were, individually.

"Call the galley," Leo said to one of the others. "Have food brought up here."

The beta rose, came, moved very carefully while he was at the com board. He spoke precisely the request and retreated again among his fellows. Leo stood watching them.

Moriah and the shuttle called again, on the quarter hour; and again.

Then a light flashed at the door, and a cart arrived from the galleys, redolent with food and drink. Azi brought it, unloaded it, bent to unload the lower tray.

Suddenly a gun was in one azi hand and a bolt flew for comp, raked it. Leo fired, and the azi spun back against the doorway, slid down. Others froze in dismay, died so.

Lights flickered. Sirens started sounding, lights all over the board flaring red.

"He's a plant," one said, bending over the azi who had fired. He wiped with his thumb at the too-bright tattoo. "A ringer."

The sirens multiplied. The betas rushed to the boards and worked at them frantically, and Leo hesitated from one threat to the other, null-mind pressing at him. "Get away!" he shouted at the betas. One of his men fired, and a beta died at the main board, slumped over it.

A sign began flashing in the overhead. DISENGAGE ALL SHIPS, it ordered.

The ship. Sanity returned with that responsibility. Leo fired, taking out the betas who would not obey his shouted orders, and leaned over com, punched it wide-broadcast. *"Eros* crew." His voice fed from the corridors outside and throughout the station. "This is Leo. Return to the ship at once. Return to the ship at once."

It was necessary to hold that, above all else. Morn would expect it. "Go," he shouted at the others with him.

And then because it occurred to him that he dared not leave betas near controls, he killed them, every one.

"They're running," the young Upcoaster said, leaning against the glass and pressed to it, staring up the outside concourse.

"Don't!" another cried, when he pushed the door open.

There were no shots, only a breath of cold air off the docks.

"Come on!" Itavvy cried at his wife, snatched Meris from her arms; and the Upcoasters sprang for the doors too, all of them starting to run, baggage left, everything left.

The floodlights on the vast docks were flickering, red lights flashing warnings, sirens braying. Itavvy sucked a lungful of the thin cold air and pelted after the artist, cast a look over his shoulder to see that Velin followed. Tears blurred the lights when he looked round again, a flickering that spelled out *Phoenix*. The ramp was ahead of them, through a tangle of lines. Someone fell behind him, scrambled up again. The artist took the ramp; Itavvy did, Meris wailing in his ear, and for that, for *her* he did not fall, although he felt pain in his side and his chest. They ran the frozen ramp, over the plates that should have moved to help them.

And the hatch was shut.

"*Let us in!*" he screamed at it. Others caught up with him, hammered at the metal with their fists. Itavvy wept, tears streaming his face, and Velin flung her arms about them both, him and Meris.

It was the oldest Upcoaster who found the intercom recessed in the ramp housing. He shouted into it. "Shut up!" he yelled back at them when they added their voices; and from the intercom: "*Stand by.*"

The hatch hummed, parted. Azi crewmen, their faces sober and unamazed, stood waiting to help them aboard.

They stood inside, with trembling hands proffered tickets, evidence of passage.

The hatch sealed behind them.

"Brace where you are," a voice grated from the intercom overhead. "We're disengaging and getting out of here."

9

THE SHRILLING WAS LOUDER, front walls, back walls, on all sides of them, and what had begun in the dark of night refused to go away by day, when light streamed over the garden. It should dispel the nightmare. It instead made it real, picking out the shapes of poised Warriors, the husks and bodies of the dead piled in the corner of the garden, and the cracks in the outer wall where assault had already been made and repulsed.

Jim wiped at his face, crouching by Max's side among the rocks. Pol was by him: they spared one young azi to keep a gun in Pol's ribs constantly, for whatever the Kontrin was, he was a born-man and old in such maneuverings, able to forwarn them what the hives might do . . . most of all what the human mind among them might do.

He's there, Pol had said, when the last assault had nearly carried to them, when cracks had appeared in the wall and fire from the gate had distracted them. *That's Morn behind that. The next thing is to watch our backs.*

And that proved true.

"He's delayed over-long," Pol said after a time. "I'm surprised. He should have tried by now. That means he and his allies are up to something that takes a little time."

Jim looked at him. The Kontrin's accustomed manner was mockery; Pol used little of that in recent hours. His gaunt face was yet more hollowed, his eyes shadowed with the exhaustion which sat on them all. The high heat would come by mid-morning; they wore sunsuits, but neither masks nor visors in place, and the sleeves were all unfastened for comfort. Azi rested in their places, slumped against rocks or walls, seeking what sleep could be gotten, for they had had little in the night. Pol leaned his head back against the rock that sheltered them, eyes shut.

"What would take time?" Max wondered aloud.

"Tunnels," Jim said, the thought leaping unwanted into his mind. He swallowed heavily and tried to reason around it. "But Warriors don't dig and Workers don't fight."

Pol lifted his head. "Azi do both," he said, and shifted around to face forward. "Look at the cracks in that wall. They're wider."

It was so. Jim bit at his lips, rose and went aside, where one of the Warriors crouched . . . touched its offered scent-patches.

"Jim. Yess."

"Warrior, the wall's cracking over there. Pol Hald thinks there could be digging."

The great head rotated, body shifted, directed toward the wall. "Human eyess . . . certain, Jim?"

"I can see it, Warrior. A crack in the shape of a tree, spreading and branching. It gets wider."

Chelae brushed him; palps flicked over his cheek. "Good, good," Warrior approved, and scuttled off. It sought and locked jaws with the next, and that one moved off into the house, while Warrior continued, touching jaws with each of the Warriors nearest, who spread in turn to pass the message further.

Jim slid back into position next Max and Pol. "It's disturbed about it," he panted. He shivered despite the warmth, suddenly realizing that he was terrified. They had fought in the night; he had never fired his gun. Now at the prospect of their shelter breached by daylight he sat trembling.

"Easy," Pol said, put out a thin hand and closed it on his leg until it hurt. The pain focused things. He looked at the Kontrin, suddenly aware of a vast silence, that the shrilling which had surrounded them had fallen away.

"You're always with Morn," Jim said hoarsely, for it did not make sense, the tapes with the behavior of Pol Hald. "You're out of his house. You wouldn't go against him."

"A long partnership." The hand did not move, though it was gentler. "In the Family, such are rare."

Treachery, what he had learned warned him. He stared at the Kontrin, paralyzed by the touch he should never have allowed.

"Strange," Pol said, "that at times you have even her look about you."

The shrilling erupted again; and a portion of the garden sank away, gaping darkness aboil with earth and majat bodies. Blues sprang, engaged; shots streaked from azi weapons.

The wall went down, collapsed in a cloud of dust: through it came a horde of majat, azi among them.

Jim braced the gun and sighted, tried to pull the trigger. Beside him a body collapsed, limp.

It was Max. A shot had gone through his brain. Jim stared down at him, numb with horror.

The azi on the other side cried warning, sprawled back unconscious. Pol had Max's rifle and whipped it from a backward blow at his guard to aim it up, putting shots into the majat horde, dropping azi and majat with no distinction.

Jim sighted amid them and pulled the trigger, firing into the oncoming mass, unsure what damage he did, his eyes blurred so that it was impossible to see anything clearly.

The sound swelled in his ears, a horrid chirring that ascended out of range. Majat poured from the house behind them, more Warriors than he had known were there. Majat swarmed from the pit before them and through the breached wall, and came on them like a living wave. Pol fired indiscriminately; he did; more came to replace the fallen, as a wider portion of the wall collapsed, exposing their flank.

"Move back!" Pol shouted at him. "Get your men back!" The Kontrin sprang up low and took a new position.

Jim shouted a half-coherent order and scrambled after, slid in at Pol's side and started firing again.

Then eerie figures appeared among the majat, like majat in the mold of men, bearing each an insignia on the shoulder.

And one was among them that was clearly a man, in Hald Color.

"Morn," Pol said, and stopped firing.

Jim sighted for that target, missed; and fire came back, grazed his arm. Pol seized him, pulled him over as a lacery of fire cut overhead.

Majat voices boomed, and stone cracked. One of the portico pillars came down in the sudden rush of majat from the house, a sea of bodies; and among them ran naked majat-azi and azi in sunsuits brown with mud and blood.

Fire cut both ways. Majat and azi fell dying and were trampled by those behind. And one there was slighter than most, with black hair flying and a gun in a chitined fist. The azi by her died, rolled sprawling.

Jim fought to loose himself, flung himself over and saw Morn in the center of the yard. Raen was blind to him. "Look out!" he screamed.

"Morn!" Pol yelled, hurled himself to his feet and fired.

Morn crumpled, the look of startlement still on his face. And startlement was on Raen's face too, horror as she averted the gun. Pol sank to one knee, swore, and Jim seized at him, but Pol stood without his help, braced, fired a flurry of shots into the armored invaders, who stood as if paralyzed.

Raen did the same, and majat swept past the lines of her men, who hurled accurate fire into the opposing tide, majat meeting body to body, waves that collided and broke upon each other, with shrilling and booming. Heads rolled. Bodies thrashed in convulsions. More of the wall collapsed, and again they were flanked. Jim turned fire in that direction, and saw to his horror the majat sweeping down on them.

Pol's accurate fire cut into them, shots pelting one after the other, precisely timed.

A body slid in from their rear: Merry, putting shots where they counted; and Raen next, whose fire was, like Pol's, accurate. The shrilling died away; majat rushed from their rear, narrowly missing them in their blinding rush, and they dropped, tucked for protection.

But Pol did not go on firing. He laid his head against the rock, staring blankly before him. Raen touched him, bent, pressed a gentle touch of her lips to his brow.

"That's once," Pol said faintly, and the face lost its life; a shudder went through his limbs, and ceased.

Raen averted her face, looked instead at the wave of majat that was breaking, flooding back toward the walls.

And with a curse she sprang up and ran; Merry followed, and other azi. Jim slipped his hand from Pol's shoulder and snatched at his rifle to follow, past the cover of the rocks.

A dark body hurtled into him, spurs ripping. He sprawled, went under, body upon body rushing over him, until pain stopped.

10

AGONY . . . MOTHER EXISTED IN IT, in each powerful drive of Her legs that drove Her vast weight another half-length. Drones moved, themselves unaccustomed to such exertions, their breathing harsh pipings. Workers danced back and forth, offering nourishment from their jaws, the depleted fluids of their own bodies, feeding Her and the Drones.

Their colors grew strange, the blue mottled light and dark, with here and there a blackness. The sight disturbed Her, and She moaned as She thrust Her way along, following the new tunnel, the making of the Workers.

Mother, the Workers sang, *Mother, Mother.*

And She led them.

I have made the way, the Warrior-mind reported, one of its units touching at Her. *Enemies are retreating. Need of Workers now to move the stones.*

Well done, She said, tasting of life-fluids and of victory.

Warrior scurried away, staggering in its exhaustion and its haste. *Follow this-unit,* Warrior gave taste to Workers. *Follow, follow me.*

11

"SERA?"

Raen caught herself, caught her breath between the wall and Merry's solid body. An azi-light swung from her wrist. She blinked clear the subway, the vacant tracks coursed by majat. One of the men offered her a flask. She drank a mouthful; it went the round among them, forlorn humans huddled at the side of the arching tunnel. They panted for breath, lost in the strange sounds, the rush of chitined bodies, of spurred feet. One of them, hurt, slumped in a knot against the wall. Raen reached and touched him, obtained a lifting of the head, an attempt to focus. Another gave him a drink.

They were twelve, only twelve, out of all of them. She swallowed heavily and rested her hand on Merry's shoulder, breathing in slower and slower gasps.

"City central's up there," she said. "Blues have A branch. The reds are probably in E, that goes to the port. Greens . . . I don't know. Golds . . . likely C, due south. They'll mass in central, under ITAK headquarters."

"Three hives against them," Merry said faintly. "Sera, the blues can't do it."

She slid her hand down, pressed his arm. "I don't think so either, but there's no stopping them. We've kept them alive this long. Merry, take the men, go back. Go back from here. I'll not throw the rest of you away."

"Sera—send them back, not me."

Other voices protested, faces anxious in the blue glow.

"Any of you who wants to stay back, stay," she said, and rose up and started to walk again, slung the burden of the riflestrap to her shoulder.

They came. Perhaps it was fear of the majat without her. She thought that it might be. She suspected something else, that she was too rational to believe. She wiped at her face, struck the tears away with no realization of hurt or grief, only that she was very tired and her eyes watered. The tunnel smelled of majat, like musty paper; and they passed strange sights as they walked, found vehicles frozen on the tracks, wherever they had been when power failed; and terrible sights, the sweet-sour reek of death, where betas had died, some sprawled on the tracks, some in vehicles the glass of which had shattered, dead of majat bite or terror—brushed constantly now by the steady rush of Warriors.

But now there appeared other types amid the press . . . blue-hive azi, staggering with exhaustion and mindless with haste; and after them, Workers, fluting shrill, plaintive cries.

"They're all going," Merry breathed beside her. "Even the queen will follow. Sera, is it wise to be here at all?"

"No," she said plainly, "it's not."

But she did not stop walking, or hesitate. The Worker-cries became song, that filled her ears, ran through her nerves, and banished thought.

Daylight shafted down ahead, where bodies milled, that vast terminal that was central, zero, with day falling down from skylights. Song came up from that heaving mass, and Warriors within it surged this way and that. Workers added themselves, climbing over the bodies of others.

More, Raen thought, far more than blue-hive alone: all, all hives, met there.

And majat died there, of weakness and wounds, crushed down. The song numbed. Merry held his ears and cried out soundlessly in the chaos; and Raen pressed hands to her own, all of them seeking the retreat of the walls, any place aside from that flood of bodies which kept coming.

The ground shook, the walls quivered.

A faint far glimmering in jewels and azi-lights, Mother came, struggling forward.

Mother drew breath, heaved forward, breathed again, dazed with pain. Her own limbs, reaching out and shifting again out of view, were mottled now, bright blue and dark. About Her moved insanity, Warriors whose colors had gone mad, whose bodies glowed blue and extremities red, whose midlimbs gold, all mottled with green.

Queens were at hand: She heard Them, others, other-hives. Desperation possessed Her, the instinct certain now of direction.

There was nothing else.

She saw Them, in a seething mass of colors, among Warriors and Workers and Drones who had gone mad. One of the queens was red, with darker mottlings: She, fiercest; one gold, tinged with red; one green, with shadings of blue, incipient chaos.

Red queen shifted forward, ominous, and went for green, for the tainted and nearest one, breathing out hate.

Red was the killer, the Warrior-fragment, as green was the Worker-mind.

Mother hesitated, trembling, and saw green die, life-fluids drunk.

Blue, red queen breathed, and the Warriors quivered aside, pressing themselves out of the way in terror.

A second queen was dead. Raen shuddered, the hard grip of her azi about her, putting their own bodies between her and the press, a small knot of humanity, blue-lit. Other azi sheltered with them, naked creatures male and female, trembling and holding their ears against the battering sound. Lighter majat clambered over them, Drones, glittering with living jewels, perhaps adding their own screams to the thunder of the queens.

Merry shivered against her. Raen caught his hand and held it, that crushed bone against bone in hers: likely he had no wit left to know; she had none to care.

The battle raged in ponderous slow-motion, hazy shafts of sunlight enveloping the queens atop the living hill, reflecting jewel-colors. Strength held against strength: then came a darting move.

The third queen died, head severed.

The hill of bodies came undone about the survivor, sweeping over and about Her. Drones streamed through, to gather with other Drones; and Workers with Workers; and Warriors with Warriors, ringed about the living queen. The dead were hauled away. The living circles widened, spread throughout the terminal.

The queen moved, shifted position; so did all the others. She breathed out a note that made the walls shake, and after that was quiet.

A human wept, audible, soft sobs.

Raen leaned against Merry a moment, then gathered herself from him, from all the azi, and rose—walked among the still shapes of majat, Warriors, Workers, with the badges of blue-hive, red-hive, green and gold commingled. The rifle was still slung from her shoulder. She realized it, and dropped it echoing to the pavement, for there was no way out but to kill a queen, the last Mother of a world, and that she would not do.

She walked within reach of Her, without weapons in hand, and gazed up into the great jewelled face, the moiré'd eyes, heard the sough of Her breathing.

It was a gold. The pattern was on Her, for those who could read it.

"Mother," she said, "I'm Raen a Sul, Meth-maren."

Air sucked in. "Meth-maren," She sighed, and the huge head lowered, sought taste.

Raen kissed Her, touched the scent-patches, waited for the vast jaws to close; and they did not.

"Meth-maren," Mother said. "Kethiuy-queen."

It was blue queen's memory.

12

THE SUN WAS UNBEARABLE. Jim felt the burn of it before he felt anything more, and struggled to shade his face from it. He was held, and had to think which way to turn; and that meant consciousness.

His hands met spines and hair and chitin. He focused at that, and shoved in horror at the stiffening limbs that lay over him, the intertwined corpses of a majat and an azi.

All about him were corpses, shimmering and running in the tears the sun brought to his eyes. He struggled to pull the visor which hung about his neck up to his eyes, to see—and found nothing living anywhere.

The house was ruined, gaping rubble; and bodies lay thickly over the garden, save in one vast track which led to the broken walls . . . bodies majat and human, naked and clothed. Insects flitted about him as they settled on the dead; he batted at them, fought with fingers stiffening with sunburn to fasten the sunsuit.

Rock moved, a shifting outside the wall. He gathered up a rifle, staggered in that direction, his senses wavering in and out of focus.

He climbed over the rubble, blinked, saw a shadow on the ground and whirled, whipped the rifle up, but the majat's leap was faster.

The gun went off, torn from his hands. Another was on him, pulling from the other side. Chelae gripped his arm, cutting flesh.

Red: he saw the badge and tried to pull from it; the badge of the second was green. It lowered its head, jaws wide, and the palps brushed his lips, his face.

And it drew back. "Jim," it intoned.

He lived. The fact numbed him. He ceased to struggle, understanding nothing any longer.

"Meth-maren sendss," red Warrior said.

"Let me go," he asked then, his heart lurching a beat. "Let me go, Warrior; I'll come with you."

It released him. He clutched his injured arm and followed it, trailed by the green, down into the circle of the street, into the dark entry of the subway, into the deep places of the city, where no lights shone at all. At times he stumbled, blind, and his hands met bodies, yielding ones of majat-azi or the spiny hardness of majat. Chelae urged at him, hastening him, lifting him each time he fell.

Blue lights drifted toward him. At first he shrank from meeting them, not wanting delay, not wanting to be left: but he saw *her* bearing one of those lights, and he thrust his way free of the Warriors and ran, stumbling, toward her.

She met him, held him off at arm's length to look at him. "You're all right," she said, a question in her impatient manner; but her voice trembled. There was Merry by her, and other faces that he knew.

She hugged him then, and he nearly wept for joy; but she did not know, he thought, the things that he must admit, the knowledge that he had stolen, the thing he had made of himself.

He tried to tell her. "I used all the tapes," he said, "even the black ones. I didn't know what else to do." She touched his face and told him to be quiet, with a shift of her eyes toward Merry and the others.

"It's ruined back there," he said then. "Everything's ruined. Where will we go now?"

"In, for a time. Till the cycle completes itself." Her hand entwined with his: he felt the jewels rough and warm beneath his fingers. She gestured, walked with assurance the way from which she had come. Warriors walked about them; armed majat-azi followed. "It's going to be a while before I think of outside, a long while, perhaps. Majat-time."

"I've nineteen years," he said, anticipating all of them, and well-content.

Her fingers tightened on his.

Soft singing filled the air, the peaceful sound of Workers, with the stirrings and movings of many bodies in the tunnels.

"Hive-song," she said. "They've long lives. A turning of nature, a pulse of the cycle, to merge all colors, to divide again. *This-sun,* they say now. *Home-hive.* Against those cycles, my own life is nothing at all. Wait with me."

There was a ship, he thought, recalling Pol. There were betas who might live, who might serve her. He objected to these things one by one, and she shook her head, silent.

He asked no more.

13

MOTH, THE VOICES SHOUTED, *Moth, Moth!*

Eggs, she thought back at them, and mocked them for what they were.

A different sound came through the speakers, the shrilling of majat voices, the crash of metal and wood.

From the vents came a curious paper-scent. Human voices had ceased long ago.

Moth poured the last of the wine, drank it.

And pushed the button.

BOOK TEN

1

THE HATCH OPENED, let in the flood of evening air, the gentle light of the setting sun.

"Stay put," Tallen heard. *"Sir, we're picking up movement out there."*

"Wouldn't do to run," he said into the com unit. "Whatever happens—no response, hear me?"

"Be careful."

Majat. He heard the ominous chirring, and walked forward, very slowly.

Newhope had stood here. Weeds had taken the ruins. At center rose a hill, monstrous, where no hill had been. He had seen the pictures smuggled out, heard the reports and memorized them, along with family tales.

And in the long passage of years, in the fading of the Wars, *this* waited, where no Outsider dared trespass, until now.

We were wrong, the one side argued, ever to have relied on them.

But governments rose and fell and rose again, and rumors persisted . . . that life stirred in the forbidden Reach, that the wealth which had made the Alliance what it had been was there to be had, if any power could contrive to obtain it.

And the hives refused contact.

There were human folk on Istra, farmers, who lived out across the wide plains, who told wild tales and traded occasional jewels and rolls of majat-silk.

Tallen had met with them, these sullen, furtive men, suspicious of

any ship that called; and there was warning here, for there were no
few ships resting derelict in Istran fields.

Sixty years the contact had lapsed: collapse, chaos, war . . .
worlds breaking from the Alliance in panic, warships forcing them
in again, all for the scarcity of certain goods and the widespread rumors of majat breakout.

It was told in Tallen's family that men and majat had co-existed
here, had walked together in city streets, had cooperated one with the
other.

It was told somewhere in Alliance files that this was so.

He heard the sound nearer now, and walked warily, stopped at
last as a glittering creature rose out of the rocks and brush.

A trembling came on him, a loss of will. *Natural,* he thought,
recalling the tales his grandfather had told, who claimed to have
stood close to them. *Humans react to them out of deep instinct. One
has to overcome that.*

They see differently: that too, from old Tallen, and from reports
deep in the archives. He spread his hands wide from his sides, making clear to it that he had no weapons.

It came closer. He shut his eyes, for he quite lost his courage to
look at it near at hand. He heard its loud breathing, felt the bristly
touch of its forelimbs. A shadow fell on his closed eyes; something
touched his mouth—he shuddered convulsively at that, and the
touch and the shadow drew back.

"Stranger," it said, a harmony of sounds that joined into a word.

"Friend," he said, and opened his eyes.

It was still near. The moiré eyes shifted through the spectrum at
each minute turn of the head. "Beta human?" it asked him.

2

A STIRRING RAN THROUGH the hive. Raen lifted her head, read it in
the voices, the shift of bodies, needing no vision in the dark.

Stranger-human, the message came to her, and that pricked at curiosity, for betas would never come this far: they did their grain-
trading far out on the riverside, where they brought their sick, such
as majat could heal.

And the azi had gone long ago.

She missed them sorely. The hives did, likewise, mourning them in Drone-songs.

Merry had gone, neither first nor last, a sudden seizure of the heart. And she had wept for that, though Merry would hardly have understood it. *I am azi,* he had said once, refusing to be otherwise. *I would not want to outlive my time.* And so, one by one, the others had chosen.

It was strange, now, that a beta would have ventured into majat land, under the great Hill.

"Jim," she said.

"I hear." He found her hand, needing sight no more than she, as he was in other ways skilled with her skills.

Of all of them, Jim remained, a costly gift of Worker lives, and of his own will, more than Merry had had, who had wanted things his own way, in old patterns, in terms he understood.

For a long time she had cared for nothing beyond that, to know that there was one human to share the dark with her.

Now Warrior came, immortal as she, as he, in one of its many persons. "Outsider," it said, troubled, perhaps, in the perception of changes. "Unit called *Tallen.*"

3

TALLEN BLINKED IN the twilight, watching them come . . . two, woman and man, robed in gauzy majat-silk. They wore it as if it were nothing, priceless though it was, as if their own will were cloak enough.

They stopped near to him, and Tallen shivered in their regard, that strange coolness and lack of fear. There was a mark on the man, beneath the eye and on the shoulder: *azi.* The old Tallen had reported such, but not such as he, whose gaze he could not bear. The mark on the woman was of jewels; of her kind too there were remembrances.

"Ab Tallen," she said, strangely accented, "would be an old, old man."

"Dead," Tallen answered. "I'm his grandson. Your people remember him?"

Her eyes flickered, seemed possessive of secrets. She held out her right hand and he took it, hesitating at the strange warmth of the jewels that covered it.

"Raen Meth-maren," she said. "Yes, there's memory of him. Kind memory."

"Your name is hers, that he mentioned."

She smiled faintly, and questions of kinship went uninvited. She nodded to the man beside her. "Jim," she said, and that was all.

Tallen took the other offered hand, regarded them both anxiously, for majat hovered about, escort, guards, soldiery—there was no knowing what.

"You delayed longer than you should," she said.

"We had our years of trouble. I'm afraid there may have been landings here of a sort we'd not have allowed. Our apologies, for such intrusions."

She shrugged. "Most have learned, have they not?"

That was truth, and chilling in her manner. "We've come here twice—peacefully, hunting some contact."

"Now," she said, "we're pleased to answer you. Is it trade you want?"

He nodded, all his careful speeches destroyed, forgotten in that direct stare.

"I'm Meth-maren. Hive-friend. Intermediary. I can arrange what you want." She looked about her, and at him. "I speak and translate."

"We need lab-goods, more than the jewels the farmers have been trading."

"Then give us computers. You'll get your lab products."

"And some sort of licensing for regular trade."

She nodded toward the plains, the beta-holds. "There are those who will deal with you as we arrange."

"There's no station any longer. It's gone."

"Crashed. We saw it, Jim and I. It fell into the sea, a long time ago. But stations can be rebuilt."

"Come aboard my ship," he invited her. "We'll talk specifics."

She shook her head, smiled faintly. "No, ser. Take your ship from the vicinity of the hive tonight, within the hour. Go to riverside. I'll find you there with no trouble. But don't linger near the hive."

And she walked away, leaving him standing. The majat remained, and the man, who looked at him with remotely curious eyes and then walked away.

"All things end," she said. "Does the Outside frighten you, Jim?"

"No," he said. She thought it truth. Their minds were much alike.

"There's *Moriah*." She nodded in the direction of the port, where the only whole buildings in Newhope remained. "There's the Reach or Outside. We're human. There's a time to remember that."

He looked at her, saying nothing.

She linked her fingers in his, chitined hand in human one.

"It begins again," she said.

RULES FOR SEJ

RULES FOR SEJ

PIECES: ONE PAIR SIX-SIDED DICE; trio of four-sided wands: first wand face black, second blue with ship symbol; third white; fourth orange with star symbol.

Object: first player to accumulate 100 points wins.

To start play: high roll of dice determines starting player. The Starting Player throws the wands, and play proceeds.

To score: The players roll dice for possession of the points represented by the wands. The casting of wands proceeds in alternation, one player and the next. The wand-thrower has the option of the first cast of dice; the dice then proceed in alternation during the Hand (this particular casting of the wands). High roll takes the wand or wands in contention, and points are recorded as follows.

Value of wands: stars are 12 points each; ships are ten; white and white with black are 5 points for the white pair combined, but the black is played separately and with its own value; white assumes the value of any wand-of-color, always the highest in the Hand . . . and assumes the value of black only if both other wands in the Hand are black; black cancels all points in the possession of whichever player "wins" the black wand, but cancellation of points is limited to the Game itself. Play always proceeds from ships to stars to black: that is, in a Hand, the dice must be rolled first for possession of the ships, then for the stars, and last of all for possession of the black. If a tie occurs in the roll of the dice, the dice are rolled again. If the wands come up doubled or tripled stars or ships or white, the winner

of the first of the double or triple set automatically takes the others of that color; for this purpose also, white matches the highest wand of the Hand. Should triple white show, the winner automatically takes Game. Should triple black show, the winner automatically loses Game.

Passing: In this matter rests the skill of the game, judging when to pass and when to risk play. A Hand containing a single black wand or any number of black wands may be declined by the thrower of wands, thus entirely voiding the Hand: the dice will not be rolled; the wands pass into the hand of the next player, who will cast again, with all privileges of the wand-thrower. Further, a player with the option to throw either wands or dice may voluntarily pass that option to the next player, who is not, however, obliged to accept: the player who has passed will receive the wands or dice again in alternation. The latter is a matter of courtesy and custom of the game: highest or decisive points are played last.